ALISTAIR MACLEAN

Alistair MacLean, the son of a Scots minister, was brought up in the Scottish Highlands. In 1941, at the age of eighteen, he joined the Royal Navy. After the war he read English at Glasgow University and became a schoolmaster. The two and a half years he spent aboard a wartime cruiser were to give him the background for HMS *Ulysses,* his remarkably successful first novel, published in 1955. He is now recognized as one of the outstanding popular writers of the 20th century, the author of twenty-nine worldwide bestsellers, many of which have been filmed, including *The Guns of Navarone, Where Eagles Dare, Fear Is the Key* and *Ice Station Zebra.* In 1983, he was awarded a D.Litt. from Glasgow University. Alistair MacLean died in 1987.

By Alistair MacLean

HMS Ulysses
The Guns of Navarone
South by Java Head
The Last Frontier
Night Without End
Fear Is the Key
The Dark Crusader
The Golden Rendezvous
The Satan Bug
Ice Station Zebra
When Eight Bells Toll
Where Eagles Dare
Force 10 from Navarone
Puppet on a Chain
Caravan to Vaccares
Bear Island
The Way to Dusty Death
Breakheart Pass
Circus
The Golden Gate
Seawitch
Goodbye California
Athabasca
River of Death
Partisans
Floodgate
San Andreas
The Lonely Sea (stories)
Santorini

ALISTAIR MACLEAN

HMS *Ulysses*

STERLING
New York

An Imprint of Sterling Publishing
387 Park Avenue South
New York, NY 10016

STERLING and the distinctive Sterling logo are registered trademarks of Sterling Publishing Co., Inc.

First Sterling edition 2011

First published in Great Britain by Collins in 1955

ISBN 978-1-4027-9034-8 (trade paperback)
ISBN 978-1-4027-9038-6 (ebook)

For information about custom editions, special sales, and premium and corporate purchases, please contact Sterling Special Sales at 800-805-5489 or specialsales@sterlingpublishing.com.

Manufactured in the United States of America

2 4 6 8 10 9 7 5 3 1

www.sterlingpublishing.com

To Gisela

Come, my friends,
'Tis not too late to seek a newer world.
Push off, and sitting well in order smite
The sounding furrows; for my purpose holds
To sail beyond the sunset, and the baths
Of all the western stars, until I die.
It may be that the gulfs will wash us down:
It may be we shall touch the Happy Isles,
And see the great Achilles, whom we knew.
Though much is taken, much abides; and though
We are not now that strength which in old days
Moved earth and heaven; that which we are, we are;
One equal temper of heroic hearts,
Made weak by time and fate, but strong in will
To strive, to seek, to find, and not to yield.

ALFRED LORD TENNYSON

Table of Contents

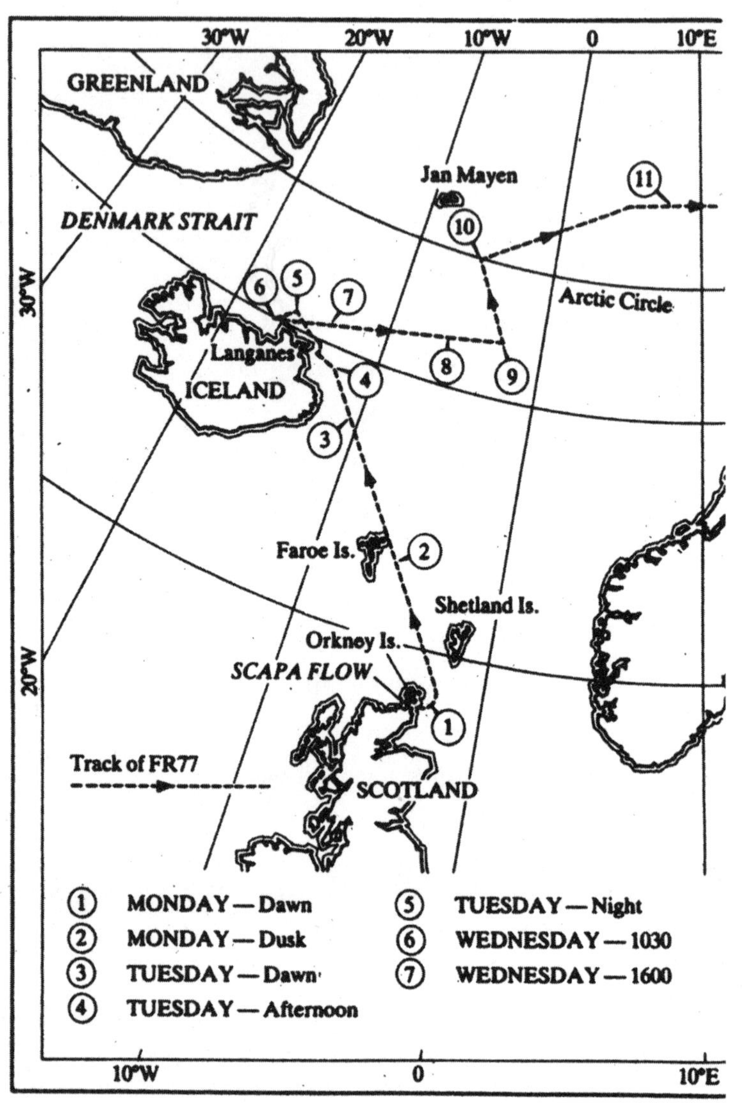

30°W
20°W
10°W
0
10°E
GREENLAND
DENMARK STRAIT
Jan Mayen
Arctic Circle
Langanes
ICELAND
Faroe Is.
Shetland Is.
Orkney Is.
SCAPA FLOW
SCOTLAND
Track of FR77
30°W
20°W
10°W
0
10°E
1
2
3
4
5
6
7
8
9
10
11
① MONDAY — Dawn
② MONDAY — Dusk
③ TUESDAY — Dawn
④ TUESDAY — Afternoon
⑤ TUESDAY — Night
⑥ WEDNESDAY — 1030
⑦ WEDNESDAY — 1600

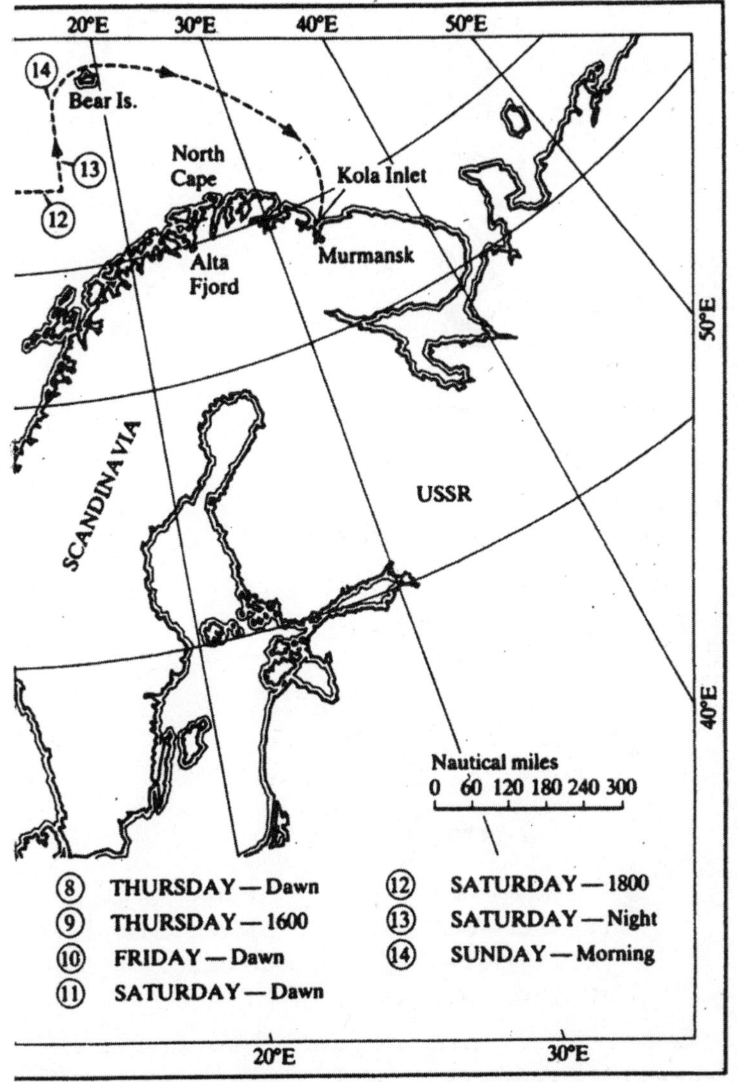
20°E
30°E
40°E
50°E
14
Bear Is.
13
12
North Cape
Kola Inlet
Alta Fjord
Murmansk
50°E
SCANDINAVIA
USSR
40°E
Nautical miles
0 60 120 180 240 300
8 THURSDAY — Dawn
9 THURSDAY — 1600
10 FRIDAY — Dawn
11 SATURDAY — Dawn
12 SATURDAY — 1800
13 SATURDAY — Night
14 SUNDAY — Morning
20°E
30°E

ONE

Prelude: Sunday Afternoon

Slowly, deliberately, Starr crushed out the butt of his cigarette. The gesture, Captain Vallery thought, held a curious air of decision and finality. He knew what was coming next, and, just for a moment, the sharp bitterness of defeat cut through that dull ache that never left his forehead nowadays. But it was only for a moment—he was too tired really, far too tired to care.

'I'm sorry, gentlemen, genuinely sorry.' Starr smiled thinly. 'Not for the orders, I assure you—the Admiralty decision, I am personally convinced, is the only correct and justifiable one in the circumstances. But I do regret your—ah—inability to see our point of view.'

He paused, proffered his platinum cigarette case to the four men sitting with him round the table in the Rear-Admiral's day cabin. At the four mute headshakes the smile flickered again. He selected a cigarette, slid the case back into the breast pocket of his double-breasted grey suit. Then he sat back in his chair, the smile quite gone. It was not difficult to visualize, beneath that pin-stripe sleeve, the more accustomed broad band and golden stripes of Vice-Admiral Vincent Starr, Assistant Director of Naval Operations.

'When I flew north from London this morning,' he continued evenly, 'I was annoyed. I was very annoyed. I am—well, I am a fairly busy man. The First Sea Lord, I thought, was wasting my time as well as his own. When I return, I must apologize. Sir Humphrey was right. He usually is . . . '

His voice trailed off to a murmur, and the flintwheel of his lighter rasped through the strained silence. He leaned forward on the table and went on softly.

'Let us be perfectly frank, gentlemen. I expected—I surely had a right to expect—every support and full co-operation from you in settling this unpleasant business with all speed. Unpleasant business?' He smiled wryly. 'Mincing words won't help. Mutiny, gentlemen, is the generally accepted term for it—a capital offence, I need hardly remind you. And yet what do I find?' His glance travelled slowly round the table.

'Commissioned officers in His Majesty's Navy, including a Flag-Officer, sympathising with—if not actually condoning—a lower-deck mutiny!'

He's overstating it, Vallery thought dully. He's provoking us. The words, the tone, were a question, a challenge inviting reply.

There was no reply. The four men seemed apathetic, indifferent. Four men, each an individual, each secure in his own personality—yet, at that moment, so strangely alike, their faces heavy and still and deeply lined, their eyes so quiet, so tired, so very old.

'You are not convinced, gentlemen?' he went on softly. 'You find my choice of words a trifle—ah—disagreeable?' He leaned back. 'Hm . . . "mutiny".' He savoured the word slowly, compressed his lips, looked round the table again. 'No, it doesn't sound too good, does it, gentlemen? You would call it something else again, perhaps?' He shook his head, bent forward, smoothed out a signal sheet below his fingers.

'"Returned from strike on Lofotens,"' he read out: '"1545—boom passed: 1610—finished with engines: 1630—provisions, stores lighters alongside, mixed seaman-stoker party detailed unload lubricating drums: 1650—reported to Captain stokers refused to obey CPO Hartley, then successively Chief Stoker Hendry, Lieutenant (E.) Grierson and Commander (E.): ringleaders apparently Stokers Riley and Petersen: 1705—refused to obey Captain: 1715—Master at Arms and Regulating PO assaulted in performance of duties."' He looked up. 'What duties? Trying to arrest the ringleaders?'

Vallery nodded silently.

'"1715—seaman branch stopped work, apparently in sympathy: no violence offered: 1725—broadcast by Captain, warned of consequences: ordered to return to work: order disobeyed: 1730—signal to C-in-C *Duke of Cumberland*, for assistance."'

Starr lifted his head again, looked coldly across at Vallery.

'Why, incidentally, the signal to the Admiral? Surely your own marines—'

'My orders,' Tyndall interrupted bluntly. 'Turn our own marines against men they've sailed with for two and half years? Out of the question! There's no matelot—boot-neck antipathy on *this* ship, Admiral Starr: they've been through far too much together . . . Anyway,' he added dryly, 'it's wholly possible that the marines would have refused. And don't forget that if we had used our own men, and they had quelled this—ah—mutiny, the *Ulysses* would have been finished as a fighting ship.'

Starr looked at him steadily, dropped his eyes to the signal again.

'"1830—Marine boarding party from *Cumberland*: no resistance offered to boarding: attempted to arrest, six, eight suspected ringleaders: strong resistance by stokers and seamen, heavy fighting poop-deck, stokers' mess-deck and engineers' flat till 1900: no firearms used, but 2 dead, 6 seriously injured, 35-40 minor casualties."' Starr finished reading, crumpled the paper in an almost savage gesture. 'You know, gentlemen, I believe you have a point after all.' The voice was heavy with irony. '"Mutiny" is hardly the term. Fifty dead and injured: "pitched battle" would be much nearer the mark.'

The words, the tone, the lashing bite of the voice provoked no reaction whatsoever. The four men still sat motionless, expressionless, unheeding in a vast indifference.

Admiral Starr's face hardened.

'I'm afraid you have things just a little out of focus, gentlemen. You've been up here a long time and isolation distorts perspective. Must I remind senior officers that, in wartime, individual feelings, trials and sufferings are of no moment at all? The Navy, the country—they come first, last and all the time.' He pounded the table softly, the gesture insistent in its restrained urgency. 'Good

God, gentlemen,' he ground out, 'the future of the world is at stake—and you, with your selfish, your inexcusable absorption in your own petty affairs, have the colossal effrontery to endanger it!'

Commander Turner smiled sardonically to himself. A pretty speech, Vincent boy, very pretty indeed—although perhaps a touch reminiscent of Victorian melodrama: the clenched teeth act was definitely overdone. Pity he didn't stand for Parliament—he'd be a terrific asset to any Government Front Bench. Suppose the old boy's really too honest for that, he thought in vague surprise.

'The ringleaders will be caught and punished—heavily punished.' The voice was harsh now, with a biting edge to it. 'Meantime the 14th Aircraft Carrier Squadron will rendezvous at Denmark Strait as arranged, at 1030 Wednesday instead of Tuesday—we radioed Halifax and held up the sailing. You will proceed to sea at 0600 tomorrow.' He looked across at Rear-Admiral Tyndall. 'You will please advise all ships under your command at once, Admiral.'

Tyndall—universally known throughout the Fleet as Farmer Giles—said nothing. His ruddy features, usually so cheerful and crinkling, were set and grim: his gaze, heavy-lidded and troubled, rested on Captain Vallery and he wondered just what kind of private hell that kindly and sensitive man was suffering right then. But Vallery's face, haggard with fatigue, told him nothing: that lean and withdrawn asceticism was the complete foil. Tyndall swore bitterly to himself.

'I don't really think there's more to say, gentlemen,' Starr went on smoothly. 'I won't pretend you're in for an easy trip—you know yourselves what happened to the last three major convoys—PQ 17, FR 71 and 74. I'm afraid we haven't yet found the answer to acoustic torpedoes and glider bombs. Further, our intelligence in Bremen and Kiel—and this is substantiated by recent experience in the Atlantic—report that the latest U-boat policy is to get the escorts first . . . Maybe the weather will save you.'

You vindictive old devil, Tyndall thought dispassionately. Go on, damn you—enjoy yourself.

'At the risk of seeming rather Victorian and melodramatic'—impatiently Starr waited for Turner to stifle his sudden fit of coughing—'we may say that the *Ulysses* is being given the opportunity of—ah—redeeming herself.' He pushed back his chair. 'After that, gentlemen, the Med. But first—FR 77 to Murmansk, come hell or high water!' His voice broke on the last word and lifted into stridency, the anger burring through the thin veneer of suavity. 'The *Ulysses* must be made to realize that the Navy will never tolerate disobedience of orders, dereliction of duty, organized revolt and sedition!'

'Rubbish!'

Starr jerked back in his chair, knuckles whitening on the armrest. His glance whipped round and settled on Surgeon-Commander Brooks, on the unusually vivid blue eyes so strangely hostile now under that magnificent silver mane.

Tyndall, too, saw the angry eyes. He saw, also, the deepening colour in Brooks's face, and moaned softly to himself. He knew the signs too well—old Socrates was about to blow his Irish top. Tyndall made to speak, then slumped back at a sharp gesture from Starr.

'What did you say, Commander?' The Admiral's voice was very soft and quite toneless.

'Rubbish,' repeated Brooks distinctly. 'Rubbish. That's what I said. "Let's be perfectly frank," you say. Well, sir, I'm being frank. "Dereliction of duty, organized revolt and sedition" my foot! But I suppose you have to call it something, preferably something well within your own field of experience. But God only knows by what strange association and slight-of-hand mental transfer, you equate yesterday's trouble aboard the *Ulysses* with the only clearly-cut code of behaviour thoroughly familiar to yourself.' Brooks paused for a second: in the silence they heard the thin, high wail of a bosun's pipe—a passing ship, perhaps. 'Tell me, Admiral Starr,' he went on quietly, 'are we to drive out the devils of madness by whipping—a quaint old medieval custom—or maybe, sir, by drowning—remember the Gadarene swine? Or perhaps a month or two in cells, you think, is the best cure for tuberculosis?'

'What in heaven's name are you talking about, Brooks?' Starr demanded angrily. 'Gadarene swine, tuberculosis—what *are* you getting at, man? Go on—explain.' He drummed his fingers impatiently on the table, eyebrows arched high into his furrowed brow. 'I hope, Brooks,' he went on silkily, 'that you can justify this—ah—insolence of yours.'

'I'm quite sure that Commander Brooks intended no insolence, sir.' It was Captain Vallery speaking for the first time. 'He's only expressing—'

'Please, Captain Vallery,' Starr interrupted. 'I am quite capable of judging these things for myself, I think.' His smile was very tight. 'Well, go on, Brooks.'

Commander Brooks looked at him soberly, speculatively.

'Justify myself?' He smiled wearily. 'No, sir, I don't think I can.' The slight inflection of tone, the implications, were not lost on Starr, and he flushed slightly. 'But I'll try to explain,' continued Brooks. 'It may do some good.'

He sat in silence for a few seconds, elbow on the table, his hand running through the heavy silver hair—a favourite mannerism of his. Then he looked up abruptly.

'When were you last at sea, Admiral Starr?' he inquired.

'Last at sea?' Starr frowned heavily. 'What the devil has that got to do with you, Brooks—or with the subject under discussion?' he asked harshly.

'A very great deal,' Brooks retorted. 'Would you please answer my question, Admiral?'

'I think you know quite well, Brooks,' Starr replied evenly, 'that I've been at Naval Operations HQ in London since the outbreak of war. What are you implying, sir?'

'Nothing. Your personal integrity and courage are not open to question. We all know that. I was merely establishing a fact.' Brooks hitched himself forward in his chair.

'I'm a naval doctor, Admiral Starr—I've been a doctor for over thirty years now.' He smiled faintly. 'Maybe I'm not a very good doctor, perhaps I don't keep quite so abreast of the latest medical developments as I might, but I believe I can claim to know a great deal about human nature—this is no time for modesty—about how the mind works, about the wonderfully intricate interaction of mind and body.

'"Isolation distorts perspective"—these were your words, Admiral Starr. "Isolation" implies a cutting off, a detachment from the world, and your implication was partly true. But—and this, sir, is the point—there are more worlds than one. The Northern Seas, the Arctic, the black-out route to Russia—these are another world, a world utterly distinct from yours. It is a world, sir, of which you cannot possibly have any conception. In effect, you are completely isolated from *our* world.'

Starr grunted, whether in anger or derision it was difficult to say, and cleared his throat to speak, but Brooks went on swiftly.

'Conditions obtain there without either precedent or parallel in the history of war. The Russian Convoys, sir, are something entirely new and quite unique in the experience of mankind.'

He broke off suddenly, and gazed out through the thick glass of the scuttle at the sleet slanting heavily across the grey waters and dun hills of the Scapa anchorage. No one spoke. The Surgeon-Commander was not finished yet: a tired man takes time to marshal his thoughts.

'Mankind, of course, can and does adapt itself to new conditions.' Brooks spoke quietly, almost to himself. 'Biologically and physically, they have had to do so down the ages, in order to survive. But it takes time, gentlemen, a great deal of time. You can't compress the natural changes of twenty centuries into a couple of years: neither mind nor body can stand it. You can try, of course, and such is the fantastic resilience and toughness of man that he can tolerate it—for extremely short periods. But the limit, the saturation capacity for adaption is soon reached. Push men beyond that limit and anything can happen. I say "anything" advisedly, because we don't yet know the precise form the crack-up will take—but crack-up there always is. It may be physical, mental, spiritual—I don't know. But this I do know, Admiral Starr—the crew of the *Ulysses* has been pushed to the limit—and clear beyond.'

'Very interesting, Commander.' Starr's voice was dry, sceptical. 'Very interesting indeed—and most instructive. Unfortunately, your theory—and it's only that, of course—is quite untenable.'

Brooks eyed him steadily.

'That, sir, is not even a matter of opinion.'

'Nonsense, man, nonsense!' Starr's face was hard in anger. 'It's a matter of fact. Your premises are completely false.' Starr leaned forward, his forefinger punctuating every word. 'This vast gulf you claim to lie between the convoys to Russia and normal operational work at sea—it just doesn't exist. Can you point out any one factor or condition present in these Northern waters which is not to be found somewhere else in the world? Can you, Commander Brooks?'

'No, sir.' Brooks was quite unruffled. 'But I can point out a frequently overlooked fact—that differences of degree and association can be much greater and have far more far-reaching effects than differences in kind. Let me explain what I mean.

'Fear can destroy a man. Let's admit it—fear is a natural thing. You get it in every theatre of war—but nowhere, I suggest, so intense, so continual as in the Arctic convoys.

'Suspense, tension can break a man—any man. I've seen it happen too often, far, far too often. And when you're keyed up to snapping point, sometimes for seventeen days on end, when you have constant daily reminders of what may happen to you in the shape of broken, sinking ships and broken, drowning bodies—well, we're men, not machines. Something has to go—and does. The Admiral will not be unaware that after the last two trips we shipped nineteen officers and men to sanatoria—mental sanatoria?'

Brooks was on his feet now, his broad, strong fingers splayed over the polished table surface, his eyes boring into Starr's.

'Hunger burns out a man's vitality, Admiral Starr. It saps his strength, slows his reactions, destroys the will to fight, even the will to survive. You are surprised, Admiral Starr? Hunger, you think—surely that's impossible in the wellprovided ships of today? But it's not impossible, Admiral Starr. It's inevitable. You keep on sending us out when the Russian season's over, when the nights are barely longer than the days, when twenty hours out of the twenty-four are spent on watch or at action stations, and you expect us to feed well!' He smashed the flat of his hand on the table. 'How the hell can we, when the cooks spend nearly all their time in the magazines, serving the turrets, or in damage control parties? Only the baker and butcher are excused—and so we live on corned-beef sandwiches. For weeks on end! Corned-beef sandwiches!' Surgeon-Commander Brooks almost spat in disgust.

Good old Socrates, thought Turner happily, give him hell. Tyndall, too, was nodding his ponderous approval. Only Vallery was uncomfortable—not because of what Brooks was saying, but because Brooks was saying it. He, Vallery, was the captain: the coals of fire were being heaped on the wrong head.

'Fear, suspense, hunger.' Brooks's voice was very low now. 'These are the things that break a man, that destroy him as surely as fire or steel or pestilence could. These are the killers.

'But they are nothing, Admiral Starr, just nothing at all. They are only the henchmen, the outriders, you might call them, of the Three Horsemen of the Apocalypse—cold, lack of sleep, exhaustion.

'Do you know what it's like up there, between Jan Mayen and Bear Island on a February night, Admiral Starr? Of course you don't. Do you know what it's like when there's sixty degrees of frost in the Arctic—and it still doesn't freeze? Do you know what it's like when the wind, twenty degrees below zero, comes screaming off the Polar and Greenland ice-caps and slices through the thickest clothing like a scalpel? When there's five hundred tons of ice on the deck, where five minutes' direct exposure means frostbite, where the bows crash down into a trough and the spray hits you as solid ice, where even a torch battery dies out in the intense cold? Do you, Admiral Starr, do you?' Brooks flung the words at him, hammered them at him.

'And do you know what it's like to go for days on end without sleep, for weeks with only two or three hours out of the twenty-four? Do you know the sensation, Admiral Starr? That fine-drawn feeling with every nerve in your body and cell in your brain stretched taut to breaking point, pushing you over the screaming edge of madness. Do you know it, Admiral Starr? It's the most exquisite agony in the world, and you'd sell your friends, your family, your hopes of immortality for the blessed privilege of closing your eyes and just letting go.

'And then there's the tiredness, Admiral Starr, the desperate weariness that never leaves you. Partly it's the debilitating effect of the cold, partly lack of sleep, partly the result of incessantly bad weather. You know yourself how exhausting it can be to brace yourself even for a few hours on a rolling, pitching deck: our boys have been doing it for months—gales are routine on the Arctic run. I can show you a dozen, two dozen old men, not one of them a day over twenty.'

Brooks pushed back his chair and paced restlessly across the cabin. Tyndall and Turner glanced at each other, then over at Vallery, who sat with head and shoulders bowed, eyes resting vacantly on his clasped hands on the table. For the moment, Starr might not have existed.

'It's a vicious, murderous circle,' Brooks went on quickly. He was leaning against the bulkhead now, hands deep in his pockets, gazing out sightlessly through the misted scuttle. 'The less sleep you have, the tireder you are: the more tired you become, the more you feel cold. And so it goes on. And then, all the time, there's the hunger and the terrific tension. Everything interacts with everything else: each single factor conspires with the others to crush a man, break him physically and mentally, and lay him wide open to disease. Yes, Admiral—disease.' He smiled into Starr's face, and there was no laughter in his smile. 'Pack men together like herring in a barrel, deprive 'em of every last ounce of resistance, batten 'em below decks for days at a time, and what do you get? TB It's inevitable.' He shrugged. 'Sure, I've only isolated a few cases so far—but I *know* that active pulmonary TB is rife in the lower deck.

'I saw the break-up coming months ago.' He lifted his shoulders wearily. 'I warned the Fleet Surgeon several times. I wrote the Admiralty twice. They were sympathetic—and that's all. Shortage of ships, shortage of men . . .

'The last hundred days did it, sir—on top of the previous months. A hundred days of pure bloody hell and not a single hour's shore leave. In port only twice—for ammunitioning: all oil and provisions from the carriers at sea. And every day an eternity of cold and hunger and danger and suffering. In the name of God,' Brooks cried, 'we're not machines!'

He levered himself off the wall and walked over to Starr, hands still thrust deep in his pockets.

'I hate to say this in front of the Captain, but every officer in the ship—except Captain Vallery—knows that the men would have mutinied, as you call it, long ago, but for one thing—Captain Vallery. The intense personal loyalty of the crew to the Captain, the devotion almost to the other side of idolatry is something quite unique in my experience, Admiral Starr.'

Tyndall and Turner both murmured approval. Vallery still sat motionless.

'But there was a limit even to that. It had to come. And now you talk of punishing, imprisoning these men. Good God above, you might as well hang a man for having leprosy, or send him to penal servitude for developing ulcers!' Brooks shook his head in despair. 'Our crew are equally guiltless. They just couldn't help it. They can't see right from wrong any more. They can't think straight. They just want a rest, they just want peace, a few days' blessed quiet. They'll give anything in the world for these things and they *can't* see beyond them. Can't you see that Admiral Starr? Can't you? Can't you?'

For perhaps thirty seconds there was silence, complete, utter silence, in the Admiral's cabin. The high, thin whine of the wind, the swish of the hail seemed unnaturally loud. Then Starr was on his feet, his hands stretching out for his gloves: Vallery looked up, for the first time, and he knew that Brooks had failed.

'Have my barge alongside, Captain Vallery. At once, please.' Starr was detached, quite emotionless. 'Complete oiling, provisioning and ammunitioning as soon as possible. Admiral Tyndall, I wish you and your squadron a successful voyage. As for you, Commander Brooks, I quite see the point of your argument—at least, as far as you are concerned.' His lips parted in a bleak, wintry smile. 'You are quite obviously overwrought, badly in need of some leave. Your relief will be aboard before midnight. If you will come with me, Captain . . . '

He turned to the door and had taken only two steps when Vallery's voice stopped him dead, poised on one foot.

'One moment, sir, if you please.'

Starr swung round. Captain Vallery had made no move to rise. He sat still, smiling. It was a smile compounded of deference, of understanding—and of a curious inflexibility. It made Starr feel vaguely uncomfortable.

'Surgeon-Commander Brooks,' Vallery said precisely, 'is a quite exceptional officer. He is invaluable, virtually irreplaceable and the *Ulysses* needs him badly. I wish to retain his services.'

'I've made my decision, Captain,' Starr snapped. 'And it's final. You know, I think, the powers invested in me by the Admiralty for this investigation.'

'Quite, sir.' Vallery was quiet, unmoved. 'I repeat, however, that we cannot afford to lose an officer of Brooks's calibre.'

The words, the tone, were polite, respectful; but their significance was unmistakable. Brooks stepped forward, distress in his face, but before he could speak, Turner cut in smoothly, urbanely.

'I assume I wasn't invited to this conference for purely decorative purposes.' He tilted back in his chair, his eyes fixed dreamily on the deckhead. 'I feel it's time I said something. I unreservedly endorse old Brooks's remarks—every word of them.'

Starr, white-mouthed and motionless, looked at Tyndall. 'And you, Admiral?'

Tyndall looked up quizzically, all the tenseness and worry gone from his face. He looked more like a West Country Farmer Giles than ever. He supposed wryly, that his career was at stake; funny, he thought how suddenly unimportant a career could become.

'As Officer Commanding, maximum squadron efficiency is my sole concern. Some people *are* irreplaceable. Captain Vallery suggests Brooks is one of these. I agree.'

'I see, gentlemen, I see,' Starr said heavily. Two spots of colour burned high up on his cheekbones. 'The convoy has sailed from Halifax, and my hands are tied. But you make a great mistake, gentlemen, a great mistake, in pointing pistols at the head of the Admiralty. We have long memories in Whitehall. We shall—ah—discuss the matter at length on your return. Good day, gentlemen, good day.'

Shivering in the sudden chill, Brooks clumped down the ladder to the upper deck and turned for'ard past the galley into the Sick

Bay. Johnson, the Leading Sick Bay Attendant, looked out from the dispensary.

'How are our sick and suffering, Johnson?' Brooks inquired. 'Bearing up manfully?'

Johnson surveyed the eight beds and their occupants morosely.

'Just a lot of bloody chancers, sir. Half of them are a damned sight fitter than I am. Look at Stoker Riley there—him with the broken finger and whacking great pile of *Reader's Digest*s. Going through all the medical articles, he is, and roaring out for sulph., penicillin and all the latest antibiotics. Can't pronounce half of them. Thinks he's dying.'

'A grievous loss,' the Surgeon-Commander murmured. He shook his head. 'What Commander Dodson sees in him I don't know . . . What's the latest from hospital?'

The expression drained out of Johnson's face.

'They're just off the blower, sir,' he said woodenly. 'Five minutes ago. Ordinary Seaman Ralston died at three o'clock.'

Brooks nodded heavily. Sending that broken boy to hospital had only been a gesture anyway. Just for a moment he felt tired, beaten. 'Old Socrates' they called him, and he was beginning to feel his age these days—and a bit more besides. Maybe a good night's sleep would help, but he doubted it. He sighed.

'Don't feel too good about all this, Johnson, do you?'

'Eighteen, sir. Exactly eighteen.' Johnson's voice was low, bitter. 'I've just been talking to Burgess—that's him in the next bed. Says Ralston steps out across the bathroom coaming, a towel over his arm. A mob rushes past, then this bloody great ape of a bootneck comes tearing up and bashes him over the skull with his rifle. Never knew what hit him, sir—and he never knew why.'

Brooks smiled faintly.

'That's what they call—ah—seditious talk, Johnson,' he said mildy.

'Sorry, sir. Suppose I shouldn't—it's just that I—'

'Never mind, Johnson. I asked for it. Can't stop anyone from thinking. Only, don't think out loud. It's—it's prejudicial to naval discipline . . . I think your friend Riley wants you. Better get him a dictionary.'

He turned and pushed his way through the surgery curtains. A dark head—all that could be seen behind the dentist's chair—twisted round. Johnny Nicholls, Acting Surgeon Lieutenant, rose quickly to his feet, a pile of report cards dangling from his left hand.

'Hallo, sir. Have a pew.'

Brooks grinned.

'An excellent thing, Lieutenant Nicholls, truly gratifying, to meet these days a junior officer who knows his place. Thank you, thank you.'

He climbed into the chair and sank back with a groan, fiddling with the neck-rest.

'If you'll just adjust the foot-rest, my boy . . . so. Ah—thank you.' He leaned back luxuriously, eyes closed, head far back on the rest, and groaned again. 'I'm an old man, Johnny, my boy, just an ancient has-been.'

'Nonsense, sir,' Nicholls said briskly. 'Just a slight malaise. Now, if you'll let me prescribe a suitable tonic . . . '

He turned to a cupboard, fished out two toothglasses and a dark-green, ribbed bottle marked 'Poison'. He filled the glasses and handed one to Brooks. 'My personal recommendation. Good health, sir!'

Brooks looked at the amber liquid, then at Nicholls.

'Heathenish practice they taught you at these Scottish Universities, my boy . . . Admirable fellers, some of these old heathens. What is it this time, Johnny?'

'First-class stuff,' Nicholls grinned. 'Produce of the Island of Coll.'

The old surgeon looked at him suspiciously.

'Didn't know they had any distilleries up there.'

'They haven't. I only said it was made in Coll . . . How did things go up top, sir?'

'Bloody awful. His nibs threatened to string us all from the yardarm. Took a special dislike to me—said I was to be booted off the ship instanter. Meant it, too.'

'You!' Nicholls's brown eyes, deep-sunk just now and red-rimmed from sleeplessness, opened wide. 'You're joking, sir, of course.'

'I'm not. But it's all right—I'm not going. Old Giles, the skipper and Turner—the crazy idiots—virtually told Starr that if I went he'd better start looking around for another Admiral, Captain and Commander as well. They shouldn't have done it, of course—but it shook old Vincent to the core. Departed in high dudgeon, muttering veiled threats . . . not so veiled, either, come to think of it.'

'Damned old fool!' said Nicholls feelingly.

'He's not really, Johnny. Actually, he's a brilliant bloke. You don't become a DNO for nothing. Master strategist and tactician, Giles tells me, and he's not really as bad as we're apt to paint him; to a certain extent we can't blame old Vincent for sending us out again. Bloke's up against an insoluble problem. Limited resources at his disposal, terrific demands for ships and men in half a dozen other theatres. Impossible to meet half the claims made on him; half the time he's operating on little better than a shoe-string. But he's still an inhuman, impersonal sort of cuss—doesn't understand men.'

'And the upshot of it all?'

'Murmansk again. Sailing at 0600 tomorrow.'

'What! Again? This bunch of walking zombies?' Nicholls was openly incredulous. 'Why, they can't do that, sir! They—they just can't!'

'They're doing it anyway, my boy. The *Ulysses* must—ah—redeem itself.' Brooks opened his eyes. 'Gad the very thought appals me. If there's any of that poison left, my boy . . . '

Nicholls shoved the depleted bottle back into the cupboard, and jerked a resentful thumb in the direction of the massive battleship clearly visible through the porthole, swinging round her anchor three or four cable-lengths away.

'Why always us, sir? It's always us. Why don't they send that useless floating barracks out once in a while? Swinging round that bloody great anchor, month in, month out—'

'Just the point,' Brooks interrupted solemnly. 'According to the Kapok Kid, the tremendous weight of empty condensed-milk cans and herring-intomato-sauce tins accumulated on the ocean bed over the past twelve months completely defeats all attempts to weigh anchor.'

Nicholls didn't seem to hear him.

'Week in, week out, months and months on end, they send

the *Ulysses* out. They change the carriers, they rest the screen destroyers—but never the *Ulysses*. There's no let-up. Never, not once. But the *Duke of Cumberland*—all it's fit for is sending hulking great brutes of marines on board here to massacre sick men, crippled men, men who've done more in a week than—'

'Easy, boy, easy,' the Commander chided. 'You can't call three dead men and the bunch of wounded heroes lying outside there a massacre. The marines were only doing their job. As for the *Cumberland*—well, you've got to face it. We're the only ship in the Home Fleet equipped for carrier command.'

Nicholls drained his glass and regarded his superior officer moodily.

'There are times, sir, when I positively love the Germans.'

'You and Johnson should get together sometime,' Brooks advised. 'Old Starr would have you both clapped in irons for spreading alarm and . . . Hallo, hallo!' He straightened up in his chair and leaned forward. 'Observe the old *Duke* there, Johnny! Yards of washing going up from the flagdeck and matelots running—actually running—up to the fo'c'sle head. Unmistakable signs of activity. By Gad, this *is* uncommon surprising! What d'ye make of it, boy?'

'Probably learned that they're going on leave,' Nicholls growled. 'Nothing else could possibly make that bunch move so fast. And who are we to grudge them the just rewards for their labours? After so long, so arduous, so dangerous a spell of duty in Northern waters . . . '

The first shrill blast of a bugle killed the rest of the sentence. Instinctively, their eyes swung round on the crackling, humming loudspeaker, then on each other in sheer, shocked disbelief. And then they were on their feet, tense, expectant: the heart-stopping urgency of the bugle-call to action stations never grows dim.

'Oh, my God, no!' Brooks moaned. 'Oh, no, no! Not again! Not in Scapa Flow!'

'Oh, God, no! Not again—*not in Scapa Flow*!'

These were the words in the mouths, the minds, the hearts of 727 exhausted, sleep-haunted, bitter men that bleak winter evening in Scapa Flow. That they thought of, and that only could they think of as the scream of the bugle stopped dead all work on decks and below decks, in engine-rooms and boiler-rooms, on ammunition lighters and fuel tenders, in the galleys and in the offices. And that only could the watch below think of—and that with an even more poignant despair—as the strident blare seared through the bliss of oblivion and brought them back, sick at heart, dazed in mind and stumbling on their feet, to the iron harshness of reality.

It was, in a strangely indefinite way, a moment of decision. It was the moment that could have broken the *Ulysses*, as a fighting ship, for ever. It was the moment that bitter, exhausted men, relaxed in the comparative safety of a landlocked anchorage, could have chosen to make the inevitable stand against authority, against that wordless, mindless compulsion and merciless insistence which was surely destroying them. If ever there was such a moment, this was it.

The moment came—and passed. It was no more than a fleeting shadow, a shadow that flitted lightly across men's minds and was gone, lost in the rush of feet pounding to action stations. Perhaps self-preservation was the reason. But that was unlikely—the *Ulysses* had long since ceased to care. Perhaps it was just naval discipline, or loyalty to the captain, or what the psychologists call conditioned reflex—you hear the scream of brakes and you immediately jump for your life. Or perhaps it was something else again.

Whatever it was, the ship—all except the port watch anchor party—was closed up in two minutes. Unanimous in their disbelief that this could be happening to them in Scapa Flow, men went to their stations silently or vociferously, according to their nature. They went reluctantly, sullenly, resentfully, despairingly. But they went.

Rear-Admiral Tyndall went also. He was not one of those who went silently. He climbed blasphemously up to the bridge, pushed his way through the port gate and clambered into his high-legged armchair in the for'ard port corner of the compass platform. He looked at Vallery.

'What's the flap, in heaven's name, Captain?' he demanded testily. 'Everything seems singularly peaceful to me.'

'Don't know yet, sir.' Vallery swept worried eyes over the

anchorage. 'Alarm signal from C-in-C, with orders to get under way immediately.'

'Get under way! But why, man, why?'

Vallery shook his head.

Tyndall groaned. 'It's all a conspiracy, designed to rob old men like myself of their afternoon sleep,' he declared.

'More likely a brainwave of Starr's to shake us up a bit,' Turner grunted.

'No.' Tyndall was decisive. 'He wouldn't try that—wouldn't dare. Besides, by his lights, he's not a vindictive man.'

Silence fell, a silence broken only by the patter of sleet and hail, and the weird haunting pinging of the Asdic. Vallery suddenly lifted his binoculars.

'Good lord, sir, look at that! The *Duke*'s slipped her anchor!'

There was no doubt about it. The shackle-pin had been knocked out and the bows of the great ship were swinging slowly round as it got under way.

'What in the world—?' Tyndall broke off and scanned the sky. 'Not a plane, not a paratrooper in sight, no radar reports, no Asdic contacts, no sign of the German Grand Fleet steaming through the boom—'

'She's signalling us, sir!' It was Bentley speaking, Bentley the Chief Yeoman of Signals. He paused and went on slowly: 'Proceed to our anchorage at once. Make fast to north buoy.'

'Ask them to confirm,' Vallery snapped. He took the fo'c'sle phone from the communication rating.

'Captain here, Number One. How is she? Up and down? Good.' He turned to the officer of the watch. 'Slow ahead both: Starboard 10.' He looked over at Tyndall's corner, brows wrinkled in question.

'Search me,' Tyndall growled. 'Could be the latest in parlour games—a sort of nautical musical chairs, you know . . . Wait a minute, though! Look! The *Cumberland*—all her 5.25's are at maximum depression!'

Vallery's eyes met his.

'No, it can't be! Good God, do you think—?'

The blare of the Asdic loudspeaker, from the cabinet immediately abaft of the bridge, gave him his answer. The voice of Leading Asdic Operation Chrysler was clear, unhurried.

'Asdic—bridge. Asdic—bridge. Echo, Red 30. Repeat, Red 30. Strengthening. Closing.'

The captain's incredulity leapt and died in the same second.

'Alert Director Control! Red 30. All AA guns maximum depression. Underwater target. Torps'—this to Lieutenant Marshall, the Canadian Torpedo Officer—"depth charge stations".'

He turned back to Tyndall.

'It can't be, sir—it just can't! A U-boat—I presume it is—in Scapa Flow. Impossible!'

'Prien didn't think so,' Tyndall grunted.

'Prien?'

'Kapitan-Leutnant Prien—gent who scuppered the *Royal Oak*.'

'It couldn't happen again. The new boom defences—'

'Would keep out any normal submarines,' Tyndall finished. His voice dropped to a murmur. 'Remember what we were told last month about our midget two-man subs—the chariots? The ones to be taken over to Norway by Norwegian fishing-boats operating from the Shetlands. Could be that the Germans have hit on the same idea.'

'Could be,' Vallery agreed. He nodded sardonically. 'Just look at the *Cumberland* go—straight for the boom.' He paused for a few seconds, his eyes speculative, then looked back at Tyndall. 'How do you like it, sir?'

'Like what, Captain?'

'Playing Aunt Sally at the fair.' Vallery grinned crookedly. 'Can't afford to lose umpteen million pounds worth of capital ship. So the old *Duke* hares out to sea and safety, while we moor near her anchor berth. You can bet German Naval Intelligence has the bearing of her anchorage down to a couple of inches. These midget subs carry detachable warheads and if there's going to be any fitted, they're going to be fitted to us.'

Tyndall looked at him. His face was expressionless. Asdic reports were continuous, reporting steady bearing to port and closing distances.

'Of course, of course,' the Admiral murmured. 'We're the

whipping boy. Gad, it makes me feel bad!' His mouth twisted and he laughed mirthlessly. 'Me? This is the final straw for the crew. That hellish last trip, the mutiny, the marine boarding party from the *Cumberland,* action stations in harbour—and now this! Risking our necks for that—that . . . ' He broke off, spluttering, swore in anger, then resumed quietly:

'What are you going to tell the men, Captain? Good God, it's fantastic! I feel like mutiny myself . . . ' He stopped short, looked inquiringly past Vallery's shoulder.

The Captain turned round.

'Yes, Marshall?'

'Excuse me, sir. This—er—echo.' He jerked a thumb over his shoulder. 'A sub, sir—possibly a pretty small one?' The transatlantic accent was very heavy.

'Likely enough, Marshall. Why?'

'Just how Ralston and I figured it, sir.' He grinned. 'We have an idea for dealing with it.'

Vallery looked out through the driving sleet, gave helm and engine orders, then turned back to the Torpedo Officer. He was coughing heavily, painfully, as he pointed to the glassed-in anchorage chart.

'If you're thinking of depth-charging our stern off in these shallow waters—'

'No, sir. Doubt whether we could get a shallow enough setting anyway. My idea—Ralston's to be correct—is that we take out the motor-boat and a few 25-lb. scuttling charges, 18-second fuses and chemical igniters. Not much of a kick from these, I know, but a miniature sub ain't likely to have helluva—er—very thick hulls. And if the crews are sitting on top of the ruddy things instead of inside—well, it's curtains for sure. It'll kipper 'em.'

Vallery smiled.

'Not bad at all, Marshall. I think you've got the answer there. What do you think, sir?'

'Worth trying anyway,' Tyndall agreed. 'Better than waiting around like a sitting duck.'

'Go ahead then, Torps.' Vallery looked at him quizzically. 'Who are your explosives experts?'

'I figured on taking Ralston—'

'Just what I thought. You're taking nobody, laddie,' said Vallery firmly. 'Can't afford to lose my torpedo officer.'

Marshall looked pained, then shrugged resignedly.

'The chief TGM and Ralston—he's the senior LTO. Good men both.'

'Right. Bentley—detail a man to accompany them in the boat. We'll signal Asdic bearings from here. Have him take a portable Aldis with him.' He dropped his voice. 'Marshall?'

'Sir?'

'Ralston's young brother died in hospital this afternoon.' He looked across at the Leading Torpedo Operator, a tall, blond, unsmiling figure dressed in faded blue overalls beneath his duffel. 'Does he know yet?'

The Torpedo Officer stared at Vallery, then looked round slowly at the LTO. He swore, softly, bitterly, fluently.

'Marshall!' Vallery's voice was sharp, imperative, but Marshall ignored him, his face a mask, oblivious alike to the reprimand in the Captain's voice and the lashing bite of the sleet.

'No, sir,' he stated at length, 'he doesn't know. But he did receive some news this morning. Croydon was pasted last week. His mother and three sisters live there—lived there. It was a land-mine, sir—there was nothing left.' He turned abruptly and left the bridge.

Fifteen minutes later it was all over. The starboard whaler and the motor-boat on the port side hit the water with the *Ulysses* still moving up to the mooring. The whaler, buoy-jumper aboard, made for the buoy, while the motor-boat slid off at a tangent.

Four hundred yards away from the ship, in obedience to the flickering instructions from the bridge, Ralston fished out a pair of pliers from his overalls and crimped the chemical fuse. The Gunner's Mate stared fixedly at his stop-watch. On the count of twelve the scuttling charge went over the side.

Three more, at different settings, followed it in close succession, while the motor-boat cruised in a tight circle. The first three explosions lifted the stern and jarred the entire length of the boat, viciously—and that was all. But with the fourth, a great gout of air came gushing to the surface, followed by a long stream of viscous bubbles. As the turbulence subsided, a thin slick of oil spread over a hundred square yards of sea . . .

Men, fallen out from Action Stations, watched with expressionless faces as the motor-boat made it back to the *Ulysses* and hooked on to the falls just in time: the Hotchkiss steering-gear was badly twisted and she was taking in water fast under the counter.

The *Duke of Cumberland* was a smudge of smoke over a far headland.

Cap in hand, Ralston sat down opposite the Captain. Vallery looked at him for a long time in silence. He wondered what to say, how best to say it. He hated to have to do this.

Richard Vallery also hated war. He always had hated it and he cursed the day it had dragged him out of his comfortable retirement. At least, 'dragged' was how he put it; only Tyndall knew that he had volunteered his services to the Admiralty on 1st September, 1939, and had had them gladly accepted.

But he hated war. Not because it interfered with his lifelong passion for music and literature, on both of which he was a considerable authority, not even because it was a perpetual affront to his aestheticism, to his sense of rightness and fitness. He hated it because he was a deeply religious man, because it grieved him to see in mankind the wild beasts of the primeval jungle, because he thought the cross of life was already burden enough without the gratuitous infliction of the mental and physical agony of war, and, above all, because he saw war all too clearly as the wild and insensate folly it was, as a madness of the mind that settled nothing, proved nothing—except the old, old truth that God was on the side of the big battalions.

But some things he had to do, and Vallery had clearly seen that this war had to be his also. And so he had come back to the service, and had grown older as the bitter years passed, older and frailer, and more kindly and tolerant and understanding. Among Naval Captains, indeed among men, he was unique. In his charity, in his humility, Captain Richard Vallery walked alone. It was a measure of the man's greatness that this thought never occurred to him.

He sighed. All that troubled him just now was what he ought to say to Ralston. But it was Ralston who spoke first.

'It's all right, sir.' The voice was a level monotone, the face very still. 'I know. The Torpedo Officer told me.'

Vallery cleared his throat.

'Words are useless, Ralston, quite useless. Your young brother—and your family at home. All gone. I'm sorry, my boy, terribly sorry about it all.' He looked up into the expressionless face and smiled wryly. 'Or maybe you think that these are all words—you know, something formal, just a meaningless formula.'

Suddenly, surprisingly, Ralston smiled briefly.

'No, sir, I don't. I can appreciate how you feel, sir. You see, my father—well, he's a captain too. He tells me he feels the same way.'

Vallery looked at him in astonishment.

'Your father, Ralston? Did you say—'

'Yes, sir.' Vallery could have sworn to a flicker of amusement in the blue eyes, so quiet, so selfpossessed, across the table. 'In the Merchant Navy, sir—a tanker captain—16,000 tons.'

Vallery said nothing. Ralston went on quietly:

'And about Billy, sir—my young brother. It's—it's just one of these things. It's nobody's fault but mine—I asked to have him aboard here. I'm to blame, sir—only me.' His lean brown hands were round the brim of his hat, twisting it, crushing it. How much worse will it be when the shattering impact of the double blow wears off, Vallery wondered, when the poor kid begins to think straight again?

'Look, my boy, I think you need a few days' rest, time to think things over.' God, Vallery thought, what an inadequate, what a futile thing to say. 'PRO is making out your travelling warrant just now. You will start fourteen days' leave as from tonight.'

'Where is the warrant made out for, sir?' The hat was crushed now, crumpled between the hands. 'Croydon?'

'Of course. Where else—' Vallery stopped dead; the enormity of the blunder had just hit him.

'Forgive me, my boy. What a damnably stupid thing to say!'

'Don't send me away, sir,' Ralston pleaded quietly. 'I know it sounds—well, it sounds corny, selfpitying, but the truth is I've nowhere to go I belong here—on the *Ulysses*. I can do things all the time—I'm busy—working, sleeping—I don't have to talk about things—I can do things . . . ' The self-possession was only the thinnest veneer, taut and frangible, with the quiet desperation immediately below.

'I can get a chance to help pay 'em back,' Ralston hurried on. 'Like crimping these fuses today—it—well, it was a privilege. It was more than that—it was—oh, I don't know. I can't find the words, sir.'

Vallery knew. He felt sad, tired, defenceless. What could he offer this boy in place of this hate, this very human, consuming flame of revenge? Nothing, he knew, nothing that Ralston wouldn't despise, wouldn't laugh at. This was not the time for pious platitudes. He sighed again, more heavily this time.

'Of course you shall remain, Ralston. Go down to the Police Office and tell them to tear up your warrant. If I can be of any help to you at any time—'

'I understand, sir. Thank you very much. Good night, sir.'

'Good night, my boy.'

The door closed softly behind him.

TWO

Monday Morning

'Close all water-tight doors and scuttles. Hands to stations for leaving harbour.' Impersonally, inexorably, the metallic voice of the broadcast system reached into every farthest corner of the ship.

And from every corner of the ship men came in answer to the call. They were cold men, shivering involuntarily in the icy north wind, sweating pungently as the heavy falling snow drifted under collars and cuffs, as numbed hands stuck to frozen ropes and metal. They were tired men, for fuelling, provisioning and ammunitioning had gone on far into the middle watch: few had had more than three hours' sleep.

And they were still angry, hostile men. Orders were obeyed, to be sure, with the mechanical efficiency of a highly-trained ship's company; but obedience was surly, acquiescence resentful, and insolence lay ever close beneath the surface. But Divisional officers and NCOs handled the men with velvet gloves: Vallery had been emphatic about that.

Illogically enough, the highest pitch of resentment had not been caused by the *Cumberland's* prudent withdrawal. It had been produced the previous evening by the routine broadcast. 'Mail will close at 2000 tonight.' Mail! Those who weren't working non-stop round the clock were sleeping like the dead with neither the heart nor the will even to think of writing. Leading Seaman Doyle, the doyen of 'B' mess-deck and a venerable three-badger (thirteen years' undiscovered crime, as he modestly explained his good-conduct stripes) had summed up the matter succinctly: 'If my old Missus was Helen of Troy and Jane Russell rolled into one—and all you blokes wot have seen the old dear's photo know that the very idea's a shocking libel on either of them ladies—I still wouldn't send her even a bleedin' postcard. You gotta draw a line somewhere. Me, for my scratcher.' Whereupon he had dragged his hammock from the rack, slung it with millimetric accuracy beneath a hot-air louvre—seniority carries its privileges—and was asleep in two minutes. To a man, the port watch did likewise: the mail bag had gone ashore almost empty . . .

At 0600, exactly to the minute, the *Ulysses* slipped her moorings and steamed slowly towards the boom. In the grey half-light, under leaden, lowering clouds, she slid across the anchorage like an insubstantial ghost, more often than not half-hidden from view under sudden, heavy flurries of snow.

Even in the relatively clear spells, she was difficult to locate. She lacked solidity, substance, definition of outline. She had a curious air of impermanence, of volatility. An illusion, of course, but an illusion that accorded well with a legend—for a legend the *Ulysses* had become in her own brief lifetime. She was known and cherished by merchant seamen, by the men who sailed the bitter seas of the North, from St John's to Archangel, from the Shetlands to Jan Mayen, from Greenland to far reaches of Spitzbergen, remote on the edge of the world. Where there was danger, where there was death, there you might look to find the *Ulysses*, materializing wraith-like from a fog-bank, or just miraculously being there when the bleak twilight of an Arctic dawn brought with it only the threat, at times almost the certainty, of never seeing the next.

A ghost-ship, almost, a legend. The *Ulysses* was also a young ship, but she had grown old in the Russian Convoys and on the Arctic patrols. She had been there from the beginning, and had known no other life. At first she had operated alone, escorting single ships or groups of two or three: later, she had operated without her squadron, the 14th Escort Carrier group.

But the *Ulysses* had never really sailed alone. Death had been, still was, her constant companion. He laid his finger on a tanker, and there was the erupting hell of a high-octane detonation; on a cargo liner, and she went to the bottom with her load of war supplies, her back broken by a German torpedo; on a destroyer, and she knifed her way into the grey-black depths of the Barents Sea, her still-racing engines her own executioners; on a U-boat, and she surfaced violently to be destroyed by gunfire, or slid down gently to the bottom of the sea, the dazed, shocked crew hoping for a cracked pressure hull and merciful instant extinction, dreading the endless gasping agony of suffocation in their iron tomb on the ocean floor. Where the *Ulysses* went, there also went death. But death never touched her. She was a lucky ship. A lucky ship and a ghost ship and the Arctic was her home.

Illusion, of course, this ghostliness, but a calculated illusion. The *Ulysses* was designed specifically for one task, for one ocean, and the camouflage experts had done a marvellous job. The special Arctic camouflage, the broken, slanting diagonals of grey and white and washed-out blues merged beautifully, imperceptibly into the infinite shades of grey and white, the cold, bleak grimness of the barren northern seas.

And the camouflage was only the outward, the superficial indication of her fitness for the north.

Technically, the *Ulysses* was a light cruiser. She was the only one of her kind, a 5,500-ton modification of the famous *Dido* type, a forerunner of the *Black Prince* class. Five hundred and ten feet long, narrow in her fifty-foot beam with a raked stem, square cruiser stern and long fo'c'sle deck extending well abaft the bridge—a distance of over two hundred feet, she looked and was a lean, fast and compact warship, dangerous and durable.

'Locate: engage: destroy.' These are the classic requirements of a naval ship in wartime, and to do each, and to do it with maximum speed and efficiency, the *Ulysses* was superbly equipped.

Location, for instance. The human element, of course, was indispensable, and Vallery was far too experienced and battlewise a captain to underestimate the value of the unceasing vigil of lookouts and signalmen. The human eye was not subject to blackouts, technical hitches or mechanical breakdowns. Radio reports, too, had their place and Asdic, of course, was the only defence against submarines.

But the *Ulysses*'s greatest strength in location lay elsewhere. She was the first completely equipped radar ship in the world. Night and day, the radar scanners atop the fore and main tripod masts swept ceaselessly in a 360° arc, combing the far horizons, searching, searching. Below, in the radar rooms—eight in all—and in the Fighter Direction rooms, trained eyes, alive to the slightest abnormality, never left the glowing screens. The radar's efficiency and range were alike fantastic. The makers, optimistically, as they had thought, had claimed a 40-45 mile operating range for their equipment. On the *Ulysses*'s first trials after her refit for its installation, the radar had located a Condor, subsequently destroyed by a Blenheim, at a range of eighty-five miles.

Engage—that was the next step. Sometimes the enemy came to you, more often you had to go after him. And then, one thing alone mattered—speed.

The *Ulysses* was tremendously fast. Quadruple screws powered by four great Parsons singlereduction geared turbines—two in the for'ard, two in the after engine-room—developed an unbelievable horsepower that many a battleship, by no means obsolete, could not match. Officially, she was rated at 33.5 knots. Off Arran, in her full-power trials, bows lifting out of the water, stern dug in like a hydroplane, vibrating in every Clyde-built rivet, and with the tortured, seething water boiling whitely ten feet above the level of the poop-deck, she had covered the measured mile at an incredible 39.2 knots—the nautical equivalent of 45 mph. And the 'Dude'—Engineer-Commander Dobson—had smiled knowingly, said he wasn't half trying and just wait till the *Abdiel* or the *Manxman* came along, and he'd show them something. But as these famous mine-laying cruisers were widely believed to be capable of 44 knots, the wardroom had merely sniffed 'Professional jealousy' and ignored him. Secretly, they were as proud of the great engines as Dobson himself.

Locate, engage—and destroy. Destruction. That was the be-all, the end-all. Lay the enemy along the sights and destroy him. The *Ulysses* was well equipped for that also.

She had four twin gun-turrets, two for'ard, two aft, 5.25 quick-firing and dual-purpose—equally effective against surface targets and aircraft. These were controlled from the Director Towers, the main one for'ard, just above and abaft of the bridge, the auxiliary aft. From these towers, all essential data about bearing, wind-speed, drift, range, own speed, enemy speed, respective angles of course were fed to the giant electronic computing tables in the Transmitting Station, the fighting heart of the ship, situated, curiously enough, in the very bowels of the *Ulysses*, deep below the water-line, and thence automatically to the turrets as two simple factors—elevation and training. The turrets, of course, could also fight independently.

These were the main armament. The remaining guns were purely AA—the batteries of multiple pompoms, firing two-pounders in rapid succession, not particularly accurate but producing a blanket curtain sufficient to daunt any enemy pilot, and isolated clusters of twin Oerlikons, high-precision, highvelocity weapons, vicious and deadly in trained hands.

Finally, the *Ulysses* carried her depth-charges and torpedoes—36 charges only, a negligible number compared to that carried by many corvettes and destroyers, and the maximum number that could be dropped in one pattern was six. But one depthcharge carries 450 lethal pounds of Amatol, and the *Ulysses* had destroyed two U-boats during the preceding winter. The 21-inch torpedoes, each with its 750-pound warhead of TNT, lay sleek and menacing, in the triple tubes on the main deck, one set on either side of the after funnel. These had not yet been blooded.

This, then, was the *Ulysses*. The complete, the perfect fighting machine, man's ultimate, so far, in his attempt to weld science and savagery into an instrument of destruction. The perfect fighting machine—but only so long as it was manned and serviced by a perfectly-integrating, smoothlyfunctioning team. A ship—any ship—can never be better than its crew. And the crew of the *Ulysses* was disintegrating, breaking up: the lid was clamped on the volcano, but the rumblings never ceased.

The first signs of further trouble came within three hours of clearing harbour. As always, minesweepers swept the channel ahead of them, but, as always, Vallery left nothing to chance. It was one of the reasons why he—and the *Ulysses*—had survived thus far. At 0620 he streamed paravanes—the slender, torpedo-shaped bodies which angled out from the bows, one on either side, on special paravane wire. In theory the wires connecting mines to their moorings on the floor of the sea were deflected away from the ship, guided out to the paravanes themselves and severed by cutters: the mines would then float to the top to be exploded or sunk by small arms.

At 0900, Vallery ordered the paravanes to be recovered. The *Ulysses* slowed down. The First Lieutenant, Lieutenant Commander Carrington, went to the fo'c'sle to supervise operations: seamen, winch drivers, and the Subs in charge of either side closed up to their respective stations.

Quickly the recovery booms were freed from their angled crutches, just abaft the port and starboard lights, swung out and rigged with recovery wires. Immediately, the three ton winches on 'B' gun-deck took the strain, smoothly, powerfully; the paravanes cleared the water.

Then it happened. It was A.B. Ferry's fault that it happened. And it was just ill-luck that the port winch was suspect, operating on a power circuit with a defective breaker, just ill-luck that Ralston was the winch-driver, a taciturn, bitter-mouthed Ralston to whom, just then, nothing mattered a damn, least of all what he said and did. But it was Carslake's responsibility that the affair developed into what it did.

Sub-Lieutenant Carslake's presence there, on top of the Carley floats, directing the handling of the port wire, represented the culmination of a series of mistakes. A mistake on the part of his father, Rear-Admiral, Rtd, who had seen in his son a man of his own calibre, had dragged him out of Cambridge in 1939 at the advanced age of twenty-six and practically forced him into the Navy: a weakness on the part of his first CO, a corvette captain who had known his father and recommended him as a candidate for a commission: a rare error of judgment on the part of the selection board of the *King Alfred*, who had granted him his commission; and a temporary lapse on the part of the Commander, who had assigned him to this duty, in spite of Carslake's known incompetence and inability to handle men.

He had the face of an overbred racehorse, long, lean and narrow, with prominent pale-blue eyes and protruding upper teeth. Below his scanty fair hair, his eyebrows were arched in a perpetual question mark: beneath the long, pointed nose, the supercilious curl of the upper lip formed the perfect complement to the eyebrows. His speech was a shocking caricature of the King's English: his short vowels were long, his long ones interminable: his grammar was frequently execrable. He resented the Navy, he resented his long overdue promotion to Lieutenant, he resented the way the men resented him. In brief, Sub-Lieutenant Carslake was the quintessence of the worst by-product of the English public-school system. Vain, superior, uncouth and ill-educated, he was a complete ass.

He was making an ass of himself now. Striving to maintain balance on the rafts, feet dramatically braced at a wide angle, he shouted unceasing, unnecessary commands at his men. CPO Hartley groaned aloud, but kept otherwise silent in the interests of discipline. But AB Ferry felt himself under no such restraints.

''Ark at his Lordship,' he murmured to Ralston. 'All for the Skipper's benefit.' He nodded at where Vallery was leaning over the bridge, twenty feet above Carslake's head. 'Impresses him no end, so his nibs reckons.'

'Just you forget about Carslake and keep your eyes on that wire,' Ralston advised. 'And take these damned great gloves off. One of these days—'

'Yes, yes, I know,' Ferry jeered. 'The wire's going to snag 'em and wrap me round the drum.' He fed in the hawser expertly. 'Don't you worry, chum, it's never going to happen to me.'

But it did. It happened just then. Ralston, watching the swinging paravane closely, flicked a glance inboard. He saw the broken strand inches from Ferry, saw it hook viciously into the gloved hand and drag him towards the spinning drum before Ferry had a chance to cry out.

Ralston's reaction was immediate. The footbrake was only six inches away—but that was too far. Savagely he spun the control wheel, full ahead to full reverse in a split second. Simultaneoulsy with Ferry's cry of pain as his forearm crushed against the lip of the drum came a muffled explosion and clouds of acrid smoke from the winch as £500-worth of electric motor burnt out in a searing flash.

Immediately the wire began to run out again, accelerating momentarily under the dead weight of the lunging paravane. Ferry went with it. Twenty feet from the winch the wire passed through a snatch-block on the deck: if Ferry was lucky, he might lose only his hand.

He was less than four feet away when Ralston's foot stamped viciously on the brake. The racing drum screamed to a shuddering stop, the paravane crashed down into the sea and the wire, weightless now, swung idly to the rolling of the ship.

Carslake scrambled down off the Carley, his sallow face suffused with anger. He strode up to Ralston.

'You bloody fool!' he mouthed furiously. 'You've lost us that paravane. By God, LTO, you'd better explain yourself! Who the hell gave you orders to do anything?'

Ralston's mouth tightened, but he spoke civilly enough.

'Sorry, sir. Couldn't help it—it had to be done. Ferry's arm—'

'To hell with Ferry's arm!' Carslake was almost screaming with rage. 'I'm in charge here—and I give the orders. Look! Look!' He pointed to the swinging wire. 'Your work, Ralston, you—you blundering idiot! It's gone, gone, do you understand, *gone*?'

Ralston looked over the side with an air of large surprise.

'Well, now, so it is.' The eyes were bleak, the tone provocative, as he looked back at Carslake and patted the winch. 'And don't forget this—it's gone too, and it costs a ruddy sight more than any paravane.'

'I don't want any of your damned impertinence!' Carslake shouted. His mouth was working, his voice shaking with passion. 'What you need is to have some discipline knocked into you and, by God, I'm going to see you get it, you insolent young bastard!'

Ralston flushed darkly. He took one quick step forward, his fist balled, then relaxed heavily as the powerful hands of CPO Hartley caught his swinging arm. But the damage was done now. There was nothing for it but the bridge.

Vallery listened calmly, patiently, as Carslake made his outraged report. He felt far from patient. God only knew, he thought wearily, he had more than enough to cope with already. But the unruffled professional mask of detachment gave no hint of his feelings.

'Is this true, Ralston?' he asked quietly, as Carslake finished his tirade. 'You disobeyed orders, swore at the Lieutenant and insulted him?'

'No, sir.' Ralston sounded as weary as the Captain felt. 'It's not true.' He looked at Carslake, his face expressionless, then turned back to the Captain. 'I didn't disobey orders—there were none. Chief Petty Officer Hartley knows that.' He nodded at the burly impassive figure who had accompanied them to the bridge. 'I didn't swear at him. I hate to sound like a sea-lawyer, sir, but there are plenty of witnesses that Sub-Lieutenant Carslake swore at me—several times. And if I insulted him'—he smiled faintly—'it was pure self-defence.'

'This is no place for levity, Ralston.' Vallery's voice was cold. He was puzzled—the boy baffled him. The bitterness, the brittle composure—he could understand these; but not the flickering humour. 'As it happens, I saw the entire incident. Your promptness, your resource, saved the rating's arm, possibly even his life—and against that a lost paravane and wrecked winch are nothing.' Carslake whitened at the implied rebuke. 'I'm grateful for that—thank you. As for the rest, Commander's Defaulters tomorrow morning. Carry on, Ralston.'

Ralston compressed his lips, looked at Vallery for a long moment, then saluted abruptly and left the bridge.

Carslake turned round appealingly.

'Captain, sir . . . ' He stopped at the sight of Vallery's upraised hand.

'Not now, Carslake. We'll discuss it later.' He made no attempt to conceal the dislike in his voice. 'You may carry on, Lieutenant. Hartley—a word with you.'

Hartley stepped forward. Forty-four years old, CPO Hartley was the Royal Navy at its best. Very tough, very kindly and very competent, he enjoyed the admiration of all, ranging from the vast awe of the youngest Ordinary Seaman to the warm respect of the Captain himself. They had been together from the beginning.

'Well, Chief, let's have it. Between ourselves.'

'Nothing to it really, sir.' Hartley shrugged. 'Ralston did a fine job. Sub-Lieutenant Carslake lost his head. Maybe Ralston *was* a bit sassy, but he was provoked. He's only a kid, but he's a professional—and he doesn't like being pushed around by amateurs.' Hartley paused and looked up at the sky. 'Especially bungling amateurs.'

Vallery smothered a smile.

'Could that be interpreted as—er—a criticism, Chief?'

'I suppose so, sir.' He nodded forward. 'A few ruffled feathers down there, sir. Men are pretty sore about this. Shall I—?'

'Thanks, Chief. Play it down as much as possible.'

When Hartley had gone, Vallery turned to Tyndall.

'Well, you heard it, sir? Another straw in the wind.'

'A straw?' Tyndall was acid. 'Hundreds of straws. More like a bloody great cornstack . . . Find out who was outside my door last night?'

During the middle watch, Tyndall had heard an unusual scraping noise outside the wardroom entry to his day cabin, had gone to investigate himself: in his hurry to reach the door, he'd knocked a chair over, and seconds later he had heard a clatter and the patter of running feet in the passage outside; but, when he had thrown the door open, the passage had been empty. Nothing there, nothing at all—except a file on the deck, below the case of Navy Colt .445s; the chain on the trigger guards was almost through.

Vallery shook his head.

'No idea at all, sir.' His face was heavy with worry. 'Bad, really bad.'

Tyndall shivered in an ice flurry. He grinned crookedly.

'Real Captain Teach stuff, eh? Pistols and cutlasses and black eyepatches, storming the bridge . . . '

Vallery shook his head impatiently.

'No, not that. You know it, sir. Defiance, maybe, but—well, no more. The point is, a marine is on guard at the keyboard—just round the corner of that passage. Night and day. Bound to have seen him. He denies—'

'The rot has gone that far?' Tyndall whistled softly. 'A black day, Captain. What does our fireeating young Captain of Marines say to that?'

'Foster? Pooh-poohs the very idea—and just about twists the ends of his moustache off. Worried to hell. So's Evans, his Colour-Seargeant.'

'So am I!' said Tyndall feelingly. He glared into space. The Officer of the Watch, who happened to be in his direct line of vision, shifted uncomfortably. 'Wonder what old Socrates thinks of it all, now? Maybe only a pill-roller, but the wisest head we've got . . . Well, speak of the devil!'

The gate had just swung open, and a burly, unhappy-looking figure, duffel-coated, oilskinned and wearing a Russian beaverskin helmet—the total effect was of an elderly grizzly bear caught in a thunderstorm—shuffled across the duckboards of the bridge. He brought up facing the Kent screen—an inset, circular sheet of glass which revolved at high speed and offered a clear view in all weather conditions—rain, hail, snow. For half a minute he peered miserably through this and obviously didn't like what he saw.

He sniffed loudly and turned away, beating his arms against the cold.

'Ha! A deck officer on the bridge of HM Cruisers. The romance, the glamour! Ha!' He hunched his oilskinned shoulders, and looked more miserable than ever. 'No place this for a civilized man like myself. But you know how it is, gentlemen—the clarion call of duty . . .'

Tyndall chuckled.

'Give him plenty of time, Captain. Slow starters, these medics, you know, but—'

Brooks cut in, voice and face suddenly serious.

'Some more trouble, Captain. Couldn't tell it over the phone. Don't know how much it's worth.'

'Trouble?' Vallery broke off, coughed harshly into his handkerchief. 'Sorry,' he apologized. 'Trouble? There's nothing else, old chap. Just had some ourselves.'

'That bumptious young fool, Carslake? Oh, I know all right. My spies are everywhere. Bloke's a bloody menace . . . However, my story.

'Young Nicholls was doing some path. work late last night in the dispensary—on TB specimens. Two, three hours in there. Lights out in the bay, and the patients either didn't know or had forgotten he was there. Heard Stoker Riley—a real trouble-maker, that Riley—and the others planning a locked-door, sit-down strike in the boiler-room when they return to duty. A sit-down strike in a boiler-room. Good lord, it's fantastic! Anyway, Nicholls let it slide—pretended he hadn't heard.'

'What!' Vallery's voice was sharp, edged with anger. 'And Nicholls ignored it, didn't report it to me! Happened last night, you say. Why wasn't I told—immediately? Get Nicholls up here—now. No, never mind.' He reached out to pick up the bridge phone. 'I'll get him myself.'

Brooks laid a gauntleted hand on Vallery's arm.

'I wouldn't do that, sir. Nicholls is a smart boy—very smart indeed. He knew that if he let the men know they had been overheard, they would know that he must report it to you. And then you'd have been bound to take action—and open provocation of trouble is the last thing you want. You said so yourself in the ward-room last night.'

Vallery hesitated. 'Yes, yes, of course I said that, but—well, Doc, this is different. It could be a focal point for spreading the idea to—'

'I told you, sir,' Brooks interrupted softly. 'Johnny Nicholls is a very smart boy. He's got a big notice, in huge red letters, outside the Sick Bay door: "Keep clear: Suspected scarlet fever infection." Kills me to watch 'em. Everybody avoids the place like the plague. Not a hope of communicating with their pals in the Stokers' Mess.'

Tyndall guffawed at him, and even Vallery smiled slightly.

'Sounds fine, Doc. Still, I should have been told last night.'

'Why should you be woken up and told every little thing in the middle of the night?' Brooks's voice was brusque. 'Sheer selfishness on my part, but what of it? When things get bad, you damn well carry this ship on your back—and when we've all got to depend on you, we can't afford to have you anything less than as fit as possible. Agreed, Admiral?'

Tyndall nodded solemnly. 'Agreed, O Socrates. A very complicated way of saying that you wish the Captain to have a good night's sleep. But agreed.'

Brooks grinned amiably. 'Well, that's all, gentlemen. See you all at the court-martial—I hope.' He cocked a jaundiced eye over a shoulder, into the thickening snow. 'Won't the Med be wonderful, gentlemen?' He sighed and slid effortlessly into his native Galway brogue. 'Malta in the spring. The beach at Sliema—with the white houses behind—where we picnicked, a hundred years ago. The soft winds, me darlin' boys, the *warm* winds, the blue skies and Chianti under a striped umbrealla—'

'Off!' Tyndall roared. 'Get off this bridge, Brooks, or I'll—'

'I'm gone already,' said Brooks. 'A sit-down strike in the boiler-room! Ha! First thing you know, there'll be a rash of male suffragettes chaining themselves to the guardrails!' The gate clanged shut behind him.

Vallery turned to the Admiral, his face grave.

'Looks as if you were right about that cornstack, sir.'

Tyndall grunted, non-commitally.

'Maybe. Trouble is, the men have nothing to do right now except brood and curse and feel bitter about everything. Later on it'll be all right—perhaps.'

'When we get—ah—busier, you mean?'

'Mmm. When you're fighting for your life, to keep the ship afloat—well, you haven't much time for plots and pondering over the injustices of fate. Self-preservation is still the first law of nature . . . Speaking to the men tonight. Captain?'

'Usual routine broadcast, yes. In the first dog, when we're all closed up to dusk action stations.' Vallery smiled briefly. 'Make sure that they're all awake.'

'Good. Lay it on thick and heavy. Give 'em plenty to think about—and, if I'm any judge of Vincent Starr's hints, we're going to *have* plenty to think about this trip. It'll keep 'em occupied.'

Vallery laughed. The laugh transformed his thin sensitive face.

He seemed genuinely amused.

Tyndall lifted an interrogatory eyebrow. Vallery smiled back at him.

'Just passing thoughts, sir. As Spencer Faggot would have said, things have come to a pretty pass . . . Things are bad indeed, when only the enemy can save us.'

THREE

Monday Afternoon

All day long the wind blew steadily out of the nor'nor'-west. A strong wind, and blowing stronger. A cold wind, a sharp wind full of little knives, it carried with it snow and ice and the strange dead smell born of the forgotten ice-caps that lie beyond the Barrier. It wasn't a gusty, blowy wind. It was a settled, steady kind of wind, and it stayed fine on the starboard bow from dawn to dusk. Slowly, stealthily, it was lifting a swell. Men like Carrington, who knew every sea and port in the world, like Vallery and Hartley, looked at it and were troubled and said nothing.

The mercury crept down and the snow lay where it fell. The tripods and yardarms were great, glistening Xmas trees, festooned with woolly stays and halliards. On the mainmast, a brown smear appeared now and then, daubed on by a wisp of smoke from the after funnel, felt rather than seen: in a moment, it would vanish. The snow lay on the deck and drifted. It softened the anchor-cables on the fo'c'sle deck into great, fluffy ropes of cottonwool, and drifted high against the breakwater before 'A' turret. It piled up against the turrets and superstructure, swished silently into the bridge and lay there slushily underfoot. It blocked the great eyes of the Director's range-finder, it crept unseen along passages, it sifted soundlessly down hatches. It sought out the tiniest unprotected chink in metal and wood, and made the mess-decks dank and clammy and uncomfortable: it defied gravity and slid effortlessly up trouser legs, up under the skirts of coats and oilskins, up under duffel hoods, and made men thoroughly miserable. A miserable world, a wet world, but always and predominately a white world of softness and beauty and strangely muffled sound. All day long it fell, this snow, fell steadily and persistently, and the *Ulysses* slid on silently through the swell, a ghost ship in a ghost world.

But not alone in her world. She never was, these days. She had companionship, a welcome, reassuring companionship, the company of the 14th Aircraft Squadron, a tough, experienced and battle-hardened escort group, almost as legendary now as that fabulous Force 8, which had lately moved South to take over that other suicide run, the Malta convoys.

Like the *Ulysses,* the squadron steamed NNW all day long. There were no dog-legs, no standard course alterations. Tyndall abhorred the zig-zag, and, except on actual convoy and then only in known U-boat waters, rarely used it. He believed—as many captains did—that the zig-zag was a greater potential source of danger than the enemy. He had seen the *Curaçoa,* 4,200 tons of cockle-shell cruiser, swinging on a routine zig-zag, being trampled into the grey depths of the Atlantic under the mighty forefoot of the *Queen Mary.* He never spoke of it, but the memory stayed with him.

The *Ulysses* was in her usual position—the position dictated by her role of Squadron flagship—as nearly as possible in the centre of the thirteen warships.

Dead ahead steamed the cruiser *Stirling.* An old Cardiff class cruiser, she was a solid, reliable ship, many years older and many knots slower than the *Ulysses,* adequately armed with five single six-inch guns, but hardly built to hammer her way through the Arctic gales: in heavy seas, her wetness was proverbial. Her primary role was squadron defence: her secondary, to take over the squadron if the flagship were crippled or sunk.

The carriers—*Defender, Invader, Wrestler* and *Blue Ranger*—were in position to port and starboard, the *Defender* and *Wrestler* slightly ahead of the *Ulysses,* the others slightly astern. It seemed *de rigeur* for these escort carriers to have names ending in -er and the fact that the Navy already had a *Wrestler*—a Force 8 destroyer (and a *Defender,* which had been sunk some time previously off Tobruk)—

was blithely ignored. These were not the 35,000-ton giants of the regular fleet—ships like the *Indefatigable* and the *Illustrious*—but 1520,000 ton auxiliary carriers, irreverently known as banana boats. They were converted merchantmen, American-built: these had been fitted out at Pascagoula, Mississippi, and sailed across the Atlantic by mixed British-American crews.

They were capable of eighteen knots, a relatively high speed for a single-screw ship—the *Wrestler* had two screws—but some of them had as many as four Busch-Sulzer Diesels geared to the one shaft. Their painfully rectangular flight-decks, 450 feet in length, were built up above the open fo'c'sle—one could see right under the flight-deck for'ard of the bridge—and flew off about thirty fighters—Grummans, Seafires or, most often, Corsairs—or twenty light bombers. They were odd craft, awkward, ungainly and singularly unwarlike; but over the months they had done a magnificent job of providing umbrella cover against air attack, of locating and destroying enemy ships and submarines: their record of kills, above, on and below the water was impressive and frequently disbelieved by the Admiralty.

Nor was the destroyer screen calculated to inspire confidence among the naval strategists at Whitehall. It was a weird hodgepodge, and the term 'destroyer' was a purely courtesy one.

One, the *Nairn*, was a River class frigate of 1,500 tons: another, the *Eager*, was a Fleet Minesweeper, and a third, the *Gannet*, better known as *Huntley and Palmer*, was a rather elderly and very tired Kingfisher corvette, supposedly restricted to coastal duties only. There was no esoteric mystery as to the origin of her nickname—a glance at her silhouette against the sunset was enough. Doubtless her designer had worked within Admiralty specifications: even so, he must have had an off day.

The *Vectra* and the *Viking* were twin-screwed, modified 'V' and 'W' destroyers, in the superannuated class now, lacking in speed and firepower, but tough and durable. The *Baliol* was a diminutive Hunt class destroyer which had no business in the great waters of the north. The *Portpatrick*, a skeleton-lean four stacker, was one of the fifty lend-lease World War I destroyers from the United States.

No one even dared guess at her age. An intriguing ship at any time, she became the focus of all eyes in the fleet and a source of intense interest whenever the weather broke down. Rumour had it that two of her sister ships had overturned in the Atlantic during a gale; human nature being what it is, everyone wanted a grandstand view whenever weather conditions deteriorated to an extent likely to afford early confirmation of these rumours. What the crew of the *Portpatrick* thought about it all was difficult to say.

These seven escorts, blurred and softened by the snow, kept their screening stations all day—the frigate and minesweeper ahead, the destroyers at the sides, and the corvette astern. The eight escort, a fast, modern 'S' class destroyer, under the command of the Captain (Destroyers), Commander Orr, prowled restlessly around the fleet. Every ship commander in the squadron envied Orr his roving commission, a duty which Tyndall had assigned him in self-defence against Orr's continual pestering. But no one objected, no one grudged him his privilege: the *Sirrus* had an uncanny nose for trouble, an almost magnetic affinity for U-boats lying in ambush.

From the warmth of the *Ulysses*'s wardroom—long, incongruously comfortable, running fifty feet along the starboard side of the fo'c'sle deck—Johnny Nicholls gazed out through the troubled grey and white of the sky. Even the kindly snow, he reflected, blanketing a thousand sins, could do little for these queer craft, so angular, so graceless, so obviously out-dated.

He supposed he ought to feel bitter at My Lords of the Admiralty, with their limousines and armchairs and elevenses, with their big wall-maps and pretty little flags, sending out this raggle-taggle of squadron to cope with the pick of the U-boat packs, while they sat comfortably, luxuriously at home. But the thought died at birth: it was he knew, grotesquely unjust. The Admiralty would have given them a dozen brand-new destroyers—if they had them. Things, he knew were pretty bad, and the demands of the Atlantic and the Mediterranean had first priority.

He supposed, too, he ought to feel cynical, ironic, at the sight of these old and worn-out ships. Strangely, he couldn't. He knew what they could do, what they had done. If he felt anything at all towards them, it was something uncommonly close to admiration—perhaps even pride. Nicholls stirred uncomfortably and turned away from the porthole. His gaze fell on the somnolent form of the Kapok Kid, flat on his back in an arm-chair, an enormous pair of fur-lined flying-boots perched above the electric fire.

The Kapok Kid, Lieutenant the Honourable Andrew Carpenter, RN, Navigator of the *Ulysses* and his best friend—he was the one to feel proud, Nicholls thought wryly. The most glorious extrovert Nicholls had ever known, the Kapok Kid was equally at home anywhere—on a dance floor or in the cockpit of a racing yacht at Cowes, at a garden party, on a tennis court or at the wheel of his big crimson Bugatti, windscreen down and the loose ends of a seven-foot scarf streaming out behind him. But appearances were never more deceptive. For the Kapok Kid, the Royal Navy was his whole life, and he lived for that alone. Behind that slightly inane façade lay, besides a first-class brain, a deeply romantic streak, an almost Elizabethan love for sea and ships which he sought, successfully, he imagined, to conceal from all his fellow-officers. It was so patently obvious that no one ever thought it worth the mentioning.

Theirs was a curious friendship, Nicholls mused. An attraction of opposites, if ever there was one. For Carpenter's hail-fellow ebullience, his natural reserve and reticence were the perfect foil: over against his friend's near-idolatry of all things naval stood his own thorough-going detestation of all that the Kapok Kid so warmly admired. Perhaps because of that over-developed sense of individuality and independence, that bane of so many highland Scots, Nicholls objected strongly to the thousand and one pin-pricks of discipline, authority and bureaucratic naval stupidity which were a constant affront to his intelligence and self-respect. Even three years ago, when the war had snatched him from the wards of a great Glasgow hospital, his first year's internship barely completed, he had had his dark suspicions that the degree of compatibility between himself and the Senior Service would prove to be singularly low. And so it had proved. But, in spite of this antipathy—or perhaps because of it and the curse of a Calvinistic conscience—

Nicholls had become a first-class officer. But it still disturbed him vaguely to discover in himself something akin to pride in the ships of his squadron.

He sighed. The loudspeaker in the corner of the wardroom had just crackled into life. From bitter experience, he knew that broadcast announcements seldom presaged anything good.

'Do you hear there? Do you hear there?' The voice was metallic, impersonal: the Kapok Kid slept on in magnificent oblivion. 'The Captain will broadcast to the ship's company at 1730 tonight. Repeat. The Captain will broadcast to the ship's company at 1730 tonight. That is all.'

Nicholls prodded the Kapok Kid with a heavy toe. 'On your feet, Vasco. Now's the time if you want a cuppa char before getting up there and navigating.' Carpenter stirred, opened a red-rimmed eye: Nicholls smiled down encouragingly. 'Besides, it's lovely up top now—sea rising, temperature falling and a young blizzard blowing. Just what you were born for, Andy, boy!'

The Kapok Kid groaned his way back to consciousness, struggled to a sitting position and remained hunched forward, his straight flaxen hair falling over his hands.

'What's the matter now?' His voice was querulous, still slurred with sleep. Then he grinned faintly. 'Know where I was, Johnny?' he asked reminiscently. 'Back on the Thames, at the Grey Goose, just up from Henley. It was summer, Johnny, late in summer, warm and very still. Dressed all in green, she was—'

'Indigestion,' Nicholls cut in briskly. 'Too much easy living . . . It's four-thirty, and the old man's speaking in an hour's time. Dusk stations at any time—we'd better eat.'

Carpenter shook his head mournfully. 'The man has no soul, no finer feelings.' He stood up and stretched himself. As always, he was dressed from head to foot in a one-piece overall of heavy, quilted kapok—the silk fibres encasing the seeds of the Japanese and Malayan silk-cotton tree: there was a great, golden 'J' embroidered on the right breast pocket: what it stood for was anyone's guess. He glanced out through the porthole and shuddered.

'Wonder what's the topic for tonight, Johnny?'

'No idea. I'm curious to see what his attitude, his tone is going to be, how he's going to handle it. The situation, to say the least, is somewhat—ah—delicate.' Nicholls grinned, but the smile didn't touch his eyes. 'Not to mention the fact that the crew don't know that they're off to Murmansk again—although they must have a pretty good idea.'

'Mmm.' The Kapok Kid nodded absently. 'Don't suppose the old man'll try to play it down—the hazards of the trip, I mean, or to excuse himself—you know, put the blame where it belongs.'

'Never.' Nicholls shook his head decisively. 'Not the skipper. Just not in his nature. Never excuses himself—and never spares himself.' He stared into the fire for a long time, then looked up quietly at the Kapok Kid. 'The skipper's a very sick man, Andy—very sick indeed.'

'What!' The Kapok Kid was genuinely startled. 'A very sick . . . Good lord, you're joking! You must be. Why—'

'I'm not,' Nicholls interrupted flatly, his voice very low. Winthrop, the padre, an intense, enthusiastic, very young man with an immense zest for life and granitic convictions on every subject under the sun, was in the far corner of the wardroom. The zest was temporarily in abeyance—he was sunk in exhausted slumber. Nicholls liked him, but preferred that he should not hear—the padre would talk. Winthrop, Nicholls had often thought, would never have made a successful priest—confessional reticence would have been impossible for him.

'Old Socrates says he's pretty far through—and he knows,' Nicholls continued. 'Old man phoned him to come to his cabin last night. Place was covered in blood and he was coughing his lungs up. Acute attack of hæmoptysis. Brooks has suspected it for a long time, but the Captain would never let him examine him. Brooks says a few more days of this will kill him.' He broke off, glanced briefly at Winthrop. 'I talk too much,' he said abruptly. 'Getting as bad as the old padre there. Shouldn't have told you, I suppose—violation of professional confidence and all that. All this under your hat, Andy.'

'Of course, of course.' There was a long pause. 'What you mean is, Johnny—he's dying?'

'Just that. Come on, Andy—char.'

Twenty minutes later, Nicholls made his way down to the Sick Bay. The light was beginning to fail and the *Ulysses* was pitching heavily. Brooks was in the surgery.

'Evening, sir. Dusk stations any minute now. Mind if I stay in the bay tonight?'

Brooks eyed him speculatively.

'Regulations,' he intoned, 'say that the Action Stations position of the Junior Medical Officer is aft in the Engineer's Flat. Far be it from me—'

'Please.'

'Why? Lonely, lazy or just plain tired?' The quirk of the eyebrows robbed the words of all offence.

'No. Curious. I want to observe the reactions of Stoker Riley and his—ah—confederates to the skipper's speech. Might be most instructive.'

'Sherlock Nicholls, eh? Right-o, Johnny. Phone the Damage Control Officer aft. Tell him you're tied up. Major operation, anything you like. Our gullible public and how easily fooled. Shame.'

Nicholls grinned and reached for the phone.

When the bugle blared for dusk Action Stations, Nicholls was sitting in the dispensary. The lights were out, the curtains almost drawn. He could see into every corner of the brightly lit Sick Bay. Five of the men were asleep. Two of the others—Petersen, the giant, slow-spoken stoker, half Norwegian, half Scots, and Burgess, the dark little cockney—were sitting up in bed, talking softly, their eyes turned towards the swarthy, heavily-built patient lying between them. Stoker Riley was holding court.

Alfred O'Hara Riley had, at a very early age indeed, decided upon a career of crime, and beset, though he subsequently was, by innumerable vicissitudes, he had clung to this resolve with an unswerving determination: directed towards almost any other sphere of activity, his resolution would have been praiseworthy, possibly even profitable. But praise and profit had passed Riley by.

Every man is what environment and heredity make him. Riley

was no exception, and Nicholls, who knew something of his upbringing, appreciated that life had never really given the big stoker a chance. Born of a drunken, illiterate mother in a filthy, overcrowded and fever-ridden Liverpool slum, he was an outcast from the beginning: allied to that, his hairy, ape-like figure, the heavy prognathous jaw, the twisted mouth, the wide flaring nose, the cunning black eyes squinting out beneath the negligible clearance between hairline and eyebrows that so accurately reflected the mental capacity within, were all admirably adapted to what was to become his chosen vocation. Nicholls looked at him and disapproved without condemning; for a moment, he had an inkling of the tragedy of the inevitable.

Riley was never at any time a very successful criminal—his intelligence barely cleared the moron level. He dimly appreciated his limitations, and had left the higher, more subtle forms of crime severely alone. Robbery—preferably robbery with violence—was his *métier*. He had been in prison six times, the last time for two years.

His induction into the Navy was a mystery which baffled both Riley and the authorities responsible for his being there. But Riley had accepted this latest misfortune with equanimity, and gone through the bomb-shattered 'G' and 'H' blocks in the Royal Naval Barracks, Portsmouth, like a high wind through a field of corn, leaving behind him a trail of slashed suitcases and empty wallets. He had been apprehended without much difficulty, done sixty days' cells, then been drafted to the *Ulysses* as a stoker.

His career of crime aboard the *Ulysses* had been brief and painful. His first attempted robbery had been his last—a clumsy and incredibly foolish rifling of a locker in the marine sergeants' mess. He had been caught red-handed by Colour-Sergeant Evans and Sergeant MacIntosh. They had preferred no charges against him and Riley had spent the next three days in the Sick Bay. He claimed to have tripped on the rung of a ladder and fallen twenty feet to the boiler-room floor. But the actual facts of the case were common knowledge, and Turner had recommended his discharge. To everyone's astonishment, not least that of Stoker Riley, Dodson, the Engineer Commander, had insisted he be given a last chance, and Riley had been reprieved.

Since that date, four months previously, he had confined his activities to stirring up trouble. Illogically but understandably, his brief encounter with the marines had swept away his apathetic tolerance of the Navy: a smouldering hatred took its place. As an agitator, he had achieved a degree of success denied him as a criminal. Admittedly, he had a fertile field for operations; but credit—if that is the word—was due also to his shrewdness, his animal craft and cunning, his hold over his crew-mates. The husky, intense voice, his earnestness, his deep-set eyes, lent Riley a strangely elemental power—a power he had used to its maximum effect a few days previously when he had precipitated the mutiny which had led to the death of Ralston, the stoker, and the marine—mysteriously dead from a broken neck. Beyond any possible doubt, their deaths lay at Riley's door; equally beyond doubt, that could never be proved. Nicholls wondered what new devilment was hatching behind these lowering, corrugated brows, wondered how on earth it was that the same Riley was continually in trouble for bringing aboard the *Ulysses* and devotedly tending every stray kitten, every broken-winged bird he found.

The loudspeaker crackled, cutting through his thoughts, stilling the low voices in the Sick Bay. And not only there, but throughout the ship, in turrets and magazines, in engine-rooms and boiler-rooms, above and below deck everywhere, all conversation ceased. Then there was only the wind, the regular smash of the bows into the deepening troughs, the muffled roar of the great boiler-room intake fans and the hum of a hundred electric motors. Tension lay heavy over the ship, over 730 officers and men, tangible, almost, in its oppression.

'This is the Captain speaking. Good evening.' The voice was calm, well modulated, without a sign of strain or exhaustion. 'As you all know, it is my custom at the beginning of every voyage to inform you as soon as possible of what lies in store for you. I feel that you have a right to know, and that it is my duty. It's not always a pleasant duty—it never has been during recent months. This time, however, I'm almost glad.' He paused, and the words came, slow and measured. 'This is our last operation as a unit of the Home Fleet. In a month's time, God willing, we will be in the Med.'

Good for you, thought Nicholls. Sweeten the pill, lay it on, thick and heavy. But the Captain had other ideas.

'But first, gentlemen, the job on hand. It's the mixture as before—Murmansk again. We rendezvous at 1030 Wednesday, north of Iceland, with a convoy from Halifax. There are eighteen ships in this convoy—big and fast—all fifteen knots and above. Our third Fast Russian convoy, gentlemen—FR77, in case you want to tell your grandchildren about it,' he added dryly. 'These ships are carrying tanks, planes, aviation spirit and oil—nothing else.

'I will not attempt to minimize the dangers. You know how desperate is the state of Russia today, how terribly badly she needs these weapons and fuel. You can also be sure that the Germans know too—and that her Intelligence agents will already have reported the nature of this convoy and the date of sailing.' He broke off short, and the sound of his harsh, muffled coughing into a handkerchief echoed weirdly through the silent ship. He went on slowly. 'There are enough fighter planes and petrol in this convoy to alter the whole character of the Russian war. The Nazis will stop at nothing—I repeat, nothing—to stop this convoy from going through to Russia.

'I have never tried to mislead or deceive you. I will not now. The signs are not good. In our favour we have, firstly, our speed, and secondly—I hope—the element of surprise. We shall try to break through direct for the North Cape.

'There are four major factors against us. You will all have noticed the steady worsening of the weather. We are, I'm afraid, running into abnormal weather conditions—abnormal even for the Arctic. It may—I repeat "may"—prevent U-boat attacks: on the other hand it may mean losing some of the smaller units of our screen—we have no time to heave to or run before bad weather. FR77 is going straight through . . . And it almost certainly means that the carriers will be unable to fly off fighter cover.'

Good God, has the skipper lost his senses, Nicholls wondered. He'll wreck any morale that's left. Not that there *is* any left. What in the world—

'Secondly,' the voice went on, calm, inexorable, 'we are taking no rescue ships on this convoy. There will be no time to stop. Besides, you all know what happened to the *Stockport* and the *Zafaaran*. You're safer where you are.[1]

'Thirdly, two—possibly three—U-boat packs are known to be strung out along latitude seventy degrees and our Northern Norway agents report a heavy mustering of German bombers of all types in their area.

'Finally, we have reason to believe that the *Tirpitz* is preparing to move out.' Again he paused, for an interminable time, it seemed. It was as if he knew the tremendous shock carried in these few words, and wanted to give it time to register. 'I need not tell you what that means. The Germans may risk her to stop the convoy. The Admiralty hope they will. During the latter part of the voyage, capital units of the Home Fleet, including possibly the aircraft-carriers *Victorious* and *Furious*, and three cruisers, will parallel our course at twelve hours' steaming distance. They have been waiting a long time, and we are the bait to spring the trap . . .

'It is possible that things may go wrong. The best-laid plans . . . or the trap may be late in springing shut. This convoy must still get through. If the carriers cannot fly off cover, the *Ulysses* must cover the withdrawal of FR77. You will know what that means. I hope this is all perfectly clear.'

There was another long bout of coughing, another long pause, and when he spoke again the tone had completely changed. He was very quiet.

'I know what I am asking of you. I know how tired, how hopeless, how sick at heart you all feel. I know—no one knows better—what you have been through, how much you need, how much you deserve a rest. Rest you shall have. The entire ship's company goes on ten days' leave from Portsmouth on the eighteenth, then for refit in Alexandria.' The words were casual, as if they carried no significance for him. 'But before that—well, I know it seems cruel, inhuman—it must seem so to you—to ask you to go through it all again, perhaps

---

1. Rescue ships, whose duties were solely what their name implies, were a feature of many of the earlier convoys. The *Zafaaran* was lost in one of the war's worst convoys. The *Stockport* was torpedoed. She was lost with all hands, including all those survivors rescued from other sunken ships.

worse than you've ever gone through before. But I can't help it—no one can help it.' Every sentence, now, was punctuated by long silences: it was difficult to catch his words, so low and far away.

'No one has any right to ask you to do it, I least of all . . . least of all. I know you *will* do it. I know you will not let me down. I know you will take the *Ulysses* through. Good luck. Good luck and God bless you. Good night.'

The loudspeakers clicked off, but the silence lingered on. Nobody spoke and nobody moved. Not even the eyes moved. Those who had been looking at the speakers still gazed on, unseeingly; or stared down at their hands; or down into the glowing butts of forbidden cigarettes, oblivious to the acrid smoke that laced exhausted eyes. It was strangely as if each man wanted to be alone, to look into his own mind, follow his thoughts out for himself, and knew that if his eyes caught another's he would no longer be alone. A strange hush, a supernatural silence, the wordless understanding that so rarely touches mankind: the veil lifts and drops again and a man can never remember what he has seen but knows that he has seen something and that nothing will ever be quite the same again. Seldom, all too seldom it comes: a sunset of surpassing loveliness, a fragment from some great symphony, the terrible stillness which falls over the huge rings of Madrid and Barcelona as the sword of the greatest of the matadors sinks inevitably home. And the Spaniards have the word for it—'the moment of truth'.

The Sick Bay clock, unnaturally loud, ticked away one minute, maybe two. With a heavy sigh—it seemed ages since he had breathed last—Nicholls softly pulled to the sliding door behind the curtains and switched on the light. He looked round at Brooks, looked away again.

'Well, Johnny?' The voice was soft, almost bantering.

'I just don't know, sir, I don't know at all.' Nicholls shook his head. 'At first I thought he was going to—well, make a hash of it. You know, scare the lights out of 'em. And good God!' he went on wonderingly, 'that's exactly what he did do. Piled it on—gales, *Tirpitz*, hordes of subs—and yet . . . ' His voice trailed off.

'And yet?' Brooks echoed mockingly. 'That's just it. Too much intelligence—that's the trouble with the young doctors today. I saw you—sitting there like a bogus psychiatrist, analysing away for all you were worth at the probable effect of the speech on the minds of the wounded warriors without, and never giving it a chance to let it register on yourself.' He paused and went on quietly.

'It was beautifully done, Johnny. No, that's the wrong word—there was nothing premeditated about it. But don't you see? As black a picture as man could paint: points out that this is just a complicated way of committing suicide: no silver lining, no promises, even Alex thrown in as a casual afterthought. Builds 'em up, then lets 'em down. No inducements, no hope, no appeal—and yet the appeal was tremendous . . . What was it, Johnny?'

'I don't know.' Nicholls was troubled. He lifted his head abruptly, then smiled faintly. 'Maybe there *was* no appeal. Listen.' Noiselessly, he slid the door back, flicked off the lights. The rumble of Riley's harsh voice, low and intense, was unmistakable.

'—just a lot of bloody clap-trap. Alex? The Med? Not on your—life, mate. You'll never see it. You'll never even see Scapa again. Captain Richard Vallery, DSO! Know what the old bastard wants, boys? Another bar to his DSO. Maybe even a VC. Well, by Christ's, he's not going to have it! Not at my expense. Not if I can—well help it. "I know you won't let me down,"' he mimicked, his voice high-pitched. 'Whining old bastard!' He paused a moment, then rushed on.

'The *Tirpitz*! Christ Almighty! The *Tirpitz*! We're going to stop it—us! This bloody toy ship! Bait, he says, bait!' His voice rose. 'I tell you, mates, nobody gives a damn about us. Direct for the North Cape! They're throwing us to the bloody wolves! And that old bastard up to—'

'Shaddap!' It was Petersen who spoke, his voice a whisper, low and fierce. His hand stretched out, and Brooks and Nicholls in the surgery winced as they heard Riley's wristbones crack under the tremendous pressure of the giant's hand. 'Often I wonder about you, Riley,' Petersen went on slowly. 'But not now, not any more. You make me sick!' He flung Riley's hand down and turned away.

Riley rubbed his wrist in agony, and turned to Burgess.

'For God's sake, what's the matter with him? What the hell . . .' He broke off abruptly. Burgess was looking at him steadily, kept looking for a long time. Slowly, deliberately, he eased himself down in bed, pulled the blankets up to his neck and turned his back on Riley.

Brooks rose quickly to his feet, closed the door and pressed the light switch.

'Act I, Scene I. Cut! Lights!' he murmured. 'See what I mean, Johnny?'

Yes, sir,' Nicholls nodded slowly. 'At least, I think so.'

'Mind you, my boy, it won't last. At least, not at that intensity.' He grinned. But maybe it'll take us the length of Murmansk. You never know.'

'I hope so, sir. Thanks for the show.' Nicholls reached up for his duffel-coat. 'Well, I suppose I'd better make my way aft.'

'Off you go, then. And, oh—Johnny—'

'Sir?'

'That scarlet-fever notice-board of yours. On your way aft you might consign it to the deep. I don't think we'll be needing it any more.' Nicholls grinned and closed the door softly behind him.

FOUR

Monday Night

Dusk Action Stations dragged out its interminable hour and was gone. That night, as on a hundred other nights, it was just another nagging irritation, a pointless precaution that did not even justify its existence, far less its meticulous thoroughness. Or so it seemed. For although at dawn enemy attacks were routine, at sunset they were all but unknown. It was not always so with other ships, indeed it was rarely so, but then, the *Ulysses* was a lucky ship. Everyone knew that. Even Vallery knew it, but he also knew why. Vigilance was the first article of his sailor's creed.

Soon after the Captain's broadcast, radar had reported a contact, closing. That it was an enemy plane was certain: Commander Westcliffe, Senior Air Arm Officer, had before him in the Fighter Direction Room a wall map showing the operational routes of all Coastal and Ferry Command planes, and this was a clear area. But no one paid the slightest attention to the report, other than Tyndall's order for a 45° course alteration. This was as routine as dusk Action Stations themselves. It was their old friend Charlie coming to pay his respects again.

'Charlie'—usually a four-engine Focke-Wulf Condor—was an institution on the Russian Convoys. He had become to the seamen on the Murmansk run very much what the albatross had been the previous century to sailing men, far south in the Roaring Forties: a bird of ill-omen, half feared but almost amicably accepted, and immune from destruction—though with Charlie, for a different reason. In the early days, before the advent of cam-ships and escort carriers, Charlie frequently spent the entire day, from first light to last, circling a convoy and radioing to base pin-point reports of its position.[1]

Exchanges of signals between British ships and German reconnaissance planes were not unknown, and apocryphal stories were legion. An exchange of pleasantries about the weather was almost commonplace. On several occasions Charlie had plaintively asked for his position and been given highly-detailed latitude and longitude bearings which usually placed him somewhere in the South Pacific; and, of course, a dozen ships claimed the authorship of the story wherein the convoy Commodore sent the signal, 'Please fly the other way round. You are making us dizzy,' and Charlie had courteously acknowledged and turned in his tracks.

Latterly, however, amiability had been markedly absent, and Charlie, grown circumspect with the passing of the months and the appearance of shipborne fighters, rarely appeared except at dusk. His usual practice was to make a single circle of the convoy at a prudent distance and then disappear into the darkness.

That night was no exception. Men caught only fleeting glimpses of the Condor in the driving snow, then quickly lost it in the gathering gloom. Charlie would report the strength, nature and course of the Squadron, although Tyndall had little hope that the German Intelligence would be deceived as to their course. A naval squadron, near the sixty-second degree of latitude, just east of the Faroes, and heading NNE, wouldn't make sense to them—especially as they almost certainly knew of the departure of the convoy from Halifax. Two and two, far too obviously totted up to four.

No attempt was made to fly off Seafires—the only plane with a chance to overhaul the Condor before it disappeared into the night. To locate the carrier again in almost total darkness, even on a radio

---

1. Cam-ships were merchant ships with specially strengthened fo'c'sles. On these were fitted fore-and-aft angled ramps from which fighter planes, such as modified Hurricanes, were catapulted for convoy defence. After breaking off action, the pilot had either to bale out or land in the sea. 'Hazardous' is rather an inadequate word to describe the duties of this handful of very gallant pilots: the chances of survival were not high.

beam, was difficult: to land at night, extremely dangerous; and to land, by guess and by God, in the snow and blackness on a pitching, heaving deck, a suicidal impossibility. The least miscalculation, the slightest error of judgment and you had not only a lost plane but a drowned pilot. A ditched Seafire, with its slender, torpedo-shaped fuselage and the tremendous weight of the great Rolls-Royce Merlin in its nose, was a literal deathtrap. When it went down into the sea, it just kept on going.

Back on to course again, the *Ulysses* pushed blindly into the gathering storm. Hands fell out from Action Stations, and resumed normal Defence Stations—watch and watch, four on, four off. Not a killing routine, one would think: twelve hours on, twelve hours off a day—a man could stand that. And so he could, were that all. But the crew also spent three hours a day at routine Action Stations, every second morning—the forenoon watch—at work (this when they were off-watch) and God only knew how many hours at Action Stations. Beyond all this, all meals—when there were meals—were eaten in their off-duty time. A total of three to four hours' sleep a day was reckoned unusual: forty-eight hours without sleep hardly called for comment.

Step by step, fraction by menacing fraction, mercury and barograph crept down in a deadly dualism. The waves were higher now, their troughs deeper, their shoulders steeper, and the bonechilling wind lashed the snow into a blinding curtain. A bad night, a sleepless night, both above deck and below, on watch and off.

On the bridge, the First Lieutenant, the Kapok Kid, signalmen, the Searchlight LTO, look-outs and messengers peered out miserably into the white night and wondered what it would be like to be warm again. Jerseys, coats, overcoats, duffels, oilskins, scarves, balaclavas, helmets—they wore them all, completely muffled except for a narrow eye-slit in the woollen cocoon, and still they shivered. They wrapped arms and forearms round, and rested their feet on the steam pipes which circled the bridge, and froze. Pom-pom crews huddled miserably in the shelter of their multiple guns, stamped their feet, swung their arms and swore incessantly. And the lonely Oerlikon gunners, each jammed in his lonely cockpit, leaned against the built-in 'black' heaters and fought off the Oerlikon gunner's most insidious enemy—sleep.

The starboard watch, in the mess-decks below, were little happier. There were no bunks for the crew of the *Ulysses*, only hammocks, and these were never slung except in harbour. There were good and sufficient reasons for this. Standards of hygiene on a naval warship are high, compared even to the average civilian home: the average matelot would never consider climbing into his hammock fully dressed—and no one in his senses would have dreamed of undressing on the Russian Convoys. Again, to an exhausted man, the prospect and the actual labour of slinging and then lashing a hammock were alike appalling. And the extra seconds it took to climb out of a hammock in an emergency could represent the margin between life and death, while the very existence of a slung hammock was a danger to all, in that it impeded quick movement. And finally, as on that night of a heavy head sea, there could be no more uncomfortable place than a hammock slung fore and aft.

And so the crew slept where it could, fully clothed even to duffel coats and gloves. On tables and under tables, on narrow nine-inch stools, on the floor, in hammock racks—anywhere. The most popular place on the ship was on the warm steel deck-plates in the alleyway outside the galley, at night-time a weird and spectral tunnel, lit only by a garish red light. A popular sleeping billet, made doubly so by the fact that only a screen separated it from the upper-deck, a scant ten feet away. The fear of being trapped below decks in a sinking ship was always there, always in the back of men's minds.

Even below decks, it was bitterly cold. The hot-air systems operated efficiently only on 'B' and 'C' mess-decks, and even there the temperature barely cleared freezing point. Deckheads dripped constantly and the condensation on the bulkheads sent a thousand little rivulets to pool on the corticene floor. The atmosphere was dank and airless and terribly chill—the ideal breeding ground for the TB, so feared by Surgeon-Commander Brooks. Such conditions, allied with the constant pitching of the ship and the sudden jarring vibrations which were beginning to develop every time the bows crashed down, made sleep almost impossible, at best a fitful, restless unease.

Almost to a man, the crew slept—or tried to sleep—with heads pillowed on inflated lifebelts. Blown up, bent double then tied with tape, these lifebelts made very tolerable pillows. For this purpose, and for this alone, were these lifebelts employed, although standing orders stated explicitly that lifebelts were to be worn at all times during action and in known enemy waters. These orders were completely ignored, not least of all by those Divisional Officers whose duty it was to enforce them. There was enough air trapped in the voluminous and bulky garments worn in these latitudes to keep a man afloat for at least three minutes. If he wasn't picked up in that time, he was dead anyway. It was shock that killed, the tremendous shock of a body at 96° F being suddenly plunged into a liquid temperature some 70° lower—for in the Arctic waters, the sea temperature often falls below normal freezing point. Worse still, the sub-zero wind lanced like a thousand stilettos through the saturated clothing of a man who had been submerged in the sea, and the heart, faced with an almost instantaneous 100° change in body temperature, just stopped beating. But it was a quick death, men said, quick and kind and merciful.

At ten minutes to midnight the Commander and Marshall made their way to the bridge. Even at this late hour and in the wicked weather, the Commander was his usual self, imperturbable and cheerful, lean and piratical, a throw-back to the Elizabethan buccaneers, if ever there was one. He had an unflagging zest for life. The duffel hood, as always, lay over his shoulders, the braided peak of this cap was tilted at a magnificent angle. He groped for the handle of the bridge gate, passed through, stood for a minute accustoming his eyes to the dark, located the First Lieutenant and thumped him resoundingly on the back.

'Well, watchman, and what of the night?' he boomed cheerfully. 'Bracing, yes, decidely so. Situation completely out of control as usual, I suppose? Where are all our chickens this lovely evening?' He peered out into the snow, scanned the horizon briefly, then gave up. 'All gone to hell and beyond, I suppose.'

'Not too bad,' Carrington grinned. An RNR officer and an ex-

Merchant Navy captain in whom Vallery reposed complete confidence, Lieutenant-Commander Carrington was normally a taciturn man, grave and unsmiling. But a particular bond lay between him and Turner, the professional bond of respect which two exceptional seamen have for each other. 'We can see the carriers now and then. Anyway, Bowden and his backroom boys have 'em all pinned to an inch. At least, that's what they say.'

'Better not let old Bowden hear you say that,' Marshall advised. 'Thinks radar is the only step forward the human race has taken since the first man came down from the trees.' He shivered uncontrollably and turned his back on the driving wind. 'Anyway, I wish to God I had his job,' he added feelingly. 'This is worse than winter in Alberta!'

'Nonsense, my boy, stuff and nonsense!' the Commander roared. 'Decadent, that's the trouble with you youngsters nowadays. This is the only life for a self-respecting human being.' He sniffed the icy air appreciatively and turned to Carrington. 'Who's on with you tonight, Number One?'

A dark figure detached itself from the binnacle and approached him.

'Ah, there you are. Well, well, 'pon my soul, if it isn't our navigating officer, the Honourable Carpenter, lost as usual and dressed to kill in his natty gent's suiting. Do you know, Pilot, in that outfit you look like a cross between a deep-sea diver and that advert for Michelin tyres?'

'Ha!' said the Kapok Kid aggrievedly. 'Sniff and scoff while you may, sir.' He patted his quilted chest affectionately. 'Just wait till we're all down there in the drink together, everybody else dragged down or frozen to death, me drifting by warm and dry and comfortable, maybe smoking the odd cigarette—'

'Enough. Be off. Course, Number One?'

'Three-twenty, sir. Fifteen knots.'

'And the Captain?'

'In the shelter.' Carrington jerked his head towards the reinforced steel circular casing at the after end of the bridge. This supported the Director Tower, the control circuits to which ran through a central shaft in the casing. A sea-bunk—a spartan, bare settee—was kept there for the Captain's use. 'Sleeping, I hope,' he added, 'but I very much doubt it. Gave orders to be called at midnight.'

'Why?' Turner demanded.

'Oh, I don't know. Routine, I suppose. Wants to see how things are.'

'Cancel the order,' Turner said briefly. 'Captain's got to learn to obey orders like anybody else—especially doctor's orders. I'll take full responsibility. Good night, Number One.'

The gate clanged shut and Marshall turned uncertainly towards the Commander.

'The Captain, sir. Oh, I know it's none of my business, but'—he hesitated—'well, is he all right?'

Turner looked quickly around him. His voice was unusually quiet.

'If Brooks had his way, the old man would be in hospital.' He was silent for a moment, then added soberly, 'Even then, it might be too late.'

Marshall said nothing. He moved restlessly around, then went aft to the port searchlight control position. For five minutes, an intermittent rumble of voices drifted up to the Commander. He glanced up curiously on Marshall's return.

'That's Ralston, sir,' the Torpedo Officer explained. 'If he'd talk to anybody, I think he'd talk to me.'

'And does he?'

'Sure—but only what *he* wants to talk about. As for the rest, no dice. You can almost see the big notice round his neck—"Private—Keep off". Very civil, very courteous and completely unapproachable. I don't know what the hell to do about him.'

'Leave him be,' Turner advised. 'There's nothing anyone can do.' He shook his head. 'My God, what a lousy break life's given that boy!'

Silence fell again. The snow was lifting now, but the wind still strengthening. It howled eerily through masts and rigging, blending with a wild and eldritch harmony into the haunting pinging of the Asdic. Weird sounds both, weird and elemental and foreboding, that rasped across the nerves and stirred up nameless, atavistic dreads of a thousand ages past, long buried under the press of civilization. An unholy orchestra, and, over years, men grew to hate it with a deadly hatred.

Half-past twelve came, one o'clock, then half-past one. Turner's thought turned fondly towards coffee and cocoa. Coffee or cocoa? Cocoa, he decided, a steaming potent brew, thick with melted chocolate and sugar. He turned to Chrysler, the bridge messenger, young brother of the Leading Asdic Operator.

'WT—Bridge. WT—Bridge.' The loudspeaker above the Asdic cabinet crackled urgently, the voice hurried, insistent. Turner jumped for the hand transmitter, barked an acknowledgement.

'Signal from *Sirrus*. Echoes, port bow, 300, strong, closing. Repeat, echoes, port bow, strong, closing.'

'Echoes, WT? Did you say "echoes"?'

'Echoes, sir. I repeat, echoes.'

Even as he spoke, Turner's hand cut down on the gleaming phosphorescence of the Emergency Action Stations switch.

Of all sounds in this earth, there is none so likely to stay with a man to the end of his days as the EAS. There is no other sound even remotely like it. There is nothing noble or martial or bloodstirring about it. It is simply a whistle, pitched near the upper limit of audio-frequency, alternating, piercing, atonic, alive with a desperate urgency and sense of danger: knife-like, it sears through the most sleep-drugged brain and has a man—no matter how exhausted, how weak, how deeply sunk in oblivion—on his feet in seconds, the pulse-rate already accelerating to meet the latest unknown, the adrenalin already pumping into his blood-stream.

Inside two minutes, the *Ulysses* was closed up to Action Stations. The Commander had moved aft to the After Director Tower, Vallery and Tyndall were on the bridge.

The *Sirrus*, two miles away to port, remained in contact for half an hour. The *Viking* was detached to help her, and, below-deck in the *Ulysses*, the peculiar, tinny clanging of depth-charging was clearly heard at irregular intervals. Finally, the *Sirrus* reported. 'No success: contact lost: trust you have not been disturbed.' Tyndall ordered the recall of the two destroyers, and the bugle blew the stand-down.

Back on the bridge, again, the Commander sent for his long overdue cocoa. Chrysler departed to the seaman's for'ard galley—the Commander would have no truck with the wishy-washy liquid concocted for the officers' mess—and returned with a steaming jug and a string of heavy mugs, their handles threaded on a bent wire. Turner watched with approval the reluctance with which the heavy, viscous liquid poured glutinously over the lip of the jug, and nodded in satisfaction after a preliminary taste. He smacked his lips and sighed contentedly.

'Excellent, young Chrysler, excellent! You have the gift. Torps, an eye on the ship, if you please. Must see where we are.'

He retired to the chart-room on the port side, just aft of the compass platform, and closed the black-out door. Relaxed in his chair, he put his mug on the chart-table and his feet beside it, drew the first deep inhalation of cigarette smoke into his lungs. Then he was on his feet, cursing: the crackle of the WT loudspeaker was unmistakable.

This time it was the *Portpatrick*. For one reason and another, her reports were generally treated with a good deal of reserve, but this time she was particularly emphatic. Commander Turner had no option; again he reached for the EAS switch.

Twenty minutes later the stand-down sounded again, but the Commander was to have no cocoa that night. Three times more during the hours of darkness all hands closed up to Action Stations, and only minutes, it seemed, after the last stand-down, the bugle went for dawn stations.

There was no dawn as we know it. There was a vague, imperceptible lightening in the sky, a bleak, chill greyness, as the men dragged themselves wearily back to their action stations. This, then, was war in the northern seas. No death and glory heroics, no roaring guns and spitting Oerlikons, no exaltation of the spirit, no glorious defiance of the enemy: just worn-out sleepless men, numbed with cold and sodden duffels, grey and drawn and stumbling on their feet with weakness and hunger and lack of rest, carrying with them the memories, the tensions, the cumulative physical exhaustion of a hundred such endless nights.

Vallery, as always, was on the bridge. Courteous, kind and considerate as ever, he looked ghastly. His face was haggard, the colour of putty, his bloodshot eyes deep-sunk in hollowed sockets, his lips bloodless. The severe hæmorrhage of the previous night and the sleepless night just gone had taken terrible toll of his slender strength.

In the half-light, the squadron came gradually into view. Miraculously, most of them were still in position. The frigate and minesweeper were together and far ahead of the fleet—during the night they had been understandably reluctant to have their tails tramped on by a heavy cruiser or a carrier. Tyndall appreciated this and said nothing. The *Invader* had lost position during the night, and lay outside the screen on the port quarter. She received a very testy signal indeed, and came steaming up to resume station, corkscrewing violently in the heavy cross seas.

Stand-down came at 0800. At 0810 the port watch was below, making tea, washing, queueing up at the galley for breakfast trays, when a muffled explosion shook the *Ulysses*. Towels, soap, cups, plates and trays went flying or were left where they were: blasphemous and bitter, the men were on their way before Vallery's hand closed on the Emergency switch.

Less than half a mile away the *Invader* was slewing round in a violent half-circle, her flight-deck tilted over at a crazy angle. It was snowing heavily again now, but not heavily enough to obscure the great gouts of black oily smoke belching up for'ard of the *Invader*'s bridge. Even as the crew of the *Ulysses* watched, she came to rest, wallowing dangerously in the troughs between the great waves.

'The fools, the crazy fools!' Tyndall was terribly bitter, unreasonably so; even to Vallery, he would not admit how much he was now feeling the burden, the strain of command that sparked off his now almost chronic irritability. 'This is what happens, Captain, when a ship loses station! And it's as much my fault as theirs—should have sent a destroyer to escort her back.' He peered through his binoculars, turned to Vallery. 'Make a signal please: "Estimate of damage—please inform." . . . That damned U-boat must have trailed her from first light, waiting for a line-up.'

Vallery said nothing. He knew how Tyndall must feel to see one of his ships heavily damaged, maybe sinking. The *Invader* was still lying over at the same unnatural angle, the smoke rising in a steady column now. There was no sign of flames.

'Going to investigate, sir?' Vallery inquired.

Tyndall bit his lip thoughtfully and hesitated.

'Yes, I think we'd better do it ourselves. Order squadron to proceed, same speed, same course. Signal the *Baliol* and the *Nairn* to stand by the *Invader*.'

Vallery, watching the flags fluttering to the yardarm, was aware of someone at his elbow. He half-turned.

'That was no U-boat, sir.' The Kapok Kid was very sure of himself. 'She can't have been torpedoed.'

Tyndall overheard him. He swung round in his chair, glared at the unfortunate navigator.

'What the devil do you know about it, sir?' he growled. When the Admiral addressed his subordinates as 'sir', it was time to take to the boats. The Kapok Kid flushed to the roots of his blond hair, but he stood his ground.

'Well, sir, in the first place the *Sirrus* is covering the *Invader*'s port side, though well ahead, ever since your recall signal. She's been quartering that area for some time. I'm sure Commander Orr would have picked her up. Also, it's far too rough for any sub to maintain periscope depth, far less line up a firing track. And if the U-boat did fire, it wouldn't only fire one—six more likely, and, from that firing angle, the rest of the squadron must have been almost a solid wall behind the *Invader*. But no one else has been hit . . . I did three years in the trade, sir.'

'I did ten,' Tyndall growled. 'Guesswork, Pilot, just guesswork.'

'No, sir,' Carpenter persisted. 'It's not. I can't swear to it'—he had his binoculars to his eyes—'but I'm almost sure the *Invader* is going astern. Could only be because her bows—below the waterline, that is—have been damaged or blown off. Must have been a mine, sir, probably acoustic.'

'Ah, of course, of course!' Tyndall was very acid. 'Moored in 6,000 feet of water, no doubt?'

'A *drifting* mine, sir,' the Kapok Kid said patiently. 'Or an old acoustic torpedo—spent German torpedoes don't always sink. Probably a mine, though.'

'Suppose you'll be telling me next what mark it is and when it was laid,' Tyndall growled. But he was impressed in spite of himself. And the *Invader* was going astern, although slowly, without enough speed to give her steerage way. She still wallowed helplessly in the great troughs.

An Aldis clacked acknowledgement to the winking light on the *Invader*. Bentley tore a sheet off a signal pad, handed it to Vallery.

'"*Invader* to Admiral,"' the Captain read. '"Am badly holed, starboard side for'ard, very deep. Suspect drifting mine. Am investigating extent of damage. Will report soon."'

Tyndall took the signal from him and read it slowly. Then he looked over his shoulder and smiled faintly.

'You were dead right, my boy, it seems. Please accept an old curmudgeon's apologies.'

Carpenter murmured something and turned away, brick-red again with embarrassment. Tyndall grinned faintly at the Captain, then became thoughtful.

'I think we'd better talk to him personally, Captain. Barlow, isn't it? Make a signal.'

They climbed down two decks to the Fighter Direction room. Westcliffe vacated his chair for the Admiral.

'Captain Barlow?' Tyndall spoke into the handpiece.

'Speaking.' The sound came from the loudspeaker above his head.

'Admiral here, Captain. How are things?'

'We'll manage, sir. Lost most of our bows, I'm afraid. Several casualties. Oil fires, but under conrol. WT doors all holding, and engineers and damage control parties are shorting up the crossbulkheads.'

'Can you go ahead at all, Captain?'

'Could do, sir, but risky—in this, anyway.'

'Think you could make it back to base?'

'With this wind and sea behind us, yes. Still take three-four days.'

'Right-o, then.' Tyndall's voice was gruff. 'Off you go. You're no good to us without bows! Damned hard luck, Captain Barlow. My commiserations. And oh! I'm giving you the *Baliol* and *Nairn* as escorts and radioing for an ocean-going tug to come out to meet you—just in case.'

'Thank you, sir. We appreciate that. One last thing—permission to empty starboard squadron fuel tanks. We've taken a lot of water, can't get rid of it all—only way to recover our trim.'

Tyndall sighed. 'Yes, I was expecting that. Can't be helped and we can't take it off you in this weather. Good luck, Captain. Goodbye.'

'Thank you very much, sir. Goodbye.'

Twenty minutes later, the *Ulysses* was back on station in the squadron. Shortly afterwards, they saw the *Invader*, not listing quite so heavily now, head slowly round to the southeast, the little Hunt class destroyer and the frigate, one on either side, rolling wickedly as they came round with her. In another ten minutes, watchers on the *Ulysses* had lost sight of them, buried in a flurrying snow squall. Three gone and eleven left behind; but it was the eleven who now felt so strangely alone.

FIVE

Tuesday

The *Invader* and her troubles were soon forgotten. All too soon, the 14th Aircraft Carrier Squadron had enough, and more than enough, to worry about on their own account. They had their own troubles to overcome, their own enemy to face—an enemy far more elemental and far more deadly than any mine or U-boat.

Tyndall braced himself more firmly against the pitching, rolling deck and looked over at Vallery. Vallery, he thought for the tenth time that morning, looked desperately ill.

'What do you make of it, Captain? Prospects aren't altogether healthy, are they?'

'We're for it, sir. It's really piling up against us. Carrington has spent six years in the West Indies, has gone through a dozen hurricanes. Admits he's seen a barometer lower, but never one so low with the pressure still falling so fast—not in these latitudes. This is only a curtain-raiser.'

'This will do me nicely, meantime, thank you.' Tyndall said dryly. 'For a curtain-raiser, it's doing not so badly.'

It was a masterly understatement. For a curtain-raiser, it was a magnificent performance. The wind was fairly steady, about Force 9 on the Beaufort scale, and the snow had stopped. A temporary cessation only, they all knew—far ahead to the north-west the sky was a peculiarly livid colour. It was a dull glaring purple, neither increasing nor fading, faintly luminous and vaguely menacing in its uniformity and permanence. Even to men who had seen everything the Arctic skies had to offer, from pitchy darkness on a summer's noon, right through the magnificent displays of Northern Lights to that wonderfully washed-out blue that so often smiles down on the stupendous calms of the milk-white seas that lap edge of the Barrier, this was something quite unknown.

But the Admiral's reference had been to the sea. It had been building up, steadily, inexorably, all during the morning. Now, at noon, it looked uncommonly like an eighteenth-century print of a barque in a storm—serried waves of greenish-grey, straight, regular and marching uniformly along, each decoratively topped with frothing caps of white. Only here, there were 500 feet between crest and crest, and the squadron, heading almost directly into it, was taking hearty punishment.

For the little ships, already burying their bows every fifteen seconds in a creaming smother of cascading white, this was bad enough, but another, a more dangerous and insidious enemy was at work—the cold. The temperature had long sunk below freezing point, and the mercury was still shrinking down, close towards the zero mark.

The cold was now intense: ice formed in cabins and mess-decks: fresh-water systems froze solid: metal contracted, hatch-covers jammed, door hinges locked in frozen immobility, the oil in the searchlight controls gummed up and made them useless. To keep a watch, especially a watch on the bridge was torture: the first shock of that bitter wind seared the lungs, left a man fighting for breath: if he had forgotten to don gloves—first the silk gloves, then the woollen mittens, then the sheepskin gauntlets—and touched a handrail, the palms of the hands seared off, the skin burnt as by white-hot metal: on the bridge; if he forgot to duck when the bows smashed down into a trough, the flying spray, solidified in a second into hurtling slivers of ice, lanced cheek and forehead open to the bone: hands froze, the very marrow of the bones numbed, the deadly chill crept upwards from feet to calves to thighs, nose and chin turned white with frostbite and demanded immediate attention: and then, by far the worst of all, the end of the watch, the return below deck, the writhing, excruciating agony of returning circulation. But, for all this, words are useless things, pale shadows of reality. Some things lie beyond the knowledge and the experience of the majority of mankind, and here imagination finds itself in a world unknown.

But all these things were relatively trifles, personal inconveniences to be shrugged aside. The real danger lay elsewhere. It lay in the fact of ice.

There were over three hundred tons of it already on the decks of the *Ulysses*, and more forming every minute. It lay in a thick, even coat over the main deck, the fo'c'sle, the gun-decks and the bridges: it hung in long, jagged icicles from coamings and turrets and rails: it trebled the diameter of every wire, stay and halliard, and turned slender masts into monstrous trees, ungainly and improbable. It lay everywhere, a deadly menace, and much of the danger lay in the slippery surface it presented—a problem much more easily overcome on a coalfired merchant ship with clinker and ashes from its boilers, than in the modern, oil-fired warships. On the *Ulysses*, they spread salt and sand and hoped for the best.

But the real danger of the ice lay in its weight. A ship, to use technical terms, can be either stiff or tender. If she's stiff, she has a low centre of gravity, rolls easily, but whips back quickly and is extremely stable and safe. If she's tender, with a high centre of gravity, she rolls reluctantly but comes back even more reluctantly, is unstable and unsafe. And if a ship were tender, and hundreds of tons of ice piled high on its decks, the centre of gravity rose to a dangerous height. It could rise to a fatal height . . .

The escort carriers and the destroyers, especially the *Portpatrick*, were vulnerable, terribly so. The carriers, already unstable with the great height and weight of their reinforced flight-decks, provided a huge, smooth, flat surface to the falling snow, ideal conditions for the formation of ice. Earlier on, it had been possible to keep the flight-decks relatively clear—working parties had toiled incessantly with brooms and sledges, salt and steam hoses. But the weather had deteriorated so badly now that to send out a man on that wildly pitching, staggering flight-deck, glassy and infinitely treacherous, would be to send him to his death. The *Wrestler* and *Blue Ranger* had modified heating systems under the flight-decks—modified, because, unlike the British ships, these Mississippi carriers had planked flight-decks: in such extreme conditions, they were hopelessly inefficient.

Conditions aboard the destroyers were even worse. They had to contend not only with the ice from the packed snow, but with ice from the sea itself. As regularly as clockwork, huge clouds of spray broke over the destroyers' fo'c'sles as the bows crashed solidly, shockingly into the trough and rising shoulder of the next wave: the spray froze even as it touched the deck, even before it touched the deck, piling up the solid ice, in places over a foot thick, from the stem aft beyond the breakwater. The tremendous weight of the ice was pushing the little ships down by their heads; deeper, with each successive plunge ever deeper, they buried their noses in the sea, and each time, more and more sluggishly, more and more reluctantly, they staggered laboriously up from the depths. Like the carrier captains, the destroyer skippers could only look down from their bridges, helpless, hoping.

Two hours passed, two hours in which the temperature fell to zero, hesitated, then shrank steadily beyond it, two hours in which the barometer tumbled crazily after it. Curiously, strangely, the snow still held off, the livid sky to the north-west was as far away as ever, and the sky to the south and east had cleared completely. The squadron presented a fantastic picture now, little toy-boats of sugar-icing, dazzling white, gleaming and sparkling in the pale, winter sunshine, pitching crazily through the everlengthening, ever-deepening valleys of grey and green of the cold Norwegian Sea, pushing on towards that far horizon, far and weird and purply glowing, the horizon of another world. It was an incredibly lovely spectacle.

Rear-Admiral Tyndall saw nothing beautiful about it. A man who was wont to claim that he never worried, he was seriously troubled now. He was gruff, to those on the bridge, gruff to the point of discourtesy and the old geniality of the Farmer Giles of even two months ago was all but gone. Ceaselessly his gaze circled the fleet; constantly, uncomfortably, he twisted in his chair. Finally he climbed down, passed through the gate and went into the Captain's shelter.

Vallery had no light on and the shelter was in semi-darkness. He lay there on his settee, a couple of blankets thrown over him. In the half-light, his face looked ghastly, corpse-like. His right hand clutched a balled handkerchief, spotted and stained: he made no attempt to hide it. With a painful effort, and before Tyndall could stop him, he had swung his legs over the edge of the settee and pulled forward a chair. Tyndall choked off his protest, sank gracefully into the seat.

'I think your curtain's just about to go up, Dick . . . What on earth ever induced me to become a squadron commander?'

Vallery grinned sympathetically. 'I don't particularly envy you, sir. What are you going to do now?'

'What would *you* do?' Tyndall countered dolefully.

Vallery laughed. For a moment his face was transformed, boyish almost, then the laugh broke down into a bout of harsh, dry coughing. The stain spread over his handkerchief. Then he looked up and smiled.

'The penalty for laughing at a superior officer. What would I do? Heave to, sir. Better still, tuck my tail between my legs and run for it.'

Tyndall shook his head.

'You never were a very convincing liar, Dick.'

Both men sat in silence for a moment, then Vallery looked up.

'How far to go, exactly, sir?'

'Young Carpenter makes it 170 miles, more or less.'

'One hundred and seventy.' Vallery looked at his watch. 'Twenty hours to go—in this weather. We *must* make it!'

Tyndall nodded heavily. 'Eighteen ships sitting out there—nineteen, counting the sweeper from Hvalfjord—not to mention old Starr's blood pressure . . .'

He broke off as a hand rapped on the door and a head looked in.

'Two signals, Captain, sir.'

'Just read them out, Bentley, will you?'

'First is from the *Portpatrick*: "Sprung bow-plates: making water fast: pumps coming: fear further damage: please advise."'

Tyndall swore. Vallery said calmly: 'And the other?'

'From the *Gannet*, sir. "Breaking up."'

'Yes, yes. And the rest of the message?'

'Just that, sir. "Breaking up."'

'Ha! One of these taciturn characters,' Tyndall growled. 'Wait a minute, Chief, will you?' He sank back in his chair, hand rasping his chin, gazing at his feet, forcing his tired mind to think.

Vallery murmured something in a low voice, and Tyndall looked up, his eyebrows arched.

'Troubled waters, sir. Perhaps the carriers—'

Tyndall slapped his knee. 'Two minds with but a single thought. Bentley, make two signals. One to all screen vessels—tell 'em to take position—astern—close astern—of the carriers. Other to the carriers. Oil hose, one each through port and starboard loading ports, about—ah—how much would you say, Captain?'

'Twenty gallons a minute, sir?'

'Twenty gallons it is. Understand, Chief? Right-o, get 'em off at once. And Chief—tell the Navigator to bring his chart here.' Bentley left, and he turned to Vallery. 'We've got to fuel later on, and we can't do it here. Looks as if this might be the last chance of shelter this side of Murmansk . . . And if the next twenty-four hours are going to be as bad as Carrington forecasts, I doubt whether some of the little ships could live through it anyway . . . Ah! Here you are, Pilot. Let's see where we are. How's the wind, by the way?'

'Force 10, sir.' Bracing himself against the wild lurching of the *Ulysses*, the Kapok Kid smoothed out the chart on the Captain's bunk. 'Backing slightly.'

'North-west, would you say, Pilot?' Tyndall rubbed his hands. 'Excellent. Now, my boy, our position?'

'12.40 west. 66.15 north,' said the Kapok Kid precisely. He didn't even trouble to consult the chart. Tyndall lifted his eyebrows but made no comment.

'Course?'

'310, sir.'

'Now, if it were necessary for us to seek shelter for fuelling—'

'Course exactly 290, sir. I've pencilled it in—there. Four and a half hours' steaming, approximately.'

'How the devil—' Tyndall exploded. 'Who told you to—to—' He spluttered into a wrathful silence.

'I worked it out five minutes ago, sir. It—er—seemed inevitable. 290 would take us a few miles inside the Langanes peninsula. There should be plenty shelter there.' Carpenter was grave, unsmiling.

'Seemed inevitable!' Tyndall roared. 'Would you listen to him, Captain Vallery? Inevitable! And it's only just occurred to me! Of all the . . . Get out! Take yourself and that damned comic-opera fancy dress elsewhere!'

The Kapok Kid said nothing. With an air of injured innocence he gathered up his charts and left. Tyndall's voice halted him at the door.

'Pilot!'

'Sir?' The Kapok Kid's eyes were fixed on a point above Tyndall's head.

'As soon as the screen vessels have taken up position, tell Bentley to send them the new course.'

'Yes, sir. Certainly.' He hesitated, and Tyndall chuckled. 'All right, all right,' he said resignedly. 'I'll say it again—I'm just a crusty old curmudgeon . . . and shut that damned door! We're freezing in here.'

The wind was rising more quickly now and long ribbons of white were beginning to streak the water. Wave troughs were deepening rapidly, their sides steepening, their tops blown off and flattened by the wind. Gradually, but perceptibly to the ear now, the thin, lonely whining in the rigging was climbing steadily up the register. From time to time, large chunks of ice, shaken loose by the increasing vibration, broke off from the masts and stays and spattered on the deck below.

The effect of the long oil-slicks trailing behind the carriers was almost miraculous. The destroyers, curiously mottled with oil now, were still plunging astern, but the surface tension of the fuel held the water and spray from breaking aboard. Tyndall, justifiably, was feeling more than pleased with himself.

Towards half-past four in the afternoon, with shelter still a good fifteen miles away, the elation had completely worn off. There was a whole gale blowing now and Tyndall had been compelled to signal for a reduction in speed.

From deck level, the seas now were more than impressive. They were gigantic, frightening. Nicholls stood with the Kapok Kid, off watch now, on the main deck, under the port whaler, sheltering in the lee of the fo'c'sle deck. Nicholls, clinging to a davit to steady himself, and leaping back now and then to avoid a deluge of spray, looked over to where the *Defender*, the *Vultra* and *Viking* tailing behind, were pitching madly, grotesquely, under that serene blue sky. The blue sky above, the tremendous seas below. There was something almost evil, something literally spine-chilling, in that macabre contrast.

'They never told me anything about this in the Medical School,' Nicholls observed at last. 'My God, Andy,' he added in awe, 'have you ever seen anything like this?'

'Once, just once. We were caught in a typhoon off the Nicobars. I don't think it was as bad as this. And Number One says this is damn all compared to what's coming tonight—and he knows. God, I wish I was back in Henley!'

Nicholls looked at him curiously.

'Can't say I know the First Lieutenant well. Not a very—ah—approachable customer, is he? But everyone—old Giles, the skipper, the Commander, yourself—they all talk about him with bated breath. What's so extra special about him? I respect him, mind you—everyone seems to—but dammit to hell, he's no superman.'

'Sea's beginning to break up,' the Kapok Kid murmured absently. 'Notice how every now and again we're beginning to get a wave half as big again as the others? Every seventh wave, the old sailors say. No, Johnny, he's not a superman. Just the greatest seaman you'll ever see. Holds two master's-tickets—square-rigged and steam. He was going round the Horn in Finnish barques when we were still in our prams. Commander could tell you enough stories about him to fill a book.' He paused then went on quietly.

'He really is one of the few great seamen of today. Old Blackbeard Turner is no slouch himself, but he'll tell anyone that he can't hold a candle to Jimmy . . . I'm no hero-worshipper, Johnny. You know that. But you can say about Carrington what they used to say about Shackleton—when there's nothing left and all hope is gone, get down on your knees and pray for him. Believe me, Johnny, I'm damned glad he's here.'

Nicholls said nothing. Surprise held him silent. For the Kapok Kid, flippancy was a creed, derogation second nature: seriousness was a crime and anything that smacked of adulation bordered on blasphemy. Nicholls wondered what manner of man Carrington must be.

The cold was vicious. The wind was tearing great gouts of water off the wave-tops, driving the atomized spray at bullet speed against fo'c'sle and sides. It was impossible to breathe without turning one's back, without wrapping layers of wool round mouth and nose. Faces blue and white, shaking violently with the cold, neither suggested, neither even thought of going below. Men hypnotized, men fascinated by the tremendous seas, the towering waves, 1,000, 2,000 feet in length, long, sloping on the lee side, steep-walled and terrifying on the other, pushed up by a sixty knot wind and by some mighty force lying far to the north-west. In these gigantic troughs, a church steeple would be lost for ever.

Both men turned round as they heard the screen door crashing behind them. A duffel-coated figure, cursing fluently, fought to shut the heavy door against the pitching of the *Ulysses*, finally succeeded in heaving the clips home. It was Leading Seaman Doyle, and even though his beard hid three-quarters of what could be seen of his face, he still looked thoroughly disgusted with life.

Carpenter grinned at him. He and Doyle had served a commission together on the China Station. Doyle was a very privileged person.

'Well, well, the Ancient Mariner himself! How are things down below, Doyle?'

'Bloody desperate, sir!' His voice was as lugubrious as his face. 'Cold as charity, sir, and everything all over the bloody place. Cups, saucers, plates in smithereens. Half the crew—'

He broke off suddenly, eyes slowly widening in blank disbelief. He was staring out to sea between Nicholls and Carpenter.

'Well, what about half the crew? . . . What's the matter, Doyle?'

'Christ Almighty!' Doyle's voice was slow, stunned: it was almost a prayer. 'Oh, Christ Almighty!' The voice rose sharply on the last two syllables.

The two officers twisted quickly round. The *Defender* was climbing—all 500 feet of her was literally climbing—up the lee side of a wave that staggered the imagination, whose immensity completely defied immediate comprehension. Even as they watched, before shocked minds could grasp the significance of it all, the *Defender* reached the crest, hesitated, crazily tilted up her stern till screw and rudder were entirely clear of the water, then crashed down, down, down . . .

Even at two cable-lengths' distance in that high wind the explosive smash of the plummeting bows came like a thunder-clap. An aeon ticked by, and still the *Defender* seemed to keep on going under, completely buried now, right back to the bridge island, in a sea of foaming white. How long she remained like that, arrowed down into the depths of the Arctic, no one could afterwards say: then slowly, agonizingly, incredibly, great rivers of water cascaded off her bows, she broke surface again. Broke surface, to present to frankly disbelieving eyes a spectacle entirely without precedent, anywhere, at any time. The tremendous, instantaneous, upthrusting pressure of unknown thousands of tons of water had torn the flight-deck completely off its mountings and bent it backwards, in a great, sweeping 'U', almost as far as the bridge. It was a sight to make men doubt their sanity, to leave them stupefied, to leave them speechless—all, that is, except the Kapok Kid. He rose magnificently to the occasion.

'My word!' he murmured thoughtfully. 'That *is* unusual.'

Another such wave, another such shattering impact, and it would have been the end for the *Defender*. The finest ships, the stoutest, most powerful vessels, are made only of thin, incredibly thin, sheets of metal, and metal, twisted and tortured as was the *Defender*'s, could never have withstood another such impact.

But there were no more such waves, no more such impacts. It had been a freak wave, one of these massive, inexplicable contortions of the sea which have occurred, with blessed infrequency, from time immemorial, in all the great seas of the world whenever Nature wanted to show mankind, an irreverent, over-venturesome mankind, just how puny and pitifully helpless a thing mankind really is . . . There were no more such waves and, by five o'clock, although land was still some eight to ten miles away, the squadron had moved into comparative shelter behind the tip of the Langanes peninsula.

From time to time, the captain of the *Defender,* who seemed to be enjoying himself hugely, sent reassuring messages to the Admiral. He was making a good deal of water, but he was managing nicely, thank you. He thought the latest shape in flight-decks very fashionable, and a vast improvement on the old type; straight flight-decks lacked imagination, he thought, and didn't the Admiral think so too. The vertical type, he stated, provided excellent protection against wind and weather, and would make a splendid sail with the wind in the right quarter. With his last message, to the effect that he thought that it would be rather difficult to fly off planes, a badly-worried Tyndall lost his temper and sent back such a blistering signal that all communications abruptly ceased.

Shortly before six o'clock, the squadron hove-to under the shelter of Langanes, less than two miles offshore. Langanes is low-lying, and the wind, still climbing the scale, swept over it and into the bay beyond, without a break; but the sea, compared to an hour ago, was mercifully calm, although the ships still rolled heavily. At once the cruisers and the screen vessels—except the *Portpatrick* and the *Gannet*—moved alongside the carriers, took oil hoses aboard. Tyndall relucantly and after much heart-searching, had decided that the *Portpatrick* and *Gannet* were suspect, a potential liability: they were to escort the crippled carrier back to Scapa.

Exhaustion, an exhaustion almost physical, almost tangible, lay heavily over the mess-decks and the wardroom of the *Ulysses.* Behind lay another sleepless night, another twenty-four hours with peace unknown and rest impossible. With dull, tired minds, men heard the broadcast that the *Defender,* the *Portpatrick* and the *Gannet* were to return to Scapa when the weather moderated. Six gone now, only eight left—half the carrier force gone. Little wonder that men felt sick at heart, felt as if they were being deserted, as if, in Riley's phrase, they were being thrown to the wolves.

But there was remarkably little bitterness, a puzzling lack of resentment which, perhaps, sprung only from the sheer passive acceptance. Brooks was aware of it, this inaction of feeling, this unnatural extinction of response, and was lost for a reason to account for it. Perhaps, he thought, this was the nadir, the last extremity when sick men and sick minds cease altogether to function, the last slow-down of all vital processes, both human and animal. Perhaps this was just the final apathy. His intellect told him that was reasonable, more, it was inevitable . . . And all the time some fugitive intuition, some evanescent insight, was thrusting upon him an awareness, a dim shadowy awareness of something altogether different; but his mind was too tired to grasp it.

Whatever it was, it wasn't apathy. For a brief moment that evening, a white-hot anger ran through the ship like a flame, then resentment of the injustice which had provoked it. That there had been cause for anger even Vallery admitted; but his hand had been forced.

It had all happened simply enough. During routine evening tests, it had been discovered that the fighting lights on the lower yardarm were not working. Ice was at once suspected as being the cause.

The lower yardarm, on this evening dazzling white and heavily coated with snow and ice, paralleled the deck, sixty feet above it, eighty feet above the waterline. The fighting lights were suspended below the outer tip: to work on these, a man had either to sit on the yardarm—a most uncomfortable position as the heavy steel WT transmission aerial was bolted to its upper length—or in a bosun's chair suspended from the yardarm. It was a difficult enough task at any time: tonight, it had to be done with the maximum speed, because the repairs would interrupt radio transmission—the 3,000-volt steel 'Safe-to-Transmit' boards (which broke the electrical circuits) had to be withdrawn and left in the keeping of the Officer of the Watch during the repair: it had to be done—very precise, finicky work had to be done—in that sub-zero temperature: it had to be done on that slippery, glasssmooth yardarm, with the *Ulysses* rolling regularly through a thirty-degree arc: the job was more than ordinarily difficult—it was highly dangerous.

Marshall did not feel justified in detailing the duty LTO for the job, especially as that rating was a middle-aged and very much overweight reservist, long past his climbing prime. He asked for volunteers. It was inevitable that he should have picked Ralston, for that was the kind of man Ralston was.

The task took half an hour—twenty minutes to climb the mast, edge out to the yardarm tip, fit the bosun's chair and lifeline, and ten minutes for the actual repair. Long before he was finished, a hundred, two hundred tired men, robbing themselves of sleep and supper, had come on deck and huddled there in the bitter wind, watching in fascination.

Ralston swung in a great arc across the darkening sky, the gale plucking viciously at his duffel and hood. Twice, wind and wave flung him out, still in his chair, parallel to the yardarm, forcing him to wrap both arms around the yardarm and hang on for his life. On the second occasion he seemed to strike his face against the aerial, for he held his head for a few seconds afterwards, as if he were dazed. It was then that he lost his gauntlets—he must have had them in his lap, while making some delicate adjustment: they dropped down together, disappeared over the side.

A few minutes later, while Vallery and Turner were standing amidships examining the damage the motorboat had suffered in Scapa Flow, a short, stocky figure came hurriedly out of the after screen door, made for the fo'c'sle at an awkward stumbling run. He pulled up abruptly at the sight of the Captain and the Commander: they saw it was Hastings, the Master-at-Arms.

'What's the matter, Hastings?' Vallery asked curtly. He always found it difficult to conceal his dislike for the Master-at-Arms, his dislike for his harshness, his uncalled-for severity.

'Trouble on the bridge, sir,' Hastings jerked out breathlessly. Vallery could have sworn to a gleam of satisfaction in his eye. 'Don't know exactly what—could hardly hear a thing but the wind on the phone . . . I think you'd better come, sir.'

They found only three people on the bridge: Etherton, the Gunnery Officer, one hand still clutching a phone, worried, unhappy: Ralston, his hands hanging loosely by his sides, the palms raw and torn, the face ghastly, the chin with the dead pallor of frostbite, the forehead masked in furrowed, frozen blood: and, lying in a corner, Sub-Lieutenant Carslake, moaning in agony, only the whites of his eyes showing, stupidly fingering his smashed mouth, the torn, bleeding gaps in his prominent upper teeth.

'Good God!' Vallery ejaculated. 'Good God above!' He stood there, his hand on the gate, trying to grasp the significance of the scene before him. Then his mouth clamped shut and he swung round on the Gunnery Officer.

'What the devil's happened here, Etherton?' he demanded harshly. 'What *is* all this? Has Carslake—'

'Ralston hit him, sir.' Etherton broke in.

'Don't be so bloody silly, Guns!' Turner grunted.

'Exactly!' Vallery's voice was impatient. 'We can see that. Why?'

'A WT messenger came up for the "Safe-to-Transmit" boards. Carslake gave them to him—about ten minutes ago, I—I think.'

'You think! Where were you, Etherton, and why did you permit it? You know very well . . . ' Vallery broke off short, remembering the presence of Ralston and the MAA.

Etherton muttered something. His words were inaudible in the gale.

Vallery bent forward. 'What did you say, Etherton?'

'I was down below, sir.' Etherton was looking at the deck. 'Just—just for a moment, sir.'

'I see. You were down below.' Vallery's voice was controlled now, quiet and even; his eyes held an expression that promised ill for Etherton. He looked round at Turner. 'Is he badly hurt, Commander?'

'He'll survive,' said Turner briefly. He had Carslake on his feet now, still moaning, his hand covering his smashed mouth.

For the first time, the Captain seemed to notice Ralston. He looked at him for a few seconds—an eternity on that bitter, storm-lashed bridge—then spoke, monosyllabic, ominous, thirty years of command behind the word.

'Well?'

Ralston's face was frozen, expressionless. His eyes never left Carslake.

'Yes, sir. I did it. I hit him—the treacherous, murdering bastard!'

'Ralston!' The MAA's voice was a whiplash.

Suddenly Ralston's shoulders sagged. With an effort, he looked away from Carslake, looked wearily at Vallery.

'I'm sorry. I forgot. He's got a stripe on his arm—only ratings are bastards.' Vallery winced at the bitterness. 'But he—'

'You've got frostbite.'

'Rub your chin, man!' Turner interrupted sharply.

Slowly, mechanically, Ralston did as he was told. He used the back of his hand. Vallery winced again as he saw the palm of the hand, raw and mutilated, skin and flesh hanging in strips. The agony of that bare-handed descent from the yardarm . . .

'He tried to murder me, sir. It was deliberate.' Ralston sounded tired.

'Do you realize what you are saying?' Vallery's voice was as icy as the wind that swept over Langanes. But he felt the first, faint chill of fear.

'He tried to murder me, sir,' Ralston repeated tonelessly. 'He returned the boards five minutes before I left the yardarm. WT must have started transmitting just as soon as I reached the mast, coming down.'

'Nonsense, Ralston. How dare you—'

'He's right, sir.' It was Etherton speaking. He was replacing the receiver carefully, his voice unhappy. 'I've just checked.'

The chill of fear settled deeper on Vallery's mind. Almost desperately he said, 'Anyone can make a mistake. Ignorance may be culpable, but—'

'Ignorance!' The weariness had vanished from Ralston as if it had never been. He took two quick steps forward. 'Ignorance! I gave him these boards, sir, when I came to the bridge. I asked for the Officer of the Watch and he said *he* was—I didn't know the Gunnery Officer was on duty, sir. When I told him that the boards were to be returned only to me, he said: "I don't want any of your damned insolence, Ralston. I know my job—you stick to yours. Just you get up there and perform your heroics." He *knew*, sir.'

Carslake burst from the Commander's supporting arm, turned

and appealed wildly to the Captain. The eyes were white and staring, the whole face working.

'That's a lie, sir! It's a damned, filthy lie!' He mouthed the words, slurred them through smashed lips. 'I never said . . . '

The words crescendoed into a coughing, choking scream as Ralston's fist smashed viciously, terribly into the torn, bubbling mouth. He staggered drunkenly through the port gate, crashed into the chart house, slid down to lie on the deck, huddled and white and still. Both Turner and the MAA had at once leapt forward to pinion the LTO's arms, but he made no attempt to move.

Above and beyond the howl of the wind, the bridge seemed strangely silent. When Vallery spoke, his voice was quite expressionless.

'Commander, you might phone for a couple of our marines. Have Carslake taken down to his cabin and ask Brooks to have a look at him. Master-at-Arms?'

'Sir?'

'Take this rating to the Sick Bay, let him have any necessary treatment. Then put him in cells. With an armed guard, Understand?'

'I understand, sir.' There was no mistaking the satisfaction in Hastings's voice.

Vallery, Turner and the Gunnery Officer stood in silence as Ralston and the MAA left, in silence as two burly marines carried Carslake, still senseless, off the bridge and below. Vallery moved after them, broke step at Etherton's voice behind him.

'Sir?'

Vallery did not even turn round. 'I'll see you later, Etherton.'

'No, sir. Please. This is important.'

Something in the Gunnery Officer's voice held Vallery. He turned back, impatiently.

'I'm not concerned with excusing myself, sir. There's no excuse.' The eyes were fixed steadily on Vallery. 'I was standing at the Asdic door when Ralston handed the boards to Carslake. I overheard them—every word they said.'

Vallery's face became very still. He glanced at Turner, saw that he, too, was waiting intently.

'And Ralston's version of the conversation?' In spite of himself,

Vallery's voice was rough, edged with suspense.

'Completely accurate, sir.' The words were hardly audible. 'In every detail. Ralston told the exact truth.'

Vallery closed his eyes for a moment, turned slowly, heavily away. He made no protest as he felt Turner's hand under his arm, helping him down the steep ladder. Old Socrates had told him a hundred times that he carried the ship on his back. He could feel the weight of it now, the crushing burden of every last ounce of it.

Vallery was at dinner with Tyndall, in the Admiral's day cabin, when the message arrived. Sunk in private thought, he gazed down at his untouched food as Tyndall smoothed out the signal.

The Admiral cleared his throat.

'On course. On time. Sea moderate, wind freshening. Expect rendezvous as planned. Commodore 77.'

He laid the signal down. 'Good God! Seas moderate, fresh wind! Do you reckon he's in the same damned ocean as us?'

Vallery smiled faintly.

'This is it, sir.'

'This is it,' Tyndall echoed. He turned to the messenger.

'Make a signal. "You are running into severe storm. Rendezvous unchanged. You may be delayed. Will remain at rendezvous until your arrival." That clear enough, Captain?'

'Should be, sir. Radio silence?'

'Oh, yes. Add "Radio silence. Admiral, 14th ACS." Get it off at once, will you? Then tell WT to shut down themselves.'

The door shut softly. Tyndall poured himself some coffee, looked across at Vallery.

'That boy still on your mind, Dick?'

Vallery smiled non-committally, lit a cigarette. At once he began to cough harshly.

'Sorry, sir,' he apologized. There was silence for some time, then he looked up quizzically.

'What mad ambition drove me to become a cruiser captain?' he asked sadly.

Tyndall grinned. 'I don't envy you . . . I seem to have heard this conversation before. What are you going to do about Ralston, Dick?'

'What would you do, sir?' Vallery countered.

'Keep him locked up till we return from Russia. On a bread-and-water diet, in irons if you like.'

Vallery smiled.

'You never were a very good liar, John.'

Tyndall laughed. '*Touché*!' He was warmed, secretly pleased. Rarely did Richard Vallery break through his self-imposed code of formality. 'A heinous offence, we all know, to clout one of HM commissioned officers, but if Etherton's story is true, my only regret is that Ralston didn't give Brooks a really large-scale job of replanning that young swine's face.'

'It's true, all right, I'm afraid,' said Vallery soberly. 'What it amounts to is that naval discipline—oh, how old Starr would love this—compels me to punish a would-be murderer's victim!' He broke off in a fresh paroxysm of coughing, and Tyndall looked away: he hoped the distress wasn't showing in his face, the pity and anger he felt that Vallery—that very perfect, gentle knight, the finest gentleman and friend he had ever known—should be coughing his heart out, visibly dying on his feet, because of the blind inhumanity of an SNO in London, two thousand miles away. 'A Victim,' Vallery went on at last, 'who has already lost his mother, brother and three sisters . . . I believe he has a father at sea somewhere.'

'And Carslake?'

'I shall see him tomorrow. I should like you to be there, sir. I will tell him that he will remain an officer of this ship till we return to Scapa, then resign his commission . . . I don't think he'd care to appear at a court-martial, even as a witness,' he finished dryly.

'Not if he's sane, which I doubt,' Tyndall agreed. A sudden thought struck him. 'Do you think he *is* sane?' He frowned.

'Carslake,' Vallery hesitated. 'Yes, I think so, sir. At least, he was. Brooks isn't so sure. Says he didn't like the look of him tonight—something queer about him, he thinks, and in these abnormal conditions small provocations are magnified out of all proportion.' Vallery smiled briefly. 'Not that Carslake is liable to regard the twin assaults on pride and person as a small provocation.'

Tyndall nodded agreement. 'He'll bear watching . . . Oh, damn! I wish the ship would stay still. Half my coffee on the tablecloth. Young Spicer'—he looked towards the pantry—'will be as mad as hell. Nineteen years old and a regular tyrant . . . I thought these would be sheltered waters, Dick?'

'So they are, compared to what's waiting for us. Listen!' He cocked his head to the howling of the wind outside. 'Let's see what the weather man has to say about it.'

He reached for the desk phone, asked for the transmitting station. After a brief conversation he replaced the receiver.

'TS says the anemometer is going crazy. Gusting up to eighty knots. Still north-west. Temperature steady at ten below.' He shivered. 'Ten below!' Then looked consideringly at Tyndall. 'Barometer almost steady at 27.8.'

'What!'

'27.8. That's what they say. It's impossible, but that's what they say.' He glanced at his wristwatch. 'Forty-five minutes, sir . . . This is a very complicated way of committing suicide.'

They were silent for a minute, then Tyndall spoke for both of them, answering the question in both their minds.

'We must go, Dick. We must. And by the way, our fire-eating young Captain (D), the doughty Orr, wants to accompany us in the *Sirrus* . . . We'll let him tag along a while. He has things to learn, that young man.'

At 2020 all ships had completed oiling. Hove to, they had had the utmost difficulty in keeping position in that great wind; but they were infinitely safer than in the open sea. They were given orders to proceed when the weather moderated, the *Defender* and escorts to Scapa, the squadron to a position 100 miles ENE of rendezvous. Radio silence was to be strictly observed.

At 2030 the *Ulysses* and *Sirrus* got under way to the East. Lights winked after them, messages of good luck. Fluently, Tyndall cursed the squadron for the breach of darken-ship regulations, realized that, barring themselves, there was no one on God's earth to see the signals anyway, and ordered a courteous acknowledgement.

At 2045, still two miles short of Langanes point, the *Sirrus* was plunging desperately in mountainous seas, shipping great masses of water over her entire fo'c'sle and main deck, and, in the darkness, looking far less like a destroyer than a porpoising submarine.

At 2050, at reduced speed, she was observed to be moving in close to such slight shelter as the land afforded there. At the same time, her six-inch Aldis flashed her signal: 'Screen doors stove in: "A" turret not tracking: flooding port boiler-room intake fans.' And on the *Sirrus's* bridge Commander Orr swore in chagrin as he received the *Ulysses*'s final message: 'Lesson without words, No 1. Rejoin squadron at once. You can't come out to play with the big boys.' But he swallowed his disappointment, signalled: 'Wilco. Just you wait till I grow up,' pulled the *Sirrus* round in a madly swinging half-circle and headed thankfully back for shelter. Aboard the flagship, it was lost to sight almost immediately.

At 2100, the *Ulysses* moved out into the Denmark Strait.

SIX

Tuesday Night

It was the worst storm of the war. Beyond all doubt, had the records been preserved for Admiralty inspection, that would have proved to be incomparably the greatest storm, the most tremendous convulsion of nature since these recordings began. Living memory aboard the *Ulysses* that night, a vast accumulation of experience in every corner of the globe, could certainly recall nothing even remotely like it, nothing that would even begin to bear comparison as a parallel or precedent.

At ten o'clock, with all doors and hatches battened shut, with all traffic prohibited on the upper deck, with all crews withdrawn from gun-turrets and magazines and all normal deck watchkeeping stopped for the first time since her commissioning, even the taciturn Carrington admitted that the Caribbean hurricanes of the autumns of '34 and '37—when he'd run out of sea-room, been forced to heave-to in the dangerous right-hand quadrant of both these murderous cyclones—had been no worse than this. But the two ships he had taken through these—a 3,000-ton tramp and a superannuated tanker on the New York asphalt run—had not been in the same class for seaworthiness as the *Ulysses*. He had little doubt as to her ability to survive. But what the First Lieutenant did not know, what nobody had any means of guessing, was that this howling gale was still only the deadly overture. Like some mindless and dreadful beast from an ancient and other world, the Polar monster crouched on its own doorstep, waiting. At 2230, the *Ulysses* crossed the Arctic Circle. The monster struck.

It struck with a feral ferocity, with an appalling savagery that smashed minds and bodies into a stunned unknowingness. Its claws were hurtling rapiers of ice that slashed across a man's face and left it welling red: its teeth were that sub-zero wind, gusting over 120 knots, that ripped and tore through the tissue paper of Arctic clothing and sank home to the bone: its voice was the devil's orchestra, the roar of a great wind mingled with the banshee shrieking of tortured rigging, a requiem for fiends: its weight was the crushing power of the hurricane wind that pinned a man helplessly to a bulkhead, fighting for breath, or flung him off his feet to crash in some distant corner, broken-limbed and senseless. Baulked of prey in its 500-mile sweep across the frozen wastes of the Greenland ice-cap, it goaded the cruel sea into homicidal alliance and flung itself, titanic in its energy, ravenous in its howling upon the cockleshell that was the *Ulysses*.

The *Ulysses* should have died then. Nothing built by man could ever have hoped to survive. She should just have been pressed under to destruction, or turned turtle, or had her back broken, or disintegrated under these mighty hammerblows of wind and sea. But she did none of these things.

How she ever survived the insensate fury of that first attack, God only knew. The great wind caught her on the bow and flung her round in a 45° arc and pressed her far over on her side as she fell—literally fell—forty heart-stopping feet over and down the precipitous walls of a giant trough. She crashed into the valley with a tremendous concussion that jarred every plate, every Clyde-built rivet in her hull. The vibration lasted an eternity as overstressed metal fought to re-adjust itself, as steel compressed and stretched far beyond specified breaking loads. Miraculously she held, but the sands were running out. She lay far over on her starboard side, the gunwales dipping: half a mile away, towering high above the masttop, a great wall of water was roaring down on the helpless ship.

The 'Dude' saved the day. The 'Dude', alternatively known as 'Persil', but officially as Engineer-Commander Dodson, immaculately clad as usual in overalls of the most dazzling white, had been at his control position in the engine-room when that tremendous gust had struck. He had no means of knowing what had happened. He had no means of knowing that the ship was not under command, that no one on the bridge had as yet recovered from that first shattering impact: he had no means of knowing that the quartermaster had been thrown unconscious into a corner of the wheelhouse, that his mate, almost a child in years, was too panic-stricken to dive for the madlyspinning wheel. But he did know that the *Ulysses* was listing crazily, almost broadside on, and he suspected the cause.

His shouts on the bridge tube brought no reply. He pointed to the port controls, roared 'Slow' in the ear of the Engineer WO—then leapt quickly for the starboard wheel.

Fifteen seconds later and it would have been too late. As it was, the accelerating starboard screw brought her round just far enough to take that roaring mountain of water under her bows, to dig her stern in to the level of the depth-charge rails, till forty feet of her airborne keel lay poised above the abyss below. When she plunged down, again that same shuddering vibration enveloped the entire hull. The fo'c'sle disappeared far below the surface, the sea flowing over and past the armoured side of 'A' turret. But she was bows on again. At once the 'Dude' signalled his WO for more revolutions, cut back the starboard engine.

Below decks, everything was an unspeakable shambles. On the mess-decks, steel lockers in their scores had broken adrift, been thrown in a dozen different directions, bursting hasps, and locks, spilling their contents everywhere. Hammocks had been catapulted from their racks, smashed crockery littered the decks: tables were twisted and smashed, broken stools stuck up at crazy angles, books, papers, teapots, kettles and crockery were scattered in insane profusion. And amidst this jumbled, sliding wreckage, hundreds of shouting, cursing, frightened and exhausted men struggled to their feet, or knelt, or sat, or just lay still.

Surgeon-Commander Brooks and Lieutenant Nicholls, with an inspired, untiring padre as good as a third doctor, were worked off their feet. The veteran Leading SBA Johnson, oddly enough, was almost useless—he was violently sick much of the time, seemed to have lost all heart: no one knew why—it was just one of these things and he had taken all he could.

Men were brought in to the Sick Bay in their dozens, in their scores, a constant trek that continued all night long as the *Ulysses* fought for her life, a trek that soon overcrowded the meagre space available and turned the wardroom into an emergency hospital. Bruises, cuts, dislocations, concussions, fractures—the exhausted doctors experienced everything that night. Serious injuries were fortunately rare, and inside three hours there were only nine bed-patients in the Sick Bay, including A.B. Ferry, his already mangled arm smashed in two places—a bitterly protesting Riley and his fellow-mutineers had been unceremoniously turfed out to make room for the more seriously injured.

About 2330, Nicholls was called to treat the Kapok Kid. Lurching, falling and staggering in the wildly gyrating ship he finally found the Navigator in his cabin. He looked very unhappy. Nicholls eyed him speculatively, saw the deep, ugly gash on his forehead, the swollen ankle peeping out below the Kapok Kid's Martian survival suit. Bad enough, but hardly a borderline case, although one wouldn't have thought so from the miserable, worried expression. Nicholls grinned inwardly.

'Well, Horatio,' he said unkindly, 'what's supposed to be the matter with you? Been drinking again?'

'It's my back, Johnny,' he muttered. He turned facedown on the bunk. 'Have a look at it, will you?'

Nicholl's expression changed. He moved forward, then stopped short.

'How the hell can I,' he demanded irritably, 'when you're wearing that damned ugly suit of yours?'

'That's what I mean,' said the Kapok Kid anxiously. 'I was thrown against the searchlight controls—all knobs and nasty, sharp projections. Is it torn? Is it ripped, cut in any way? Are the seams—'

'Well, for God's sake! Do you mean to tell me—?' Nicholls sank back incredulously on a locker.

The Kapok Kid looked at him hopefully.

'Does that mean it's all right?'

'Of course it's all right! If it's a blasted tailor you want, why the hell—'

'Enough!' The Kapok Kid swung briskly on to the side of his bunk, lifting an admonitory hand. 'There is work for you, sawbones.' He touched his bleeding forehead. 'Stitch this up and waste no time about it. A man of my calibre is urgently needed on the bridge . . . I'm the only man on this ship who has the faintest idea where we are.'

Busy with a swab, Nicholls grinned. 'And where are we?'

'I don't know,' said the Kapok Kid frankly. 'That's what's so urgent about it . . . But I do know where I was! Back in Henley. Did I ever tell you . . . ?'

The *Ulysses* did not die. Time and again that night, hove to with the wind fine of her starboard bow, as her bows crashed into and under the far shoulder of a trough, it seemed that she could never shake free from the great press of water. But time and again she did just that, shuddering, quivering under the fantastic strain. A thousand times before dawn officers and men blessed the genius of the Clyde ship-yard that had made her: a thousand times they cursed the blind malevolence of that great storm that put the *Ulysses* on the rack.

Perhaps 'blind' was not the right word. The storm wielded its wild hate with an almost human cunning. Shortly after the first onslaught, the wind had veered quickly, incredibly so and in defiance of all the laws, back almost to the north again. The *Ulysses* was on a lee shore, forced to keep pounding into gigantic seas.

Gigantic—and cunning also. Roaring by the *Ulysses*, a huge comber would suddenly whip round and crash on deck, smashing a boat to smithereens. Inside an hour, the barge, motor-boat and two whalers were gone, their shattered timbers swept away in the boiling cauldron. Carley rafts were broken off by the sudden hammer-blows of the same cunning waves, swept over the side and gone for ever: four of the Balsa floats went the same way.

But the most cunning attack of all was made right aft on the poop-deck. At the height of the storm a series of heavy explosions, half a dozen in as many seconds, almost lifted the stern out of the water. Panic spread like wildfire in the after mess-decks: practically every light abaft the after engine-room smashed or failed, in the darkness of the mess-decks, above the clamour, high-pitched cries of 'Torpedoed!' 'Mined!' 'She's breaking up!' galvanized exhausted, injured men, even those—more than half—in various degrees of prostration from seasickness, into frantic stampeding towards doors and hatches, only to find doors and hatches jammed solidly by the intense cold. Here and there, the automatic battery lamps had clicked on when the lighting circuits failed: glowing little pin-points, they played on isolated groups of white, contorted faces, sunken-eyed and straining, as they struggled through the yellow pools of light. Conditions were ripe for disaster when a voice, harsh, mocking, cut cleanly through the bedlam. The voice was Ralston's: he had been released before nine o'clock, on the Captain's orders: the cells were in the very forepeak of the ship, and conditions there were impossible in a head sea: even so, Hastings had freed him only with the worst possible grace.

'It's our own depth charges! Do you hear me, you bloody fools—it's our own depth charges!' It was not so much the words as the biting mockery, that stopped short the panic, halted dazed, unthinking men in their tracks. 'They're *our* depth charges, I tell you! They must have been washed over the side!'

He was right. The entire contents of a rack had broken adrift, lifted from their cradles by some freak wave, and tumbled over the side. Through some oversight, they had been left set at their shallow setting—those put on for the midget submarine in Scapa—and had gone off almost directly under the ship. The damage, it seemed, was only minor.

Up in 'A' mess-deck, right for'ard, conditions were even worse. There was more wreckage on the decks and far more seasickness—not the green-faced, slightly ludicrous malaise of the crosschannel steamer, but tearing rendering conversions, dark and heavy with blood—for the bows had been rearing and lunging, rearing and plunging, thirty, forty, fifty feet at a time for endless, hopeless hours; but there was an even more sinister agent at work, rapidly making the mess-deck untenable.

At the for'ard end of the capstan flat, which adjoined the mess-deck, was the battery-room. In here were stored, or on charge, a hundred and one different batteries, ranging from the heavy lead-acid batteries weighing over a hundred pounds to the tiny nickel-calmium cells for the emergency lighting. Here, too, were stored earthenware jars of prepared acid and big, glass carboys of undiluted sulphuric. These last were permanently stored: in heavy weather, the big batteries were lashed down.

No one knew what had happened. It seemed likely—certain, indeed—that acid spilt from the batteries by the tremendous pitching had eaten through the lashings. Then a battery must have broken loose and smashed another, and another, and another, and then the jars and carboys until the entire floor—fortunately of acid-resisting material—was awash to a depth of five or six inches in sulphuric acid.

A young torpedoman, on a routine check, had opened the door and seen the splashing sea of acid inside. Panicking, and recalling vaguely that caustic soda, stored in quantities just outside, was a neutralizer for sulphuric, he had emptied a fortypound carton of it into the battery-room: he was in the Sick Bay now, blinded. The acid fumes saturated the capstan flat, making entry impossible without breathing equipment, and was seeping back, slowly, insidiously, into the mess-deck: more deadly still hundreds of gallons of salt water from sprung deck-plates and broken capstan speaking tubes were surging crazily around the flat: already the air was tainted with the first traces of chlorine gas. On the deck immediately above, Hartley and two seamen, belayed with ropes, had made a brief, hopelessly gallant attempt to plug the gaping holes: all three, battered into near senselessness by the great waves pounding the fo'c'sle, were dragged off within a minute.

For the men below, it was discomfort, danger and desperate physical illness: for the bare handful of men above, the officers and ratings on the bridge, it was pure undiluted hell. But a hell not of our latter-day imagining, a strictly Eastern and Biblical conception, but the hell of our ancient North-European ancestors, of the Vikings, the Danes, the Jutes, of Beowulf and the monsterhaunted meres—the hell of eternal cold.

True, the temperature registered a mere 10° below zero –42° of frost. Men have been known to live, even to work in the open, at far lower temperatures. What is not so well known, what is barely realized at all, is that when freezing point has been passed, every extra mile per hour of wind is *equivalent,* in terms of pure cold as it reacts on a human being, to a 1° drop in temperature. Not once, but several times that night, before it had finally raced itself to destruction, the anemometer had recorded gusts of over 125 mph, wave-flattening gusts that sundered stays and all but tore the funnels off. For minutes on end, the shrieking, screaming wind held steady at 100 mph and above—the total equivalent, for these numbed, paralysed creatures on the bridge, of something well below 100° below zero.

Five minutes at a time was enough for any man on the bridge, then he had to retire to the Captain's shelter. Not that manning the bridge was more than a gesture anyway—it was impossible to look into that terrible wind: the cold would have seared the eyeballs blind, the ice would have gouged them out. And it was impossible even to see through the Kent Clear-view windscreens. They still spun at high speed but uselessly: the ice-laden storm, a gigantic sand-blaster, had starred and abraded the plate glass until it was completely opaque.

It was not a dark night. It was possible to see above, abeam and astern. Above, patches of nightblue sky and handfuls of stars could be seen at fleeting intervals, obscured as soon as seen by the scudding, shredded cloud-wrack. Abeam and astern, the sea was an inky black, laced with boiling white. Gone now were the serried ranks of yesterday, gone, too, the decorative white-caps: here now were only massive mountains of water, broken and confused, breaking this way and that, but always tending south. Some of these moving ranges of water—by no stretch of the imagination, only by proxy, could they be called waves—were small, insignificant—in size of a suburban house: others held a million tons of water, towered seventy to eighty feet, looming terrifyingly against the horizon, big enough to drown a cathedral . . . As the Kapok Kid remarked, the best thing to do with these waves was to look the other way. More often than not, they passed harmlessly by, plunging the *Ulysses* into the depths:

rarely, they curled over and broke their tops into the bridge, soaking the unfortunate Officer of the Watch. He had then to be removed at once or he would literally have frozen solid within a minute.

So far they had survived, far beyond the expectation of any man. But, as they were blind ahead, there was always the worry of what would come next. Would the next sea be normal—for that storm, that was—or some nameless juggernaut that would push them under for ever? The suspense never lifted, a suspense doubled by the fact that when the *Ulysses* reared and crashed down, it did so soundlessly, sightlessly. They could judge its intensity only by movement and vibration: the sound of the sea, everything, was drowned in the Satanic cacophony of that howling wind in the upper works and rigging.

About two in the morning—it was just after the depth-charge explosions—some of the senior officers had staged their own private mutiny. The Captain, who had been persuaded to go below less than an hour previously, exhausted and shaking uncontrollably with cold, had been wakened by the depth-charging and had returned to the bridge. He found his way barred by the Commander and Commander Westcliffe, who bundled him quietly but firmly into the shelter. Turner heaved the door to, switched on the light. Vallery was more puzzled than angry.

'What—what in the world does this mean?' he demanded.

'Mutiny!' boomed Turner happily. His face was covered in blood from flying splinters of ice. 'On the High Seas, is the technical term, I believe. Isn't that so, Admiral?'

'Exactly,' the Admiral agreed. Vallery swung round, startled: Tyndall was lying in state on the bunk. 'Mind you, I've no jurisdiction over a Captain in his own ship; but I can't see a thing.' He lay back on the bunk, eyes elaborately closed in seeming exhaustion. Only Tyndall knew that he wasn't pretending.

Vallery said nothing. He stood there clutching a handrail, his face grey and haggard, his eyes bloodred and drugged with sleep. Turner felt a knife twist inside him as he looked at him. When he spoke, his voice was low and earnest, so unusual for him that he caught and held Vallery's attention.

'Sir, this is no night for a naval captain. Danger from any quarter except the sea itself just doesn't exist. Agreed?'

Vallery nodded silently.

'It's a night for a seaman, sir. With all respect, I suggest that neither of us is in the class of Carrington—he's just a different breed of man.'

'Nice of you to include yourself, Commander,' Vallery murmured. 'And quite unnecessary.'

'The first Lieutenant will remain on the bridge all night. So will Westcliffe here. So will I.'

'Me, too,' grunted Tyndall. 'But I'm going to sleep.' He looked almost as tired, as haggard as Vallery.

Turner grinned. 'Thank you, sir. Well, Captain, I'm afraid it's going to be a bit overcrowded here tonight . . . We'll see you after breakfast.'

'But—'

'But me no buts,' Westcliffe murmured.

'Please,' Turner insisted. 'You will do us a favour.'

Vallery looked at him. 'As Captain of the *Ulysses* . . . ' His voice tailed off. 'I don't know what to say.'

'I do,' said Turner briskly, his hand on Vallery's elbow. 'Let's go below.'

'Don't think I can manage by myself, eh?' Vallery smiled faintly.

'I do. But I'm taking no chances. Come along, sir.'

'All right, all right.' He sighed tiredly. 'Anything for a quiet life . . . and a night's sleep!'

Reluctantly, with a great effort, Lieutenant Nicholls dragged himself up from the mist-fogged depths of exhausted sleep. Slowly, reluctantly, he opened his eyes. The *Ulysses*, he realized, was still rolling as heavily, plunging as sickeningly as ever. The Kapok Kid, forehead swathed in bandages, the rest of his face pocked with blood, was bending over him. He looked disgustingly cheerful.

'Hark, hark, the lark, et cetera,' the Kapok Kid grinned. 'And how are we this morning?' he mimicked unctuously. The Hon. Carpenter held the medical profession in low esteem.

Nicholls focused blurred eyes on him.

'What's the matter, Andy? Anything wrong?'

'With Messrs Carrington and Carpenter in charge,' said the Kapok Kid loftily, 'nothing could be wrong. Want to come up top, see Carrington do his stuff? He's going to turn the ship round. In this little lot, it should be worth seeing!'

'What! Dammit to hell! Have you woken me just—'

'Brother, when this ship turns, you would wake up anyway—probably on the deck with a broken neck. But as it so happens, Jimmy requires your assistance. At least, he requires one of these heavy plate-glass squares which I happen to know you have in great numbers in the dispensary. But the dispensary's locked—I tried it,' he added shamelessly.

'But what—I mean—plate glass—'

'Come and see for yourself,' the Kapok Kid invited.

It was dawn now, a wild and terrible dawn, fit epilogue for a nightmare. Strange, trailing bands of misty-white vapour swept by barely at mast-top level, but high above the sky was clear. The seas, still gigantic, were shorter now, much shorter, and even steeper: the *Ulysses* was slowed right down, with barely enough steerage way to keep her head up—and even then, taking severe punishment in the precipitous head seas. The wind had dropped to a steady fifty knots—gale force: even at that, it seared like fire in Nicholls's lungs as he stepped out on the flap-deck, blinded him with ice and cold. Hastily he wrapped scarves over his entire face, clambered up to the bridge by touch and instinct. The Kapok Kid followed with the glass. As they climbed, they heard the loudspeakers crackling some unintelligible message.

Turner and Carrington were alone on the twilit bridge, swathed like mummies. Not even their eyes were visible—they wore goggles.

'Morning, Nicholls,' boomed the Commander. 'It *is* Nicholls, isn't it?' He pulled off his goggles, his back turned to the bitter wind, threw them away in disgust. 'Can't see damn all through these bloody things . . . Ah, Number One, he's got the glass.'

Nicholls crouched in the for'ard lee of the compass platform. In a corner, the duckboards were littered with goggles, eye-shields and gas-masks. He jerked his head towards them.

'What's this—a clearance sale?'

'We're turning round, Doc.' It was Carrington who answered, his voice calm and precise as ever, without a trace of exhaustion. 'But we've got to see where we're going, and as the Commander says, all these damn things there are useless—mist up immediately they're put on—it's too cold. If you'll just hold it—so—and if you would wipe it, Andy?'

Nicholls looked at the great seas. He shuddered.

'Excuse my ignorance, but why turn round at all?'

'Because it will be impossible very shortly,' Carrington answered briefly. Then he chuckled. 'This is going to make me the most unpopular man in the ship. We've just broadcast a warning. Ready, sir?'

'Stand by, engine-room: stand by, wheelhouse. Ready, Number One.'

For thirty seconds, forty-five, a whole minute, Carrington stared steadily, unblinkingly through the glass. Nicholls's hands froze. The Kapok Kid rubbed industriously. Then:

'Half-ahead, port!'

'Half-ahead, port!' Turner echoed.

'Starboard 20!'

'Starboard 20!'

Nicholls risked a glance over his shoulder. In the split second before his eyes blinded, filled with tears, he saw a huge wave bearing down on them, the bows already swinging diagonally away from it. Good God! Why hadn't Carrington waited until that was past?

The great wave flung the bows up, pushed the *Ulysses* far over to starboard, then passed under. The *Ulysses* staggered over the top, corkscrewed wickedly down the other side, her masts, great gleaming tree trunks thick and heavy with ice, swinging in a great arc as she rolled over, burying her port rails in the rising shoulder of the next sea.

'Full ahead port!'

'Full ahead port!'

'Starboard 30!'

'Starboard 30!'

The next sea, passing beneath, merely straightened the *Ulysses* up. And then, at last, Nicholls understood. Incredibly, because it had been impossible to see so far ahead, Carrington had known that two opposing wave systems were due to interlock in an area of comparative calm: how he had sensed it, no one knew, would ever know, not even Carrington himself: but he was a great seaman, and he had known. For fifteen, twenty seconds, the sea was a seething white mass of violently disturbed, conflicting waves—of the type usually found, on a small scale, in tidal races and overfalls—and the *Ulysses* curved gracefully through. And then another great sea, towering almost to bridge height, caught her on the far turn of the quarter circle. It struck the entire length of the *Ulysses*—for the first time that night—with tremendous weight. It threw her far over on her side, the lee rails vanishing. Nicholls was flung off his feet, crashed heavily into the side of the bridge, the glass shattering. He could have sworn he heard Carrington laughing. He clawed his way back to the middle of the compass platform.

And still the great wave had not passed. It towered high above the trough into which the *Ulysses*, now heeled far over to 40°, had been so contemptuously flung, bore down remorselessly from above and sought, in a lethal silence and with an almost animistic savagery, to press her under. The inclinometer swung relentlessly over—45°, 50°, 53°, and hung there an eternity, while men stood on the side of the ship, braced with their hands on the deck, numbed minds barely grasping the inevitable. This was the end. The *Ulysses* could never come back.

A lifetime ticked agonizingly by. Nicholls and Carpenter looked at each other, blank-faced, expressionless. Tilted at that crazy angle, the bridge was sheltered from the wind. Carrington's voice, calm, conversational, carried with amazing clarity.

'She'd go to 65° and still come back,' he said matter-of-factly. 'Hang on to your hats, gentlemen. This is going to be interesting.'

Just as he finished, the *Ulysses* shuddered, then imperceptibly, then slowly, then with vicious speed lurched back and whipped through an arc of 90°, then back again. Once more Nicholls found himself in the corner of the bridge. But the *Ulysses* was almost round.

The Kapok Kid, grinning with relief, picked himself up and tapped Carrington on the shoulder.

'Don't look now, sir, but we have lost our mainmast.'

It was a slight exaggeration, but the top fifteen feet, which had carried the after radar scanner, were undoubtedly gone. That wicked, double whip-lash, with the weight of the ice, had been too much.

'Slow ahead both! Midships!'

'Slow ahead both! Midships!'

'Steady as she goes!'

The *Ulysses* was round.

The Kapok Kid caught Nicholls's eye, nodded at the First Lieutenant.

'See what I mean, Johnny?'

'Yes,' Nicholls was very quiet. 'Yes, I see what you mean.' Then he grinned suddenly. 'Next time you make a statement, I'll just take your word for it, if you don't mind. These demonstrations of proof take too damn much out of a person!'

Running straight before the heavy stern sea, the *Ulysses* was amazingly steady. The wind, too, was dead astern now, the bridge in magical shelter. The scudding mist overhead had thinned out, was almost gone. Far away to the south-east a dazzling white sun climbed up above a cloudless horizon. The long night was over.

An hour later, with the wind down to thirty knots, radar reported contacts to the west. After another hour, with the wind almost gone and only a heavy swell running, smoke plumes tufted above the horizon. At 1030, in position, on time, the *Ulysses* rendezvoused with the convoy from Halifax.

SEVEN

Wednesday Night

The convoy came steadily up from the west, rolling heavily in cross seas, a rich argosy, a magnificent prize, for any German wolf-pack. Eighteen ships in this argosy, fifteen big, modern cargo ships, three 16,000-ton tankers, carrying a freight far more valuable, infinitely more vital, than any fleet of quinqueremes or galleons had ever known. Tanks, planes and petrol—what were gold and jewels, silks and the rarest of spices compared to these? £10,000,000, £20,000,000—the total worth of that convoy was difficult to estimate: in any event, its real value was not to be measured in terms of money.

Aboard the merchant ships, crews lined the decks as the *Ulysses* steamed up between the port and centre lines. Lined the decks and looked and wondered—and thanked their Maker they had been wide of the path of that great storm. The *Ulysses*, seen from another deck, was a strange sight: broken-masted, stripped of her rafts, with her boat falls hauled taut over empty cradles, she glistened like crystal in the morning light: the great wind had blown away all snow, had abraded and rubbed and polished the ice to a stain-smooth, transparent gloss: but on either side of the bows and before the bridge were huge patches of crimson, where the hurricane sand-blaster of that long night had stripped off camouflage and base coats, exposing the red lead below.

The American escort was small—a heavy cruiser with a seaplane for spotting, two destroyers and two near-frigates of the coastguard type. Small, but sufficient: there was no need of escort carriers (although these frequently sailed with the Atlantic convoys) because the Luftwaffe could not operate so far west, and the wolf-packs, in recent months, had moved north and east of Iceland: there, they were not only nearer base—they could more easily lie astride the converging convoy routes to Murmansk.

ENE they sailed in company, freighters, American warships and the *Ulysses* until, late in the afternoon, the box-like silhouette of an escort carrier bulked high against the horizon. Half an hour later, at 1600, the American escorts slowed, dropped astern and turned, winking farewell messages of good luck. Aboard the *Ulysses*, men watched them depart with mixed feelings. They knew these ships had to go, that another convoy would already be mustering off the St Lawrence. There was none of the envy, the bitterness one might expect—and had indeed been common enough only a few weeks ago—among these exhausted men who carried the brunt of the war. There was instead a careless acceptance of things as they were, a quasi-cynical bravado, often a queer, high nameless pride that hid itself beneath twisted jests and endless grumbling.

The 14th Aircraft Carrier Squadron—or what was left of it—was only two miles away now. Tyndall, coming to the bridge, swore fluently as he saw that a carrier and minesweeper were missing. An angry signal went out to Captain Jeffries of the *Stirling*, asking why orders had been disobeyed, where the missing ships were.

An Aldis flickered back its reply. Tyndall sat grim-faced and silent as Bentley read out the signal to him. The *Wrestler*'s steering gear had broken down during the night. Even behind Langanes the weather position had been severe, had worsened about midnight when the wind had veered to the north. The *Wrestler*, even with two screws, had lost almost all steering command, and, in zero visibility and an effort to maintain position, had gone too far ahead and grounded on the Vejle bank. She had grounded on the top of the tide. She had still been there, with the minesweeper *Eager* in attendance, when the squadron had sailed shortly after dawn.

Tyndall sat in silence for some minutes. He dictated a WT signal to the *Wrestler*, hesitated about breaking radio silence, countermanded the signal, and decided to go to see for himself. After all, it was only three hours' steaming distance. He signalled the *Stirling*: 'Take over squadron command: will rejoin in the morning,' and ordered Vallery to take the *Ulysses* back to Langanes.

Vallery nodded unhappily, gave the necessary orders. He was worried, badly so, was trying hard not to show it. The least of his worries was himself, although he knew, but never admitted to anyone, that he was a very sick man. He thought wryly that he didn't have to admit it anyway—he was amused and touched by the elaborate casualness with which his officers sought to lighten his load, to show their concern for him.

He was worried, too, about his crew—they were in no fit state to do the lightest work, to survive that killing cold, far less sail the ship and fight her through to Russia. He was depressed, also, over the series of misfortunes that had befallen the squadron since leaving Scapa: it augured ill for the future, and he had no illusions as to what lay ahead for the crippled squadron. And always, a gnawing torment at the back of his mind, he worried about Ralston.

Ralston—that tall throwback to his Scandinavian ancestors, with his flaxen hair and still blue eyes. Ralston, whom nobody understood, with whom nobody on the ship had an intimate friendship, who went his own unsmiling, self-possessed way. Ralston, who had nothing left to fight for, except memories, who was one of the most reliable men in the *Ulysses*, extraordinarily decisive, competent and resourceful in any emergency—and who again found himself under lock and key. And for nothing that any reasonable and just man could call fault of his own.

Under lock and key—that was what hurt. Last night, Vallery had gladly seized the excuse of bad weather to release him, had intended to forget the matter, to let sleeping dogs lie. But Hastings, the Master-At-Arms, had exceeded his duty and returned him to cells during the forenoon watch. Masters-At-Arms—disciplinary Warrant Officers, in effect—had never been particularly noted for a humane, tolerant and ultra-kindly attitude to life in general or the lower deck in particular—they couldn't afford to be. But even amongst such men, Hastings was an exception—a machinelike, seemingly emotionless creature, expressionless, unbending, strict, fair according to his lights, but utterly devoid of heart and sympathy. If Hastings were not careful, Vallery mused, he might very well go the same way as Lister, until recently the highly unpopular Master-At-Arms of the *Blue Ranger*. Not, when he came to think of it, that anyone knew what had happened to Lister, except that he had been so misguided as to take a walk on the flight-deck on a dark and starless night . . .

Vallery sighed. As he had explained to Foster, his hands were tied. Foster, the Captain of Marines, with an aggrieved and incensed Colour-Sergeant Evans standing behind him, had complained bitterly at having his marines withdrawn for guard duty, men who needed every minute of sleep they could snatch. Privately, Vallery had sympathized with Foster, but he couldn't afford to countermand his original order—not, at least, until he had held a Captain's Defaulters and placed Ralston under open arrest . . . He sighed again, sent for Turner and asked him to break out grass lines, a manila and a five-inch wire on the poop. He suspected that they would be needed shortly, and, as it turned out, his preparations were justified.

Darkness had fallen when they moved up to the Vejle bank, but locating the *Wrestler* was easy—her identification challenge ten minutes ago had given her approximate position, and now her squat bulk loomed high before them, a knife-edged silhouette against the pale afterglow of sunset. Ominously, her flight-deck raked perceptibly towards the stern, where the *Eager* lay, apparently at anchor. The sea was almost calm here—there was only a gentle swell running.

Aboard the *Ulysses*, a hooded pin-hole Aldis started to chatter.

'Congratulations! How are you fast?'

From the *Wrestler*, a tiny light flickered in answer. Bentley read aloud as the message came.

'Bows aft 100 feet.'

'Wonderful,' said Tyndall bitterly. 'Just wonderful! Ask him, "How is steering-gear?"'

Back came the answer: 'Diver down: transverse fracture of post: dockyard job.'

'My God!' Tyndall groaned. 'A dockyard job! That's handy. Ask him, "What steps have you taken?"'

'All fuel and water pumped aft. Kedge anchor. *Eager* towing. Full astern, 1200-1230.'

The turn of the high tide, Tyndall knew. 'Very successful, very successful indeed,' he growled. 'No, you bloody fool, don't send that. Tell him to prepare to receive towing wire, bring own towing chain aft.'

'Message understood,' Bentley read.

'Ask him, "How much excess squadron fuel have you?"'

'800 tons.'

'Get rid of it.'

Bentley read, 'Please confirm.'

'Tell him to empty the bloody stuff over the side!' Tyndall roared.

The light on the *Wrestler* flickered and died in hurt silence.

At midnight the *Eager* steamed slowly ahead of the *Ulysses*, taking up the wire that led back to the cruiser's fo'c'sle capstan: two minutes later, the *Ulysses* began to shudder as the four great engines boiled up the shallow water into a seething mudstained cauldron. The chain from the poop-deck to the *Wrestler*'s stern was a bare fifteen fathoms in length, angling up at 30°. This would force the carrier's stern down—only a fraction, but in this situation every ounce counted—and give more positive buoyancy to the grounded bows. And much more important—for the racing screws were now aerating the water, developing only a fraction of their potential thrust—the proximity of the two ships helped the *Ulysses*'s screws reinforce the action of the *Wrestler*'s in scouring out a channel in the sand and mud beneath the carrier's keel.

Twenty minutes before high tide, easily, steadily, the *Wrestler* slid off. At once the blacksmith on the *Ulysses*'s bows knocked off the shackle securing the *Eager*'s towing wire, and the *Ulysses* pulled the carrier, her engines shut down, in a big half-circle to the east.

By one o'clock the *Wrestler* was gone, the *Eager* in attendance and ready to pass a head rope for bad weather steering. On the bridge of the *Ulysses*, Tyndall watched the carrier vanish into the night, zig-zagging as the captain tried to balance the steering on the two screws.

'No doubt they'll get the hang of it before they get to Scapa,' he growled. He felt cold, exhausted and only the way an Admiral can feel when he has lost three-quarters of his carrier force. He sighed wearily and turned to Vallery.

'When do you reckon we'll overtake the convoy?'

Vallery hesitated: not so the Kapok Kid.

'0805,' he answered readily and precisely. 'At twenty-seven knots, on the intersection course I've just pencilled out.'

'Oh, my God!' Tyndall groaned. 'That stripling again. What did I ever do to deserve him. As it happens, young man, it's imperative that we overtake before dawn.'

'Yes, sir.' The Kapok Kid was imperturbable. 'I thought so myself. On my alternative course, 33 knots, thirty minutes before dawn.'

'I thought so myself! Take him away!' Tyndall raved. 'Take him away or I'll wrap his damned dividers round . . . ' He broke off, climbed stiffly out of his chair, took Vallery by the arm. 'Come on, Captain. Let's go below. What the hell's the use of a couple of ancient has-beens like us getting in the way of youth?' He passed out the gate behind the Captain, grinning tiredly to himself.

The *Ulysses* was at dawn Action Stations as the shadowy shapes of the convoy, a bare mile ahead, lifted out of the greying gloom. The great bulk of the *Blue Ranger*, on the starboard quarter of the convoy, was unmistakable. There was a moderate swell running, but not enough to be uncomfortable: the breeze was light, from the west, the temperature just below zero, the sky chill and cloudless. The time was exactly 0700.

At 0702, the *Blue Ranger* was torpedoed. The *Ulysses* was two cable-lengths away, on her starboard quarter: those on the bridge felt the physical shock of the twin explosions, heard them shattering the stillness of the dawn as they saw two searing columns of flame fingering skywards, high above the *Blue Ranger*'s bridge and well aft of it. A second later they heard a signalman shouting something unintelligible, saw him pointing forwards and downwards. It was another torpedo, running astern of the carrier, trailing its evil phosphorescent wake across the heels of the convoy, before spending itself in the darkness of the Arctic.

Vallery was shouting down the voice-pipe, pulling round the *Ulysses*, still doing upwards of twenty knots, in a madly heeling, skidding turn, to avoid collision with the slewing carrier. Three sets of Aldis lamps and the fighting lights were already stuttering out the 'Maintain Position' code signal to ships in the convoy. Marshall, on the phone, was giving the stand-by order to the depth-charge LTO: gun barrels were already depressing, peering hungrily into the treacherous sea. The signal to the *Sirrus* stopped short, unneeded: the destroyer, a half-seen blue in the darkness, was already knifing its way through the convoy, white water piled high at its bows, headed for the estimated position of the U-boat.

The *Ulysses* sheered by parallel to the burning carrier, less than 150 feet away; travelling so fast, heeling so heavily and at such close range, it was impossible to gather more than a blurred impression, a tangled, confused memory of heavy black smoke laced with roaring columns of flame, appalling in that near-darkness, of a drunkenly listing flight-deck, of Grummans and Corsairs cartwheeling grotesquely over the edge to splash icy clouds of spray in shocked faces, as the cruiser slewed away; and then the *Ulysses* was round, heading back south for the kill.

Within a minute, the signal-lamp of the *Vectra*, up front with the convoy, started winking: 'Contact, Green 70, closing: Contact, Green 70, closing.'

'Acknowledge,' Tyndall ordered briefly.

The Aldis had barely begun to clack when the *Vectra* cut through the signal.

'Contacts, repeat contacts. Green 90, Green 90. Closing. Very close. Repeat contacts, contacts.'

Tyndall cursed softly.

'Acknowledge. Investigate.' He turned to Vallery. 'Let's join him, Captain. This is it. Wolf-pack Number One—and in force. No bloody right to be here,' he added bitterly. 'So much for Admiralty Intelligence!'

The *Ulysses* was round again, heading for the *Vectra*. It should have been growing lighter now, but the *Blue Ranger*, her squadron fuel tanks on fire, a gigantic torch against the eastern horizon, had the curious effect of throwing the surrounding sea into heavy darkness. She lay almost athwart of the flagship's course for the *Vectra*, looming larger every minute. Tyndall had his night glasses to his eyes, kept on muttering: 'The poor bastards, the poor bastards!'

The *Blue Ranger* was almost gone. She lay dead in the water, heeled far over to starboard, ammunition and petrol tanks going up in a constant series of crackling reports. Suddenly, a succession of dull, heavy explosions rumbled over the sea: the entire bridge island structure lurched crazily sideways, held, then slowly, ponderously, deliberately, the whole massive body of it toppled majestically into the glacial darkness of the sea. God only knew how many men perished with it, deep down in the Arctic, trapped in its iron walls. They were the lucky ones.

The *Vectra*, barely two miles ahead now, was pulling round south in a tight circle. Vallery saw her, altered course to intercept. He heard Bentley shouting something unintelligible from the fore corner of the compass platform. Vallery shook his head, heard him shouting again, his voice desperate with some nameless urgency, his arm pointing frantically over the windscreen, and leapt up beside him.

The sea was on fire. Flat, calm, burdened with hundreds of tons of fuel oil, it was a vast carpet of licking, twisting flames. That much, for a second, and that only, Vallery saw: then with heartstopping shock, with physically sickening abruptness, he saw something else again: the burning sea was alive with swimming, struggling men. Not a handful, not even dozens, but literally hundreds, soundlessly screaming, agonizingly dying in the barbarous contrariety of drowning and cremation.

'Signal from *Vectra*, sir.' It was Bentley speaking, his voice abnormally matter-of-fact. '"Depth-charging. 3, repeat 3 contacts. Request immediate assistance."'

Tyndall was at Vallery's side now. He heard Bentley, looked a long second at Vallery, following his sick, fascinated gaze into the sea ahead.

For a man in the sea, oil is an evil thing. It clogs his movements, burns his eyes, sears his lungs and tears away his stomach in uncontrollable paroxysms of retching; but oil on fire is a hellish thing, death by torture, a slow, shrieking death by drowning, by burning, by asphyxiation—for the flames devour all the life-giving oxygen on the surface of the sea. And not even in the bitter Arctic is there the merciful extinction by cold, for the insulation of an oil-soaked body stretches a dying man on the rack for eternity, carefully preserves him for the last excruciating refinement of agony. All this Vallery knew.

He knew, too, that for the *Ulysses* to stop, starkly outlined against the burning carrier, would have been suicide. And to come sharply round to starboard, even had there been time and room to clear the struggling, dying men in the sea ahead, would have wasted invaluable minutes, time and to spare for the U-boats ahead to line up firing-tracks on the convoy; and the *Ulysses*'s first responsibility was to the convoy. Again all this Vallery knew. But at that moment, what weighed most heavily with him was common humanity. Fine off the port bow, close in to the *Blue Ranger*, the oil was heaviest, the flames fiercest, the swimmers thickest: Vallery looked back over his shoulder at the Officer of the Watch.

'Port 10!'

'Port 10, sir.'

'Midships!'

'Midships, sir.'

'Steady as she goes!'

For ten, fifteen seconds the *Ulysses* held her course, arrowing through the burning sea to the spot where some gregariously atavistic instinct for self-preservation held two hundred men knotted together in a writhing, seething mass, gasping out their lives in hideous agony. For a second a great gout of flame leapt up in the centre of the group, like a giant, incandescent magnesium flare, a flame that burnt the picture into the hearts and minds of the men on the bridge with a permanence and searing clarity that no photographic plate could ever have reproduced: men on fire, human torches beating insanely at the flames that licked, scorched and then incinerated clothes, hair and skin: men flinging themselves almost out of the water, backs arched like tautened bows, grotesque in convulsive crucifixion: men lying dead in the water, insignificant, featureless little oil-stained mounds in an oil-soaked plain: and a handful of fear-maddened men, faces inhumanly contorted, who saw the *Ulysses* and knew what was coming, as they frantically thrashed their way to a safety that offered only a few more brief seconds of unspeakable agony before they gladly died.

'Starboard 30!' Vallery's voice was low, barely a murmur, but it carried clearly through the shocked silence on the bridge.

'Starboard 30, sir.'

For the third time in ten minutes, the *Ulysses* slewed crazily round in a racing turn. Turning thus, a ship does not follow through the line of the bows cutting the water; there is a pronounced sideways or lateral motion, and the faster and sharper the turn, the more violent the broadside skidding motion, like a car on ice. The side of the *Ulysses*, still at an acute angle, caught the edge of the group on the port bow: almost on the instant, the entire length of the swinging hull smashed into the heart of the fire, into the thickest press of dying men.

For most of them, it was just extinction, swift and glad and merciful. The tremendous concussion and pressure waves crushed the life out of them, thrust them deep down into the blessed oblivion of drowning, thrust them down and sucked them back into the thrashing vortex of the four great screws . . .

On board the *Ulysses*, men for whom death and destruction had become the stuff of existence, to be accepted with the callousness and jesting indifference that alone kept them sane—these men clenched impotent fists, mouthed meaningless, useless curses over and over again and wept heedlessly like little children. They wept as pitiful, charred faces, turned up towards the *Ulysses* and alight with joy and hope, petrified into incredulous staring horror, as realization dawned and the water closed over them; as hate-filled men screamed insane invective, both arms raised aloft, shaking fists white-knuckled through the dripping oil as the *Ulysses* trampled them under: as a couple of young boys were sucked into the maelstrom of the propellers, still giving the thumbs-up sign: as a particularly shocking case, who looked as if he had been barbecued on a spit and had no right to be alive, lifted a scorified hand to the blackened hole that had been his mouth, flung to the bridge a kiss in token of endless gratitude; and wept, oddly, most of all, at the inevitable humorist who lifted his fur cap high above his head and bowed gravely and deeply, his face into the water as he died.

Suddenly, mercifully, the sea was empty. The air was strangely still and quiet, heavy with the sickening stench of charred flesh and burning Diesel, and the *Ulysses*'s stern was swinging wildly almost under the black pall overhanging the *Blue Ranger* amidships, when the shells struck her.

The shells—three 3.7s—came from the *Blue Ranger*. Certainly, no living gun-crews manned these 3.7s—the heat must have ignited the bridge fuses in the cartridge cases. The first shell exploded harmlessly against the armour-plating: the second wrecked the bosun's store, fortunately empty: the third penetrated No 3 Low Power Room via the deck. There were nine men in there—an officer, seven ratings and Chief-Torpedo Gunner's Mate Noyes. In that confined space, death was instantaneous.

Only seconds later a heavy rumbling explosion blew out a great hole along the waterline of the *Blue Ranger* and she fell slowly, wearily right over on her starboard side, her flight-deck vertical to the water, as if content to die now that, dying, she had lashed out at the ship that had destroyed her crew.

On the bridge, Vallery still stood on the yeoman's platform, leaning over the starred, opaque windscreen. His head hung down, his eyes were shut and he was retching desperately, the gushing blood—arterial blood—ominously bright and scarlet in the erubescent glare of the sinking carrier. Tyndall stood there helplessly beside him, not knowing what to do, his mind numbed and sick. Suddenly, he was brushed unceremoniously aside by the Surgeon-Commander, who pushed a white towel to Vallery's mouth and led him gently below. Old Brooks, everyone knew, should have been at his Action Stations position in the Sick Bay: no one dared say anything.

Carrington straightened the *Ulysses* out on course, while he waited for Turner to move up from the after Director tower to take over the bridge. In three minutes the cruiser was up with the *Vectra,* methodically quartering for a lost contact. Twice the ships regained contact, twice they dropped heavy patterns. A heavy oil slick rose to the surface: possibly a kill, probably a ruse, but in any event, neither ship could remain to investigate further. The convoy was two miles ahead now, and only the *Stirling* and *Viking* were there for its protection—a wholly inadequate cover and powerless to save the convoy from any determined attack.

It was the *Blue Ranger* that saved FR77. In these high latitudes, dawn comes slowly, interminably: even so, it was more than half-light, and the merchant ships, line ahead through that very gentle swell, lifted clear and sharp against a cloudless horizon, a U-boat Commander's dream—or would have been, had he been able to see them. But, by this time, the convoy was completely obscured from the wolf-pack lying to the south: the light westerly wind carried the heavy black smoke from the blazing carrier along the southern flank of the convoy, at sea level, the perfect smoke-screen, dense, impenetrable. Why the U-boats had departed from their almost invariable practice of launching dawn attacks from the north, so as to have their targets between themselves and the sunrise, could only be guessed. Tactical surprise, probably, but whatever the reason it was the saving of the convoy. Within an hour, the thrashing screws of the convoy had left the wolf-pack far behind—and FR77, having slipped the pack, was far too fast to be overtaken again.

Aboard the flagship, the WT transmitter was chattering out a coded signal to London. There was little point, Tyndall had decided, in maintaining radio silence now; the enemy knew their position to a mile. Tyndall smiled grimly as he thought of the rejoicing in the German Naval High Command at the news that FR77 was without any air cover whatsoever; as a starter, they could expect Charlie within the hour.

The signal read: 'Admiral, 14 ACS: To DNC, London. Rendezvoused FR77 1030 yesterday. Weather conditions extreme. Severe damage to Carriers: *Defender, Wrestler* unserviceable, returning base under escort: *Blue Ranger* torpedoed 0702, sunk 0730 today: Convoy Escorts now *Ulysses, Stirling, Sirrus, Vectra, Viking*: no minesweepers—*Eager* to base, minesweeper from Hvalfjord failed rendezvous: Urgently require air support: Can you detach carrier battle squadron: Alternatively, permission return base. Please advise immediately.'

The wording of the message, Tyndall pondered, could have been improved. Especially the bit at the end—probably sounded sufficiently like a threat to infuriate old Starr, who would only see in it pusillanimous confirmation of his conviction of the *Ulysses*'s—and Tyndall's—unfitness for the job . . . Besides, for almost two years now—since long before the sinking of the *Hood* by the *Bismarck*—it had been Admiralty policy not to break up the Home Fleet squadrons by detaching capital ships or carriers. Old battleships too slow for modern inter-naval surface action—vessels such as the *Ramillies* and the *Malaya*—were used for selected Arctic convoys: with that exception, the official strategy was based on keeping the Home Fleet intact, containing the German Grand Fleet—and risking the convoys . . . Tyndall took a last look round the convoy, sighed warily and eased himself down to the duckboards. What the hell, he thought, let it go. If it wasted his time sending it, it would also waste old Starr's time reading it.

He clumped his way heavily down the bridge ladders, eased his bulk through the door of the Captain's cabin, hard by the FDR. Vallery, partly undressed, was lying in his bunk, between very clean, very white sheets: their knife-edged ironing crease-marks contrasted oddly with the spreading crimson stain. Vallery himself, gaunt-cheeked and cadaverous beneath dark stubble of beard, red eyes sunk deep in great hollow sockets, looked corpse-like, already dead. From one corner of his mouth blood trickled down a parchment cheek. As Tyndall shut the door, Vallery lifted a wasted hand, all ivory knuckles and blue veins, in feeble greeting.

Tyndall closed the door carefully, quietly. He took his time, time and to spare to allow the shock to drain out of his face. When he turned round, his face was composed, but he made no attempt to disguise his concern.

'Thank God for old Socrates!' he said feelingly. 'Only man in the ship who can make you see even a modicum of sense.' He parked himself on the edge of the bed. 'How do you feel, Dick?'

Vallery grinned crookedly. There was no humour in his smile.

'All depends what you mean, sir. Physically or mentally? I feel a bit worn out—not really ill, you know. Doc says he can fix me up—temporarily anyway. He's going to give me a plasma transfusion—says I've lost too much blood.'

'Plasma?'

'Plasma. Whole blood would be a better coagulant. But he thinks it may prevent—or minimize—future attacks . . .' He paused, wiped some froth off his lips, and smiled again, as mirthlessly as before. 'It's not really a doctor and medicine I need, John—it's a padre—and forgiveness.' His voice trailed off into silence. The cabin was very quiet.

Tyndall shifted uncomfortably and cleared his throat noisily. Rarely had he been so conscious that he was, first and last, a man of action.

'Forgiveness? What on earth do you mean, Dick?' He hadn't meant to speak so loudly, so harshly.

'You know damn well what I mean,' Vallery said mildly. He was a man who was rarely heard to swear, to use the most innocuous oath. 'You were with me on the bridge this morning.'

For perhaps two minutes neither man said a word. Then Vallery broke into a fresh paroxysm of coughing. The towel in his hand grew dark, sodden, and when he leaned back on his pillow Tyndall felt a quick stab of fear. He bent quickly over the sick man, sighed in soundless relief as he heard the quick, shallow breathing.

Vallery spoke again, his eyes still closed.

'It's not so much the men who were killed in the Low Power Room.' He seemed to be talking to himself, his voice a drifting murmur. 'My fault, I suppose—I took the *Ulysses* too near the *Ranger*. Foolish to go near a sinking ship, especially if she's burning . . . But just one of these things, just one of the risks . . . they happen . . . ' The rest was a blurred, dying whisper. Tyndall couldn't catch it.

He rose abruptly to his feet, pulling his gloves on.

'Sorry, Dick,' he apologized. 'Shouldn't have come—shouldn't have stayed so long. Old Socrates will give me hell.'

'It's the others—the boys in the water.' Vallery might never have heard him. 'I hadn't the right—I mean, perhaps some of them would . . . ' Again his voice was lost for a moment, then he went on strongly: 'Captain Richard Vallery, DSO—judge, jury and executioner. Tell me, John, what am I going to say when *my* turn comes?'

Tyndall hesitated, heard the authoritative rap on the door and jerked round, his breath escaping in a long, inaudible sigh of thankfulness.

'Come in,' he called.

The door opened and Brooks walked in. He stopped short at the sight of the Admiral, turned to the white-coated assistant behind him, a figure weighed down with stands, bottles, tubing and various paraphernalia.

'Remain outside, Johnson, will you?' he asked. 'I'll call you when I want you.'

He closed the door, crossed the cabin and pulled a chair up to the Captain's bunk. Vallery's wrist between his fingers, he looked coldly across at Tyndall. Nicholls, Brooks remembered, was insistent that the Admiral was far from well. He looked tired, certainly, but more unhappy than tired . . . The pulse was very fast, irregular.

'You've been upsetting him,' Brooks accused.

'Me? Good God, no!' Tyndall was injured. 'So help me, Doc, I never said—'

'Not guilty, Doc.' It was Vallery who spoke, his voice stronger now. 'He never said a word. *I'm* the guilty man—guilty as hell.'

Brooks looked at him for a long moment. Then he smiled, smiled in understanding and compassion.

'Forgiveness, sir. That's it, isn't it?' Tyndall started in surprise, looked at him in wonder.

Vallery opened his eyes. 'Socrates!' he murmured. 'You would know.'

'Forgiveness,' Brooks mused. 'Forgiveness. From whom—the living, the dead—or the Judge?'

Again Tyndall started. 'Have you—have you been listening outside? How can you—?'

'From all three, Doc. A tall order, I'm afraid.'

'From the dead, sir, you are quite right. There would be no forgiveness: only their blessing, for there is nothing to forgive. I'm a doctor, don't forget—I saw those boys in the water . . . you sent them home the easy way. As for the Judge—you know, "The Lord giveth, the Lord taketh away. Blessed be the name of the Lord"—the Old Testament conception of the Lord who takes away in His own time and His own way, and to hell with mercy and charity.' He smiled at Tyndall. 'Don't look so shocked, sir. I'm not being blasphemous. If that were the Judge, Captain, neither you nor I—nor the Admiral—would ever want any part of him. But you know, it isn't so . . . '

Vallery smiled faintly, propped himself up on his pillow. 'You make good medicine, Doctor. It's a pity you can't speak for the living also.'

'Oh, can't I?' Brooks smacked his hand on his thigh, guffawed in sudden recollection. 'Oh, my word, it was magnificent!' He laughed again in genuine amusement. Tyndall looked at Vallery in mock despair.

'Sorry,' Brooks apologized. 'Just fifteen minutes ago a bunch of sympathetic stokers deposited on the deck of the Sick Bay the prone and extremely unconscious form of one of their shipmates. Guess who? None other than our resident nihilist, our old friend Riley. Slight concussion and assorted facial injuries, but he should be restored to the bosom of his mess-deck by nightfall. Anyway, he insists on it—claims his kittens need him.'

Vallery looked up, amused, curious.

'Fallen down the stokehold again, I presume?'

'Exactly the question I put, sir—although it looked more as if he had fallen into a concrete mixer. "No, sir," says one of the stretcher-bearers. "He tripped over the ship's cat." "Ship's cat?" I says. "What ship's cat?" So he turns to his oppo and says: "Ain't we got a ship's cat, Nobby?" Whereupon the stoker looks at him pityingly and says: "E's got it all wrong, sir. Poor old Riley just came all over queer—took a weak turn, 'e did. I 'ope 'e ain't 'urt 'isself?" He sounded quite anxious.'

'What had happened?' Tyndall queried.

'I let it go at that. Young Nicholls took two of them aside, promised no action and had it out of them in a minute flat. Seems that Riley saw in this morning's affair a magnificent opportunity for provoking trouble. Cursed you for an inhuman, cold-blooded murderer and, I regret to say, cast serious aspersions on your immediate ancestors—and all of this, mind you, where he thought he was safe—among his own friends. His friends half-killed him . . . You know, sir, I envy you . . . '

He broke off, rose abruptly to his feet.

'Now, sir, if you'll just lie down and roll up your sleeve . . . Oh, damn!'

'Come in.' It was Tyndall who answered the knock. 'Ah, for me, young Chrysler. Thank you.'

He looked up at Vallery. 'From London—in reply to my signal.' He turned it over in his hand two or three times. 'I suppose I have to open it some time,' he said reluctantly.

The Surgeon-Commander half-rose to his feet.

'Shall I—'

'No, no, Brooks. Why should you? Besides, it's from our mutual friend, Admiral Starr. I'm sure you'd like to hear what he's got to say, wouldn't you?'

'No, I wouldn't.' Brooks was very blunt. 'I can't imagine it'll be anything good.'

Tyndall opened the signal, smoothed it out.

'DNO to Admiral Commanding 14 ACS,' he read slowly. '*Tirpitz* reported preparing to move out. Impossible detach Fleet carrier: FR77 vital: proceed Murmansk all speed: good luck: Starr.' Tyndall paused, his mouth twisted. 'Good luck! He might have spared us that!'

For a long time the three men looked at each other, silently, without expression. Characteristically, it was Brooks who broke the silence.

'Speaking of forgiveness,' he murmured quietly, 'what I want to know is—who on God's earth, above or below it, is ever going to forgive that vindictive old bastard?'

EIGHT

Thursday Night

It was still only afternoon, but the grey Arctic twilight was already thickening over the sea as the *Ulysses* dropped slowly astern. The wind had died away completely; again the snow was falling, steadily, heavily, and visibility was down to a bare cable-length. It was bitterly cold.

In little groups of three and four, officers and men made their way aft to the starboard side of the poop-deck. Exhausted, bone-chilled men, mostly sunk in private and bitter thought, they shuffled wordlessly aft, dragging feet kicking up little puffs of powdery snow. On the poop, they ranged themselves soundlessly behind the Captain or in a line inboard and aft of the long, symmetrical row of snow-covered hummocks that heaved up roundly from the unbroken whiteness of the poop.

The Captain was flanked by three of his officers—Carslake, Etherton and the Surgeon-Commander. Carslake was by the guard-rail, the lower half of his face swathed in bandages to the eyes. For the second time in twenty-four hours he had waylaid Vallery, begged him to reconsider the decision to deprive him of his commission. On the first occasion Vallery had been adamant, almost contemptuous: ten minutes ago he had been icy and abrupt, had threatened Carslake with close arrest if he annoyed him again. And now Carslake just stared unseeingly into the snow and gloom, pale-blue eyes darkened and heavy with hate.

Etherton stood just behind Vallery's left shoulder, shivering uncontrollably. Above the white, jerking line of compressed mouth, cheek and jaw muscles were working incessantly: only his eyes were steady, dulled in sick fascination at the curious mound at his feet. Brooks, too, was tight-lipped, but there the resemblance ended: red of face and wrathful blue of eye, he fumed and seethed as can only a doctor whose orders have been openly flouted by the critically ill. Vallery, as Brooks had told him, forcibly and insubordinately, had no bloody right to be there, was all sorts of a damned fool for leaving his bunk. But, as Vallery had mildly pointed out, somebody had to conduct a funeral service, and that was the Captain's duty if the padre couldn't do it. And this day the padre couldn't do it, for it was the padre who lay dead at his feet . . . At his feet, and at the feet of Etherton—the man who had surely killed him.

The padre had died four hours ago, just after Charlie had gone. Tyndall had been far out in his estimate. Charlie had not appeared within the hour. Charlie had not appeared until mid-morning, but when he did come he had the company of three of his kind. A long haul indeed from the Norwegian coast to this, the 10th degree west of longitude, but nothing for these giant Condors—Foke-Wulf 200s—who regularly flew the great dawn to dusk half-circle from Trondheim to Occupied France, round the West Coast of the British Isles.

Condors in company always meant trouble, and these were no exception. They flew directly over the convoy, approaching from astern: the barrage from merchant ships and escorts was intense, and the bombing attack was pressed home with a marked lack of enthusiasm: the Condors bombed from a height of 7,000 feet. In that clear, cold morning air the bombs were in view almost from the moment they cleared the bomb-bays: there was time to spare to take avoiding action. Almost at once the Condors had broken off the attack and disappeared to the east impressed, but apparently unharmed, by the warmth of their reception.

In the circumstances, the attack was highly suspicious. Circumspect Charlie might normally be on reconnaissance, but on the rare occasions that he chose to attack he generally did so with courage and determination. The recent sally was just too timorous, the tactics too obviously hopeless. Possibly, of course, recent entrants to the Luftwaffe were given to a discretion so signally lacking in their predecessors, or perhaps they were under strict orders not to risk their valuable craft. But probably, almost certainly, it was thought, that futile attack was only diversionary and the main danger lay elsewhere. The watch over and under the sea was intensified.

Five, ten, fifteen minutes passed and nothing had happened. Radar and Asdic screens remained obstinately clear. Tyndall finally decided that there was no justification for keeping the entire ship's company, so desperately in need of rest, at Action Stations for a moment longer and ordered the stand-down to be sounded.

Normal Defence Stations were resumed. All forenoon work had been cancelled, and officers and ratings off watch, almost to a man, went to snatch what brief sleep they could. But not all. Brooks and Nicholls had their patients to attend to: the Navigator returned to the chart-house: Marshall and his Commissioned Gunner, Mr Peters, resumed their interrupted routine rounds: and Etherton, nervous, anxious, over-sensitive and desperately eager to redeem himself for his share in the Carslake-Ralston episode, remained huddled and watchful in the cold, lonely eyrie of the Director Tower.

The sharp, urgent call from the deck outside came to Marshall and Peters as they were talking to the Leading Wireman in charge of No 2 Electrical Shop. The shop was on the port side of the fo'c'sle deck cross-passage which ran athwartships for'ard of the wardroom, curving aft round the trunking of 'B' turret. Four quick steps had them out of the shop, through the screen door and peering over the side through the freshly falling snow, following the gesticulating finger of an excited marine. Marshall glanced at the man, recognized him immediately: it was Charteris, the only ranker known personally to every officer in the ship—in port, he doubled as wardroom barman.

'What is it, Charteris?' he demanded. 'What are you seeing? Quickly, man!'

'There, sir! Look! Out there—no, a bit more to your right! It's—it's a sub, sir, a U-boat!'

'What? What's that? A U-boat?' Marshall halfturned as the Rev

Winthrop, the padre, squeezed to the rail between himself and Charteris. 'Where? Where is it? Show me, show me!'

'Straight ahead, padre. I can see it now—but it's a damned funny shape for a U-boat—if you'll excuse the language,' Marshall added hastily. He caught the war-like, un-Christian gleam in Winthrop's eye, smothered a laugh and peered through the snow at the strange squat shape which had now drifted almost abreast of them.

High up in the Tower, Etherton's restless, hunting eyes had already seen it, even before Charteris. Like Charteris, he immediately thought it was a U-boat caught surfacing in a snowstorm—the pay-off of the attack by the Condors: the thought that Asdic or radar would certainly have picked it up never occurred to him. Time, speed—that was the essence, before it vanished. Unthinkingly, he grabbed the phone to the for'ard multiple pom-pom.

'Director—pom-pom!' he barked urgently. 'U-boat, port 60. Range 100 yards, moving aft. Repeat, port 60. Can you see it? . . . No, no, port 60-70 now!' he shouted desperately. 'Oh, good, good! Commence tracking.'

'On target, sir,' the receiver crackled in his ear.

'Open fire—continuous!'

'Sir—but, sir—Kingston's not here. He went—'

'Never mind Kingston!' Etherton shouted furiously. Kingston, he knew, was Captain of the Gun. 'Open fire, you fools—now! I'll take full responsibility.' He thrust the phone back on the rest, moved across to the observation panel . . . Then realization, sickening, shocking, fear seared through his mind and he lunged desperately for the phone.

'Belay the last order!' he shouted wildly. 'Cease fire! Cease fire! Oh, my God, my God, my God!' Through the receiver came the staccato, angry bark of the two-pounder. The receiver dropped from his hand, crashed against the bulkhead. It was too late.

It was too late because he had committed the cardinal sin—he had forgotten to order the removal of the muzzle-covers—the metal plates that sealed off the flash-covers of the guns when not in use. And the shells were fused to explode on contact . . .

The first shell exploded inside its barrel, killing the trainer and seriously wounding the communication number: the other three smashed through their flimsy covers and exploded within a second of each other, a few feet from the faces of the four watchers on the fo'c'sle deck.

All four were untouched, miraculously untouched by the flying, screaming metal. It flew outwards and downwards, a red-hot iron hail sizzling into the sea. But the blast of the explosion was backwards, and the power of even a few pounds of high explosive detonating at arm's length is lethal.

The padre died instantly, Peters and Charteris within seconds, and all from the same cause—telescoped occiputs. The blast hurled them backwards off their feet, as if flung by a giant hand, the backs of their heads smashing to an eggshell pulp against the bulkhead. The blood seeped darkly into the snow, was obliterated in a moment.

Marshall was lucky, fantastically so. The explosion—he said afterwards that it was like getting in the way of the driving piston of the Coronation Scot—flung him through the open door behind him, ripped off the heels of both shoes as they caught on the storm-sill: he braked violently in mid-air, described a complete somersault, slithered along the passage and smashed squarely into the trunking of 'B' turret, his back framed by the four big spikes of the butterfly nuts securing an inspection hatch. Had he been standing a foot to the right or the left, had his heels been two inches higher as he catapulted through the doorway, had he hit the turret a hair's-breadth to the left or right—Lieutenant Marshall had no right to be alive. The laws of chance said so, overwhelmingly. As it was, Marshall was now sitting up in the Sick bay, strapped, broken ribs making breathing painful, but otherwise unharmed.

The upturned lifeboat, mute token of some earlier tragedy on the Russian Convoys, had long since vanished into the white twilight.

Captain Vallery's voice, low and husky, died softly away. He stepped back, closing the Prayer Book, and the forlorn notes of the bugle echoed briefly over the poop and died in the blanketing snow. Men stood silently, unmovingly, as, one by one, the thirteen figures shrouded in weighted canvas, slid down the tipped plank, down from under the Union Flag, splashed heavily into the Arctic and were gone. For long seconds, no one moved. The unreal, hypnotic effect of that ghostly ritual of burial held tired, sluggish minds in unwilling thrall, held men oblivious to cold and discomfort. Even when Etherton half-stepped forward, sighed, crumpled down quietly, unspectacularly in the snow, the trance-like hiatus continued. Some ignored him, others glanced his way, incuriously. It seemed absurd, but it struck Nicholls, standing in the background, that they might have stayed there indefinitely, the minds and the blood of men slowing up, coagulating, freezing, while they turned to pillars of ice. Then suddenly, with exacerbating abruptness, the spell was shattered: the strident scream of the Emergency Stations whistle seared through the gathering gloom.

It took Vallery about three minutes to reach the bridge. He rested often, pausing on every second or third step of the four ladders that reached up to the bridge: even so, the climb drained the last reserves of his frail strength. Brooks had to half-carry him through the gate. Vallery clung to the binnacle, fighting for breath through foam-flecked lips; but his eyes were alive, alert as always, probing through the swirling snow.

'Contact closing, closing: steady on course, interception course: speed unchanged.' The radar loudspeaker was muffled, impersonal; but the calm precise tones of Lieutenant Bowden were unmistakable.

'Good, good! We'll fox him yet!' Tyndall, his tired, sagging face lit up in almost beaming anticipation, turned to the Captain. The prospect of action always delighted Tyndall.

'Something coming up from the SSW, Captain. Good God above, man, what are you doing here?' He was shocked at Vallery's appearance. 'Brooks! Why in heaven's name—?'

'Suppose *you* try talking to him?' Brooks growled wrathfully. He slammed the gate shut behind him, stalked stiffly off the bridge.

'What's the matter with him?' Tyndall asked of no one in particular. 'What the hell am I supposed to have done?'

'Nothing, sir,' Vallery pacified him. 'It's all my fault—disobeying doctor's orders and what have you. You were saying—?'

'Ah, yes. Trouble, I'm afraid, Captain.' Vallery smiled secretly as he saw the satisfaction, the pleased anticipation creep back into the Admiral's face. 'Radar reports a surface vessel approaching, big, fast, more or less on interception course for us.'

'And not ours, of course?' Vallery murmured. He looked up suddenly. 'By jove, sir, it couldn't be—?

'The *Tirpitz*?' Tyndall finished for him. He shook his head in decision. 'My first thought, too, but no. Admiralty and Air Force are watching her like a broody hen over her eggs. If she moves a foot, we'll know . . . Probably some heavy cruiser.'

'Closing. Closing. Course unaltered.' Bowden's voice, clipped, easy, was vaguely reminiscent of a cricket commentator's. 'Estimates speed 24, repeat 24 knots.'

His voice crackled into silence as the WT speaker came to life.

'WT—bridge. WT—bridge. Signal from convoy: *Stirling*—Admiral. Understood. Wilco. Out.'

'Excellent, excellent! From Jeffries,' Tyndall explained. 'I sent him a signal ordering the convoy to alter course to NNW. That should take 'em well clear of our approaching friend.'

Vallery nodded. 'How far ahead is the convoy, sir?'

'Pilot!' Tyndall called and leaned back expectantly.

'Six—six and a half miles.' The Kapok Kid's face was expressionless.

'He's slipping,' Tyndall said mournfully. 'The strain's telling. A couple of days ago he'd have given us the distance to the nearest yard. Six miles—far enough, Captain. He'll never pick 'em up. Bowden says he hasn't even picked us up yet, that the intersection of courses must be pure coincidence . . . I gather Lieutenant Bowden has a poor opinion of German radar.'

'I know. I hope he's right. For the first time the question is of rather more than academic interest.' Vallery gazed to the South, his binoculars to his eyes: there was only the sea, the thinning snow. 'Anyway, this came at a good time.'

Tyndall arched a bushy eyebrow.

'It was strange, down there on the poop.' Vallery was hesitant. 'There was something weird, uncanny in the air. I didn't like it, sir. It was desperately—well, almost frightening. The snow, the silence, the dead men—thirteen dead men—I can only guess how the men felt, about Etherton, about anything. But it wasn't good—don't know how it would have ended—'

'Five miles,' the loudspeaker cut in. 'Repeat, five miles. Course, speed, constant.'

'Five miles,' Tyndall repeated in relief. Intangibles bothered him. 'Time to trail our coats a little, Captain. We'll soon be in what Bowden reckons is his radar range. Due east, I think—it'll look as if we're covering the tail of the convoy and heading for the North Cape.'

'Starboard 10,' Vallery ordered. The cruiser came gradually round, met, settled on her new course: engine revolutions were cut down till the *Ulysses* was cruising along at 26 knots.

One minute, five passed, then the loudspeaker blared again.

'Radar—bridge. Constant distance, altering on interception course.'

'Excellent! Really excellent!' The Admiral was almost purring. 'We have him, gentlemen. He's missed the convoy . . . Commence firing by radar!'

Vallery reached for the Director handset.

'Director? Ah, it's you, Courtney . . . good, good . . . you just do that.'

Vallery replaced the set, looked across at Tyndall.

'Smart as a whip, that boy. He's had "X" and "Y" lined up, tracking for the past ten minutes. Just a matter of pressing a button, he says.'

'Sounds uncommon like our friends here.' Tyndall jerked his head in the direction of the Kapok Kid, then looked up in surprise. 'Courtney? Did you say "Courtney"? Where's Guns?'

'In his cabin, as far as I know. Collapsed on the poop. Anyway, he's in no fit state to do his job . . . Thank God I'm not in that boy's shoes. I can imagine . . . '

The *Ulysses* shuddered, and the whip-like crash of 'X' turret drowned Vallery's voice as the 5.25 shells screamed away into the twilight. Seconds later, the ship shook again as the guns of 'Y' turret joined in. Thereafter the guns fired alternately, one shell at a time, every half-minute: there was no point in wasting ammunition when the fall of shot could not be observed; but it was probably the bare minimum necessary to infuriate the enemy and distract his attention from everything except the ship ahead.

The snow had thinned away now to a filmy curtain of gauze that blurred, rather than obscured the horizon. To the west, the clouds were lifting, the sky lightening in sunset. Vallery ordered 'X' turret to cease fire, to load with star-shell.

Abruptly, the snow was gone and the enemy was there, big and menacing, a black featureless silhouette with the sudden flush of sunset striking incongruous golden gleams from the water creaming high at her bows.

'Starboard 30!' Vallery snapped. 'Full ahead. Smokescreen!' Tyndall nodded compliance. It was no part of his plan to become embroiled with a German heavy cruiser or pocket battleship . . . especially at an almost point-blank range of four miles.

On the bridge, half a dozen pairs of binoculars peered aft, trying to identify the enemy. But the fore-and-aft silhouette against the reddening sky was difficult to analyse, exasperatingly vague and ambiguous. Suddenly, as they watched, white gouts of flame lanced out from the heart of the silhouette: simultaneously, the starshell burst high up in the air, directly above the enemy, bathing him in an intense, merciless white glare, so that he appeared strangely naked and defenceless.

An illusory appearance. Everyone ducked low, in reflex instinct, as the shells whistled just over their heads and plunged into the sea ahead. Everyone, that is, except the Kapok Kid. He bent an impassive eye on the Admiral as the latter slowly straightened up.

'Hipper Class, sir,' he announced. '10,000 tons, 8-inch guns, carries aircraft.'

Tyndall looked at his unsmiling face in long suspicion. He cast around in his mind for a suitably crushing reply, caught sight of the German cruiser's turrets belching smoke in the sinking glare of the starshell.

'My oath!' he exclaimed. 'Not wasting much time, are they? And damned good shooting!' he added in professional admiration as the shells hissed into the sea through the *Ulysses's* boiling wake, about 150 feet astern. 'Bracketed in the first two salvoes. They'll straddle us next time.'

The *Ulysses* was still heeling round, the black smoke beginning to pour from the after funnel, when Vallery straightened, clapped his binoculars to his eyes. Heavy clouds of smoke were mushrooming from the enemy's starboard deck, just for'ard of the bridge.

'Oh, well done, young Courtney!' he burst out. 'Well done indeed!'

'Well done indeed!' Tyndall echoed. 'A beauty! Still, I don't think we'll stop to argue the point with me . . . Ah! Just in time, gentlemen! Gad, that was close!' The stern of the *Ulysses*, swinging round now almost to the north, disappeared from sight as a salvo crashed into the sea, dead astern, one of the shells exploding in a great eruption of water.

The next salvo—obviously the hit on the enemy cruiser hadn't affected her fire-power—fell a cable length's astern. The German was now firing blind. Engineer Commander Dodson was making smoke with a vengeance, the oily, black smoke flattening down on the surface of the sea, rolling, thick, impenetrable. Vallery doubled back on course, then headed east at high speed.

For the next two hours, in the dusk and darkness, they played cat and mouse with the 'Hipper' class cruiser, firing occasionally, appearing briefly, tantalizingly, then disappearing behind a smoke-screen, hardly needed now in the coming night. All the time, radar was their eyes and their ears and never played them false. Finally, satisfied that all danger to the convoy was gone, Tyndall laid a double screen in a great curving 'U', and vanished to the south-west, firing a few final shells, not so much in token of farewell as to indicate direction of depature.

Ninety minutes later, at the end of a giant halfcircle to port, the *Ulysses* was sitting far to the north, while Bowden and his men tracked the progress of the enemy. He was reported as moving steadily east, then, just before contact was lost, as altering course to the south-east.

Tyndall climbed down from his chair, numbed and stiff. He stretched himself luxuriantly.

'Not a bad night's work, Captain, not bad at all. What do you bet our friend spends the night circling to the south and east at high speed, hoping to come up ahead of the convoy in the morning?' Tyndall felt almost jubilant, in spite of his exhaustion. 'And by that time FR77 should be 200 miles to the north of him . . . I suppose, Pilot, you have worked out intersection courses for rejoining the convoy at all speeds up to a hundred knots?'

'I think we should be able to regain contact without much difficulty,' said the Kapok Kid politely.

'It's when he is at his most modest,' Tyndall announced, 'that he sickens me most . . . Heavens above, I'm froze to death . . . Oh, damn! Not more trouble, I hope?'

The communication rating behind the compass platform picked up the jangling phone, listened briefly.

'For you, sir,' he said to Vallery. 'The Surgeon Lieutenant.'

'Just take the message, Chrysler.'

'Sorry, sir. Insists on speaking to you himself.' Chrysler handed the receiver into the bridge. Vallery smothered an exclamation of annoyance, lifted the receiver to his ear.

'Captain, here. Yes, what is it? . . . What? . . . *What*? Oh, God, no! . . . Why wasn't I told? . . . Oh, I see. Thank you, thank you.'

Vallery handed the receiver back, turned heavily to Tyndall. In the darkness, the Admiral felt, rather than saw the sudden weariness; the hunched defeat of the shoulders.

'That was Nicholls.' Vallery's voice was flat, colourless. 'Lieutenant Etherton shot himself in his cabin, five minutes ago.'

At four o'clock in the morning, in heavy snow, but in a calm sea, the *Ulysses* rejoined the convoy.

By mid-morning of that next day, a bare six hours later Admiral Tyndall had become an old weary man, haggard, haunted by remorse and bitter self-criticism, close, very close, to despair. Miraculously, in a matter of hours, the chubby cheeks had collapsed in shrunken flaccidity, draining blood had left the florid cheeks a parchment grey, the sunken eyes had dulled in blood and exhaustion. The extent and speed of the change wrought in that tough and jovial sailor, a sailor seemingly impervious to the most deadly vicissitudes of war, was incredible: incredible and disturbing in itself, but infinitely more so in its wholly demoralising effect on the men. To every arch there is but one keystone . . . or so any man must inevitably think.

Any impartial court of judgment would have cleared Tyndall of all guilt, would have acquitted him without a trial. He had done what he thought right, what any commander would have done in his place. But Tyndall sat before the merciless court of his own conscience. He could not forget that it was he who had re-routed the convoy so far to the north, that it was he who had ignored official orders to break straight for the North Cape, that it was exactly on latitude 70 N—where their Lordships had told him they would be—that FR77 had, on that cold, clear windless dawn, blundered straight into the heart of the heaviest concentration of U-boats encountered in the Arctic during the entire course of the war.

The wolf-pack had struck at its favourite hour—the dawn—and from its favourite position—the north-east, with the dawn in its eyes. It struck cruelly, skilfully and with a calculated ferocity. Admittedly, the era of Kapitan Leutnant Prien—his U-boat long ago sent to the bottom with all hands by the destroyer *Wolverine*—and his illustrious contemporaries, the hey-day of the great U-boat Commanders, the high noon of individual brilliance and great personal gallantry, was gone. But in its place—and generally acknowledged to be even more dangerous, more deadly—were the concerted, highly integrated mass attacks of the wolf-packs, methodical, machine-like, almost reduced to a formula, under a single directing command.

The *Cochella*, third vessel in the port line, was the first to go. Sister ship to the *Vytura* and the *Varella*, also accompanying her in FR77, the *Cochella* carried over 3,000,000 gallons of 100-octane petrol. She was hit by at least three torpedoes: the first two broke her almost in half, the third triggered off a stupendous detonation that literally blew her out of existence. One moment she was there, sailing serenely through the limpid twilight of sunrise: the next moment she was gone. Gone, completely, utterly gone, with only a seething ocean, convulsed in boiling white, to show where she had been: gone, while stunned eardrums and stupefied minds struggled vainly to grasp the significance of what had happened: gone, while blind reflex instinct hurled men into whatever shelter offered as a storm of lethal metal swept over the fleet.

Two ships took the full force of the explosion. A huge mass of metal—it might have been a winch—passed clear through the superstructure of the *Sirrus,* a cable-length away on the starboard: it completely wrecked the radar office. What happened to the other ship immediately astern, the impossibly-named *Tennessee Adventurer,* was not clear, but almost certainly her wheelhouse and bridge had been severely damaged: she had lost steering control, was not under command.

Tragically, this was not at first understood, simply because it was not apparent. Tyndall, recovering fast from the sheer physical shock of the explosion, broke out the signal for an emergency turn to port. The wolf-pack, obviously, lay on the port hand, and the only action to take to minimize further losses, to counter the enemy strategy, was to head straight towards them. He was reasonably sure that the U-boats would be bunched—generally, they strung out only for the slow convoys. Besides, he had adopted this tactic several times in the past with a high degree of success. Finally, it cut the U-boats' target to an impossible tenth, forcing on them the alternative of diving or the risk of being trampled under.

With an immaculate precision and co-ordination of Olympic equestrians, the convoy heeled steadily over to starboard, slewed majestically round, trailing curved, white wakes phosphorescently alive in the near-darkness that still clung to the surface of the sea. Too late, it was seen that the *Tennessee Adventurer* was not under command. Slowly, then with dismaying speed, she came round to the east, angling directly for another merchantman, the *Tobacco Planter.* There was barely time to think, to appreciate the inevitable: frantically, the *Planter's* helm went hard over in an attempt to clear the other astern, but the wildly swinging *Adventurer,* obviously completely out of control, matched the *Planter's* tightening circle, foot by inexorable foot, blind malice at the helm.

She struck the *Planter* with sickening violence just for'ard of the bridge. The *Adventurer's* bows, crumpling as they went, bit deeply into her side, fifteen, twenty feet in a chaos of tearing, rending metal: the stopping power of 10,000 tons deadweight travelling at 15 knots is fantastic. The wound was mortal, and the *Planter*'s own momentum, carrying her past, wrenched her free from the lethal bows, opening the wound to the hungry sea and hastened her own end. Almost at once she began to fill, to list heavily to starboard. Aboard the *Adventurer*, someone must have taken over command: her engine stopped, she lay almost motionless alongside the sinking ship, slightly down by the head.

The rest of the convoy cleared the drifting vessels, steadied west by north. Far out on the starboard hand, Commander Orr, in the *Sirrus*, clawed his damaged destroyer round in a violent turn, headed back towards the crippled freighters. He had gone less than half a mile when he was recalled by a vicious signal from the flagship. Tyndall was under no illusions. The *Adventurer*, he knew, might remain there all day, unharmed—it was obvious that the *Planter* would be gone in a matter of minutes—but that would be a guarantee neither of the absence of U-boats nor of the sudden access of misguided enemy chivalry: the enemy would be there, would wait to the last possible second before dark in the hope that some rescue destroyer would heave to alongside the *Adventurer*.

In that respect, Tyndall was right. The *Adventurer* was torpedoed just before sunset. Threequarters of the ship's company escaped in lifeboats, along with twenty survivors picked up from the *Planter*. A month later the frigate *Esher* found them, in three lifeboats tied line ahead, off the bitter, iron coast of Bear Island, heading steadily north. The Captain alert and upright, was still sitting in the sternsheets, empty eye-sockets searching for some lost horizon, a withered claw locked to the tiller. The rest were sitting or lying about the boats, one actually standing, his arm cradled around the mast, and all with shrunken sun-blackened lips drawn back in hideous mirth. The log-book lay beside the Captain, empty: all had frozen to death on that first night. The young frigate commander had cast them adrift, watched them disappear over the northern rim of the world, steering for the Barrier. And the Barrier is the region of the great silence, the seas of incredible peace, so peaceful, so calm, so cold that they may be there yet, the dead who cannot rest. A mean and shabby end for the temple of the spirit . . . It is not known whether the Admiralty approved the action of the captain of the frigate.

But in the major respect, that of anticipating enemy disposition, the Admiral was utterly wrong. The wolf-pack commander had outguessed him and it was arguable that Tyndall should have foreseen this. His tactic of swinging an entire convoy into the face of a torpedo attack was well known to the enemy: it was also well known that his ship was the *Ulysses*, and the *Ulysses*, the only one of her kind, was familiar, by sight or picture silhouette, to every U-boat commander in the German Navy: and it had been reported, of course, that it was the *Ulysses* that was leading FR77 through to Murmansk. Tyndall should have expected, expected and forestalled the long overdue counter.

For the submarine that had torpedoed the *Cochella* had been the last, not the first, of the pack. The others had lain to the south of the U-boat that had sprung the trap, and well to the west of the track of FR77—clear beyond the reach of Asdic. And when the convoy wheeled to the west, the U-boats lined up leisurely firing tracks as the ships steamed up to cross their bows at right angles. The sea was calm, calm as a millpond, an extraordinary deep, Mediterranean blue. The snow-squalls of the night had passed away. Far to the south-east a brilliant sun was shouldering itself clear of the horizon, its level rays striking a great band of silver across the Arctic, highlighting the ships, shrouded white in snow, against the darker sea and sky beyond. The conditions were ideal, if one may use the word 'ideal' to describe the prologue to a massacre.

Massacre, an almost total destruction there must inevitably have been but for the warning that came almost too late. A warning given neither by radar nor Asdic, nor by any of the magically efficient instruments of modern detection, but simply by the keen eyes of an eighteen-year-old Ordinary Seaman—and the God-sent rays of the rising sun.

'Captain, sir! Captain, sir!' It was young Chrysler who shouted. His voice broke in wild excitement, his eyes were glued to the powerful binoculars clamped on the port searchlight control position. 'There's something flashing to the south, sir! It flashed twice—there it goes again!'

'Where, boy?' Tyndall shouted. 'Come on, where, where?' In his agitation, Chrysler had forgotten the golden rule of the reporting look-out—bearing must come first.

'Port 50, sir—no, port 60 . . . I've lost sight of it now, sir.'

Every pair of glasses on the bridge swung round on the given bearing. There was nothing to be seen, just nothing at all. Tyndall shut his telescope slowly, shrugged his shoulders eloquent in disbelief.

'Maybe there *is* something,' said the Kapok Kid doubtfully. 'How about the sea catching a periscope making a quick circle sweep?'

Tyndall looked at him, silent, expressionless, looked away, stared straight ahead. To the Kapok Kid he seemed strange, different. His face was set, stonily impassive, the face of a man with twenty ships and 5,000 lives in his keeping, the face of a man who has already made one wrong decision too many.

'There they go again!' Chrysler screamed. 'Two flashes—no, *three* flashes!' He was almost beside himself with excitement, literally dancing in an agony of frustration. 'I did see them, sir, I *did*. I *did*. Oh, please, sir, please!'

Tyndall had swung round again. Ten long seconds he gazed at Chrysler, who had left his binoculars, and was gripping the gate in gauntleted hands, shaking it in anguished appeal. Abruptly, Tyndall made up his mind.

'Hard aport, Captain. Bentley—the signal!'

Slowly, on the unsupported word of an eighteen-year-old, FR77 came round to the south, slowly, just too slowly. Suddenly, the sea was alive with running torpedoes—three, five, ten—Vallery counted thirty in as many seconds. They were running shallow and their bubbling trails, evil, ever-lengthening, rose swiftly to the surface and lay there milkily on the glassy sea, delicately evanescent shafts for arrowheads so lethal. Parallel in the centre, they fanned out to the east and west to embrace the entire convoy. It was a fantastic sight: no man in that convoy had ever seen anything remotely like it.

In a moment the confusion was complete. There was no time for signals. It was every ship for itself in an attempt to avoid wholesale destruction: and confusion was worse confounded by the ships in the centre and outer lines, that had not yet seen the wakes of the streaking torpedoes.

Escape for all was impossible: the torpedoes were far too closely bunched. The cruiser *Stirling* was the first casualty. Just when she seemed to have cleared all danger—she was far ahead where the torpedoes were thickest—she lurched under some unseen hammer-blow, slewed round crazily and steamed away back to the east, smoke hanging heavily over her poop. The *Ulysses*, brilliantly handled, heeled over on maximum rudder and under the counter-thrusting of her great screws, slid down an impossibly narrow lane between four torpedoes, two of them racing by a bare boat's length from either side: she was still a lucky ship. The destroyers, fast, highly manoeuvrable, impeccably handled, bobbed and weaved their way to safety with almost contemptuous ease, straightened up and headed south under maximum power.

The merchant ships, big, clumsy, relatively slow, were less fortunate. Two ships in the port line, a tanker and a freighter, were struck: miraculously, both just staggered under the numbing shock, then kept on coming. Not so the big freighter immediately behind them, her holds crammed with tanks, her decks lined with them. She was torpedoed three times in three seconds: there was no smoke, no fire, no spectacular after-explosion: sieved and ripped from stern to stem, she sank quickly, quietly, still on even keel, dragged down by the sheer weight of metal. No one below decks had even the slightest chance of escaping.

A merchantman in the centre line, the *Belle Isle*, was torpedoed amidships. There were two separate explosions—probably she had been struck twice—and she was instantly on fire. Within seconds, the list to port was pronounced, increasing momentarily: gradually her rails dipped under, the outslung lifeboats almost touching the surface of the sea. A dozen, fifteen men were seen to be slipping, sliding down the sheering decks and hatch-covers, already half-submerged, towards the nearest lifeboat. Desperately they hacked at bellyband securing ropes, piled into the lifeboat in grotesquely comical haste, pushed it clear of the dipping davits, seized the oars and pulled frantically away. From beginning to end, hardly a minute had elapsed.

Half a dozen powerful strokes had them clear beyond their ship's counter: two more took them straight under the swinging bows of the *Walter A. Baddeley*, her companion tankcarrier in the starboard line. The consummate seamanship that had saved the *Baddeley* could do nothing to save the lifeboat: the little boat crumpled and splintered like a matchwood toy, catapulting screaming men into the icy sea.

As the big, grey hull of the *Baddeley* slid swiftly by them, they struck out with insane strength that made nothing of their heavy Arctic-clothing. At such times, reason vanishes: the thought that if, by some God-given miracle, they were to escape the guillotine of the *Baddeley*'s single great screw, they would do so only to die minutes later in the glacial cold of the Arctic, never occurred to them. But, as it happened, death came by neither metal nor cold. They were still struggling, almost abreast the poop, vainly trying to clear the rushing, sucking vortex of water, when the torpedoes struck the *Baddeley*, close together and simultaneously, just for'ard of the rudder.

For swimming men who have been in the close vicinity of an underwater high explosion there can be no shadow of hope: the effect is inhuman, revolting, shocking beyond conception: in such cases, experienced doctors, pathologists even, can with difficulty bring themselves to look upon what were once human beings . . . But for these men, as so often in the Arctic, death was kind, for they died unknowing.

The *Walter A. Baddeley*'s stern had been almost completely blown off. Hundreds of tons of water were already rushing in the gaping hole below the counter, racing through cross-bulkheads fractured by the explosion, smashing open engine-boiler room watertight doors buckled by the blast, pulling her down by the stern, steadily, relentlessly, till her taffrail dipped salute to the waiting Arctic. For a moment, she hung there. Then, in quick succession from deep inside the hull, came a muffled explosion, the ear-shattering, frightening roar of escaping high-pressure steam and the thunderous crash of massive boilers rending away from their stools as the ship upended. Almost immediately the shattered stern lurched heavily, sank lower and lower till the poop was completely gone, till the dripping forefoot was tilted high above the sea. Foot by foot the angle of tilt increased, the stern plunged a hundred, two hundred feet under the surface of the sea, the bows rearing almost as high against the blue of the sky, buoyed up by half a million cubic feet of trapped air.

The ship was exactly four degrees off the vertical when the end came. It was possible to establish this angle precisely, for it was just at that second, half a mile away aboard the *Ulysses*, that the shutter clicked, the shutter of the camera in Lieutenant Nicholls's gauntleted hands.

A camera that captured an unforgettable picture—a stark, simple picture of a sinking ship almost vertically upright against a pale-blue sky. A picture with a strange lack of detail, with the exception only of two squat shapes, improbably suspended in mid-air: these were 30-ton tanks, broken loose from their foredeck lashings, caught in midflight as they smashed down on the bridge structure, awash in the sea. In the background was the stern of the *Bell Isle*, the screw out of the water, the Red Duster trailing idly in the peaceful sea.

Bare seconds after the camera had clicked, the camera was blown from Nicholls's hands, the case crumpling against a bulkhead, the lens shattering but the film still intact. Panic-stricken the seamen in the lifeboat may have been, but it wasn't unreasoning panic: in No 2 hold, just for'ard of the fire, the *Belle Isle* had been carrying over 1,000 tons of tank ammunition . . . Broken cleanly in two, she was gone inside a minute: the *Baddeley*'s bows, riddled by the explosion, slide gently down behind her.

The echoes of the explosion were still rolling out over the sea in ululating diminuendo when they were caught up and flung back by a series of muffled reports from the South. Less than two miles away, the *Sirrus*, *Vectra* and *Viking*, dazzling white in the morning sun, were weaving a crazily intricate pattern over the sea, depth-charges cascading from either side of their poop-decks. From time to time, one or other almost disappeared behind towering mushrooms of erupting water and spray, reappearing magically as the white columns fell back into the sea.

To join in the hunt, to satisfy the flaming, primitive lust for revenge—that was Tyndall's first impulse. The Kapok Kid looked at him furtively and wondered, wondered at the hunched rigidity, the compressed lipless mouth, the face contorted in white and bitter rage—a bitterness directed not least against himself. Tyndall twisted suddenly in his seat.

'Bentley! Signal the *Sterling*—ascertain damage.' The *Stirling* was more than a mile astern now, but coming round fast, her speed at least twenty knots.

'Making water after engine-room,' Bentley read eventually. 'Store-rooms flooded, but hull damage slight. Under control. Steering gear jammed. On emergency steering. Am all right.'

'Thank God for that! Signal, "Take over: proceed east." Come on, Captain, let's give Orr a hand to deal with these murdering hounds!'

The Kapok Kid looked at him in sudden dismay.

'Sir!'

'Yes, yes, Pilot! What is it?' Tyndall was curt, impatient.

'How about that first U-boat?' Carpenter ventured. 'Can't be much more than a mile to the south, sir. Shouldn't we—?'

'God Almighty!' Tyndall swore. His face was suffused with anger. 'Are you trying to tell me . . . ?' He broke off abruptly, stared at Carpenter for a long moment. 'What did you say, Pilot?'

'The boat that sunk the tanker, sir,' the Kapok Kid said carefully. 'She could have reloaded by now and she's in a perfect position—'

'Of course, of course,' Tyndall muttered. He passed a hand across his eyes, flickered a glance at Vallery. The Captain had his head averted. Again the hand passed across the tired eyes. 'You're quite right, Pilot, quite right.' He paused, then smiled. 'As usual, damn you!'

The *Ulysses* found nothing to the north. The U-boat that had sunk the *Cochella* and sprung the trap had wisely decamped. While they were quartering the area, they heard the sound of gun-fire, saw the smoke erupting from the *Sirrus*'s 4.7s.

'Ask him what all the bloody fuss is about,' Tyndall demanded irritably. The Kapok Kid smiled secretly: the old man had life in him yet.

'*Vectra* and *Viking* damaged, probably destroyed U-boat,' the message read. '*Vectra* and self sunk surfaced boat. How about you?'

'How about you!' Tyndall exploded. 'Damn his confounded insolence! How about you? He'll have the oldest, bloody minesweeper in Scapa for his next command . . . This is all your fault, Pilot!'

'Yes, sir. Sorry, sir. Maybe he's only asking in a spirit of—ah—anxious concern.'

'How would you like to be his Navigator in his next command?' said Tyndall dangerously. The Kapok Kid retired to his charthouse.

'Carrington!'

'Sir?' The First Lieutenant was his invariable self, clear-eyed, freshly shaven, competent, alert. The sallow skin—hall-mark of all men who have spent too many years under tropical suns—was unshadowed by fatigue. He hadn't slept for three days.

'What do you make of that?' He pointed to the northwest. Curiously woolly grey clouds were blotting out the horizon; before them the sea dusked to indigo under wandering catspaws from the north.

'Hard to say, sir,' Carrington said slowly. 'Not heavy weather, that's certain . . . I've seen this before, sir—low, twisting cloud blowing up on a fine morning with a temperature rise. Very common in the Aleutians and the Bering Sea, sir—and there it means fog, heavy mist.'

'And you, Captain?'

'No idea, sir.' Vallery shook his head decisively. The plasma transfusion seemed to have helped him. 'New to me—never seen it before.'

'Thought not,' Tyndall grunted. 'Neither have I—that's why I asked Number One first . . . If you think it's fog that's coming up, Number One, let me know, will you? Can't afford to have convoy and escorts scattered over half the Arctic if the weather closes down. Although, mind you,' he added bitterly, 'I think they'd be a damned sight safer without us!'

'I can tell you now, sir.' Carrington had that rare gift—the ability to make a confident, quietly unarguable assertion without giving the slightest offence. 'It's fog.'

'Fair enough.' Tyndall never doubted him. 'Let's get the hell out of it. Bentley—signal the destroyers: "Break off engagement. Rejoin convoy." And Bentley—add the word "Immediate".' He turned to Vallery. 'For Commander Orr's benefit.'

Within the hour, merchant ships and escorts were on station again, on a north-east course at first to clear any further packs on latitude 70. To the south-east, the sun was still bright: but the first thick, writhing tendrils of the mist, chill and dank, were already swirling round the convoy. Speed had been reduced to six knots: all ships were streaming fog-buoys.

Tyndall shivered, climbed stiffly from his chair as the stand-down sounded. He passed through the gate, stopped in the passage outside. He laid a glove on Chrysler's shoulder, kept it there as the boy turned round in surprise.

'Just wanted a squint at these eyes of yours, laddie,' he smiled. 'We owe them a lot. Thank you very much—we will not forget.' He looked a long time into the young face, forgot his own exhaustion and swore softly in sudden compassion as he saw the red-rimmed eyes, the white, maculated cheeks stained with embarrassed pleasure.

'How old are you, Chrysler?' he asked abruptly.

'Eighteen, sir . . . in two days' time.' The soft West Country voice was almost defiant.

'He'll be eighteen—in two days' time!' Tyndall repeated slowly to himself. 'Good God! Good God above!' He dropped his hand, walked wearily aft to the shelter, entered, closed the door behind him.

'He'll be eighteen—in two days' time,' he repeated, like a man in a daze.

Vallery propped himself up on the settee. 'Who? Young Chrysler?'

Tyndall nodded unhappily.

'I know.' Vallery was very quiet. 'I know how it is . . . He did a fine job today.'

Tyndall sagged down in a chair. His mouth twisted in bitterness.

'The only one . . . Dear God, what a mess!' He drew heavily on a cigarette, stared down at the floor. 'Ten green bottles, hanging on a wall,' he murmured absently.

'I beg your pardon, sir?'

'Fourteen ships left Scapa, eighteen St John—the two components of FR77,' Tyndall said softly. 'Thirty-two ships in all. And now'—he paused—'now there are seventeen—and three of these damaged. I'm counting the *Tennessee Adventurer* as a dead duck.' He swore savagely. 'Hell's teeth, how I hate leaving ships like that, sitting targets for any murdering . . . ' He stopped short, drew on his cigarette again, deeply. 'Doing wonderfully, ain't I?'

'Ah, nonsense, sir!' Vallery interrupted, impatient, almost angry. 'It wasn't any fault of yours that the carriers had to return.'

'Meaning that the rest was my fault?' Tyndall smiled faintly, lifted a hand to silence the automatic protest. 'Sorry, Dick, I know you didn't mean that—but it's true, it's true. Six merchant boys gone in ten minutes—six! And we shouldn't have lost one of them.' Head bent, elbows on knees, he screwed the heels of his palms into exhausted eyes. 'Rear-Admiral Tyndall, master strategist,' he went on softly. 'Alters convoy course to run smack into the biggest wolf-pack I've ever known—and just where the Admiralty said they would be . . . No matter what old Starr does to me when I get back, I've no kick coming. Not now, not after this.'

He rose heavily to his feet. The light of the single lamp caught his face. Vallery was shocked at the change.

'Where to now, sir?' he asked.

'The bridge. No, no, stay where you are, Dick.' He tried to smile, but the smile was a grimace that flickered only to die. 'Leave me in peace while I ponder my next miscalculation.'

He opened the door; stopped dead as he heard the unmistakable whistling of shells close above, heard the EAS signal screaming urgently through the fog. Tyndall turned his head slowly, looked back into the shelter.

'It looks,' he said bitterly, 'as if I've already made it.'

NINE

Friday Morning

The fog, Tyndall saw, was all around them now. Since that last heavy snowfall during the night, the temperature had risen steadily, quickly. But it had beguiled only to deceive: the clammy, ice feathers of the swirling mist now struck doubly chill.

He hurried through the gate, Vallery close behind him. Turner, steel helmet trailing, was just leaving for the After Tower. Tyndall stretched out his hand, stopped him.

'What is it, Commander?' he demanded. 'Who fired? Where? Where did it come from?'

'I don't know, sir. Shells came from astern, more or less. But I've a damned good idea who it is.' His eyes rested on the Admiral a long, speculative moment. 'Our friend of last night is back again.' He turned abruptly, hurried off the bridge.

Tyndall looked after him, perplexed, uncomprehending. Then he swore, softly, savagely, and jumped for the radar handset.

'Bridge. Admiral speaking. Lieutenant Bowden at once!' The loudspeaker crackled into immediate life.

'Bowden speaking, sir.'

'What the devil are you doing down there?' Tyndall's voice was low, vicious. 'Asleep, or what? We are being attacked, Lieutenant Bowden. By a surface craft. This may be news to you.' He broke off, ducked low as another salvo screamed overhead and crashed into the water less than half a mile ahead: the spray cascaded over the decks of a merchantman, glimpsed momentarily in a clear lane between two rolling fog-banks. Tyndall straightened up quickly, snarled into the mouthpiece. 'He's got our range, and got it accurately. In God's name, Bowden, where is he?'

'Sorry, sir.' Bowden was cool, unruffled. 'We can't seem to pick him up. We still have the *Adventurer* on our screens, and there appears to be a very slight distortion on his bearing, sir—approximately 300 . . . I suggest the enemy ship is still screened by the *Adventurer* or, if she's closer, is on the *Adventurer*'s direct bearing.'

'How near?' Tyndall barked.

'Not near, sir. Very close to the *Adventurer*. We can't distinguish either by size or distance.'

Tyndall dangled the transmitter from his hand. He turned to Vallery.

'Does Bowden really expect me to believe that yarn?' he asked angrily. 'A million to one coincidence like that—an enemy ship accidentally chose and holds the only possible course to screen her from our radar. Fantastic!'

Vallery looked at him, his face without expression.

'Well?' Tyndall was impatient. 'Isn't it?'

'No, sir,' Vallery answered quietly. 'It's not. Not really. And it wasn't accidental. The U-pack would have radioed her, given our bearing and course. The rest was easy.'

Tyndall gazed at him through a long moment of comprehension, screwed his eyes shut and shook his head in short fierce jerks. It was a gesture compounded of self-criticism, the death of disbelief, the attempt to clear a woolly, exhausted mind. Hell, a six-year-old could have seen that . . . A shell whistled into the sea a bare fifty yards to port. Tyndall didn't flinch, might never have seen or heard it.

'Bowden?' He had the transmitter to his mouth again.

'Sir?'

'Any change in the screen?'

'No, sir. None.'

'And are you still of the same opinion?'

'Yes, sir! Can't be anything else.'

'And close to the *Adventurer*, you say?'

'Very close, I would say.'

'But, good God, man, the *Adventurer* must be ten miles astern by now!'

'Yes, sir. I know. So is the bandit.'

'What! Ten miles! But, but—'

'He's firing by radar, sir,' Bowden interrupted. Suddenly the metallic voice sounded tired. 'He must be. He's also tracking by radar, which is why he's keeping himself in line with our bearing on the *Adventurer*. And he's extremely accurate . . . I'm afraid, Admiral, that his radar is at least as good as ours.'

The speaker clicked off. In the sudden strained silence on the bridge, the crash of breaking ebonite sounded unnaturally loud as the transmitter slipped from Tyndall's hand, fractured in a hundred pieces. The hand groped forward, he clutched at a steam pipe as if to steady himself. Vallery stepped towards him, arms outstretched in concern, but Tyndall brushed by unseeingly. Like an old spent man, like a man from whose ancient bones and muscles all the pith has long since drained, he shuffled slowly across the bridge, oblivious of a dozen mystified eyes, dragged himself up on to his high stool.

You fool, he told himself bitterly, savagely, oh you bloody old fool! He would never forgive himself, never, never, never! All along the line he had been out-thought, out-guessed and outmanoeuvred by the enemy. They had taken him for a ride, made an even bigger bloody fool out of him than his good Maker had ever intended. Radar! Of course, that was it! The blind assumption that German radar had remained the limited, elementary thing that Admiralty and Air Force Intelligence had reported it to be last year! Radar—and as good as the British. As good as the *Ulysses*'s—and everybody had believed that the *Ulysses* was incomparably the most efficient—indeed the only efficient—radar ship in the world. As good as our own—probably a damned sight better. But had the thought ever occurred to him? Tyndall writhed in sheer chagrin, in agony of spirit, and knew the bitter taste of self-loathing. And so, this morning, the pay-off: six ships, three hundred men gone to the bottom. May God forgive you, Tyndall, he thought dully, may God forgive you. You sent them there . . . Radar!

Last night, for instance. When the *Ulysses* had been laying a false trail to the east, the German cruiser had obligingly tagged behind, the perfect foil to his, Tyndall's genius. Tyndall groaned in mortification. He tagged behind, firing wildly, erratically each time the *Ulysses* had disappeared behind a smoke-screen. Had done so to conceal the efficiency of her radar, to conceal the fact that, during the first half-hour at least, she must have been tracking the escaping convoy as it disappeared to the NNW—a process made all the easier by the fact that he, Tyndall, had expressly forbidden the use of the zig-zag!

And then, when the *Ulysses* had so brilliantly circled, first to the south and then to the north again, the enemy must have had her on his screen—constantly. And later, the biter bit with a vengeance, the faked enemy withdrawal to the south-east. Almost certainly, he, too, had circled to the north again, picked up the disappearing British cruiser on the edge of his screen, worked out her intersection course as a cross check on the convoy's, and radioed ahead to the wolf-pack, positioning them almost to the foot.

And now, finally, the last galling blow to whatever shattered remnants of his pride were left him. The enemy had opened fire at extreme range, but with extreme accuracy—a dead give-away to the fact that the firing was radar-controlled. And the only reason for it must be the enemy's conviction that the *Ulysses*, by this time, must have come to the inevitable conclusion that the enemy was equipped with a highly sensitive radar transmitter. The inevitable conclusion! Tyndall had never even begun to suspect it. Slowly, oblivious to the pain, he pounded his fist on the edge of the windscreen. God, what a blind, crazily stupid fool he'd been! Six ships, three hundred men. Hundreds of tanks and planes, millions of gallons of fuel lost to Russia; how many more thousands of dead Russians, soldiers and civilians, did that represent? And the broken, sorrowing families, he thought incoherently, families throughout the breadth of Britain: the telegram boys cycling to the little houses in the Welsh valleys, along the wooded lanes of Surrey, to the lonely reek of the peat-fire, remote in the Western Isles, to the lime-washed cottages of Donegal and Antrim: the empty homes across the great reaches of the New World, from Newfoundland and Maine to the far slopes of the Pacific. These families would never know that it was he, Tyndall, who had so criminally squandered the lives of husbands, brothers, sons—and that was worse than no consolation at all.

'Captain Vallery?' Tyndall's voice was only a husky whisper. Vallery crossed over, stood beside him, coughing painfully as the swirling fog caught nose and throat, lanciniated inflamed lungs. It was a measure of Tyndall's distressed preoccupation that Vallery's obvious suffering quite failed to register.

'Ah, there you are. Captain, this enemy cruiser must be destroyed.'

Vallery nodded heavily. 'Yes, sir. How?'

'How?' Tyndall's face, framed in the moisturebeaded hood of his duffel, was haggard and grey: but he managed to raise a ghost of a smile. 'As well hung for a sheep . . . I propose to detach the escorts—including ourselves—and nail him.' He stared out blindly into the fog, his mouth bitter. 'A simple tactical exercise—maybe within even my limited compass.' He broke off suddenly, stared over the side then ducked hurriedly: a shell had exploded in the water—a rare thing—only yards away, erupting spray showering down on the bridge.

'We—the *Stirling* and ourselves—will take from the south,' he continued, 'soak up his fire and radar. Orr and his death-or-glory boys will approach from the north. In this fog, they'll get very close before releasing their torpedoes. Conditions are all against a single ship—he shouldn't have much chance.'

'All the escorts,' Vallery said blankly. 'You propose to detach *all* the escorts?'

'That's exactly what I propose to do, Captain.'

'But—but—perhaps that's exactly what he wants,' Vallery protested.

'Suicide? A glorious death for the Fatherland? Don't you believe it!' Tyndall scoffed. 'That sort of thing went out with Langesdorff and Middelmann.'

'No, sir!' Vallery was impatient. 'He wants to pull us off, to leave the convoy uncovered.'

'Well, what of it?' Tyndall demanded. 'Who's going to find them in this lot?' He waved an arm at the rolling, twisting fog-banks.

'Dammit, man, if it weren't for their fog-buoys, even our ships couldn't see each other. So I'm damned sure no one else could either.'

'No?' Vallery countered swiftly. 'How about another German cruiser fitted with radar? Or even another wolf-pack? Either could be in radio contact with our friend astern—and he's got our course to the nearest minute!'

'In radio contact? Surely to God our WT is monitoring all the time?'

'Yes, sir. They are. But I'm told it's not so easy on the VHF ranges.'

Tyndall grunted non-committally, said nothing. He felt desperately tired and confused; he had neither the will nor the ability to pursue the argument further. But Vallery broke in on the silence, the vertical lines between his eyebrows etched deep with worry.

'And why's our friend sitting steadily on our tails, pumping the odd shell among us, unless he's concentrating on driving us along a particular course? It reduces his chance of a hit by 90 per cent—and cuts out half his guns.'

'Maybe he's expecting us to reason like that, to see the obvious.' Tyndall was forcing himself to think, to fight his way through a mental fog no less nebulous and confusing than the dank mist that swirled around him. 'Perhaps he's hoping to panic us into altering course—to the north, of course—where a U-pack *may* very well be.'

'Possible, possible,' Vallery conceded. 'On the other hand, he may have gone a step further. Maybe he wants us to be too clever for our own good. Perhaps he expects us to see the obvious, to avoid it, to continue on our present course—and so do exactly what he wants us to do . . . He's no fool, sir—we know that now.'

What was it that Brooks had said to Starr back in Scapa, a lifetime ago? 'That fine-drawn feeling . . . that exquisite agony . . . every cell in the brain stretched taut to breaking point, pushing you over the screaming edge of madness.' Tyndall wondered dully how Brooks could have known, could have been so damnably accurate in his description. Anyway, he knew now, knew what it was to stand on the screaming edge . . . Tyndall appreciated dimly that he was at the limit. That aching, muzzy forehead where to think was to be a blind man wading through a sea of molasses. Vaguely he realized that this must be the first—or was it the last?—symptom of a nervous breakdown . . . God only knew there had been plenty of them aboard the *Ulysses* during the past months . . . But he was still the Admiral . . . He must *do* something, *say* something.

'It's no good guessing, Dick,' he said heavily. Vallery looked at him sharply—never before had old Giles called him anything but 'Captain' on the bridge. 'And we've got to do something. We'll leave the *Vectra* as a sop to our consciences. No more.' He smiled wanly. 'We must have at least two destroyers for the dirty work. Bentley—take this signal for WT "To all escort vessels and Commander Fletcher on the *Cape Hatteras . . .* "'

Within ten minutes, the four warships, boring south-east through the impenetrable wall of fog, had halved the distance that lay between them and the enemy. The *Stirling, Viking* and *Sirrus* were in constant radio communication with the *Ulysses*—they had to be for they travelled as blind men in an invidious world of grey and she was their eyes and their ears.

'Radar—bridge. Radar—bridge.' Automatically, every eye swung round, riveted on the loudspeaker. 'Enemy altering course to south: increasing speed.'

'Too late!' Tyndall shouted hoarsely. His fists were clenched, his eyes alight with triumph. 'He's left it too late!'

Vallery said nothing. The seconds ticked by, the *Ulysses* knifed her way through cold fog and icy sea. Suddenly, the loudspeaker called again.

'Enemy 180° turn. Heading south-east. Speed 28 knots.'

'28 knots? He's on the run!' Tyndall seemed to have gained a fresh lease on life. 'Captain, I propose that the *Sirrus* and *Ulysses* proceed south-east at maximum speed, engage and slow the enemy. Ask WT to signal Orr. Ask Radar enemy's course.'

He broke off, waited impatiently for the answer.

'Radar—bridge. Course 312. Steady on course. Repeat, steady on course.'

'Steady on course,' Tyndall echoed. 'Captain, commence firing by radar. We have him, we have him!' he cried exultantly. 'He's waited too long! We have him, Captain!'

Again Vallery said nothing. Tyndall looked at him, half in perplexity, half in anger. 'Well, don't you agree?'

'I don't know, sir.' Vallery shook his head doubtfully. 'I don't know at all. Why did he wait so long? Why didn't he turn and run the minute we left the convoy?'

'Too damn sure of himself!' Tyndall growled.

'Or too sure of something else,' Vallery said slowly. 'Maybe he wanted to make good and sure that we *would* follow him.'

Tyndall growled again in exasperation, made to speak then lapsed into silence as the *Ulysses* shuddered from the recoil of 'A' turret. For a moment, the billowing fog on the fo'c'sle cleared, atomized by the intense heat and flash generated by the exploding cordite. In seconds, the grey shroud had fallen once more.

Then, magically it was clear again. A heavy fogbank had rolled over them, and through a gap in the next they caught a glimpse of the *Sirrus,* dead on the beam, a monstrous bone in her teeth, scything to the south-east at something better than 34 knots. The *Stirling* and the *Viking* were already lost in the fog astern.

'He's too close,' Tyndall snapped. 'Why didn't Bowden tell us? We can't bracket the enemy this way. Signal the *Sirrus*: "Steam 317 five minutes." Captain, same for us, five south, then back on course.'

He had hardly sunk back in his chair, and the *Ulysses,* mist-shrouded again, was only beginning to answer her helm when the WT loudspeaker switched on.

'WT—bridge. WT—bridge—'

The twin 5.25s of 'B' turret roared in deafening unison, flame and smoke lancing out through the fog. Simultaneously, a tremendous crash and explosion heaved up the duckboards beneath the feet of the men in the bridge catapulting them all ways, into each other, into flesh-bruising, bonebreaking metal, into the dazed confusion of numbed minds and bodies fighting to reorientate themselves under the crippling handicap of stunning shock, of eardrums rended by the blast, of throat and nostrils stung by acrid fumes, of eyes blinded by dense black smoke. Throughout it all, the calm impersonal voice of the WT transmitter repeated its unintelligible message.

Gradually the smoke cleared away. Tyndall pulled himself

drunkenly to his feet by the rectifying arm of the binnacle: the explosion had blown him clean out of his chair into the centre of the compass platform. He shook his head, dazed, uncomprehending. Must be tougher than he'd imagined: all that way—and he couldn't remember bouncing. And that wrist, now—that lay over at a damned funny angle. His own wrist, he realized with mild surprise. Funny, it didn't hurt a bit. And Carpenter's face there, rising up before him: the bandages were blown off, the gash received on the night of the great storm gaping wide again, the face masked with blood . . . That girl at Henley, the one he was always talking about—Tyndall wondered, inconsequently, what she would say if she saw him now . . . Why doesn't the WT transmitter stop that insane yammering? . . . Suddenly his mind was clear.

'My God! Oh, God!' He stared in disbelief at the twisted duckboards, the fractured asphalt beneath his feet. He released his grip on the binnacle, lurched forward into the windscreen: his sense of balance had confirmed what his eyes had rejected: the whole compass platform tilted forward at an angle of 15 degrees.

'What is it, Pilot?' His voice was hoarse, strained, foreign even to himself. 'In God's name, what's happened? A breech explosion in "B" turret?'

'No, sir.' Carpenter drew his forearm across his eyes: the kapok sleeve came away covered in blood. 'A direct hit, sir—smack in the superstructure.'

'He's right, sir.' Carrington had hoisted himself far over the windscreen, was peering down intently. Even at that moment, Tyndall marvelled at the man's calmness, his almost inhuman control. 'And a heavy one. It's wrecked the for'ard pom-pom and there's a hole the size of a door just below us . . . It must be pretty bad inside, sir.'

Tyndall scarcely heard the last words. He was kneeling over Vallery, cradling his head in his one good arm. The Captain lay crumpled against the gate, barely conscious, his stertorous breathing interrupted by rasping convulsions as he choked on his own blood. His face was deathly white.

'Get Brooks up here, Chrysler—the Surgeon-Commander, I mean!' Tyndall shouted. 'At once!'

'WT—bridge. WT—bridge. Please acknowledge. Please acknowledge.' The voice was hurried, less impersonal, anxiety evident even in its metallic anonymity.

Chrysler replaced the receiver, looked worriedly at the Admiral.

'Well?' Tyndall demanded. 'Is he on his way?'

'No reply, sir.' The boy hesitated. 'I think the line's gone.'

'Hell's teeth!' Tyndall roared. 'What are you doing standing there, then? Go and get him. Take over, Number One, will you? Bentley—have the Commander come to the bridge.'

'WT—bridge. WT—bridge.' Tyndall glared up at the speaker in exasperation, then froze into immobility as the voice went on. 'We have been hit aft. Damage Control reports coding-room destroyed. Number 6 and 7 Radar Offices destroyed. Canteen wrecked. After control tower severely damaged.'

'The After control tower!' Tyndall swore, pulled off his gloves, wincing at the agony of his broken hand. Carefully, he pillowed Vallery's head on the gloves, rose slowly to his feet. 'The After Tower! And Turner's there! I hope to God . . .'

He broke off, made for the after end of the bridge at a stumbling run. Once there he steadied himself, his hand on the ladder rail, and peered apprehensively aft.

At first he could see nothing, not even the after funnel and mainmast. The grey, writhing fog was too dense, too maddeningly opaque. Then suddenly, for a mere breath of time, an icy catspaw cleared away the mist, cleared away the dark, convoluted smoke-pall above the after superstructure. Tyndall's hand tightened convulsively on the rail, the knuckles whitening to ivory.

The after superstructure had disappeared. In its place was a crazy mass of jumbled twisted steel, with 'X' turret, normally invisible from the bridge, showing up clearly beyond, apparently unharmed. But the rest was gone—radar offices, coding-room, police office, canteen, probably most of the after galley. Nothing, nobody could have survived there. Miraculously, the truncated mainmast still stood, but immediately aft of it, perched crazily on top of this devil's scrap-heap, the After Tower, fractured and grotesquely askew, lay over at an impossible angle of 60°, its range-finder gone. And Commander

Turner had been in there . . . Tyndall swayed dangerously on top of the steel ladder, shook his head again to fight off the fog clamping down on his mind. There was a heavy, peculiarly dull ache just behind his forehead, and the fog seemed to be spreading from there . . . A lucky ship, they called the *Ulysses*. Twenty months on the worst run and in the worst waters in the world and never a scratch . . . But Tyndall had always known that some time, some place, her luck would run out.

He heard hurried steps clattering up the steel ladder, forced his blurred eyes to focus themselves. He recognized the dark, lean face at once: it was Leading Signalman Davies, from the flag deck. His face was white, his breathing short and quick. He opened his mouth to speak, then checked himself, his eyes staring at the handrail.

'Your hand, sir!' He switched his startled gaze from the rail to Tyndall's eyes. 'Your hand! You've no gloves on, sir!'

'No?' Tyndall looked down as if faintly astonished he had a hand. 'No, I haven't, have I? Thank you, Davies.' He pulled his hand off the smooth frozen steel, glanced incuriously at the raw, bleeding flesh. 'It doesn't matter. What is it, boy?'

'The Fighter Direction Room, sir!' Davies's eyes were dark with remembered horror. 'The shell exploded in there. It's—it's just gone, sir. And the Plot above . . . ' He stopped short, his jerky voice lost in the crash of the guns of 'A' turret. Somehow it seemed strangely unnatural that the main armament still remained effective. 'I've just come from the FDR and the Plot, sir,' Davies continued, more calmly now. 'They—well, they never had a chance.'

'Including Commander Westcliffe?' Dimly, Tyndall realised the futility of clutching at straws.

'I don't know, sir. It's—it's just bits and pieces in the FDR, if you follow me. But if he was there—'

'He would be,' Tyndall interrupted heavily. 'He never left it during Action Stations . . . '

He stopped abruptly, broken hands clenched involuntarily as the high-pitched scream and impact explosion of HE shells blurred into shattering cacophony, appalling in its closeness.

'My God!' Tyndall whispered. 'That was close! Davies! What the hell . . . !'

His voice choked off in an agonized grunt, arms flailing wildly at the empty air, as his back crashed against the deck of the bridge, driving every last ounce of breath from his body. Wordlessly, convulsively, propelled by desperately thrusting feet and launched by the powerful back-thrust of arms pivoting on the handrails, Davies had just catapulted himself up the last three steps of the ladder, head and shoulders socketing into the Admiral's body with irresistible force. And now Davies, too, was down, stretched his length on the deck, spreadeagled across Tyndall's legs. He lay very still.

Slowly, the cruel breath rasping his tortured lungs, Tyndall surfaced from the black depths of unconsciousness. Blindly, instinctively he struggled to sit up, but his broken hand collapsed under the weight of his body. His legs didn't seem to be much help either: they were quite powerless, as if he were paralysed from the waist down. The fog was gone now, and blinding flashes of colour, red, green and white were coruscating brilliantly across the darkening sky. Starshells? Was the enemy using a new type of starshell? Dimly, with a great effort of will, he realized that there must be some connection between these dazzling flashes and the now excruciating pain behind his forehead. He reached up the back of his right hand: his eyes were still screwed tightly shut . . . Then the realization faded and was gone.

'Are you all right, sir? Don't move. We'll soon have you out of this!' The voice, deep, authoritative, boomed directly above the Admiral's head. Tyndall shrank back, shook his head in imperceptible despair. It was Turner who was speaking, and Turner, he knew, was gone. Was this, then, what it was like to be dead? he wondered dully. This frightening, confused world of blackness and blinding light at the same time, a darkbright world of pain and powerlessness and voices from the past?

Then suddenly, of their own volition almost, his eyelids flickered and were open. Barely a foot above him were the lean, piratical features of the Commander, who was kneeling anxiously at his side.

'Turner! Turner?' A questioning hand reached out in tentative hope, clutched gratefully, oblivious to the pain, at the reassuring solidity of the Commander's arm. 'Turner! It *is* you! I thought—'

'The After Tower, eh?' Turner smiled briefly. 'No, sir—I wasn't within a mile of it. I was coming here, just climbing up to the fo'c'sle deck, when that first hit threw me back down to the main deck . . . How are you, sir?'

'Thank God! Thank God! I don't know how I am. My legs . . . What in the name of heaven is that?'

His eyes focusing normally again, widened in baffled disbelief. Just above Turner's head, angling for'ard and upward to port, a great white treetrunk stretched as far as he could see in either direction. Reaching up, he could just touch the massive bole with his hand.

'The foremast, sir,' Turner explained. 'It was sheared clean off by that last shell, just above the lower yardarm. The back blast flung it on to the bridge. Took most of the AA tower with it, I'm afraid—and caved in the Main Tower. I don't think young Courtney could have had much chance . . . Davies saw it coming—I was just below him at the time. He was very quick—'

'Davies!' Tyndall's dazed mind had forgotten all about him. 'Of course! Davies!' It must be Davies who was pinioning his legs. He craned his neck forward, saw the huddled figure at his feet, the great weight of the mast lying across his back. 'For God's sake, Commander, get him out of that!'

'Just lie down, sir, till Brooks gets here. Davies is all right.'

'All right? All right!' Tyndall was almost screaming, oblivious to the silent figures who were gathering around him. 'Are you mad, Turner? The poor bastard must be in agony!' He struggled frantically to rise, but several pairs of hands held him down, firmly, carefully.

'He's all right, sir.' Turner's voice was surprisingly gentle. 'Really he is, sir. He's all right. Davies doesn't feel a thing. Not any more.' And all at once the Admiral knew and he fell back limply to the deck, his eyes closed in shocked understanding.

His eyes were still shut when Brooks appeared, doubly welcome in his confidence and competence. Within seconds, almost, the Admiral was on his feet, shocked, badly bruised, but otherwise unharmed. Doggedly, and in open defiance of Brooks, Tyndall demanded that he be assisted back to the bridge. His eyes lit up momentarily as he saw Vallery standing shakily on his feet, a white towel to his mouth. But he said nothing. His head bowed, he hoisted himself painfully into his chair.

'WT—bridge. WT—bridge. Please acknowledge signal.'

'Is that bloody idiot still there?' Tyndall demanded querulously. 'Why doesn't someone—?'

'You've only been gone a couple of minutes, sir,' the Kapok Kid ventured.

'Two minutes!' Tyndall stared at him, lapsed into silence. He glanced down at Brooks, busy bandaging his right hand. 'Have you nothing better to do, Brooks?' he asked harshly.

'No, I haven't,' Brooks replied truculently. 'When shells explode inside four walls, there isn't much work left for a doctor . . . except signing death certificates,' he added brutally. Vallery and Turner exchanged glances. Vallery wondered if Brooks had any idea how far through Tyndall was.

'WT—bridge. WT—bridge. *Vectra* repeats request for instruction. Urgent. Urgent.'

'The *Vectra*!' Vallery glanced at the Admiral, silent now and motionless, and turned to the bridge messenger. 'Chrysler! Get through to WT Any way you can. Ask them to repeat the first message.'

He looked again at Turner, following the Admiral's sick gaze over the side. He looked down, recoiled in horror, fighting down the instant nausea. The gunner in the sponson below—just another boy like Chrysler—must have seen the falling mast, must have made a panic-stricken attempt to escape. He had barely cleared his cockpit when the radar screen, a hundred square feet of meshed steel carrying the crushing weight of the mast as it had snapped over the edge of the bridge, had caught him fairly and squarely. He lay still now, mangled, broken, something less than human, spreadeagled in outflung crucifixion across the twin barrels of his Oerlikon.

Vallery turned away, sick in body and mind. God, the craziness, the futile insanity of war. Damn that German cruiser, damn those German gunners, damn them, damn them! . . . But why should he? They, too, were only doing a job—and doing it terribly well. He gazed sightlessly at the wrecked shambles of his bridge. What damnably accurate gunnery! He wondered, vaguely, if the *Ulysses* had registered any hits. Probably not, and now, of course, it was impossible. It was impossible now because the *Ulysses*, still racing southeast through the fog, was completely blind, both radar eyes gone, victims to the weather and the German guns. Worse still, all the Fire Control towers were damaged beyond repair. If this goes on, he thought wryly, all we'll need is a set of grappling irons and a supply of cutlasses. In terms of modern naval gunnery, even although her main armament was intact, the *Ulysses* was hopelessly crippled. She just didn't have a chance. What was it that Stoker Riley was supposed to have said—'being thrown to the wolves'? Yes, that was it—'thrown to the wolves'. But only a Nero, he reflected wearily, would have blinded a gladiator before throwing him into the arena.

All firing had ceased. The bridge was deadly quiet. Silence, complete silence, except for the sound of rushing water, the muffled roar of the great engine-room intake fans, the monotonous, nerve-drilling pinging of the Asdic—and these, oddly enough, only served to deepen the great silence.

Every eye, Vallery saw, was on Admiral Tyndall. Old Giles was mumbling something to himself, too faint to catch. His face, shockingly grey, haggard and blotched, still peered over the side. He seemed fascinated by the site of the dead boy. Or was it the smashed Radar screen? Had the full significance of the broken scanner and wrecked Director Towers dawned on him yet? Vallery looked at him for a long moment, then turned away: he knew that it had.

'WT—bridge. WT—bridge.' Everyone on the bridge jumped, swung round in nerve-jangled startlement. Everyone except Tyndall. He had frozen into a graven immobility.

'Signal from *Vectra*. First Signal. Received 0952.' Vallery glanced at his watch. Only six minutes ago! Impossible!

'Signal reads: Contacts, contacts, 3, repeat 3. Amend to 5. Heavy concentration of U-boats, ahead and abeam. Am engaging."'

Every eye on the bridge swung back to Tyndall. His, they knew, the responsibility, his the decision—taken alone, against the advice of his senior officer—to leave the convoy almost unguarded. Impersonally, Vallery admired the baiting, the timing, the springing of the trap. How would old Giles react to this, the culmination of a series of disastrous miscalculations—miscalculations for which, in all fairness, he could not justly be blamed . . . But he would be held accountable. The iron voice of the loudspeaker broke in on his thoughts.

'Second signal reads: "Close contact. Depthcharging. Depthcharging. One vessel torpedoed, sinking. Tanker torpedoed, damaged, still afloat, under command. Please advise. Please assist. Urgent. Urgent!"'

The speaker clicked off. Again that hushed silence, strained, unnatural. Five seconds it lasted, ten, twenty—then everyone stiffened, looked carefully away.

Tyndall was climbing down from his chair. His movements were stiff, slow with the careful faltering shuffle of the very old. He limped heavily. His right hand, startling white in its snowy sheath of bandage, cradled his broken wrist. There was about him a queer, twisted sort of dignity, and if his face held any expression at all, it was the far-off echo of a smile. When he spoke, he spoke as a man might talk to himself, aloud.

'I am not well,' he said. 'I am going below.' Chrysler, not too young to have an inkling of the tragedy, held open the gate, caught Tyndall as he stumbled on the step. He glanced back over his shoulder, a quick, pleading look, caught and understood Vallery's compassionate nod. Side by side, the old and the young, they moved slowly aft. Gradually, the shuffling died away and they were gone.

The shattered bridge was curiously empty now, the men felt strangely alone. Giles, the cheerful, buoyant, indestructible Giles was gone. The speed, the extent of the collapse was not for immediate comprehension: the only sensation at the moment was that of being unprotected and defenceless and alone.

'Out of the mouths of babes and sucklings . . . ' Inevitably, the first to break the silence was Brooks. 'Nicholls always maintained that . . . ' He stopped short, his head shaking in slow incredulity. 'I must see what I can do,' he finished abruptly, and hurried off the bridge.

Vallery watched him go, then turned to Bentley. The Captain's face, haggard, shadowed with grizzled beard, the colour of death in the weird halflight of the fog, was quite expressionless.

'Three signals, Chief. First to *Vectra*. "Steer 360°. Do not disperse. Repeat, do not disperse. Am coming to your assistance."' He paused, then went on: 'Sign it, "Admiral, 14 ACS." Got it? . . . Right. No time to code it. Plain language. Send one of your men to the WT at once.'

'Second: To *Stirling, Sirrus* and *Viking*. "Abandon pursuit immediate. Course north-east. Maximum speed." Plain language also.' He turned to the Kapok Kid. 'How's your forehead, Pilot? Can you carry on?'

'Of course, sir.'

'Thank you, boy. You heard me? Convoy rerouted north—say in a few minutes' time, at 1015. Six knots. Give me an intersection course as soon as possible.'

'Third signal, Bentley: To *Stirling, Sirrus* and *Viking:* "Radar out of action. Cannot pick you up on screen. Stream fog-buoys. Siren at two-minute intervals." Have that message coded. All acknowledgements to the bridge at once. Commander!'

'Sir?' Turner was at his elbow.

'Hands to defence stations. It's my guess the pack will have gone before we get there. Who'll be off watch?'

'Lord only knows,' said Turner frankly. 'Let's call it port.'

Vallery smiled faintly. 'Port it is. Organize two parties. First of port to clear away all loose wreckage: over the side with the lot—keep nothing. You'll need the blacksmith and his mate, and I'm sure Dodson will provide you with an oxyacetylene crew. Take charge yourself. Second of port as burial party. Nicholls in charge. All bodies recovered to be laid out in the canteen when it's clear . . . Perhaps you could give me a full report of casualties and damage inside the hour?'

'Long before that, sir . . . Could I have a word with you in private?'

They walked aft. As the shelter door shut behind them, Vallery looked at the Commander curiously, half-humorously. 'Another mutiny, perhaps, Commander?'

'No, sir.' Turner unbuttoned his coat, his hand struggling into the depths of a hip-pocket. He dragged out a flat half-bottle, held it up to the light. 'Thank the Lord for that!' he said piously. 'I was afraid it got smashed when I fell . . . Rum, sir. Neat. I know you hate the stuff, but never mind. Come on, you need this!'

Vallery's brows came down in a straight line.

'Rum. Look here, Commander, do you—?'

'To hell with KRs and AFOs!' Turner interrupted rudely. 'Take it—you need it badly! You've been hurt, you've lost a lot more blood and you're almost frozen to death.' He uncorked it, thrust the bottle into Vallery's reluctant hands. 'Face facts. We need you—more than ever now—and you're almost dead on your feet—and I mean dead on your feet,' he added brutally. 'This might keep you going a few more hours.'

'You put things so nicely,' Vallery murmured. 'Very well. Against my better judgement . . . '

He paused, the bottle to his mouth.

'And you give me an idea, Commander. Have the bosun break out the rum. Pipe "Up spirits." Double ration to each man. They, too, are going to need it.' He swallowed, pulled the bottle away, and the grimace was not for the rum.

'Especially,' he added soberly, 'the burial party.'

TEN

Friday Afternoon

The switch clicked on and the harsh fluorescent light flooded the darkening surgery. Nicholls woke with a start, one hand coming up automatically to shield exhausted eyes. The light hurt. He screwed his eyes to slits, peered painfully at the hands of his wrist-watch. Four o'clock! Had he been asleep that long? God, it was bitterly cold!

He hoisted himself stiffly forward in the dentist's chair, twisted his head round. Brooks was standing with his back to the door, snow-covered hood framing his silver hair, numbed fingers fumbling with a packet of cigarettes. Finally he managed to pull one out. He looked up quizzically over a flaring match-head.

'Hallo, there, Johnny! Sorry to waken you, but the skipper wants you. Plenty of time, though.' He dipped the cigarette into the dying flame, looked up again. Nicholls, he thought with sudden compassion, looked ill, desperately tired and overstrained; but no point in telling him so. 'How are you? On second thoughts, don't tell me! I'm a damned sight worse myself. Have you any of that poison left?'

'Poison, sir?' The levity was almost automatic, part of their relationship with each other. 'Just because you make one wrong diagnosis? The Admiral will be all right—'

'Gad! The intolerance of the very young—especially on the providentially few occasions that they happen to be right . . . I was referring to that bottle of bootleg hooch from the Isle of Mull.'

'Coll,' Nicholls corrected. 'Not that it matters—you've drunk it all, anyway,' he added unkindly. He grinned tiredly at the Commander's crestfallen face, then relented. 'But we do have a bottle of Talisker left.' He crossed over to the posion cupboard, unscrewed the top of a bottle marked 'Lysol'. He heard, rather than saw, the clatter of glass against glass, wondered vaguely, with a kind of clinical detachment, why his hands were shaking so badly.

Brooks drained his glass, sighed in bliss as he felt the grateful warmth sinking down inside him.

'Thank you, my boy. Thank you. You have the makings of a first-class doctor.'

'You think so, sir? I don't. Not any longer. Not after today.' He winced, remembering. 'Forty-four of them, sir, over the side in ten minutes, one after the other, like—like so many sacks of rubbish.'

'Forty-four?' Brooks looked up. 'So many, Johnny?'

'Not really, sir. That was the number of missing. About thirty, rather, and God only knows how many bits and pieces . . . It was a brush and shovel job in the FDR' He smiled, mirthlessly. 'I had no dinner, today. I don't think anybody else in the burial party had either . . . I'd better screen that porthole.'

He turned away quickly, walked across the surgery. Low on the horizon, through the thinlyfalling snow, he caught intermittent sight of an evening star. That meant that the fog was gone—the fog that had saved the convoy, had hidden them from the U-boats when it had turned so sharply to the north. He could see the *Vectra*, her depth-charge racks empty and nothing to show for it. He could see the *Vytura*, the damaged tanker, close by, almost awash in the water, hanging grimly on to the convoy. He could see four of the Victory ships, big, powerful, reassuring, so pitifully deceptive in their indestructible permanence . . . He slammed the scuttle, screwed home the last butterfly nut, then swung round abruptly.

'Why the hell don't we turn back?' he burst out. 'Who does the old man think he's kidding—us or the Germans? No air cover, nor radar, not the faintest chance of help! The Germans have us pinned down to an inch now—and it'll be easier still for them as we go on. And there's a thousand miles to go!' His voice rose. 'And every bloody enemy ship, U-boat and plane in the Arctic smacking their lips and waiting to pick us off at their leisure.' He shook his head in despair. 'I'll take my chance with anybody else, sir. You know that. But this is just murder—or suicide. Take your pick, sir. It's all the same when you're dead.'

'Now, Johnny, you're not—'

'*Why* doesn't he turn back?' Nicholls hadn't even heard the interruption. 'He's only got to give the order. What does he want? Death or glory? What's he after? Immortality at my expense, at *our* expense?' He swore, bitterly. 'Maybe Riley was right. Wonderful headlines. "Captain Richard Vallery, DSO, has been posthumously awarded—"'

'Shut up!' Brooks's eye was as chill as the Arctic ice itself, his voice a biting lash.

'You dare to talk of Captain Vallery like that!' he said softly. 'You dare to besmirch the name of the most honourable . . . ' He broke off, shook his head in wrathful wonder. He paused to pick his words carefully, his eyes never leaving the other's white, strained face.

'He is a good officer, Lieutenant Nicholls, maybe even a great officer: and that just doesn't matter a damn. What does matter is that he is the finest gentleman—I say "gentleman"—I've ever known, that ever walked the face of this graceless, Godforsaken earth. He is not like you or me. He is not like anybody at all. He walks alone, but he is never lonely, for he has company all the way . . . men like Peter, like Bede, like St Francis of Assisi.' He laughed shortly. 'Funny, isn't it—to hear an old reprobate like myself talk like this? Blasphemy, even, you might call it—except that the truth can never be blasphemy. And I *know*.'

Nicholls said nothing. His face was like a stone.

'Death, glory, immortality,' Brooks went on relentlessly. 'These were your words, weren't they? Death?' He smiled and shook his head again. 'For Richard Vallery, death doesn't exist. Glory? Sure, he wants glory, we all want glory, but all the *London Gazettes* and Buckingham Palaces in the world can't give *him* the kind of glory he wants: Captain Vallery is no longer a child, and only children play with toys . . . As for immortality.' He laughed, without a trace of rancour now, laid a hand on Nicholls's shoulder. 'I ask you, Johnny—wouldn't it be damned stupid to ask for what he has already?'

Nicholls said nothing. The silence lengthened and deepened, the rush of the air from the ventilation louvre became oppressively loud. Finally, Brooks coughed, looked meaningfully at the 'Lysol' bottle.

Nicholls filled the glasses, brought them back. Brooks caught his eyes, held them, and was filled with sudden pity. What was that classical understatement of Cunningham's during the German invasion of Crete—'It is inadvisable to drive men beyond a certain point.' Trite but true. True even for men like Nicholls. Brooks wondered what particular private kind of hell that boy had gone through that morning, digging out the shattered, torn bodies of what had once been men. And, as the doctor in charge, he would have had to examine them all—or all the pieces he could find . . .

'Next step up and I'll be in the gutter.' Nicholls's voice was very low. 'I don't know what to say, sir. I don't know what made me say it . . . I'm sorry.'

'Me too,' Brooks said sincerely. 'Shooting off my mouth like that! And I mean it.' He lifted his glass, inspected the contents lovingly. 'To our enemies, Johnny: their downfall and confusion, and don't forget Admiral Starr.' He drained the glass at a gulp, set it down, looked at Nicholls for a long moment.

'I think you should hear the rest, too, Johnny. You know, why Vallery doesn't turn back.' He smiled wryly. 'It's not because there are as many of these damned U-boats behind us as there are in front—which there undoubtedly are.' He lit a fresh cigarette, went on quietly:

'The Captain radioed London this morning. Gave it as his considered opinion that FR77 would be a goner—"annihilated" was the word he used and, as a word, they don't come any stronger—long before it reached the North Cape. He asked at least to be allowed to go north about, instead of east for the Cape . . . Pity there was no sunset tonight, Johnny,' he added half-humorously. 'I would have liked to see it.'

'Yes, yes,' Nicholls was impatient. 'And the answer?'

'Eh! Oh, the answer. Vallery expected it immediately.' Brooks shrugged. 'It took four hours to come through.' He smiled, but there was no laughter in the eyes. 'There's something big, something on a huge scale brewing up somewhere. It can only be some major invasion—this under your hat, Johnny?'

'Of course, sir!'

'What it is I haven't a clue. Maybe even the long-awaited Second Front. Anyway, the support of the Home Fleet seems to be regarded as vital to success. But the Home Fleet is tied up—by the *Tirpitz*. And so the orders have gone out—get the *Tirpitz*. Get it at all costs.' Brooks smiled, and his face was very cold. 'We're big fish, Johnny, we're important people. We're the biggest, juiciest bait ever offered up, the biggest, juiciest prize in the world today—although I'm afraid the trap's a trifle rusty at the hinges . . . The signal came from the First Sea Lord—and Starr. The decision was taken at Cabinet level. We go on. We go east.'

'We are the "all costs",' said Nicholls flatly. 'We are expendable.'

'We are expendable,' Brooks agreed. The speaker above his head clicked on, and he groaned. 'Hell's bells, here we go again!'

He waited until the clamour of the Dusk Action Stations' bugle had died away, stretched out a hand as Nicholls hurried for the door.

'Not you, Johnny. Not yet. I told you, the skipper wants you. On the bridge, ten minutes after Stations begin.'

'What? On the bridge? What the hell for?'

'Your language is unbecoming to a junior officer,' said Brooks solemnly. 'How did the men strike you today?' he went on inconsequently. 'You were working with them all morning. Their usual selves?'

Nicholls blinked, then recovered.

'I suppose so.' He hesitated. 'Funny, they seemed a lot better a couple of days ago, but—well, now they're back to the Scapa stage. Walking zombies. Only more so—they can hardly walk now.' He shook his head. 'Five, six men to a stretcher. Kept tripping and falling over things. Asleep on their feet—eyes not focusing, too damned tired to look where they're going.'

Brooks nodded. 'I know, Johnny, I know. I've seen it myself.'

'Nothing mutinous, nothing sullen about them any more.' Nicholls was puzzled, seeking tiredly to reduce nebulous, scattered impressions to a homogeneous coherence. 'They've neither the energy nor the initiative left for a mutiny now, anyway, I suppose, but it's not that. Kept muttering to themselves in the FDR: "Lucky bastard" "He died easy"—things like that. Or "Old Giles—off his bleedin rocker." And you can imagine the shake of the head. But no humour, none, not even the grisly variety you usually . . . ' He shook his own head. 'I just don't know, sir. Apathetic, indifferent, hopeless—call 'em what you like. I'd call 'em lost.'

Brooks looked at him a long moment, then added gently:

'Would you now?' He mused. 'And do you know, Johnny, I think you'd be right . . . Anyway,' he continued briskly, 'get up there. Captain's going to make a tour of the ship.'

'What!' Nicholls was astounded. 'During action stations? Leave the bridge?'

'Just that.'

'But—but he can't, sir. It's—it's unprecedented!'

'So's Captain Vallery. That's what I've been trying to tell you all evening.'

'But he'll kill himself!' Nicholls protested wildly.

'That's what I said,' Brooks agreed wryly. 'Clinically, he's dying. He should be dead. What keeps him going God only knows—literally. It certainly isn't plasma or drugs . . . Once in a while, Johnny, it's salutary for us to appreciate the limits of medicine. Anyway, I talked him into taking you with him . . . Better not keep him waiting.'

For Lieutenant Nicholls, the next two hours were borrowed from purgatory. Two hours, the Captain took to his inspection, two hours of constant walking, of climbing over storm-sills and tangled wreckage of steel, of squeezing and twisting through impossibly narrow apertures, of climbing and descending a hundred ladders, two hours of exhausting torture in the bitter, heart-sapping cold of a sub-zero temperature. But it was a memory that was to stay with him always, that was never to return without filling him with warmth, with a strange and wonderful gratitude.

They started on the poop—Vallery, Nicholls and Chief Petty Officer Hartley—Vallery would have none of Hastings, the Master-At-Arms, who usually accompanied the Captain on his rounds.

There was something oddly reassuring about the big, competent Chief. He worked like a Trojan that night, opening and shutting dozens of watertight doors, lifting and lowering countless, heavy hatches, knocking off and securing the thousand clips that held these doors and hatches in place, and before ten minutes had passed, lending a protesting Vallery the support of his powerful arm.

They climbed down the long, vertical ladder to 'Y' magazine, a dim and gloomy dungeon thinly lit with pinpoints of garish light. Here were the butchers, bakers and candlestick makers—the non-specialists in the purely offensive branches. 'Hostilities only' ratings, almost to a man, in charge of a trained gunner, they had a cold, dirty and unglamorous job, strangely neglected and forgotten—strangely, because so terribly dangerous. The four-inch armour encasing them offered about as much protection as a sheet of newspaper to an eight-inch armour-piercing shell or a torpedo . . .

The magazine walls—walls of shells and cartridge cases—were soaking wet, dripping constantly visibly, with icy condensation. Half the crew were leaning or lying against the racks, blue, pinched, shivering with cold, their breath hanging heavily in the chill air: the others were trudging heavily round and round the hoist, feet splashing in pools of water, lurching, stumbling with sheer exhaustion, gloved hands buried in their pockets, drawn, exhausted faces sunk on their chests. Zombies, Nicholls thought wonderingly, just living zombies. Why don't they lie down?

Gradually, everyone became aware of Vallery's presence, stopped walking or struggling painfully erect, eyes too tired, minds too spent for either wonder or surprise.

'As you were, as you were,' Vallery said quickly. 'Who's in charge here?'

'I am, sir.' A stocky, overalled figure walked slowly forward, halted in front of Vallery.

'Ah, yes. Gardiner, isn't it?' He gestured to the men circling the hoist. 'What in the world is all this for, Gardiner?'

'Ice,' said Gardiner succinctly. 'We have to keep the water moving or it'll freeze in a couple of minutes. We can't have ice on the magazine floor, sir.'

'No, no, of course not! But—but the pumps, the draincocks?'

'Solid!'

'But surely—this doesn't go on all the time?'

'In flat weather—all the time, sir.'

'Good God!' Vallery shook his head incredulously, splashed his way to the centre of the group, where a slight, boyish figure was coughing cruelly into a corner of an enormous green and white muffler. Vallery placed a concerned arm across the shaking shoulders.

'Are you all right, boy?'

'Yes, sir. 'Course, Ah am!' He lifted a thin white face racked with pain. 'Ah'm fine,' he said indignantly.

'What's your name?'

'McQuater, sir.'

'And what's your job, McQuater?'

'Assistant cook, sir.'

'How old are you?'

'Eighteen, sir.' Merciful heavens, Vallery thought, this isn't a cruiser I'm running—it's a nursery!

'From Glasgow, eh?' He smiled.

'Yes, sir.' Defensively.

'I see.' He looked down at the deck, at McQuater's boots half-covered in water. 'Why aren't you wearing your sea-boots?' he asked abruptly.

'We don't get issued with them, sir.'

'But your feet, man! They must be soaking!'

'Ah don't know, sir. Ah think so. Anyway,' McQuater said simply, 'it doesna matter. Ah canna feel them.'

Vallery winced. Nicholls, looking at the Captain, wondered if he realized the distressing, pathetic picture he himself presented with his sunken, bloodless face, red, inflamed eyes, his mouth and nose daubed with crimson, the inevitable dark and sodden hand-towel clutched in his left glove. Suddenly unaccountably, Nicholls felt ashamed of himself: that thought, he knew, could never occur to this man.

Vallery smiled down at McQuater.

'Tell me son, honestly—are you tired?'

'Ah am that—Ah mean, aye, aye, sir.'

'Me too,' Vallery confessed. 'But—you can carry on a bit longer?'

He felt the frail shoulders straighten under his arm.

''Course Ah can, sir!' The tone was injured, almost truculent.' '*Course* Ah can!'

Vallery's gaze travelled slowly over the group, his dark eyes glowing as he heard a murmured chorus of assent. He made to speak, broke off in a harsh coughing and bent his head. He looked up again, his eyes wandering once more over the circle of now-anxious faces, then turned abruptly away.

'We won't forget you,' he murmured indistinctly. 'I promise you, we won't forget you.' He splashed quickly away, out of the pool of water, out of the pool of light, into the darkness at the foot of the ladder.

Ten minutes later, they emerged from 'Y' turret. The night sky was cloudless now, brilliant with diamantine stars, little chips of frozen fire in the dark velvet of that fathomless floor. The cold was intense. Captain Vallery shivered involuntarily as the turret door slammed behind them.

'Hartley?'

'Sir?'

'I smelt rum in there!'

'Yes, sir. So did I.' The Chief was cheerful, unperturbed. 'Proper stinking with it. Don't worry about it though, sir. Half the men in the ship bottle their rum ration, keep it for action stations.'

'Completely forbidden in regulations, Chief. You know that as well as I do!'

'I know. But there's no harm, sir. Warms 'em up—and if it gives them Dutch courage, all the better. Remember that night the for'ard pom-pom got two Stukas?'

'Of course.'

'Canned to the wide. Never have done it otherwise . . . And now, sir, they *need* it.'

'Suppose you're right, Chief. They do and I don't blame them.' He chuckled. 'And don't worry about my knowing—I've always known. But it smelled like a saloon bar in there . . . '

They climbed up to 'X' turret—the marine turret—then down to the magazine. Wherever he went, as in 'Y' magazine, Vallery left the men the better for his coming. In personal contact, he had some strange indefinable power that lifted men above themselves, that brought out in them something they had never known to exist. To see dull apathy and hopelessness slowly give way to resolution, albeit a kind of numbed and desperate resolve, was to see something that baffled the understanding. Physically and mentally, Nicholls knew, these men had long since passed the point of no return.

Vaguely, he tried to figure it out, to study the approach and technique. But the approach varied every time, he saw, was no more than a natural reaction to different sets of circumstances as they presented themselves, a reaction utterly lacking in calculation or finesse. There *was* no technique. Was pity, then, the activating force, pity for the heart-breaking gallantry of a man so clearly dying? Or was it shame—if *he* can do it, if *he* can still drive that wasted mockery of a body, if he can kill himself just to come to see if *we're* all right—if he can do that and smile—then, by God, we can stick it out, too? That's it, Nicholls said to himself, that's what it is, pity and shame, and he hated himself for thinking it, and not because of the thought, but because he knew he lied . . . He was too tired to think anyway. His mind was woolly, fuzzy round the edges, his thoughts disjointed, uncontrolled. Like everyone else's. Even Andy Carpenter, the last man you would suspect of it—he felt that way, too, and admitted it . . . He wondered what the Kapok Kid would have to say to this . . . The Kid was probably wandering too, but wandering in his own way, back as always on the banks of the Thames. He wondered what the girl in Henley was like. Her name started with 'J'—Joan, Jean—he didn't know: the Kapok Kid had a big golden 'J' on the right breast of his kapok suit—*she* had put it there. But what was she like? Blonde and gay, like the Kid himself? Or dark and kind and gentle, like St Francis of Assisi? St Francis of Assisi? Why in the world did he—ah, yes, old Socrates had been talking about him. Wasn't he the man of whom Axel Munthe . . .

'Nicholls! Are you all right?' Vallery's voice was sharp with anxiety.

'Yes, of course, sir.' Nicholls shook his head, as if to clear it. 'Just gathering wool. Where to now, sir?'

'Engineers' Flat, Damage Control parties, Switchboard, Number 3 Low Power room—no, of course, that's gone—Noyes was killed there, wasn't he? . . . Hartley, I'd appreciate it if you'd let my feet touch the deck occasionally . . . '

All these places they visited in turn and a dozen others besides—not even the remotest corner, the most impossible of access, did Vallery pass by, if he knew a man was there, closed up to his action station.

They came at last to the engine and boiler-rooms, to the gulping pressure changes on unaccustomed eardrums as they went through the airlocks, to the antithetically breath-taking blast of heat as they passed inside. In 'A' boiler-room, Nicholls insisted on Vallery's resting for some minutes. He was grey with pain and weakness, his breathing very distressed. Nicholls noticed Hartley talking in a corner, was dimly aware of someone leaving the boiler-room.

Then his eyes caught sight of a burly, swarthy stoker, with bruised cheeks and the remnants of a gorgeous black eye, stalking across the floor. He carried a canvas chair, set it down with a thump behind Vallery.

'A seat, sir,' he growled.

'Thank you, thank you.' Vallery lowered himself gratefully, then looked up in surprise. 'Riley?' he murmured, then switched his glance to Hendry, the Chief Stoker. 'Doing his duty with a minimum of grace, eh?'

Hendry stirred uncomfortably.

'He did it off his own bat, sir.'

'I'm sorry,' Vallery said sincerely. 'Forgive me, Riley. Thank you very much.' He stared after him in puzzled wonder, looked again at Hendry, eyebrows lifted in interrogation.

Hendry shook his head.

'Search me, sir. I've no idea. He's a queer fish. Does things like that. He'd bend a lead pipe over your skull without batting an eyelid—and he's got a mania for looking after kittens and lame dogs. Or if you get a bird with a broken wing—Riley's your man. But he's got a low opinion of his fellowmen, sir.'

Vallery nodded slowly, without speaking, leaned against the canvas back and closed his eyes in exhaustion. Nicholls bent over him.

'Look, sir,' he urged quietly, 'why not give it up? Frankly, sir, you're killing yourself. Can't we finish this some other time?'

'I'm afraid not, my boy.' Vallery was very patient. 'You don't understand. "Some other time" will be too late.' He turned to Hendry. 'So you think you'll manage all right, Chief?'

'Don't you worry about us, sir.' The soft Devon voice was grim and gentle at the same time. 'Just you look after yourself. The stokers won't let you down, sir.'

Vallery rose painfully to his feet, touched him lightly on the arm. 'Do you know, Chief, I never thought you would . . . Ready, Hartley?' He stopped short, seeing a giant duffel-coated figure waiting at the foot of the ladder, the face below the hood dark and sombre. 'Who's that? Oh, I know. Never thought stokers got so cold,' he smiled.

'Yes, sir, it's Petersen,' Hartley said softly. 'He's coming with us.'

'Who said so? And—and Petersen? Wasn't that—?'

'Yes, sir. Riley's—er—lieutenant in the Scapa business . . . Surgeon Commander's orders, sir. Petersen's going to give us a hand.'

'Us? Me, you mean.' There was no resentment, no bitterness in Vallery's voice. 'Hartley, take my advice—never let yourself get into the hands of the doctors . . . You think he's safe?' he added half-humorously.

'He'd probably kill the man who looked sideways at you,' Hartley stated matter-of-factly. 'He's a good man, sir. Simple, easily led—but good.'

At the foot of the ladder, Petersen stepped aside to let them pass, but Vallery stopped, looked up at the giant towering six inches above him, into the grave, blue eyes below the flaxen hair.

'Hallo, Petersen. Hartley tells me you're coming with us. Do you really want to? You don't have to, you know.'

'Please, Captain.' The speech was slow and precise, the face curiously dignified in unhappiness. 'I am very sorry for what has happened—'

'No, no!' Vallery was instantly contrite. 'You misunderstand. It's a bitter night up top. But I would like it very much if you would come. Will you?'

Petersen stared at him, then began slowly to smile, his face darkening with pleasure. As the Captain set foot on the first step, the giant arm came round him. The sensation, as Vallery described it later, was very much like going up in a lift.

From there they visited Engineer Commander Dodson in his engine-room, a cheerful, encouraging, immensely competent Dodson, an engineer to his finger-tips in his single-minded devotion to the great engines under his care. Then aft to the Engineers' Flat, up the companionway between the wrecked Canteen and the Police Office, out on to the upper deck. After the heat of the boiler-room, the 100° drop in temperature, a drop that strangled breath with the involuntary constriction of the throat and made a skin-crawling mockery of 'Arctic clothing,' was almost literally paralysing.

The starboard torpedo tubes—the only ones at the standby—were only four paces away. The crew, huddled in the lee of the wrecked bosun's store—the one destroyed by the *Blue Ranger*'s shells—were easily located by the stamping of frozen feet, the uncontrollable chattering of teeth.

Vallery peered into the gloom. 'LTO there?'

'Captain, sir?' Surprise, doubt in the voice.

'Yes. How are things going?'

'All right, sir.' He was still off-balance, hesitant. 'I think young Smith's left foot is gone, sir—frostbite.'

'Take him below—at once. And organize your crew into ten-minute watches: one to keep a telephone watch here, the other four in the Engineers' Flat. From now on. You understand?' He hurried away, as if to avoid the embarrassment of thanks, the murmurs of smiling gladness.

They passed the torpedo shop, where the spare torpedoes and compressed air cylinders were stored, climbed the ladder to the boat-deck. Vallery paused a moment, one hand on the boat-winch, the other holding the bloody scarf, already frozen almost solid, to mouth and nose. He could just distinguish the shadowy bulkiness of merchantmen on either side: their masts, though, were oddly visible, swinging lazily, gently against the stars as the ships rolled to a slight swell, just beginning. He shuddered, pulled his scarf higher round his neck. God, it was cold! He moved for'ard, leaning heavily on Petersen's arm. The snow, three to four inches deep, cushioned his footsteps as he came up behind an Oerlikon gun. Quietly, he laid a hand on the shoulder of the hooded gunner hunched forward in his cockpit.

'Things all right, gunner?'

No reply. The man appeared to stir, moved forward, then fell still again.

'I said, "Are you all right?"' Vallery's voice had hardened. He shook the gunner by the shoulder, turned impatiently to Hartley.

'Asleep, Chief! At Action Stations! We're all dead from lack of sleep, I know—but his mates below are depending on him. There's no excuse. Take his name!'

'Take his name!' Nicholls echoed softly, bent over the cockpit. He shouldn't speak like this, he knew, but he couldn't help it. 'Take his name,' he repeated. 'What for? His next of kin? This man is dead.'

The snow was beginning to fall again, cold and wet and feathery, the wind lifting a perceptible fraction. Vallery felt the first icy flakes, unseen in the darkness, brushing his cheeks, heard the distant moan of the wind in the rigging, lonely and forlorn. He shivered.

'His heater's gone.' Hartley withdrew an exploratory hand, straightened up. He seemed tired. 'These Oerlikons have black heaters bolted to the side of the cockpit. The gunners lean against them, sir, for hours at a time . . . I'm afraid the fuses must have blown. They've been warned against this, sir, a thousand times.'

'Good God! Good God!' Vallery shook his head slowly. He felt old, terribly tired. 'What a useless, futile way to die . . . Have him taken to the Canteen, Hartley.'

'No good, sir.' Nicholls straightened up also. 'It'll have to wait. What with the cold and the quick onset of rigor mortis—well, it'll have to wait.'

Vallery nodded assent, turned heavily away. All at once, the deck speaker aft of the winch blared into raucous life, a rude desecration that shattered the chilled hush of the evening.

'Do you hear there? Do you hear there? Captain, or notify Captain, to contact bridge immediately, please.' Three times the message was repeated, then the speaker clicked off.

Quickly Vallery turned to Hartley.

'Where's the nearest phone, Chief?'

'Right here, sir.' Hartley turned back to the Oerlikon, stripped earphones and chest mouthpiece from the dead man. 'That is, if the AA tower is still manned?'

'What's left of it is.'

'Tower? Captain to speak to bridge. Put me through.' He handed the receiver to Vallery. 'Here you are, sir.'

'Thank you. Bridge? Yes, speaking . . . Yes, yes . . . Very good. Detail the *Sirrus* . . . No, Commander, nothing I can do anyway—just maintain position, that's all.' He took the handset off, handed it back to Hartley.

'Asdic contact from *Viking*,' he said briefly. 'Red 90.' He turned, looked out over the dark sea, realized the futility of his instinctive action, and shrugged. 'We've sent the *Sirrus* after him. Come on.'

Their tour of the boat-deck gun-sites completed with a visit to the midships' pom-pom crew, bonechilled and shaking with cold, under the command of the bearded Doyle, respectfully sulphurous in his outspoken comments on the weather, they dropped down to the main deck again. By this time Vallery was making no protest at all, not even of the most token kind, against Petersen's help and support. He was too glad of them. He blessed Brooks for his foresight and thoughfulness, and was touched by the rare delicacy and consideration that prompted the big Norwegian to withdraw his supporting arm whenever they spoke to or passed an isolated group of men.

Inside the port screen door and just for'ard of the galley, Vallery and Nicholls, waiting as the others knocked the clamps off the hatch leading down to the stokers' mess, heard the muffled roar of distant depth-charges—there were four in all—felt the pressure waves strike the hull of the *Ulysses*. At the first report Vallery had stiffened, head cocked in attention, eyes fixed on infinity, in the immemorial manner of a man whose ears are doing the work for all the sense.

Hesitated a moment, shrugged, bent his arm to hook a leg over the hatch coaming. There was nothing he could do.

In the centre of the stokers' mess was another, heavier hatch. This, too, was opened. The ladder led down to the steering position, which, as in most modern warships, was far removed from the bridge, deep in the heart of the ship below the armour-plating. Here, for a couple of minutes, Vallery talked quietly to the quartermaster, while Petersen, working in the confined space just outside, opened the massive hatch—450 lbs of steel, actuated by a counter-balancing pulley weight—which gave access to the hold, to the very bottom of the *Ulysses*, to the Transmitting Station and No. 2 Low Power Room.

Amazing, confusing mystery of a place, this Low Power Room, confusing to the eye and ear. Round every bulkhead, interspersed with scores of switches, breakers and rheostats, were ranged tiered banks of literally hundreds of fuses, baffling to the untrained eye in their myriad complexity. Baffling, too, was the function of a score or more of low-power generators, nerve-drilling in the frenetic dissonance of their high-pitched hums. Nicholls straightened up at the foot of the ladder and shuddered involuntarily. A bad place, this. How easily could mind and nerves slide over the edge of insanity under the pounding, insistent clamour of the desynchronized cacophony!

Just then there were only two men there—an Electric Artificer and his assistant, bent over the big Sperry master gyro, making some latitude adjustment to the highly complex machinery of the compass. They looked up quickly, tired surprise melting into tired pleasure. Vallery had a few words with them—speech was difficult in that bedlam of sound—then moved over to the door of the TS.

He had his glove on the door handle when he froze to complete stillness. Another pattern had exploded, much closer this time, two cable lengths distant, at most. Depth-charges, they knew, but only because reason and experience told them: deep down in the heart of an armour-plated ship there is no sense of explosion, no roar of eruption from a detonating depth-charge. Instead, there is a tremendous, metallic clang, peculiarly tinny in calibre, as if some giant with a giant sledge had struck the ship's side and found the armour loose.

The pattern was followed almost immediately by another two explosions, and the *Ulysses* was still shuddering under the impact of the second when Vallery turned the handle and walked in. The others filed in after the Captain, Petersen closing the door softly behind him. At once the clamour of the electric motors died gratefully away in the hushed silence of the TS

The TS, fighting heart of the ship, lined like the Low Power Room though it was by banks of fuses, was completely dominated by the two huge electronic computing tables occupying almost half the floor space. These, the vital links between the Fire Control Towers and the turrets, were generally the scene of intense, controlled activity: but the almost total destruction of the towers that morning had made them all but useless, and the undermanned TS was strangely quiet. Altogether, there were only eight ratings and an officer manning the tables.

The air in the TS, a TS prominently behung with 'No Smoking' notices, was blue with tobacco smoke hanging in a flat, lazily drifting cloud near the deckhead—a cloud which spiralled thinly down to smouldering cigarette ends. For Nicholls there was something oddly reassuring in these burning cigarettes: in the unnatural bow-taut stillness, in the inhuman immobility of the men, it was the only guarantee of life.

He looked, in a kind of detached curiosity, at the rating nearest him. A thin, dark-haired man, he was sitting hunched forward, his elbow on the table, the cigarette clipped between his fingers a bare inch from his half-open mouth. The smoke was curling up, lacing its smarting path across vacant, sightless eyes oblivious to the irritation, the ash on the cigarette, itself almost two inches in length, drooping slightly. Vaguely, Nicholls wondered how long he had been sitting there motionless, utterly motionless . . . and why?

Expectancy, of course. That was it—expectancy. It was too obvious. Waiting, just waiting. Waiting for what? For the first time it struck Nicholls, struck him with blinding clarity, what it was to wait, to wait with the bowstring of the nerves strung down at inhuman tension, strung down far beyond quivering to the taughtened immobility of snapping point, to wait for the torpedo that would send them crashing into oblivion. For the first time he realized why it was that men who could, invariably it seemed, find something complainingly humorous in any place and every place never joked about the TS. A death trap is not funny. The TS was twenty feet below water level: for'ard of it was 'B' magazine, aft of it 'A' boiler-room, on either side of it were fuel tanks, and below it was the unprotected bottom, prime target for acoustic mines and torpedoes. They were ringed, surrounded, by the elements, the threat of death, and it needed only a flash, a wandering spark, to trigger off the annihilating reality . . . And above them, in the one in a thousand chance of survival, was a series of hatches which could all too easily warp and lock, solid under the metal-twisting shock of an explosion. Besides, the primary idea was that the hatches, deliberately heavy in construction, should *stay* shut in the event of damage, to seal off the flooded compartments below. The men in the TS knew this.

'Good evening. Everything all right down here?' Vallery's voice, quiet and calm as ever, sounded unnaturally loud. Startled faces, white and strained, twisted round, eyes opening in astonishment: the depth-charging, Nicholls realized, had masked their approach.

'Wouldn't worry too much about the racket outside,' Vallery went on reassuringly. 'A wandering U-boat, and the *Sirrus* is after him. You can thank your stars you're here and not in that sub.'

No one else had spoken. Nicholls, watching them, saw their eyes flickering back from Vallery's face to the forbidden cigarettes, understood their discomfort, their embarrassment at being caught red-handed by the Captain.

'Any reports from the main tower, Brierley?' he asked the officer in charge. He seemed unaware of the strain.

'No, sir. Nothing at all. All quiet above.'

'Fine!' Vallery sounded positively cheerful. 'No news is good news.' He brought his hand out from his pocket, proffered his cigarette case to Brierley. 'Smoke? And you, Nicholls?' He took one himself, replaced the case, absently picked up a box of matches lying in front of the nearest gunner and if he noticed the gunner's startled disbelief, the slow beginnings of a smile, the tired shoulders slumping fractionally in a long, soundless sigh of relief, he gave no sign.

The thunderous clanging of more depth-charges drowned the rasping of the hatch, drowned Vallery's harsh, convulsive coughing as the smoke reached his lungs. Only the reddening of the sodden hand-towel betrayed him. As the last vibration died away, he looked up, concern in his eyes.

'Good God! Does it always sound like that down here?'

Brierley smiled faintly. 'More or less, sir. Usually more.'

Vallery looked slowly round the men in the TS, nodded for'ard. '"B" magazine there, isn't it?'

'Yes, sir.'

'And nice big fuel tanks all round you?'

Brierley nodded. Every eye was on the captain.

'I see. Frankly, I'd rather have my own job—wouldn't have yours for a pension . . . Nicholls, I think we'll spend a few minutes down here, have our smoke in peace. Besides'—he grinned—'think of the increased fervour with which we'll count our blessings when we get out of here!'

He stayed five minutes, talking quietly to Brierley and his men. Finally, he stubbed out his cigarette, took his leave and started for the door.

'Sir.' The voice stopped him on the threshold, the voice of the thin dark gunner whose matches he had borrowed.

'Yes, what is it?'

'I thought you might like this.' He held out a clean, white towel. 'That one you've got is—well, sir, I mean it's—'

'Thank you.' Vallery took the towel without any hesitation. 'Thank you very much.'

Despite Petersen's assistance, the long climb up to the upper deck left Vallery very weak. His feet were dragging heavily.

'Look, sir, this is madness!' Nicholls was desperately anxious. 'Sorry, sir, I didn't mean that, but—well, come and see Commander Brooks. Please!'

'Certainly.' The reply was a husky whisper. 'Our next port of call anyway.'

Half a dozen paces took them to the door of the Sick Bay. Vallery insisted on seeing Brooks alone. When he came out of the surgery after some time, he seemed curiously refreshed, his step lighter. He was smiling, and so was Brooks. Nicholls lagged behind as the Captain left.

'Give him anything, sir?' he asked. 'Honest to God, he's killing himself!'

'He took something, not much.' Brooks smiled softly. 'I know he's killing himself, so does he. But he knows why, and I know why, and he knows I know why. Anyway, he feels better. Not to worry, Johnny!'

Nicholls waited at the top of the ladder outside the Sick Bay, waited for the Captain and others to come up from the telephone exchange and No. I Low Power Room. He stood aside as they climbed the coaming, but Vallery took his arm, walked him slowly for'ard past the Torpedo Office, nodding curtly to Carslake, in nominal charge of a Damage Control party. Carslake, face still swathed in white, looked back with eyes wild and staring and strange, his gaze almost devoid of recognition. Vallery hesitated, shook his head, then turned to Nicholls, smiling.

'BMA in secret session eh?' he queried. 'Never mind, Nicholls, and don't worry. *I'm* the one who should be worrying.'

'Indeed, sir? Why!'

Vallery shook his head again. 'Rum in the gun turrets, cigarettes in the TS, and now a fine old whisky in a "Lysol" bottle. Though Commander Brooks was going to poison me—and what a glorious death! Excellent stuff, and the Surgeon Commander's apologies to you for broaching your private supplies.'

Nicholls flushed darkly, began to stammer an apology but Vallery cut him off.

'Forget it, boy, forget it. What does it matter? But it makes me wonder what we're going to find next. An opium den in the Capstan Flat, perhaps, or dancing girls in "B" turret?'

But they found nothing in these or any other places, except cold, misery and hunger-haunted exhaustion. As ever, Nicholls saw, they—or rather, Vallery—left the men the better of their coming.

But they themselves were now in a pretty bad state, Nicholls realized. His own legs were made of rubber, he was exhausted by continuous shivering: where Vallery found the strength to carry on, he couldn't even begin to imagine. Even Petersen's great strength was flagging, not so much from half-carrying Vallery as from the ceaseless hammering of clips frozen solid on doors and hatches.

Leaning against a bulkhead, breathing heavily after the ascent from 'A' magazine, Nicholls looked hopefully at the Captain. Vallery saw the look, interpreted it correctly, and shook his head, smiling.

'Might as well finish it, boy. Only the Capstan Flat. Nobody there anyway, I expect, but we might as well have a look.'

They walked slowly round the heavy machinery in the middle of the Capstan Flat, for'ard past the Battery Room and Sailmaker's Shop, past the Electrical Workshop and cells to the locked door of the Painter's Shop, the most for'ard compartment in the ship.

Vallery reached his hand forward, touched the door symbolically, smiled tiredly and turned away. Passing the cell door, he casually flicked open the inspection port, glanced in perfunctorily and moved on. Then he stopped dead, wheeled round and flung open the inspection port again.

'What in the name of—Ralston! What on earth are you doing here?' he shouted.

Ralston smiled. Even through the thick plate glass it wasn't a pleasant smile and it never touched the blue eyes. He gestured to the barred grille, indicating that he could not hear.

Impatiently, Vallery twisted the grille handle.

'What are you doing here, Ralston?' he demanded. The brows were drawn down heavily over blazing eyes. 'In the cells—and at this time! Speak up, man! Tell me!' Nicholls looked at Vallery in slow surprise. The old man—angry! It was unheard of! Shrewdly, Nicholls decided that he'd rather not be the object of Vallery's fury.

'I was locked up here, sir.' The words were innocuous enough, but their tone said, 'What a damned silly question.' Vallery flushed faintly.

'When?'

'At 1030 this morning, sir.'

'And by whom, may I inquire?'

'By the Master-At-Arms, sir.'

'On what authority?' Vallery demanded furiously.

Ralston looked at him a long moment without speaking. His face was expressionless. 'On yours, sir.'

'Mine!' Vallery was incredulous. 'I didn't tell him to lock you up!'

'You never told him not to,' said Ralston evenly. Vallery winced: the oversight, the lack of consideration was his, and that hurt badly.

'Where's your night Action Station?' he asked sharply.

'Port tubes, sir.' That, Vallery realized, explained why only the starboard crew had been closed up.

'And why—why have you been left here during Action Stations? Don't you know it's forbidden, against all regulations?'

'Yes, sir.' Again the hint of the wintry smile. 'I know. But does the Master-At-Arms know?' He paused a second, smiled again. 'Or maybe he just forgot,' he suggested.

'Hartley!' Vallery was on balance again, his tone level and grim. 'The Master-At-Arms here, immediately: see that he brings his keys!' He broke into a harsh bout of coughing, spat some blood into the towel, looked at Ralston again.

'I'm sorry about this, my boy,' he said slowly. 'Genuinely sorry.'

'How's the tanker?' Ralston asked softly,

'What? What did you say?' Vallery was unprepared for the sudden switch. 'What tanker?'

'The one that was damaged this morning, sir.'

'Still with us.' Vallery was puzzled. 'Still with us, but low in the water. Any special reason for asking?'

'Just interested, sir.' The smile was wry, but this time it was a smile. 'You see—'

He stopped abruptly as a deep, muffled roar crashed through the silent night, the pressure blast listing the *Ulysses* sharply to starboard. Vallery lurched, staggered and would have fallen but for Petersen's sudden arm. He braced himself against the righting roll, looked at Nicholls in sudden dismay. The sound was all too familiar.

Nicholls gazed back at him, sorry to his heart for this fresh burden for a dying man, and nodded slowly, in reluctant agreement with the unspoken thought in Vallery's eyes.

'Afraid you're right, sir. Torpedo. Somebody's stopped a packet.'

'Do you hear there!' The capstan flat speaker was hurried, intense, unnaturally loud in the aftermath of silence. 'Do you hear there! Captain on the bridge: urgent. Captain on the bridge: urgent. Captain on the bridge: urgent . . .'

ELEVEN

Friday Evening

Bent almost double, Captain Vallery clutched the handrail of the port ladder leading up to the fo'c'sle deck. Desperately, he tried to look out over the darkened water, but he could see nothing. A mist, a dark and swirling and roaring mist flecked with blood, a mist shot through with dazzling light swam before his eyes and he was blind. His breath came in great whooping gasps that racked his tortured lungs: his lower ribs were clamped in giant pincers, pincers that were surely crushing him. That stumbling, lurching run from the forepeak, he dimly realized, had all but killed him. Close, too damn close, he thought. I must be more careful in future . . .

Slowly his vision cleared, but the brilliant light remained. Heavens above, Vallery thought, a blind man could have seen all there was to see here. For there was nothing to be seen but the tenebrous silhouette, so faint as to be almost imagined, of a tanker deep, deep in the water—and a great column of flame, hundreds of feet in height, streaking upwards from the heart of the dense mushroom of smoke that obscured the bows of the torpedoed ship. Even at the distance of half a mile, the roaring of the flames was almost intolerable. Vallery watched appalled. Behind him he could hear Nicholls swearing, softly, bitterly, continuously.

Vallery felt Petersen's hand on his arm. 'Does the Captain wish to go up to the bridge?'

'In a moment, Petersen, in a moment. Just hang on.' His mind was functioning again, his eyes, conditioned by forty years' training, automatically sweeping the horizon. Funny, he thought, you can hardly see the tanker—the *Vytura*, it must be—she's shielded by that thick pall of smoke, probably; but the other ships in the convoy, white, ghost-like, sharply etched against the indigo blue of the sky, were bathed in that deadly glare. Even the stars had died.

He became aware that Nicholls was no longer swearing in repetitious monotony, that he was talking to him.

'A tanker, isn't it, sir? Hadn't we better take shelter? Remember what happened to that other one!'

'What one?' Vallery was hardly listening.

'The *Cochella*. A few days ago, I think it was. Good God, no! It was only this morning!'

'When tankers go up, they go up, Nicholls.' Vallery seemed curiously far away. 'If they just burn, they may last long enough. Tankers die hard, terribly hard, my boy: they live where any other ship would sink.'

'But—but she must have a hole the size of a house in her side!' Nicholls protested.

'No odds,' Vallery replied. He seemed to be waiting, watching for something. 'Tremendous reserve buoyancy in these ships. Maybe 27 sealed tanks, not to mention cofferdams, pump-rooms, engine-rooms . . . Never heard of the Nelson device for pumping compressed air into a tanker's oil tanks to give it buoyancy, to keep it afloat? Never heard of Captain Dudley Mason and the *Ohio*? Never heard of . . . ' He broke off suddenly, and when he spoke again the dreaming lethargy of the voice was gone.

'I thought so!' he exclaimed, his voice sharp with excitement. 'I thought so! The *Vytura*'s still under way, still under command! Good God, she must still be going almost 15 knots! The bridge, quick!'

Vallery's feet left the deck, barely touched it again till Petersen set him down carefully on the duckboards in front of the startled Commander. Vallery grinned faintly at Turner's astonishment, at the bushy eyebrows lifting over the dark, lean buccaneer's face, leaner, more recklessly chiselled than ever in the glare of the blazing tanker. If ever a man was born 400 years too late, Vallery thought inconsequentially; but what a man to have around!

'It's all right, Commander.' He laughed shortly. 'Brooks thought I needed a Man Friday. That's Stoker Petersen. Over-enthusiastic, maybe a trifle apt to take orders too literally . . . But he was a Godsend to me tonight . . . But never mind me.' He jerked his thumb towards the tanker, blazing even more whitely now, difficult to look at, almost, as the noonday sun. 'How about him?'

'Makes a bloody fine lighthouse for any German ship or plane that happens to be looking for us,' Turner growled. 'Might as well send a signal to Trondheim giving our lat and long.'

'Exactly,' Vallery nodded. 'Besides setting up some beautiful targets for the sub that got the *Vytura* just now. A dangerous fellow, Commander. That was a brilliant piece of work—in almost total darkness, too.'

'Probably a scuttle somebody forgot to shut. We haven't the ships to keep checking them all the time. And it wasn't so damned brilliant, at least not for him . . . I sent her right away.'

'Good man!' Vallery said warmly. He turned to look at the burning tanker, looked back at Turner, his face set. 'She'll have to go, Commander.'

Turner nodded slowly. 'She'll have to go,' he echoed.

'It *is* the *Vytura*, isn't it?'

'That's her. Same one that caught it this morning.'

'Who's the master?'

'Haven't the foggiest,' Turner confessed. 'Number One, Pilot? Any idea where the sailing list is?'

'No, sir.' The Kapok Kid was hesitant, oddly unsure of himself. 'Admiral had them, I know. Probably gone, now.'

'What makes you think that?' Vallery asked sharply.

'Spicer, his pantry steward was almost choked with smoke this afternoon, found him making a whacking great fire in his bath,' the Kapok Kid said miserably. 'Said he was burning vital documents that must not fall into enemy hands. Old newspapers, mostly, but I think the list must have been among them. It's nowhere else.'

'Poor old . . .' Turner remembered just in time that he was speaking of the Admiral, broke off, shook his head in compassionate wonder. 'Shall I send a signal to Fletcher on the *Cape Hatteras*?'

'Never mind.' Vallery was impatient. 'There's no time. Bentley—to the master, *Vytura*: "Please abandon ship immediately: we are going to sink you."'

Suddenly Vallery stumbled, caught hold of Turner's arm.

'Sorry,' he apologized. 'I'm afraid my legs are going. Gone, rather.' He smiled up wryly at the anxious faces. 'No good pretending any longer, is there? Not when your legs start a mutiny on their own. Oh, dear God, I'm done!'

'And no bloody wonder!' Turner swore. 'I wouldn't treat a mad dog the way you treat yourself! Come on, sir. Admiral's chair for you—now. If you don't, I'll get Petersen to you,' he threatened, as Vallery made to protest. The protest died in a smile, and Vallery meekly allowed himself to be helped into a chair. He sighed deeply, relaxed into the God-sent support of the back and arms of the chair. He felt ghastly, powerless, his wasted body a wide sea of pain, and deadly cold; all these things, but also proud and grateful—Turner had never even suggested that he go below.

He heard the gate crash behind him, the murmur of voices, then Turner was at his side.

'The Master-At-Arms, sir. Did you send for him?'

'I certainly did.' Vallery twisted in his chair, his face grim. 'Come here, Hastings!'

The Master-At-Arms stood at attention before him. As always, his face was a mask, inscrutable, expressionless, almost inhuman in that fierce light.

'Listen carefully.' Vallery had to raise his voice above the roar of the flames: the effort even to speak was exhausting. 'I have no time to talk to you now. I will see you in the morning. Meantime, you will release Leading Seaman Ralston immediately. You will then hand over your duties, your papers and your keys to Regulating Petty Officer Perrat. Twice, now, you have overstepped the limits of your authority: that is insolence, but it can be overlooked. But you have also kept a man locked in cells during Action Stations. The prisoner would have died like a rat in a trap. You are no longer Master-At-Arms of the *Ulysses*. That is all.' For a couple of seconds Hastings stood rigidly in shocked unbelieving silence, then the iron discipline snapped. He stepped forward, arms raised in appeal, the mask collapsed in contorted bewilderment.

'Relieved of my duties? Relieved of my duties! But, sir, you can't do that! You can't . . . '

His voice broke off in a gasp of pain as Turner's iron grip closed over his elbow.

'Don't say "can't" to the Captain,' he whispered silkily in his ear. 'You heard him? Get off the bridge!'

The gate clicked behind him. Carrington said, conversationally: 'Somebody's using his head aboard the *Vytura*—fitted a red filter to his Aldis. Couldn't see it otherwise.'

Immediately the tension eased. All eyes were on the winking red light, a hundred feet aft of the flames, and even then barely distinguishable. Suddenly it stopped.

'What does he say, Bentley?' Vallery asked quickly.

Bentley coughed apologetically. 'Message reads: "Are you hell. Try it and I will ram you. Engine intact. We can make it."'

Vallery closed his eyes for a moment. He was beginning to appreciate how old Giles must have felt. When he looked up again, he made made his decision.

'Signal: "You are endangering entire convoy. Abandon ship at once. Repeat, at once."'He turned to the Commander, his mouth bitter. 'I take off my hat to him. How would you like to sit on top of enough fuel to blow you to Kingdom Come . . . Must be oil in some of his tanks . . . God, how I hate to have to threaten a man like that!'

'I know, sir,' Turner murmured. 'I know how it is . . . Wonder what the *Viking*'s doing out there? Should be hearing from her now?'

'Send a signal,' Vallery ordered. 'Ask for information.' He peered aft, searched briefly for the Torpedo Lieutenant. 'Where's Marshall?'

'Marshall?' Turner was surprised. 'In the Sick Bay, of course. Still on the injured list, remember—four ribs gone?'

'Of course, of course!' Vallery shook his head tiredly, angry with himself. 'And the Chief Torpedo Gunner's Mate—Noyes, isn't it?—he was killed yesterday in Number 3. How about Vickers?'

'He was in the FDR'

'In the FDR,' Vallery repeated slowly. He wondered why his heart didn't stop beating. He was long past the stage of chilled bone and coagulating blood. His whole body was a great block of ice . . . He had never known that such cold could exist. It was very strange, he thought, that he was no longer shivering . . .

'I'll do it myself, sir,' Turner interrupted his wandering. 'I'll take over the bridge Torpedo Control—used to be the worst Torps officer on the China Station.' He smiled faintly. 'Perhaps the hand has not lost what little cunning it ever possessed!'

'Thank you.' Vallery was grateful. 'You just do that.'

'We'll have to take him from starboard,' Turner reminded him. 'Port control was smashed this morning—foremast didn't do it any good . . . I'll go check the Dumaresq[1] . . . Good God!' His hand gripped Vallery's shoulder with a strength that made him wince. 'It's the Admiral, sir! He's coming on the bridge!'

Incredulously, Vallery twisted round in his chair. Turner was right. Tyndall was coming through the gate, heading purposefully towards him. In the deep shadow cast by the side of the bridge, he seemed disembodied. The bare head, sparsely covered with thin, straggling wisps of white, the grey, pitifully-shrunken face, the suddenly stooped shoulders, unaccountably thin under black oilskins, all these were thrown into harsh relief by the flames. Below, nothing was visible. Silently, Tyndall padded his way across the bridge, stood waiting at Vallery's side.

Slowly, leaning on Turner's ready arm, Vallery climbed down. Unsmiling, Tyndall looked at him, nodded gravely, hoisted himself into his seat. He picked up the binoculars from the ledge before him, slowly quartered the horizon.

It was Turner who noticed it first.

'Sir! You've no gloves on, sir!'

'What? What did you say?' Tyndall replaced the glasses, looked incredulously at his bloodstained, bandaged hands. 'Ah! Do you know, I *knew* I had forgotten something. That's the second time.

---

1. The Dumaresq was a miniature plotting table on which such relevant factors as corresponding speeds and courses were worked out to provide firing tracks for the torpedoes.

Thank you, Commander.' He smiled courteously, picked up the binoculars again, resumed his quartering of the horizon. All at once Vallery felt another, deadlier chill pass through him, and it had nothing to do with the bitter chill of the Arctic night.

Turner hesitated helplessly for a second, then turned quickly to the Kapok Kid.

'Pilot! Haven't I seen gauntlets hanging in your charthouse?'

'Yes, sir. Right away!' The Kapok Kid hurried off the bridge.

Turner looked up at the Admiral again.

'Your head, sir—you've nothing on. Wouldn't you like a duffel coat, a hood, sir?'

'A hood?' Tyndall was amused. 'What in the world for? I'm not cold . . . If you'll excuse me, Commander?' He turned the binoculars full into the glare of the blazing *Vytura*. Turner looked at him again, looked at Vallery, hesitated, then walked aft.

Carpenter was on his way back with the gloves when the WT loudspeaker clicked on.

'WT—bridge. WT—bridge. Signal from *Viking*: "Lost contact. Am continuing search."'

'Lost contact!' Vallery exclaimed. Lost contact—the worst possible thing that could have happened! A U-boat out there, loose, unmarked, and the whole of FR77 lit up like a fairground. A fairground, he thought bitterly, clay pipes in a shooting gallery and with about as much chance of hitting back once contact had been lost. Any second now . . .

He wheeled round, clutched at the binnacle for support. He had forgotten how weak he was, how the tilting of the shattered bridge affected balance.

'Bentley! No reply form the *Vytura* yet?'

'No, sir,' Bentley was as concerned as the Captain, as aware of the desperate need for speed. 'Maybe his power's gone—no, no, no, there he is now, sir!'

'Captain, sir.'

Vallery looked round. 'Yes, Commander, what is it? Not more bad news, I hope?'

'Fraid so, sir. Starboard tubes won't train—jammed solid.'

'Won't train,' Vallery snapped irritably. 'That's nothing new, surely. Ice, frozen snow. Chip it off, use boiling water, blowlamps, any old—'

'Sorry, sir.' Turner shook his read regretfully. 'Not that. Rack and turntable buckled. Must have been either the shell that got the bosun's store or Number 3 Lower Power Room—immediately below. Anyway—kaput!'

'Very well, then!' Vallery was impatient. 'It'll have to be the port tubes.'

'No bridge control left, sir,' Turner objected. 'Unless we fire by local control?'

'No reason why not, is there?' Vallery demanded. 'After all, that's what torpedo crews are trained for. Get on to the port tubes—I assume the communication line there is still intact—tell them to stand by.'

'Yes, sir.'

'And Turner?'

'Sir?'

'I'm sorry.' He smiled crookedly. 'As old Giles used to say of himself, I'm just a crusty old curmudgeon. Bear with me, will you?'

Turner grinned sympathetically, then sobered quickly. He jerked his head forward.

'How is he, sir?'

Vallery looked at the Commander for a long second, shook his head, almost imperceptibly. Turner nodded heavily and was gone.

'Well, Bentley? What does he say?'

'Bit confused, sir,' Bentley apologized. 'Couldn't get it all. Says he's going to leave the convoy, proceed on his own. Something like that, sir.'

Proceed on his own! That was no solution, Vallery knew. He might still burn for hours, a dead give-away, even on a different course. But to proceed on his own! An unprotected, crippled, blazing tanker—and a thousand miles to Murmansk, the worst thousand miles in all the world! Vallery closed his eyes. He felt sick to his heart. A man like that, and a ship like that—and he had to destroy them both!

Suddenly Tyndall spoke.

'Port 30!' he ordered. His voice was loud, authoritative. Vallery stiffened in dismay. Port 30! They'd turn into the *Vytura*.

There was a couple of seconds' silence, then Carrington, Officer of the Watch, bent over the speaking-tube, repeated: 'Port 30.' Vallery started forward, stopped short as he saw Carrington gesturing at the speaking-tube. He'd stuffed a gauntlet down the mouthpiece.

'Midships!'

'Midships, sir!'

'Steady! Captain?'

'Sir?'

'That light hurts my eyes,' Tyndall complained. 'Can't we put the fire out?'

'We'll try, sir.' Vallery walked across, spoke softly. 'You look tired, sir. Wouldn't you like to go below?'

'What? Go below! Me!'

'Yes, sir. We'll send for you if we need you,' he added persuasively.

Tyndall considered this for a moment, shook his head grimly.

'Won't do, Dick. Not fair to you . . . ' His voice trailed away and he muttered something that sounded like 'Admiral Tyndall', but Vallery couldn't be sure.

'Sir? I didn't catch—'

'Nothing!' Tyndall was very abrupt. He looked away towards the *Vytura*, exclaimed in sudden pain, flung up an arm to protect his eyes. Vallery, too, started back, eyes screwed up to shut out the sudden blinding flash of flame from the *Vytura*.

The explosion crashed in their ears almost simultaneously, the blast of the pressure wave sent them reeling. The *Vytura* had been torpedoed again, right aft, close to her engine-room, and was heavily on fire there. Only the bridge island, amidships, was miraculously free from smoke and flames. Even in the moment of shock, Vallery thought, 'She must go now. She can't last much longer.' But he knew he was deluding himself, trying to avoid the inevitable, the decision he must take. Tankers, as he'd told Nicholls, died hard, terribly hard. Poor old Giles, he thought unaccountably, poor old Giles.

He moved aft to the port gate. Turner was shouting angrily into the telephone.

'You'll damn well do what you're told, do you hear? Get them out immediately! Yes, I said "immediately"!'

Vallery touched his arm in surprise. 'What's the matter, Commander?'

'Of all the bloody insolence!' Turner snorted. 'Telling *me* what to do!'

'Who?'

'The LTO on the tubes. Your friend Ralston!' said Turner wrathfully.

'Ralston! Of course!' Vallery remembered now. 'He told me that was his night Action Stations. What's wrong?'

'What's wrong: Says he doesn't think he can do it. Doesn't like to, doesn't wish to do it, if you please. Blasted insubordination!' Turner fumed.

Vallery blinked at him. 'Ralston—are you sure? But of course you are . . . That boy's been through a very private hell, Turner. Do you think—'

'I don't know what to think!' Turner lifted the phone again. 'Tubes nine-oh? At last! . . . What? What did you say? . . . Why don't we . . . Gunfire! Gunfire!' He hung up the receiver with a crash, swung round on Vallery.

'Asks me, pleads with me, for gunfire instead of torpedoes! He's mad, he must be! But mad or not, I'm going down there to knock some sense into that mutinous young devil!' Turner was angrier than Vallery had ever seen him. 'Can you get Carrington to man this phone, sir?'

'Yes, yes, of course!' Vallery himself had caught up some of Turner's anger. 'Whatever his sentiments, this is no time to express them!' he snapped. 'Straighten him up . . . Maybe I've been too lenient, too easy, perhaps he thinks we're in his debt, at some psychological disadvantage, for the shabby treatment he's received . . . All right, all right, Commander!' Turner's mounting impatience was all to evident. 'Off you go. Going in to attack in three or four minutes.' He turned abruptly, passed in to the compass platform.

'Bentley!'

'Sir?'

'Last signal—'

'Better have a look, sir,' Carrington interrupted. 'He's slowing up.'

Vallery stepped forward, peered over the windscreen. The *Vytura*, a roaring mass of flames was falling rapidly astern.

'Clearing the davits, sir!' the Kapok Kid reported excitedly. 'I think—yes, yes, I can see the boat coming down!'

'Thank God for that!' Vallery whispered. He felt as though he had been granted a new lease of life. Head bowed, he clutched the screen with both hands—reaction had left him desperately weak. After a few seconds he looked up.

'WT code signal to *Sirrus*,' he ordered quietly. '"Circle well astern. Pick up survivors from the *Vytura*'s lifeboat."'

He caught Carrington's quick look and shrugged. 'It's a better than even risk, Number One, so to hell with Admiralty orders. God,' he added with sudden bitterness, 'wouldn't I love to see a boatload of the "no-survivors-will-be-picked-up" Whitehall warriors drifting about in the Barents Sea!' He turned away, caught sight of Nicholls and Petersen.

'Still here, are you, Nicholls? Hadn't you better get below?'

'If you wish, sir.' Nicholls hesitated, nodded forward towards Tyndall.

'I thought, perhaps—'

'Perhaps you're right, perhaps you're right.' Vallery shook his head in weary perplexity. 'We'll see. Just wait a bit, will you?' He raised his voice. 'Pilot!'

'Sir?'

'Slow ahead both!'

'Slow ahead both, sir!'

Gradually, then more quickly, way fell off the *Ulysses* and she dropped slowly astern of the convoy. Soon, even the last ships in the lines were ahead of her, thrashing their way to the north-east. The snow was falling more thickly now, but still the ships were bathed in that savage glare, frighteningly vulnerable in their naked helplessness.

Seething with anger, Turner brought up short at the port torpedoes. The tubes were out, their evil, gaping mouths, highlighted by the great flames, pointing out over the intermittent refulgence of the rolling swell. Ralston, perched high on the unprotected control position above the central tube, caught his eye at once.

'Ralston!' Turner's voice was harsh, imperious. 'I want to speak to you!'

Ralston turned round quickly, rose, jumped on to the deck. He stood facing the Commander. They were of a height, their eyes on a level, Ralston's still, blue, troubled, Turner's dark and stormy with anger.

'What the hell's the matter with you, Ralston?' Turner ground out. 'Refusing to obey orders, is that it?'

'No, sir.' Ralston's voice was quiet, curiously strained. 'That's not true.'

'Not true!' Turner's eyes were narrowed, his fury barely in check. 'Then what's all this bloody claptrap about not wanting to man the tubes? Are you thinking of emulating Stoker Riley? Or have you just taken leave of your senses—if any?'

Ralston said nothing.

The silence, a silence all too easily interpreted as dumb insolence, infuriated Turner. His powerful hands reached out, grasped Ralston's duffel coat. He pulled the rating towards him, thrust his face close to the other's.

'I asked a question, Ralston,' he said softly. 'I haven't had an answer. I'm waiting. What *is* all this?'

'Nothing, sir.' Distress in his eyes, perhaps, but no fear. 'I—I just don't want to, sir. I hate to do it—to send one of our own ships to the bottom!' The voice was pleading now, blurred with overtones of desperation: Turner was deaf to them. 'Why does she have to go, sir!' he cried. 'Why? Why? Why?'

'None of your bloody business—but as it so happens she's endangering the entire convoy!' Turner's face was still within inches of Ralston's. 'You've got a job to do, orders to obey. Just get up there and obey them! Go on!' he roared, as Ralston hesitated. 'Get up there!' He fairly spat the words out.

Ralston didn't move.

'There are other LTOs, sir!' His arms lifted high in appeal, something in the voice cut through Turner's blind anger: he realized, almost with shock, that this boy was desperate. 'Couldn't *they*—?'

'Let someone else do the dirty work, eh? That's what you mean, isn't it?' Turner was bitingly contemptuous. 'Get them to do what you won't do yourself, you—you contemptible young bastard! Communications Number? Give me your set. I'll take over from the bridge.' He took the phone, watched Ralston climb slowly back up and sit hunched forward, head bent over the Dumaresq.

'Number One? Commander speaking. All set here. Captain there?'

'Yes, sir. I'll call him.' Carrington put down the phone, walked through the gate.

'Captain, sir. Commander's on the—'

'Just a moment!' The upraised hand, the tenseness of the voice stopped him. 'Have a look, No. 1. What do you think?' Vallery pointed towards the *Vytura*, past the oil-skinned figure of the Admiral. Tyndall's head was sunk on his chest, and he was muttering incoherently to himself.

Carrington followed the pointing finger. The lifeboat, dimly visible through the thickening snow, had slipped her falls while the *Vytura* was still under way. Crammed with men, she was dropping quickly astern under the great twisting column of flame—dropping far too quickly astern as the First Lieutenant suddenly realized. He turned round, found Vallery's eyes, bleak and tired and old, on his own. Carrington nodded slowly.

'She's picking up, sir. Under way, under comand . . . What are you going to do, sir?

'God help me, I've no choice. Nothing from the *Viking*, nothing from the *Sirrus*, nothing from our Asdic—and that U-boat's still out there . . . Tell Turner what's happened. Bentley!'

'Sir?'

'Signal the *Vytura*.' The mouth, whitely compressed, belied the eyes—eyes dark and filled with pain. '"Abandon ship. Torpedoing you in three minutes. Last signal." Port 20, Pilot!'

'Port 20 it is, sir.'

The *Vytura* was breaking off tangentially, heading north. Slowly, the *Ulysses* came round, almost paralleling her course, now a little astern of her.

'Half-ahead, Pilot!'

'Half-ahead it is, sir.'

'Pilot!'

'Sir?'

'What's Admiral Tyndall saying? Can you make it out?'

Carpenter bent forward, listened, shook his head. Little flurries of snow fell off his fur helmet.

'Sorry, sir. Can't make him out—too much noise from the *Vytura* . . . I think he's humming, sir.'

'Oh, God!' Vallery bent his head, looked up again, slowly, painfully. Even so slight an effort was labour intolerable.

He looked across to the *Vytura*, stiffened to attention. The red Aldis was winking again. He tried to read it, but it was too fast: or perhaps his eyes were just too old, or tired: or perhaps he just couldn't think any more . . . There was something weirdly hypnotic about that tiny crimson light flickering between these fantastic curtains of flame, curtains sweeping slowly, ominously together, majestic in their inevitability. And then the little red light had died, so unexpectedly, so abruptly, that Bentley's voice reached him before the realization.

'Signal from the *Vytura*, sir.'

Vallery tightened his grip on the binnacle. Bentley guessed the nod, rather than saw it.

'Message reads: "Why don't you—off. Nuts to the Senior Service. Tell him I send all my love."' The voice died softly away, and there was only the roaring of the flames, the lost pinging of the Asdic.

'All my love.' Vallery shook his head in silent wonderment. 'All my love! He's crazy! He must be. "All my love," and I'm going to destroy him . . . Number One!'

'Sir?'

'Tell the Commander to stand by!'

Turner repeated the message from the bridge, turned to Ralston.

'Stand by, LTO!' He looked out over the side, saw that the *Vytura* was slightly ahead now, that the *Ulysses* was still angling in on an interception course. 'About two minutes now, I should say.' He felt the vibration beneath his feet dying away, knew the *Ulysses* was slowing down. Any second now, and she'd start slewing away to starboard. The receiver crackled again in his ear, the sound barely audible above the roaring of the flames. He listened, looked up. '"X" and "Y" only. Medium settings. Target 11 knots.' He spoke into the phone. 'How long?'

'How long, sir?' Carrington repeated.

'Ninety seconds,' Vallery said huskily. 'Pilot—starboard 10.' He jumped, startled, as he heard the crash of falling binoculars, saw the Admiral slump forward, face and neck striking cruelly on the edge of the windscreen, the arms dangling loosely from the shoulders.

'Pilot!'

But the Kapok Kid was already there. He slipped an arm under Tyndall, took most of the dead weight off the biting edge of the screen.

'What's the matter, sir?' His voice was urgent, blurred with anxiety. 'What's wrong?'

Tyndall stirred slightly, his cheek lying along the edge of the screen.

'Cold, cold, cold,' he intoned. The quavering tones were those of an old, a very old man.

'What? What did you say, sir?' the Kapok Kid begged.

'Cold. I'm cold. I'm terribly cold! My feet, my feet!' The old voice wandered away, and the body slipped into a corner of the bridge, the grey face upturned to the falling snow.

Intuition, an intuition amounting to a sudden sick certainty, sent the Kapok Kid plunging to his knees. Vallery heard the muffled exclamation, saw him straighten up and swing round, his face blank with horror.

'He's—he's got nothing on, sir,' he said unsteadily. 'He's barefoot! They're frozen—frozen solid!'

'Barefoot?' Vallery repeated unbelievingly. 'Barefoot! It's not possible!'

'And pyjamas, sir! That's all he's wearing!'

Vallery lurched forward, peeling off his gloves. He reached down, felt his stomach turn over in shocked nausea as his fingers closed on ice-chilled skin. Bare feet! And pyjamas! Bare feet—no wonder he'd padded so silently across the duckboards! Numbly, he remembered that the last temperature reading had shown 35° of frost. And Tyndall, feet caked in frozen snow and slush, had been sitting there for almost five minutes! . . . He felt great hands under his armpits, felt himself rising effortlessly to his feet. Petersen. It *could* only be Petersen, of course. And Nicholls behind him.

'Leave this to me, sir. Right, Petersen, take him below.' Nicholls's brisk, assured voice, the voice of a man competent in his own element, steadied Vallery, brought him back to the present, and the demands of the present, more surely than anything else could have done. He became aware of Carrington's clipped, measured voice, reeling off course, speed, directions, saw the *Vytura* 50° off the port bow, dropping slowly, steadily aft. Even at that distance, the blast of heat was barely tolerable—what in the name of heaven was it like on the bridge of the *Vytura*?

'Set course, Number One,' he called. 'Local control.'

'Set course, local control.' Carrington might have been on a peace-time exercise in the Solent.

'Local control,' Turner repeated. He hung up the set, looked round. 'You're on your own, Ralston,' he said softly.

There was no reply. The crouched figure on the control position, immobile as graved stone, gave no sign that he had heard.

'Thirty seconds!' Turner said sharply. 'All lined up?'

'Yes, sir.' The figure stirred. 'All lined up.' Suddenly, he swung round, in desperate, final appeal. 'For God's sake, sir! Is there no other—'

'Twenty seconds!' Turner said viciously. 'Do you want a thousand lives on your lily-livered conscience? And if you miss . . . '

Ralston swung slowly back. For a mere breath of time, his face was caught full in the harsh glare of the *Vytura*: with sudden shock, Turner saw that the eyes were masked with tears. Then he saw the lips move. 'Don't worry, sir. I won't miss.' The voice was quite toneless, heavy with nameless defeat.

Perplexed, now, rather than angry, and quite uncomprehending, Turner saw the left sleeve come up to brush the eyes, saw the right hand stretch forward, close round the grip of 'X' firing lever. Incongruously, there sprang to Turner's mind the famous line of Chaucer, 'In goon the spears full sadly in arrest.' In the closing of that hand there was the same heart-stopping decision, the same irrevocable finality.

Suddenly, so suddenly that Turner started in spite of himself, the hand jerked convulsively back. He heard the click of the tripping lever, the muffled roar in the explosion chamber, the hiss of compressed air, and the torpedo was gone, its evil sleekness gleaming fractionally in the light of the flames before it crashed below the surface of the sea. It was hardly gone before the tubes shuddered again and the second torpedo was on its way.

For five, ten seconds Turner stared out, fascinated, watching the arrowing wakes of bubbles vanish in the distance. A total of 1,500 lbs of Amatol in these warheads—God help the poor bastards aboard the *Vytura* . . . The deck speaker clicked on.

'Do you hear there? Do you hear there? Take cover immediately! Take cover—immediately!' Turner stirred, tore his eyes away from the sea, looked up, saw that Ralston was still crouched in his seat.

'Come down out of there, you young fool!' he shouted. 'Want to be riddled when the *Vytura* goes up? Do you hear me?'

Silence. No word, no movement, only the roaring of the flames.

'Ralston!'

'I'm all right, sir.' Ralston's voice was muffled: he did not even trouble to turn his head.

Turner swore, leapt up on the tubes, dragged Ralston from his seat, pulled him down to the deck and into shelter. Ralston offered no resistance: he seemed sunk in a vast apathy, an uncaring indifference.

Both torpedoes struck home. The end was swift, curiously unspectacular. Listeners—there were no watchers—on the *Ulysses* tensed themselves for the shattering detonation, but the detonation never came. Broken-backed and tired of fighting, the *Vytura* simply collapsed in on her stricken mid-ships, lay gradually, wearily over on her side and was gone.

Three minutes later, Turner opened the door of the Captain's shelter, pushed Ralston in before him.

'Here you are, sir,' he said grimly. Thought you might like to see what a conscientious objector looks like!'

'I certainly do!' Vallery laid down the log-book, turned a cold eye on the torpedoman, looked him slowly up and down. 'A fine job, Ralston, but it doesn't excuse your conduct. Just a minute, Commander.'

He turned back to the Kapok Kid. 'Yes, that seems all right, Pilot. It'll make good reading for their lordships,' he added bitterly. 'The ones the Germans don't get, we finish off for them . . . Remember to signal the *Hatteras* in the morning, ask for the name of the master of the *Vytura*.'

'He's dead . . . You needn't trouble yourself!' said Ralston bitterly, then staggered as the Commander's open hand smashed across his face. Turner was breathing heavily, his eyes dark with anger.

'You insolent young devil!' he said softly. 'That was just a little too much from you.'

Ralston's hand came up slowly, fingering the reddening weal on his cheek.

'You misunderstand me, sir.' There was no anger, the voice was a fading murmur, they had to strain to catch his words. 'The master of the *Vytura*—I can tell you his name. It's Ralston. Captain Michael Ralston. He was my father.'

TWELVE

Saturday

To all things an end, to every night its dawn; even to the longest night when dawn never comes, there comes at last the dawn. And so it came for FR77, as grey, as bitter, as hopeless as the night had been long. But it came.

It came to find the convoy some 350 miles north of the Arctic Circle, steaming due east along the 72nd parallel of latitude, halfway between Jan Mayen and the North Cape. 8° 45′ east, the Kapok Kid reckoned, but he couldn't be sure. In heavy snow and with ten-tenth cloud, he was relying on dead reckoning: he had to, for the shell that had destroyed the FDR had wrecked the Automatic Pilot. But roughly 600 nautical miles to go. 600 miles, 40 hours, and the convoy—or what would be left of it by that time—would be in the Kola Inlet, steaming up-river to Polyarnoe and Murmansk . . . 40 hours.

It came to find the convoy—14 ships left in all—scattered over three square miles of sea and rolling heavily in the deepening swell from the NNE: 14 ships, for another had gone in the deepest part of the night. Mine, torpedo? Nobody knew, nobody ever would know. The *Sirrus* had stopped, searched the area for an hour with hooded ten-inch signalling lamps. There had been no survivors. Not that Commander Orr had expected to find any—not with the air temperature 6° below zero.

It came after a sleepless night of never-ending alarms, of continual Asdic contacts, of constant depth-charging that achieved nothing. Nothing, that is, from the escorts' point of view: but for the enemy, it achieved a double-edged victory. It kept exhausted men at Action Stations all night long, blunting, irreparably perhaps, the last vestiges of the knife-edged vigilance on which the only hope—it was never more—of survival in the Arctic depended. More deadly still, it had emptied the last depth-charge rack in the convoy . . . It was a measure of the intensity of the attack, of the relentlessness of the persecution, that this had never happened before. But it had happened now. There was not a single depth-charge left—not one. The fangs were drawn, the defences were down. It was only a matter of time before the wolf-packs discovered that they could strike at will . . .

And with the dawn, of course, came dawn Action Stations, or what would have been dawn stations had the men not already been closed up for fifteen hours, fifteen endless hours of intense cold and suffering, fifteen hours during which the crew of the *Ulysses* had been sustained by cocoa and one bully-beef sandwich, thin, sliced and stale, for there had been no time to bake the previous day. But dawn stations were profoundly significant in themselves: they prolonged the waiting another interminable two hours—and to a man rocking on his feet from unimaginable fatigue, literally holding convulsively jerking eyelids apart with finger and thumb while a starving brain, which is less a brain than a well of fine-drawn agony, begs him to let go, let go just for a second, just this once and never again, even a minute is brutal eternity: and they were still more important in that they were recognized as the Ithuriel hour of the Russian Convoys, the testing time when every man stood out clearly for what he was. And for the crew of a mutiny ship, for men already tried and condemned, for physically broken and mentally scourged men who neither could nor would ever be the same again in body or mind, the men of the *Ulysses* had no need to stand in shame. Not all, of course, they were only human; but many had found, or were finding, that the point of no return was not necessarily the edge of the precipice: it could be the bottom of the valley, the beginning of the long climb up the far slope, and when a man had once begun that climb he never looked back to that other side.

For some men, neither precipice nor valley ever existed. Men like

Carrington, for instance. Eighteen consecutive hours on the bridge now, he was still his own indestructible self, alert with that relaxed watchfulness that never flagged, a man of infinite endurance, a man who could never crack, who you knew could never crack, for the imagination baulked at the very idea. Why he was what he was, no man could tell. Such, too, were men like Chief Petty Officer Hartley, like Chief Stoker Hendry, like Colour-Sergeant Evans and Sergeant MacIntosh; four men strangely alike, big, tough, kindly, no longer young, steeped in the traditions of the Service. Taciturn, never heard to speak of themselves, they were under no illusions as to their importance: they knew—as any Naval Officer would be the first to admit—that, as the senior NCOs, they, and not any officer, were the backbone of the Royal Navy; and it was from their heavy sense of responsibility that sprung their rock-like stability. And then, of course, there were men—a handful only—like Turner and the Kapok Kid and Dodson, whom dawn found as men above themselves, men revelling in danger and exhaustion, for only thus could they realize themselves, for only this had they been born. And finally, men like Vallery, who had collapsed just after midnight, and was still asleep in the shelter, and Surgeon Commander Brooks: wisdom was their sheet anchor, a clear appreciation of the relative insignificance both of themselves and the fate of FR77, a coldly intellectual appraisal of, married to an infinite compassion for, the follies and suffering of mankind.

At the other end of the scale, dawn found men—a few dozen, perhaps—gone beyond recovery. Gone in selfishness, in self-pity and in fear, like Carslake, gone because their armour, the trappings of authority, had been stripped off them, like Hastings, or gone, like Leading SBA Johnson and a score of others, because they had been pushed too far and had no sheet anchor to hold them.

And between the two extremes were those—the bulk of the men—who had touched zero and found that endurance can be infinite—and found in this realization the springboard for recovery. The other side of the valley *could* be climbed, but not without a staff. For Nicholls, tired beyond words from a long night standing braced against the operating table in the surgery, the staff was pride and shame. For Leading Seaman Doyle, crouched miserably into the shelter of the for'ard funnel, watching the pinched agony, the perpetual shivering of his young midships pom-pom crew, it was pity; he would, of course, have denied this, blasphemously. For young Spicer, Tyndall's devoted pantryboy, it was pity, too—pity and a savage grief for the dying man in the Admiral's cabin. Even with both legs amputated below the knee, Tyndall should not have been dying. But the fight, the resistance was gone, and Brooks knew old Giles would be glad to go. And for scores, perhaps for hundreds, for men like the tubercular-ridden McQuater, chilled to death in sodden clothes, but no longer staggering drunkenly round the hoist in 'Y' turret, for the heavy rolling kept the water on the move: like Petersen, recklessly squandering his giant strength in helping his exhausted mates: like Chrysler, whose keen young eyes, invaluable now that Radar was gone, never ceased to scan the horizons: for men like these, the staff was Vallery, the tremendous respect and affection in which he was held, the sure knowledge that they could never let him down.

These, then, were the staffs, the intangible sheet anchors that held the *Ulysses* together that bleak and bitter dawn—pride, pity, shame, affection, grief—and the basic instinct for self-preservation although the last, by now, was an almost negligible factor. Two things were never taken into the slightest account as the springs of endurance: never mentioned, never even considered, they did not exist for the crew of the *Ulysses*: two things the sentimentalists at home, the gallant leader writers of the popular press, the propagandizing purveyors of nationalistic claptrap would have had the world believe to be the source of inspiration and endurance—hatred of the enemy, love of kinsfolk and country.

There was no hatred of the enemy. Knowledge is the prelude to hate, and they did not know the enemy. Men cursed the enemy, respected him, feared him and killed him if they could: if they didn't, the enemy would kill them. Nor did men see themselves as fighting for King and country: they saw the necessity for war, but objected to camouflaging this necessity under a spurious cloak of perfervid patriotism: they were just doing what they were told, and if they didn't, they would be stuck against a wall and shot. Love of kinsfolk—that had some validity, but not much. It was natural to want to protect your kin, but this was an equation where the validity varied according to the factor of distance. It was a trifle difficult for a man crouched in his ice-coated Oerlikon cockpit off the shores of Bear Island to visualize himself as protecting that rose-covered cottage in the Cotswolds . . . But for the rest, the synthetic national hatreds and the carefully cherished myth of King and country; these are nothing and less than nothing when mankind stands at the last frontier of hope and endurance: for only the basic, simple human emotions, the positive ones of love and grief and pity and distress, can carry a man across that last frontier.

Noon, and still the convoy, closed up in tight formation now, rolled eastwards in the blinding snow. The alarm halfway through dawn stations had been the last that morning. Thirty-six hours to go, now, only thirty-six hours. And if this weather continued, the strong wind and blinding snow that made flying impossible, the near-zero visibility and heavy seas that would blind any periscope . . . there was always that chance. Only thirty-six hours.

Admiral John Tyndall died a few minutes after noon. Brooks, who had sat with him all morning, officially entered the cause of death as 'postoperative shock and exposure.' The truth was that Giles had died because he no longer wished to live. His professional reputation was gone: his faith, his confidence in himself were gone, and there was only remorse for the hundreds of men who had died: and with both legs gone, the only life he had ever known, the life he had so loved and cherished and to which he had devoted forty-five glad and unsparing years, that life, too, was gone for ever. Giles died gladly, willingly. Just on noon he recovered consciousness, looked at Brooks and Vallery with a smile from which every trace of madness had vanished. Brooks winced at that grey smile, mocking shadow of the famous guffaw of the Giles of another day. Then he closed his eyes and muttered something about his family—Brooks knew he had no family. His eyes opened again, he saw Vallery as if for the first time, rolled his eyes till he saw Spicer. 'A chair for the Captain, my boy.' Then he died.

He was buried at two o'clock, in the heart of a blizzard. The Captain's voice, reading the burial service, was shredded away by snow and wind: the Union flag was flapping emptily on the tilted board before the men knew he was gone: the bugle notes were broken and distant and lost, far away and fading like the horns of Elfland: and then the men, two hundred of them at least, turned silently away and trudged back to their frozen mess-decks.

Barely half an hour later, the blizzard had died, vanished as suddenly as it had come. The wind, too, had eased, and though the sky was still dark and heavy with snow, though the seas were still heavy enough to roll 15,000-ton ships through a 30° arc, it was clear that the deterioration in the weather had stopped. On the bridge, in the turrets, in the mess-decks, men avoided each other's eyes and said nothing.

Just before 1500, the *Vectra* picked up an Asdic contact. Vallery received the report, hesitated over his decision. If he sent the *Vectra* to investigate, and if the *Vectra* located the U-boat accurately and confined herself, as she would have to do, to describing tight circles above the submarine, the reason for this freedom from depth-charging would occur to the U-boat captain within minutes. And then it would only be a matter of time—until he decided it was safe to surface and use his radio—that every U-boat north of the Circle would know that FR77 could be attacked with impunity. Further, it was unlikely that any torpedo attack would be made under such weather conditions. Not only was periscope observation almost impossible in the heavy seas, but the U-boat itself would be a most unstable firing platform: wave motion is not confined to the surface of the water—the effects can be highly uncomfortable and unstabilizing thirty, forty, fifty feet down—and are appreciable, under extreme conditions, at a depth of almost a hundred feet. On the other hand, the U-boat captain might take a 1,000-1 chance, might strike home with a lucky hit. Vallery ordered the *Vectra* to investigate.

He was too late. The order would have been too late anyway. The *Vectra* was still winking acknowledgement of the signal, had not begun to turn, when the rumble of a heavy explosion reached the bridge of the *Ulysses*. All eyes swept round a full circle of the horizon, searching for smoke and flame, for the canted deck and slewing ship that would show where the torpedo had gone home. They found no sign, none whatsoever, until almost half a minute had passed. Then they noticed, almost casually, that the *Electra*, leading ship in the starboard line, was slowing up, coming to a powerless stop, already settling in the water on an even keel, with no trace of tilt either for'ard or aft. Almost certainly, she had been holed in the engine-room.

The Aldis on the *Sirrus* had begun to flash. Bentley read the message, turned to Vallery.

'Commander Orr requests permission to go alongside, port side, take off survivors.'

'Port, is it?' Turner nodded. 'The sub's blind side. It's a fair chance, sir—in a calm sea. As it is . . . ' He looked over at the *Sirrus*, rolling heavily in the beam sea, and shrugged. 'Won't do her paintwork any good.'

'Her cargo?' Vallery asked. 'Any idea? Explosive?' He looked round, saw the mute headshakes, turned to Bentley.

'Ask *Electra* if she's carrying any explosives as cargo.'

Bentley's Aldis chattered, fell silent. After half a minute, it was clear that there was going to be no reply.

'Power gone, perhaps, or his Aldis smashed,' the Kapok Kid ventured. 'How about one flag for explosive, two for none?'

Vallery nodded in satisfaction. 'You heard, Bentley?'

He looked over the starboard quarter as the message went out. The *Vectra* was almost a mile distant, rolling one minute, pitching the next as she came round in a tight circle. She had found the killer—and her depth-charge racks were empty.

Vallery swung back, looked across to the *Electra*. Still no reply, nothing . . . Then he saw two flags fluttering up to the yardarm.

'Signal the *Sirrus*,' he ordered. '"Go ahead: exercise extreme care."'

Suddenly he felt Turner's hand on his arm.

'Can you hear 'em?' Turner asked.

'Hear what?' Vallery demanded.

'Lord only knows. It's the *Vectra*. Look!'

Vallery followed the pointing finger. At first, he could see nothing, then all at once he saw little geysers of water leaping up in the *Vectra*'s wake, geysers swiftly extinguished by the heavy seas. Then, faintly, his straining ear caught the faraway murmur of underwater explosions, all but inaudible against the wind.

'What the devil's the *Vectra* doing?' Vallery demanded. 'And what's she using?'

'Looks like fireworks to me,' Turner grunted. 'What do you think, Number One?'

'Scuttling charges—25-pounders,' Carrington said briefly.

'He's right, sir,' Turner admitted. 'Of course that's what they are. Mind you, he might as well be using fireworks,' he added disparagingly.

But the Commander was wrong. A scuttling charge has less than a tenth part of the disruptive power of a depth-charge—but one lodged snugly in the conning-tower or exploding alongside a steering plane could be almost as lethal. Turner had hardly finished speaking when a U-boat—the first the *Ulysses* had seen above water for almost six months—porpoised high above the surface of the sea, hung there for two or three seconds, then crashed down on even keel, wallowing wickedly in the troughs between the waves.

The dramatic abruptness of her appearance—one moment the empty sea, the next a U-boat rolling in full view of the entire convoy—took every ship by surprise—including the *Vectra*. She was caught on the wrong foot, moving away on the outer leg of a figure-of-eight turn. Her pom-pom opened up immediately, but the pom-pom, a notoriously inaccurate gun in the best of circumstances, is a hopeless proposition on the rolling, heeling deck of a destroyer making a fast turn in heavy weather: the Oerlikons registered a couple of hits on the conning-tower, twin Lewises peppered the hull with as much effect as a horde of angry hornets; but by the time the *Vectra* was round, her main armament coming to bear, the U-boat had disappeared slowly under the surface.

In spite of this, the *Vectra*'s 4.7s opened up, firing into the sea where the U-boat had submerged, but stopping almost immediately when two shells in succession had ricocheted off the water and whistled dangerously through the convoy. She steadied on course, raced over the position of the submerged U-boat: watchers on the *Ulysses*, binoculars to their eyes, could just distinguish duffel-coated figures on the *Vectra*'s poop-deck hurling more scuttling charges over the side. Almost at once, the *Vectra*'s helm went hard over and she clawed her way back south again, guns at maximum depression pointing down over her starboard side.

The U-boat must have been damaged, more severely this time, by either the shells or the last charges. Again she surfaced, even more violently than before, in a seething welter of foam, and again the Vectra was caught on the wrong foot, for the submarine had surfaced off her port bow, three cable-lengths away.

And this time, the U-boat was up to stay. Whatever Captain and crew lacked, it wasn't courage. The hatch was open, and men were swarming over the side of the conning-tower to man the gun, in a token gesture of defiance against crushing odds.

The first two men over the side never reached the gun—breaking, sweeping waves, waves that towered high above the submarine's deck, washed them over the side and they were gone. But others flung themselves forward to take their place, frantically training their gun through a 90° arc to bear on the onrushing bows of the *Vectra*. Incredibly—for the seas were washing over the decks, seas which kept tearing the men from their posts, and the submarine was rolling with impossible speed and violence—their first shell, fired over open sights, smashed squarely into the bridge of the *Vectra*. The first shell and the last shell, for the crew suddenly crumpled and died, sinking down by the gun or pitching convulsively over the side.

It was a massacre. The *Vectra* had two Bolton-Paul Defiant night-fighter turrets, quadruple hydraulic turrets complete with astrodome, bolted to her fo'c'sle, and these had opened up simultaneously, firing, between them, something like a fantastic total of 300 shells every ten seconds. That often misused cliché 'hail of lead' was completely accurate here. It was impossible for a man to live two seconds on the exposed deck of that U-boat, to hope to escape that lethal storm. Man after man kept flinging himself over the coaming in suicidal gallantry, but none reached the gun.

Afterwards, no one aboard the *Ulysses* could say when they first realized that the *Vectra*, pitching steeply through the heavy seas, was going to ram the U-boat. Perhaps her Captain had never intended to do so. Perhaps he had expected the U-boat to submerge, had intended to carry away conning-tower and periscope standard, to make sure that she could not escape again. Perhaps he had been killed when that shell struck the bridge. Or perhaps he had changed his mind at the last second, for the *Vectra*, which had been arrowing in on the conning-tower, suddenly slewed sharply to starboard.

For an instant, it seemed that she might just clear the U-boat's bows, but the hope died the second it was born. Plunging heavily down the sheering side of a gaping trough, the *Vectra*'s forefoot smashed down and through the hull of the submarine, some thirty feet aft of the bows, slicing through the toughened steel of the pressure hull as if it were cardboard. She was still plunging, still driving down, when two shattering explosions, so close together as to be blurred into one giant blast, completely buried both vessels under a skyrocketing mushroom of boiling water and twisted steel. The why of the explosion was pure conjecture; but what had happened was plain enough. Some freak of chance must have triggered off the TNT—normally an extremely stable and inert disruptive—in a warhead in one of the U-boat's tubes: and then the torpedoes in the storage racks behind and possibly, probably even, the for'ard magazine of the *Vectra* had gone up in sympathetic detonation.

Slowly, deliberately almost, the great clouds of water fell back into the sea, and the *Vectra* and the U-boat—or what little was left of them—came abruptly into view. To the watchers on the *Ulysses*, it was inconceivable that either of them should still be afloat. The U-boat was very deep in the water, seemed to end abruptly just for'ards of the gun platform: the *Vectra* looked as if some great knife had sheared her athwartships, just for'ard of the bridge. The rest was gone, utterly gone. And throughout the convoy unbelieving minds were still wildly rejecting the evidence of their eyes when the shattered hull of the *Vectra* lurched into the same trough as the

U-boat, rolled heavily, wearily, over on top of her, bridge and mast cradling the conning-tower of the submarine. And then the water closed over them and they were gone, locked together to the bottom of the sea.

The last ships in the convoy were two miles away now, and in the broken seas, at that distance, it was impossible to see whether there were any survivors. It did not seem likely. And if there were, if there were men over there, struggling, swimming, shouting for help in the murderous cold of that glacial sea, they would be dying already. And they would have been dead long before any rescue ship could even have turned round. The convoy streamed on, beating steadily east. All but two, that is—the *Electra* and the *Sirrus*.

The *Electra* lay beam on to the seas, rolling slowly, sluggishly, dead in the water. She had now a list of almost 15° to port. Her decks, fore and aft of the bridge, were lined with waiting men. They had given up their attempt to abandon ship by lifeboat when they had seen the *Sirrus* rolling up behind them, fine on the port quarter. A boat had been swung out on its davits, and with the listing of the *Electra* and the rolling of the sea it had proved impossible to recover it. It hung now far out from the ship's side, swinging wildly at the end of its davits about twenty feet above the sea. On his approach, Orr had twice sent angry signals, asking the falls to be cut. But the lifeboat remained there, a menacing pendulum in the track of the *Sirrus*: panic, possibly, but more likely winch brakes jammed solid with ice. In either event, there was no time to be lost: another ten minutes and the *Electra* would be gone.

The *Sirrus* made two runs past in all—Orr had no intention of stopping alongside, of being trampled under by the 15,000-ton deadweight of a toppling freighter. On his first run he steamed slowly by at five knots, at a distance of twenty feet—the nearest he dared go with the set of the sea rolling both ships towards each other at the same instant.

As the *Sirrus*'s swinging bows slid up past the bridge of the *Electra*, the waiting men began to jump. They jumped as the *Sirrus*'s fo'c'sle reared up level with their deck, they jumped as it plunged down fifteen, twenty feet below. One man carrying a suitcase and Burberry stepped nonchalantly across both sets of guard-rails during the split second that they were relatively motionless to each other: others crashed sickeningly onto the ice-coated steel deck far below, twisting ankles, fracturing legs and thighs, dislocating hip-joints. And two men jumped and missed; above the bedlam of noise, men heard the blood-chilling, bubbling scream of one as the swinging hulls crushed the life out of him, the desperate, terror-stricken cries of the other as the great, iron wall of the *Electra* guided him into the screws of the *Sirrus*.

It was just then that it happened and there could be no possible reflection on Commander Orr's seamanship: he had handled the *Sirrus* brilliantly. But even his skill was helpless against these two successive freak waves, twice the size of the others. The first flung the *Sirrus* close in to the *Electra*, then passing under the *Electra*, lurched her steeply to port as the second wave heeled the *Sirrus* far over to starboard. There was a grinding, screeching crash. The *Sirrus*'s guard-rails and upper side plates buckled and tore along a 150-foot length: simultaneously, the lifeboat smashed endwise into the front of the bridge, shattering into a thousand pieces. Immediately, the telegraphs jangled, the water boiled whitely at the *Sirrus*'s stern—shocked realization of its imminence and death itself must have been only a merciful hair's-breadth apart for the unfortunate man in the water—and then the destroyer was clear, sheering sharply away from the *Electra*.

In five minutes the *Sirrus* was round again. It was typical of Orr's ice-cold, calculating nerve and of the luck that never deserted him that he should this time choose to rub the *Sirrus*'s shattered starboard side along the length of the *Electra*—she was too low in the water now to fall on him—and that he should do so in a momentary spell of slack water. Willing hands caught men as they jumped, cushioned their fall. Thirty seconds and the destroyer was gone again and the decks of the *Electra* were deserted. Two minutes later and a muffled roar shook the sinking ship—her boilers going. And then she toppled slowly over on her side: masts and smokestack lay along the surface of the sea, dipped and vanished: the straight-back of bottom and keel gleamed fractionally, blackly, against the grey of sea and sky, and was gone. For a minute, great gouts of air rushed turbulently to the surface. By and by the bubbles grew smaller and smaller and then there were no more.

The *Sirrus* steadied on course, crowded decks throbbing as she began to pick up speed, to overtake the convoy. Convoy No FR77. The convoy the Royal Navy would always want to forget. Thirty-six ships had left Scapa and St John's. Now there were only twelve, only twelve. And still almost thirty-two hours to the Kola Inlet . . .

Moodily, even his tremendous vitality and zest temporarily subdued, Turner watched the *Sirrus* rolling up astern. Abruptly he turned away, looked furtively, pityingly at Captain Vallery, no more now than a living skeleton driven by God only knew what mysterious force to wrest hour after impossible hour from death. And for Vallery now, death, even the hope of it, Turner suddenly realized, must be infinitely sweet. He looked, and saw the shock and sorrow in that grey mask, and he cursed, bitterly, silently. And then these tired, dull eyes were on him and Turner hurriedly cleared his throat.

'How many survivors does that make in the *Sirrus* now?' he asked.

Vallery lifted weary shoulders in the ghost of a shrug.

'No idea, Commander. A hundred, possibly more. Why?'

'A hundred,' Turner mused. 'And no-survivors-will-be-picked-up. I'm just wondering what old Orr's going to say when he dumps that little lot in Admiral Starr's lap when we get back to Scapa Flow!'

THIRTEEN

Saturday Afternoon

The *Sirrus* was still a mile astern when her Aldis started flickering. Bentley took the message, turned to Vallery.

'Signal, sir. "Have 25-30 injured men aboard. Three very serious cases, perhaps dying. Urgently require doctor."'

'Acknowledge,' Vallery said. He hesitated a moment, then: 'My compliments to Surgeon-Lieutenant Nicholls. Ask him to come to the bridge.' He turned to the Commander, grinned faintly. 'I somehow don't see Brooks at his athletic best in a breeches buoy on a day like this. It's going to be quite a crossing.'

Turner looked again at the *Sirrus*, occasionally swinging through a 40° arc as she rolled and crashed her way up from the west.

'It'll be no picnic,' he agreed. 'Besides, breeches buoys aren't made to accommodate the likes of our venerable chief surgeon.' Funny, Turner thought, how matter-of-fact and offhand everyone was: nobody had as much as mentioned the *Vectra* since she'd rammed the U-boat.

The gate creaked. Vallery turned round slowly, acknowledged Nicholls's sketchy salute.

'The *Sirrus* needs a doctor,' he said without preamble. 'How do you fancy it?'

Nicholls steadied himself against the canted bridge and the rolling of the cruiser. Leave the *Ulysses*—suddenly, he hated the thought, was amazed at himself for his reaction. He, Johnny Nicholls, unique, among the officers anyway, in his thorough-going detestation and intolerance of all things naval—to feel like that! Must be going soft in the head. And just as suddenly he knew that his mind wasn't slipping, knew why he wanted to stay. It was not a matter of pride or principle or sentiment: it was just that—well, just that he belonged. The feeling of belonging—even to himself he couldn't put it more accurately, more clearly than that, but it affected him strangely, powerfully. Suddenly he became aware that curious eyes were on him, looked out in confusion over the rolling sea.

'Well?' Vallery's voice was edged with impatience.

'I don't fancy it at all,' Nicholls said frankly. 'But of course I'll go, sir. Right now?'

'As soon as you can get your stuff together,' Vallery nodded.

'That's now. We have an emergency kit packed all the time.' He cast a jaundiced eye over the heavy sea again. 'What am I supposed to do, sir—jump?'

'Perish the thought!' Turner clamped him on the back with a large and jovial hand. 'You haven't a thing to worry about,' he boomed cheerfully, 'you positively won't feel a thing—these, if I recall rightly, were your exact words to me when you extracted that old molar of mine two-three weeks back.' He winced in painful recollection. 'Breeches buoy, laddie, breeches buoy!'

'Breeches buoy!' Nicholls protested. 'Haven't noticed the weather, have you? I'll be going up and down like a blasted yo-yo!'

'The ignorance of youth.' Turner shook his head sadly. 'We'll be turning into the sea, of course. It'll be like a ride in a Rolls, my boy! We're going to rig it now.' He turned away. 'Chrysler—get on to Chief Petty Officer Hartley. Ask him to come up to the bridge.'

Chrysler gave no sign of having heard. He was in his usual favourite position these days—gloved hands on the steam pipes, the top half of his face crushed into the rubber eyepiece of the powerful binoculars on the starboard searchlight control. Every few seconds a hand would drop, revolve the milled training rack a fraction. Then again the complete immobility.

'Chrysler!' Turner roared. 'Are you deaf?'

Three, four, five more seconds passed in silence. Every eye was on Chrysler when he suddenly jerked back, glanced down at the bearing indicator, then swung round. His face was alive with excitement.

'Green one-double-oh!' he shouted. 'Green onedouble-oh! Aircraft. Just on the horizon!' He fairly flung himself back at his binoculars. 'Four, seven—no, *ten*! Ten aircraft!' he yelled.

'Green one-double-oh?' Turner had his glasses to his eyes. 'Can't see a thing! Are you sure, boy?' he called anxiously.

'Still the same, sir.' There was no mistaking the agitated conviction in the young voice.

Turner was through the gate and beside him in four swift steps. 'Let me have a look,' he ordered. He gazed through the glasses, twisted the training rack once or twice, then stepped back slowly, heavy eyebrows lowering in anger.

'There's something bloody funny here, young man!' he growled. 'Either your eyesight or your imagination? And if you ask me—'

'He's right,' Carrington interrupted calmly. 'I've got 'em, too.'

'So have I, sir!' Bentley shouted.

Turner wheeled back to the mounted glasses, looked through them briefly, stiffened, looked round at Chrysler.

'Remind me to apologize some day!' he smiled, and was back on the compass platform before he had finished speaking.

'Signal to convoy,' Vallery was saying rapidly. 'Code H. Full ahead. Number One. Bosun's mate? Broadcaster: stand by all guns. Commander?'

'Sir?'

'Independent targets, independent fire all AA guns? Agreed? And the turrets?

'Couldn't say yet . . . Chrysler, can you make out—'

'Condors, sir,' Chrysler anticipated him.

'Condors!' Turner stared in disbelief. 'A dozen Condors! Are you sure that . . . Oh, all right, all right!' he broke off hastily. 'Condors they are.' He shook his head in wonderment, turned to Vallery. 'Where's my bloody tin hat? Condors, he says!'

'So Condors they are,' Vallery repeated, smiling. Turner marvelled at the repose, the unruffled calm.

'Bridge targets, independent fire control for all turrets?' Vallery went on.

'I think so, sir.' Turner looked at the two communication ratings just aft of the compass platform—one each on the group phones to the for'ard and after turrets. 'Ears pinned back, you two. And hop to it when you get the word.'

Vallery beckoned to Nicholls.

'Better get below, young man,' he advised. 'Sorry your little trip's been postponed.'

'I'm not,' Nicholls said bluntly.

'No?' Vallery was smiling. 'Scared?'

'No, sir,' Nicholls smiled back. 'Not scared. And you know I wasn't.'

'I know you weren't,' Vallery agreed quietly. 'I know—and thank you.'

He watched Nicholls walk off the bridge, beckoned to the WT messenger, then turned to the Kapok Kid.

'When was our last signal to the Admiralty, Pilot? Have a squint at the log.'

'Noon yesterday,' said the Kapok Kid readily.

'Don't know what I'll do without you,' Vallery murmured. 'Present position?'

'72.20 north, 13.40 east.'

'Thank you.' He looked at Turner. 'No point in radio silence now, Commander?'

Turner shook his head.

'Take this message,' Vallery said quickly. 'To DNO, London . . . How are our friends doing, Commander?'

'Circling well to the west, sir. Usual high altitude, gambit from the stern, I suppose,' he added morosely. 'Still,' he brightened, 'cloud level's barely a thousand feet.'

Vallery nodded. '"FR77. 1600. 72.20, 13.40. Steady on 090. Force 9, north, heavy swell: Situation desperate. Deeply regret Admiral Tyndall died 1200 today. Tanker *Vytura* torpedoed last night, sunk by self. *Washington State* sunk 0145 to-day. *Vectra* sunk 1515, collision U-boat. *Electra* sunk 1530. Am being heavily attacked by twelve, minimum twelve, Focke-Wulf 200s." A reasonable assumption, I think, Commander,' he said wryly, 'and it'll shake their Lordships. They're of the opinion there aren't so many Condors in the whole of

Norway. "Imperative send help. Air cover essential. Advise immediately." Get that off at once, will you?'

'Your nose, sir!' Turner said sharply.

'Thank you.' Vallery rubbed the frostbite, dead white in the haggard grey and blue of his face, gave up after a few seconds: the effort was more trouble than it was worth, drained away too much of his tiny reserves of strength.

Shivering, he pulled himself to his feet, swept his glasses over FR77. Code H was being obeyed. The ships were scattered over the sea apparently at random, broken out from the two lines ahead which would have made things far too simple for bomb-aimers in aircraft attacking from astern. They would have to aim now for individual targets. Scattered, but not too scattered—close enough together to derive mutual benefit from the convoy's concerted barrage. Vallery nodded to himself in satisfaction and twisted round, his glasses swivelling to the west.

There was no mistaking them now, he thought—they were Condors, all right. Almost dead astern now, massive wingtips dipping, the big four-engined planes banked slowly, ponderously to starboard, then straightened on a 180° overtaking course. And they were climbing, steadily climbing.

Two things were suddenly clear to Vallery, two things the *enemy* obviously knew. They had known where to find FR77—the Luftwaffe was not given to sending heavy bombers out over the Arctic on random hazard: they hadn't even bothered to send Charlie on reconnaissance. For a certainty, some submarine had located them earlier on, given their position and course: at any distance at all, their chance of seeing a periscope in that heavy sea had been remote. Further, the German *knew* that the *Ulysses*'s radar was gone. The Focke-Wulfs were climbing to gain the low cloud, would break cover only seconds before it was time to bomb. Against radar-controlled fire, at such close range, it would have been near suicide. But they *knew* it was safe.

Even as he watched, the last of the labouring Condors climbed through the low, heavy ceiling, was completely lost to sight. Vallery shrugged wearily, lowered his binoculars.

'Bentley?'

'Sir?'

'Code R. Immediate.'

The flags fluttered up. For fifteen, twenty seconds—it seemed ten times as long as that to the impatient Captain—nothing happened. And then, like rolling toy marionettes under the hand of a master puppeteer, the bows of every ship in the convoy began to swing round—those to the port of the *Ulysses* to the north, those to the starboard to the south. When the Condors broke through—two minutes, at the most, Vallery reckoned, they would find beneath them only the empty sea. Empty, that is, except for the *Ulysses* and the *Stirling*, ships admirably equipped to take care of themselves. And then the Condors would find themselves under heavy cross-fire from the merchant ships and destroyers, and too late—at that low altitude, much too late—to alter course for fore-and-aft bombing runs on the freighters. Vallery smiled wryly to himself. As a defensive tactic, it was little enough, but the best he could do in the circumstances . . . He could hear Turner barking orders through the loudspeaker, was more than content to leave the defence of the ship in the Commander's competent hands. If only he himself didn't feel so tired . . .

Ninety seconds passed, a hundred, two minutes—and still no sign of the Condors. A hundred eyes stared out into the cloud-wrack astern: it remained obstinately, tantalizingly grey and featureless.

Two and a half minutes passed. Still there was nothing.

'Anybody seen anything?' Vallery asked anxiously. His eyes never left that patch of cloud astern. 'Nothing? Nothing at all?' The silence remained oppressive, unbroken.

Three minutes. Three and a half. Four. Vallery looked away to rest his straining eyes, caught Turner looking at him, caught the growing apprehension, the slow dawn and strengthening of surmise in the lean face. Wordlessly, at the same instant, they swung round, staring out into the sky ahead.

'That's it!' Vallery said quickly. 'You're right, Commander, you must be!' He was aware that everyone had turned now, was peering ahead as intently as himself. 'They've by-passed us, they're going to take us from ahead. Warn the guns! Dear God, they almost had us!' he whispered softly.

'Eyes skinned, everyone!' Turner boomed. The apprehension was gone, the irrepressible joviality, the gratifying anticipation of action was back again. 'And I mean everyone! We're all in the same boat together. No joke intended. Fourteen days' leave to the first man to sight a Condor!'

'Effective as from when?' the Kapok Kid asked dryly.

Turner grinned at him. Then the smile died, the head lifted sharply in sudden attention.

'Can you hear 'em?' he asked. His voice was soft, almost as if he feared the enemy might be listening. 'They're up there, somewhere—damned if I can tell where, though. If only that wind—'

The vicious, urgent thudding of the boat-deck Oerlikons stopped him dead in mid-sentence, had him whirling round and plunging for the broadcast transmitter in one galvanic, concerted movement. But even then he was too late—he would have been too late anyway. The Condors—the first three in line ahead, were already visible—were already through the cloud, 500 feet up and barely half a mile away—dead astern. *Astern*. The bombers must have circled back to the west as soon as they had reached the clouds, completely fooled them as to their intentions . . . Six seconds—six seconds is time and to spare for even a heavy bomber to come less than half a mile in a shallow dive. There was barely time for realization, for the first bitter welling of mortification and chagrin when the Condors were on them.

It was almost dusk, now, the weird half-light of the Arctic twilight. Tracers, glowing hot pinpoints of light streaking out through the darkening sky, were clearly seen, at first swinging erratically, fading away to extinction in the far distance, then steadying, miraculously dying in the instant of birth as they sank home into the fuselages of the swooping Condors. But time was too short—the guns were on target for a maximum of two seconds—and these giant Focke-Wulfs had a tremendous capacity for absorbing punishment. The leading Condor levelled out about three hundred feet, its medium 250-kilo bombs momentarily paralleling its line of flight, then arching down lazily towards the *Ulysses*. At once the Condor pulled its nose up in maximum climb, the four great engines labouring in desynchronized clamour, as it sought the protection of the clouds.

The bombs missed. They missed by about thirty feet, exploding on contact with the water just abaft the bridge. For the men in the TS, engine- and boiler-rooms, the crash and concussion must have been frightful—literally ear-shattering. Waterspouts, twenty feet in diameter at their turbulent bases, streaked up whitely into the twilight, high above the truncated masts, hung there momentarily, then collapsed in drenching cascades on the bridge and boat-deck aft, soaking, saturating, every gunner on the pom-pom and in the open Oerlikon cockpits. The temperature stood at 2° above zero—30° of frost.

More dangerously, the blinding sheets of water completely unsighted the gunners. Apart from a lone Oerlikon on a sponson below the starboard side of the bridge, the next Condor pressed home its attack against a minimum of resistance. The approach was perfect, dead fore-and-aft on the centre line; but the pilot overshot, probably in his anxiety to hold course. Three bombs this time: for a second, it seemed that they must miss, but the first smashed into the fo'c'sle between the breakwater and the capstan, exploding in the flat below, heaving up the deck in a tangled wreckage of broken steel. Even as the explosion died, the men on the bridge could hear a curious clanking rattle: the explosion must have shattered the fo'c'sle capstan and Blake stopper simultaneously, and sheared the retaining shackle on the anchor cable, and the starboard anchor, completely out of control, was plummeting down to the depths of the Arctic.

The other bombs fell into the sea directly ahead, and from the *Stirling*, a mile ahead, it seemed that the *Ulysses* disappeared under the great column of water. But the water subsided, and the *Ulysses* steamed on, apparently unharmed. From dead ahead, the sweeping lift of the bows hid all damage, and there was neither flame nor smoke—hundreds of gallons of water, falling from the sky and pouring in through the great jagged holes in the deck, had killed any fire there was. The *Ulysses* was still a lucky ship . . . And then, at last, after twenty months of the fantastic escapes, the fabulous good fortune that had made her a legend, a byword for immunity throughout all the north, the luck of the *Ulysses* ran out.

Ironically, the *Ulysses* brought disaster on herself. The main armament, the 5.25s aft, had opened up now, was pumping its 100-lb shells at the diving bombers, at point-blank range and over equivalent of open sights. The very first shell from 'X' turret sheared away the starboard wing of the third Condor between the engines, tore it completely away to spin slowly like a fluttering leaf into the darkly-rolling sea. For a fraction of a second the Folke-Wulf held on course, then abruptly the nose tipped over and the giant plane screamed down in an almost vertical dive, her remaining engines inexplicably accelerating to a deafening crescendo as she hurtled arrowstraight for the deck of the *Ulysses*.

There was no time to take any avoiding action, no time to think, no time even to hope. A cluster of jettisoned bombs crashed in to the boiling wake—the *Ulysses* was already doing upwards of thirty knots—and two more crashed through the poop-deck, the first exploding in the after seamen's mess-deck, the other in the marines' mess-deck. One second later, with a tremendous roar and in a blinding sheet of gasoline flame, the Condor itself, at a speed of upwards of three hundred mph, crashed squarely into the front of 'Y' turret.

Incredibly, that was the last attack on the *Ulysses*—incredibly, because the *Ulysses* was defenceless now, wide open to any air attack from astern. 'Y' turret was gone, 'X' turret, still magically undamaged, was half-buried under the splintered wreckage of the Condor, blinded by the smoke and leaping flame. The boat-deck Oerlikons, too, had fallen silent. The gunners, half-drowned under the deluge of less than a minute ago, were being frantically dragged from their cockpits: a difficult enough task at any time, it was almost impossible with their clothes already frozen solid, their duffels cracking and crackling like splintering matchwood as the men were dragged over the side of their cockpits. With all speed, they were rushed below, thrust into the galley passage to thaw, literally to thaw: agony, excruciating agony, but the only alternative to the quick and certain death which would have come to them in their ice-bound cockpits.

The remaining Condors had pulled away in a slow climbing turn to starboard. They were surrounded, bracketed fore and aft and on either side, by scores of woolly, expanding puffs of exploding AA shells, but they flew straight through these, charmed, unhurt. Already, they were beginning to disappear into the clouds, to settle down on a south-east course for home. Strange, Vallery thought vaguely, one would have expected them to hammer home their initial advantage of surprise, to concentrate on the crippled *Ulysses*: certainly, thus far the Condor crews had shown no lack of courage . . . He gave it up, turned his attention to more immediate worries. And there was plenty to worry about.

The *Ulysses* was heavily on fire aft—a deck and mess-deck fire, admittedly, but potentially fatal for all that—'X' and 'Y' magazines were directly below. Already, dozens of men from the damage control parties were running aft, stumbling and falling on the rolling ice-covered deck, unwinding the hose drums behind them, occasionally falling flat on their faces as two ice-bound coils locked together, the abruptly tightening hose jerking them off their feet. Others stumbled past them, carrying the big, red foam-extinguishers on their shoulders or under their arms. One unfortunate seaman—A.B. Ferry who had left the Sick Bay in defiance of strict orders—running down the port alley past the shattered Canteen, slipped and fell abreast 'X' turret: the port wing of the Condor, even as it had sheared off and plunged into the sea, had torn away the guard-rails here, and Ferry, hands and feet scrabbling frantically at the smooth ice of the deck, his broken arm clawing uselessly at one of the remaining stanchions, slid slowly, inevitably over the side and was gone. For a second, the high-pitched, fear-stricken shriek rose thin and clear above the roaring of the flames, died abruptly as the water closed over him. The propellers were almost immediately below.

The men with the extinguishers were the first into action, as, indeed, they had to be when fighting a petrol fire—water would only have made matters worse, have increased the area of the fire by washing the petrol in all directions, and the petrol, being lighter than water, immiscible and so floating to the top, would have burned as furiously as ever. But the foam-extinguishers were of only limited efficiency, not so much because several release valves had jammed solid in the intense cold as because of the intense white heat which made close approach almost impossible, while the smaller carbon-tet extinguishers, directed against electrical fires below, were shockingly ineffective: these extinguishers had never been in action before and the crew of the *Ulysses* had known for a long time of the almost magical properties of the extinguisher liquid for removing the most obstinate stains and marks in clothes. You may convince a WT rating of the lethal nature of 2,000 volts: you may convince a gunner of the madness of matches in a magazine: you may convince a torpedoman of the insanity of juggling with fulminate of mercury: but you will never convince any of them of the criminal folly of draining off just a few drops of carbon-tetrachloride . . . Despite stringent periodical checks, most of the extinguishers were only half-full. Some were completely empty.

The hoses were little more effective. Two were coupled up to the starboard mains and the valves turned: the hoses remained lifeless, empty. The starboard salt-water line had frozen solid—common enough with fresh-water systems, this, but not with salt. A third hose on the port side was coupled up, but the release valve refused to turn: attacked with hammers and crowbars, it sheered off at the base—at extremely low temperatures, molecular changes occur in metals, cut tensile strength to a fraction—the high-pressure water drenching everyone in the vicinity. Spicer, the dead Admiral's pantry-boy, a stricken-eyed shadow of his former cheerful self, flung away his hammer and wept in anger and frustration. The other port valve worked, but it took an eternity for the water to force its way through the flattened frozen hose.

Gradually, the deck fire was brought under control—less through the efforts of the firefighters than the fact that there was little inflammable material left after the petrol had burnt off. Hoses and extinguishers were then directed through the great jagged rents on the poop to the figures roaring in the mess-deck below, while two asbestos-suited figures clambered over and struggled through the red-hot, jangled mass of smoking wreckage on the poop. Nicholls had one of the suits, Leading Telegraphist Brown, a specialist in rescue work, the other.

Brown was the first on the scene. Picking his way gingerly, he climbed up to the entrance of 'Y' turret. Watchers in the port and starboard alleyways saw him pause there, fighting to tie back the heavy steel door—it had been crashing monotonously backwards and forwards with the rolling of the cruiser. Then they saw him step inside. Less than ten seconds later they saw him appear at the door again, on his knees and clutching desperately at the side for support. His entire body was arching convulsively and he was being violently sick into his oxygen mask.

Nicholls saw this, wasted time neither on 'Y' turret nor on the charred skeletons still trapped in the incinerated fuselage of the Condor. He climbed quickly up the vertical steel ladders to 'X' gun-deck, moved round to the back and tried to open the door. The clips were jammed, immovable—whether from cold or metal distortion he did not know. He looked round for some lever, stepped aside as he saw Doyle, duffel coat smouldering, haggard face set and purposeful under the beard, approaching with a sledge in his hand. A dozen heavy, well-directed blows—the clanging, Nicholls thought, must be almost intolerable inside the hollow amplifier of the turret—and the door was open. Doyle secured it, stepped aside to let Nicholls enter.

Nicholls climbed inside. There had been no need to worry about that racket outside, he thought wryly. Every man in the turret was stone dead. Colour-Sergeant Evans was sitting bolt upright in his seat, rigid and alert in death as he had been in life: beside him lay Foster, the dashing, fiery Captain of Marines, whom death became so ill. The rest were all sitting or lying quietly at their stations, apparently unharmed and quite unmarked except for an occasional tiny trickle of blood from ear and mouth, trickles already coagulated in the intense cold—the speed of the *Ulysses* had carried the flames aft, away from the turret. The concussion must have been tremendous, death instantaneous. Heavily, Nicholls bent over the communications number, gently detached his headset, and called the bridge.

Vallery himself took the message, turned back to Turner. He looked old, defeated.

'That was Nicholls,' he said. Despite all he could do, the shock and sorrow showed clearly in every deeply-etched line in that pitiably wasted face. '"Y" turret is gone—no survivors. "X" turret seems intact—but everyone inside is dead. Concussion, he says. Fires in the after mess-deck still not under control . . . Yes, boy, what is it?'

'"Y" magazine, sir,' the seaman said uncertainly. 'They want to speak to the gunnery officer.'

'Tell them he's not available,' Vallery said shortly. 'We haven't time . . . ' He broke off, looked up sharply. 'Did you say "Y" magazine? Here, let me have that phone.'

He took the receiver, pushed back the hood of his duffel coat.

'Captain speaking, "Y" magazine. What is it? . . . What? Speak up man, I can't hear you . . . Oh, damn!' He swung round on the bridge LTO 'Can you switch this receiver on to the relay amplifier? I can't hear a . . . Ah, that's better.'

The amplifier above the chart-house crackled into life—a peculiarily throaty, husky life, doubly difficult to understand under the heavy overlay of a slurred Glasgow accent.

'Can ye hear me now?' the speaker boomed.

'I can hear you.' Vallery's own voice echoed loudly over the amplifier. 'McQuater, isn't it?'

'Aye, it's me, sir. How did ye ken?' Even through the speaker the surprise was unmistakable. Shocked and exhausted though he was, Vallery found himself smiling.

'Never mind that now, McQuater. Who's in charge down there—Gardiner, isn't it?'

'Yes, sir. Gardiner.'

'Put him on, will you?' There was a pause.

'Ah canna, sir. Gardiner's deid.'

'Dead!' Vallery was incredulous. 'Did you say "dead", McQuater?'

'Aye, and he's no' the only one.' The voice was almost truculent, but Vallery's ear caught the faint tremor below. 'Ah was knocked oot masel', but Ah'm fine now.'

Vallery paused, waited for the boy's bout of hoarse, harsh coughing to pass.

'But—but—what happened?'

'How should Ah know—Ah mean, Ah dinna ken—Ah don't know, sir. A helluva bang and then—ach, Ah'm no' sure whit happened . . . Gardiner's mooth's all blood.'

'How—how many of you are left?'

'Just Barker, Williamson and masel', sir. Naebody else—just us.'

'And—and they're all right, McQuater?'

'Ach, they're fine. But Barker thinks he's deein'. He's in a gey bad wey. Ah think he's gone clean aff his trolley, sir.'

'He's *what*?'

'Loony, sir,' McQuater explained patiently. 'Daft. Some bluidy nonsense aboot goin' to meet his Maker, and him wi' naething behind him but a lifetime o' swindlin' his fellowman.' Vallery heard Turner's sudden chuckle, remembered that Barker was the canteen manager. 'Williamson's busy shovin' cartridges back into the racks—floor's littered with the bluidy things.'

'McQuater!' Vallery's voice was sharp, automatic in reproof.

'Aye, Ah'm sorry, sir. Ah clean forgot . . . Whit's to be done, sir?'

'Done about what?' Vallery demanded impatiently.

'This place, sir. "Y" magazine. Is the boat on fire ootside? It's bilin' in here—hotter than the hinges o'hell!'

'What! What did you say?' Vallery shouted. This time he forgot to reprimand McQuater. 'Hot, did you say? How hot? Quickly, boy!'

'Ah canna touch the after bulkheid, sir,' McQuater answered simply. 'It 'ud tak 'the fingers aff me.'

'But the sprinklers—what's the matter with them?' Vallery shouted. 'Aren't they working? Good God, boy, the magazine will go up any minute!'

'Aye.' McQuater's voice was noncommittal. 'Aye, Ah kinna thought that might be the wey o' it. No, sir, the sprinklers arena workin'—and it's already 20 degrees above the operatin' temperature, sir.'

'Don't just stand there,' Vallery said desperately. 'Turn them on by hand! The water in the sprinklers can't possibly be frozen if it's hot as you say it is. Hurry, man, hurry. If the mag goes up, the *Ulysses* is finished. For God's sake, hurry!'

'Ah've tried them, sir,' McQuater said softly. 'It's nae bluidy use. They're solid!'

'Then break them open! There must be a tommy bar lying about somewhere. Smash them open, man! Hurry!'

'Aye, richt ye are, sir. But—but if Ah do that, sir, how am Ah to shut the valves aff again?' There was a note almost of quiet desperation in the boy's voice—some trick of reproduction in the amplifier, Vallery guessed.

'You can't! It's impossible! But never mind that!' Vallery said impatiently, his voice ragged with anxiety. 'We'll pump it all out later. Hurry, McQuater, hurry!'

There was a brief silence followed by a muffled shout and a soft thud, then they heard a thin metallic clanging echoing through the amplifier, a rapid, staccato succession of strokes. McQuater must have been raining a veritable hail of blows on the valve handles. Abruptly, the noise ceased.

Vallery waited until he heard the phone being picked up, called anxiously: 'Well, how is it? Sprinklers all right?'

'Goin' like the clappers, sir.' There was a new note in his voice, a note of pride and satisfaction. 'Ah've just crowned Barker wi' the tommy bar,' he added cheerfully.

'You've *what*?'

'Laid oot old Barker,' said McQuater distinctly. 'He tried to stop me. Windy auld bastard . . . Ach, he's no' worth mentionin' . . . My they sprinklers are grand things, sir. Ah've never seen them working' before. Place is ankle deep a'ready. And the steam's fair sizzlin' aff the bulkheid!'

'That's enough!' Vallery's voice was sharp. 'Get out at once—and make sure that you take Barker with you.'

'Ah saw a picture once. In the Paramount in Glasgow, Ah think. Ah must've been flush.' The tone was almost conversational, pleasurably reminiscent. Vallery exchanged glances with Turner, saw that he too, was fighting off the feeling of unreality. '*Rain*, it was cried. But it wasnae hauf as bad as this. There certainly wisnae hauf as much bluidy steam! Talk aboot the hothouse in the Botanic Gardens!'

'McQuater!' Vallery roared. 'Did you hear me? Leave at once, I say! At once, do you hear?'

'Up to ma knees a'ready!' McQuater said admiringly. 'It's gey cauld . . . Did you say somethin' sir?'

'I said, "Leave at once!"' Vallery ground out. 'Get out!'

'Aye, Ah see. "Get oot." Aye. Ah thought that was what ye said. Get oot. Well, it's no that easy. As a matter o'fact, we canna. Hatchway's buckled and the hatch-cover, too—jammed deid solid, sir.'

The echo from the speaker boomed softly over the shattered bridge, died away in frozen silence. Unconsciously, Vallery lowered the telephone, his eyes wandering dazedly over the bridge. Turner, Carrington, the Kapok Kid, Bentley, Chrysler and the others—they were all looking at him, all with the same curiously blank intensity blurring imperceptibly into the horror of understanding—and he knew that their eyes and faces only mirrored his own. Just for a second, as if to clear his mind, he screwed his eyes tightly shut, then lifted the phone again.

'McQuater! McQuater! Are you still there?'

'Of course Ah'm here!' Even through the speaker, the voice was peevish, the asperity unmistakable. 'Where the hell—?'

'Are you sure it's jammed, boy?' Vallery cut in desperately. 'Maybe if you took a tommy-bar to the clips—'

'Ah could take a stick o' dynamite to the bluidy thing and it 'ud make no difference,' McQuater said matter-of-factly. 'Onywey, it's just aboot red-hot a'ready—the hatch, Ah mean. There must be a bluidy great fire directly ootside it.'

'Hold on a minute,' Vallery called. He turned round. 'Commander, have Dodson send a stoker to the main magazine flooding valve aft: stand by to shut off.'

He crossed over to the nearest communication number.

'Are you on to the poop phone just now? Good! Give it to me . . . Hallo, Captain here. Is—ah, it's you, Hartley. Look, give me a report on the state of the mess-deck fires. It's desperately urgent. There are ratings trapped in "Y" magazine, the sprinklers are on and the hatch-cover's jammed . . . Yes, yes, I'll hold on.'

He waited impatiently for the reply, gloved hand tapping mechanically on top of the phone box. His eyes swept slowly over the convoy, saw the freighters steaming in to take up position again. Suddenly he stiffened, eyes unseeing.

'Yes, Captain speaking . . . Yes . . . Yes. Half an hour, maybe an hour . . . Oh, God, no! You're quite certain? . . . No, that's all.'

He handed the receiver back, looked up slowly, his face drained of expression.

'Fire in the seamen's mess is under control,' he said dully. 'The marines' mess is an inferno—directly on top of "Y" magazine. Hartley says there isn't a chance of putting it out for an hour at least . . . I think you'd better get down there, Number One.'

A whole minute passed, a minute during which there was only the pinging of the Asdic, the regular crash of the sea as the *Ulysses* rolled in the heavy troughs.

'Maybe the magazine's cool enough now,' the Kapok Kid suggested at length. 'Perhaps we could shut off the water long enough . . . ' His voice trailed away uncertainly.

'Cool enough?' Turner cleared his throat noisily. 'How do we know? Only McQuater could tell us . . . ' He stopped abruptly, as he realized the implications of what he was saying.

'We'll ask him,' Vallery said heavily. He picked up the phone again. 'McQuater?'

'Hallo!'

'Perhaps we could shut off the sprinklers outside, if it's safe. Do you think the temperature . . . ?'

He broke off, unable to complete the sentence. The silence stretched out, taut and tangible, heavy with decision. Vallery wondered numbly what McQuater was thinking, what he himself would have thought in McQuater's place.

'Hing on a minute,' the speaker boomed abruptly. 'Ah'll have a look up top.'

Again that silence, again that tense unnatural silence lay heavily over the bridge. Vallery started as the speaker boomed again.

'Jings, Ah'm b—d. Ah couldna climb that ladder again for twenty-four points in the Treble Chance . . . Ah'm on the ladder now, but Ah'm thinkin' Ah'll no' be on it much longer.'

'Never mind . . . ' Vallery checked himself, aghast at what he had been about to say. If McQuater fell off, he'd drown like a rat in that flooded magazine.

'Oh, aye. The magazine.' In the intervals between the racked bouts of coughing, the voice was strangely composed. 'The shells up top are just aboot meltin'. Worse than ever, sir.'

'I see.' Vallery could think of nothing else to say. His eyes were closed and he knew he was swaying on his feet. With an effort, he spoke again. 'How's Williamson?' It was all he could think of.

'Near gone. Up to his neck and hangin' on to the racks.' McQuater coughed again. 'Says he's a message for the Commander and Carslake.'

'A—a message?'

'Uh-huh! Tell old Blackbeard to take a turn to himself and lay off the bottle,' he said with relish. The message for Carslake was unprintable.

Vallery didn't even feel shocked.

'And yourself, McQuater?' he said. 'No message, nothing you would like . . . ' He stopped, conscious of the grotesque inadequacy, the futility of what he was saying.

'Me? Ach, there's naething Ah'd like . . . Well, maybe a transfer to the *Spartiate*, but Ah'm thinking maybe it's a wee bit ower late for that.[1] 'Williamson!' The voice had risen to a sudden urgent shout. 'Williamson! Hing on, boy, Ah'm coming!' They heard the booming clatter in the speaker as McQuater's phone crashed against metal, and then there was only the silence.

'McQuater!' Vallery shouted into the phone. 'McQuater! Answer me, man. Can you hear me? McQuater!'

But the speaker above him remained dead, finally, irrevocably dead. Vallery shivered in the icy wind. That magazine, that flooded

---

1. HMS *Spartiate* was a shore establishment. Naval HQ for the West of Scotland. It was at St Enoch's Hotel, Glasgow.

magazine . . . less than twenty-four hours since he had been there. He could see it now, see it as clearly as he had seen it last night. Only now he saw it dark, cavernous with only the pin-points of emergency lighting, the water welling darkly, slowly up the sides, saw that little, pitifully wasted Scots boy with the thin shoulders and pain-filled eyes, struggling desperately to keep his mate's head above that icy water, exhausting his tiny reserves of strength with the passing of every second. Even now, the time must be running out and Vallery knew hope was gone. With a sudden clear certainty he knew that when those two went down, they would go down together. McQuater would never let go. Eighteen years old, just eighteen years old. Vallery turned away, stumbling blindly through the gate on to the shattered compass platform. It was beginning to snow again and the darkness was falling all around them.

FOURTEEN

Saturday Evening I

The *Ulysses* rolled on through the Arctic twilight. She rolled heavily, awkwardly, in seas of the wrong critical length, a strange and stricken sight with both masts gone, with all boats and rafts gone, with shattered fore-and-aft superstructure, with a crazily tilted bridge and broken, mangled after turret, half-buried in the skeleton of the Condor's fuselage. But despite all that, despite, too, the great garish patches of red lead and gaping black holes in fo'c'sle and poop—the latter welling with dark smoke laced with flickering lances of flame—she still remained uncannily ghost-like and graceful, a creature of her own element, inevitably at home in the Arctic. Ghost-like, graceful, and infinitely enduring . . . and still deadly. She still had her guns—and her engines. Above all, she had these great engines, engines strangely blessed with endless immunity. So, at least, it seemed . . .

Five minutes dragged themselves interminably by, five minutes during which the sky grew steadily darker, during which reports from the poop showed that the firefighters were barely holding their own, five minutes during which Vallery recovered something of his normal composure. But he was now terribly weak.

A bell shrilled, cutting sharply through the silence and the gloom. Chrysler answered it, turned to the bridge.

'Captain, sir. After engine-room would like to speak to you.'

Turner looked at the Captain, said quickly: 'Shall I take it, sir?'

'Thank you.' Vallery nodded his head gratefully. Turner nodded in turn, crossed to the phone.

'Commander speaking. Who is it? . . . Lieutenant Grierson. What is it, Grierson? Couldn't be good news for a change?'

For almost a minute Turner remained silent. The others on the bridge could hear the faint crackling of the earpiece, sensed rather than saw the taut attention, the tightening of the mouth.

'Will it hold?' Turner asked abruptly. 'Yes, yes, of course . . . Tell him we'll do our best up here . . . Do that. Half-hourly, if you please.'

'It never rains, et cetera,' Turner growled, replacing the phone. 'Engine running rough, temperature hotting up. Distortion in inner starboard shaft. Dodson himself is in the shaft tunnel right now. Bent like a banana, he says.'

Vallery smiled faintly. 'Knowing Dodson, I suppose that means a couple of thou out of alignment.'

'Maybe.' Turner was serious. 'What does matter is that the main shaft bearing's damaged and the lubricating line fractured.'

'As bad as that?' Vallery asked softly.

'Dodson is pretty unhappy. Says the damage isn't recent—thinks it began the night we lost our depthcharges.' Turner shook his head. 'Lord knows what stresses that shaft's undergone since . . . I suppose tonight's performance brought it to a head . . . The bearing will have to be lubricated by hand. Wants engine revs at a minimum or engine shut off altogether. They'll keep us posted.'

'And no possibility of repair?' Vallery asked wryly.

'No, sir. None.'

'Very well, then. Convoy speed. And Commander?' 'Sir?'

'Hands to stations all night. You needn't tell 'em so—but, well, I think it would be wise. I have a feeling—'

'What's that!' Turner shouted. 'Look! What the hell's she doing?' His finger was stabbing towards the last freighter in the starboard line: her guns were blazing away at some unseen target, the tracers lancing whitely through the twilight sky. Even as he dived for the broadcaster, he caught sight of the *Viking*'s main armament belching smoke and jagged flame.

'All guns! Green 110! Aircraft! Independent fire, independent targets! Independent fire, independent targets!' He heard Vallery ordering starboard helm, knew he was going to bring the for'ard turrets to bear.

They were too late. Even as the *Ulysses* began to answer her helm, the enemy planes were pulling out of their approach dives. Great, clumsy shapes, these planes, forlorn and insubstantial in the murky gloom, but identifiable in a sickening flash by the clamour of suddenly racing engines. Condors, without a shadow of doubt. Condors that had outguessed them again, that gliding approach, throttles cut right back, muted roar of the engines drifting downwind, away from the convoy. Their timing, their judgement of distance, had been superb.

The freighter was bracketed twice, directly hit by at least seven bombs: in the near-darkness, it was impossible to see the bombs going home, but the explosions were unmistakable. And as each plane passed over, the decks were raked by savage bursts of machine-gun fire. Every gun position on the freighter was wide open, lacking all but the most elementary frontal protection: the Dems, Naval Ratings on the LA guns, Royal Marine Artillery-men on the HA weapons, were under no illusions as to their life expectancy when they joined the merchant ships on the Russian run . . . For such few gunners as survived the bombing, the vicious stuttering of these machine-guns was almost certainly their last sound on earth.

As the bombs plummeted down on the next ship in line, the first freighter was already a brokenbacked mass of licking, twisting flames. Almost certainly, too, her bottom had been torn out: she had listed heavily, and now slowly and smoothly broke apart just aft of the bridge as if both parts were hinged below the water-line, and was gone before the clamour of the last aero engine had died away in the distance.

Tactical surprise had been complete. One ship gone, a second slewing wildly to an uncontrolled stop, deep in the water by the head, and strangely disquieting and ominous in the entire absence of smoke, flame or any movement at all, a third heavily damaged but still under command. Not one Condor had been lost.

Turner ordered the cease-fire—some of the gunners were still firing blindly into the darkness: trigger-happy, perhaps, or just that the imagination plays weird tricks on woolly minds and sunken blood-red eyes that had known no rest for more hours and days than Turner could remember. And then, as the last Oerlikon fell silent, he heard it again—the drone of the heavy aero engines, the sound welling then ebbing again like breakers on a distant shore, as the wind gusted and died.

There was nothing anyone could do about it. The Focke-Wulf, although lost in the low cloud, was making no attempt to conceal its presence: the ominous drone was never lost for long. Clearly, it was circling almost directly above.

'What do you make of it, sir?' Turner asked.

'I don't know,' Vallery said slowly. 'I just don't know at all. No more visits from the Condors, I'm sure of that. It's just that little bit too dark—and they know they won't catch us again. Tailing us, like as not.'

'Tailing us! It'll be black as tar in half an hour!' Turner disagreed. 'Psychological warfare, if you ask me.'

'God knows,' Vallery sighed wearily. 'All I know is that I'd give all my chances, here and to come, for a couple of Corsairs, or radar, or fog, or another such night as we had in the Denmark Straits.' He laughed shortly, broke down in a fit of coughing. 'Did you hear me?' he whispered. 'I never thought I'd ask for that again . . . How long since we left Scapa, Commander?'

Turner thought briefly. 'Five—six days, sir.'

'Six days!' He shook his head unbelievingly. 'Six days. And—and thirteen ships—we have thirteen ships now.'

'Twelve,' Turner corrected quietly. 'Another's almost gone. Seven freighters, the tanker and ourselves. Twelve . . . I wish they'd have a go at the old *Stirling* once in a while,' he added morosely.

Vallery shivered in a sudden flurry of snow. He bent forward, head bent against the bitter wind and slanting snow, sunk in unmoving thought. Presently he stirred.

'We will be off the North Cape at dawn,' he said absently. 'Things may be a little difficult, Commander. They'll throw in everything they've got.'

'We've been round there before,' Turner conceded.

'Fifty-fifty on our chances.' Vallery did not seem to have heard him, seemed to be talking to himself '*Ulysses* and the Sirens—"it may be that the gulfs will wash us down." . . . I wish you luck, Commander.'

Turner stared at him. 'What do you mean—?'

'Oh, myself too.' Vallery smiled, his head lifting up. 'I'll need all the luck, too.' His voice was very soft.

Turner did what he had never done before, never dreamed he would do. In the near-darkness he bent over the Captain, pulled his face round gently and searched it with troubled eyes. Vallery made no protest, and after a few seconds Turner straightened up.

'Do me a favour, sir,' he said quietly. 'Go below. I can take care of things—and Carrington will be up before long. They're gaining control aft.'

'No, not tonight.' Vallery was smiling, but there was a curious finality about the voice. 'And it's no good dispatching one of your minions to summon old Socrates to the bridge. Please, Commander. I want to stay here—I want to see things tonight.'

'Yes, yes, of course.' Suddenly, strangely, Turner no longer wished to argue. He turned away. 'Chrysler! I'll give you just ten minutes to have a gallon of boiling coffee in the Captain's shelter . . . And you're going to go in there for half an hour,' he said firmly, turning to Vallery, 'and drink the damned stuff, or—or—'

'Delighted!' Vallery murmured. 'Laced with your incomparable rum, of course?'

'Of course! Eh—oh, yes, damn that Williamson!' Turner growled irritably. He paused, went on slowly: 'Shouldn't have said that . . . Poor bastards, they'll have had it by this time . . . ' He fell silent, then cocked his head listening. 'I wonder how long old Charlie means to keep stooging around up there,' he murmured.

Vallery cleared his throat, coughed, and before he could speak the WT broadcaster clicked on.

'WT—bridge. WT—bridge. Two messages.'

'One from the dashing Orr, for a fiver,' Turner grunted.

'First from the *Sirrus*. "Request permission to go alongside, take off survivors. As well hung for a sheep as a lamb."'

Vallery stared through the thinly falling snow, through the darkness of the night and over the rolling sea.

'In *this* sea?' he murmured. 'And as near dark as makes no difference. He'll kill himself!'

'That's nothing to what old Starr's going to do to him when he lays hands on him!' Turner said cheerfully.

'He hasn't a chance. I—I could never ask a man to do that. There's no justification for such a risk. Besides, the merchantman's been badly hit. There can't be many left alive aboard.'

Turner said nothing.

'Make a signal,' Vallery said clearly. '"Thank you. Permission granted. Good luck." And tell WT to go ahead.'

There was a short silence, then the speaker crackled again.

'Second signal from London to Captain. Decoding. Messenger leaving for bridge immediately.'

'To Officer Commanding, 14 ACS, FR77,' the speaker boomed after a few seconds. '"Deeply distressed at news. Imperative maintain 090. Battle squadron steaming SSE at full speed on interception course. Rendezvous approx 1400 tomorrow. Their Lordships expressly command best wishes Rear-Admiral, repeat Rear-Admiral Vallery. DNO, London."'

The speaker clicked off and there was only the lost pinging of the Asdic, the throbbing monotony of the prowling Condor's engines, the lingering memory of the gladness in the broadcaster's voice.

'Uncommon civil of their Lordships,' murmured the Kapok Kid, rising to the occasion as usual. 'Downright decent, one might almost say.'

'Bloody long overdue,' Turner growled. 'Congratulations, sir,' he added warmly. 'Signs of grace at last along the banks of the Thames.' A murmur of pleasure ran round the bridge: discipline or not, no one made any attempt to hide his satisfaction.

'Thank you, thank you.' Vallery was touched, deeply touched. Promise of help at long, long last, a promise which might hold—almost certainly held—for each and every member of his crew the difference between life and death—and they could only think to rejoice in his promotion! Dead men's shoes, he thought, and thought of saying it, but dismissed the idea immediately: a rebuff, a graceless affront to such genuine pleasure.

'Thank you very much,' he repeated. 'But gentlemen, you appear to have missed the only item of news of any real significance—'

'Oh, no, we haven't,' Turner growled. 'Battle squadron—ha! Too—late as usual. Oh, to be sure, they'll be in at the death—or shortly afterwards, anyway. Perhaps in time for a few survivors. I suppose the *Illustrious* and the *Furious* will be with them?'

'Perhaps. I don't know.' Vallery shook his head, smiling. 'Despite my recent—ah—elevation, I am not yet in their Lordships' confidence. But there'll be some carriers, and they could fly off a few hours away, give us air cover from dawn.'

'Oh, no, they won't,' said Turner prophetically. 'The weather will break down, make flying off impossible. See if I'm not right.'

'Perhaps, Cassandra, perhaps,' Vallery smiled. 'We'll see . . . What was that, Pilot? I didn't quite . . . '

The Kapok Kid grinned.

'It's just occurred to me that tomorrow's going to be a big day for our junior doctor—he's convinced that no battleship ever puts out to sea except for a Spithead review in peacetime.'

'That reminds me,' Vallery said thoughtfully. 'Didn't we promise the *Sirrus*—?'

'Young Nicholls is up to his neck in work,' Turner cut in. 'Doesn't love us—the Navy rather—overmuch, but he sure loves his job. Borrowed a fire-fighting suit, and Carrington says he's already . . . ' He broke off, looked up sharply into the thin, driving snow. 'Hallo! Charlie's getting damned nosy, don't you think?'

The roar of the Condor's engines was increasing every second: the sound rose to a clamouring crescendo as the bomber roared directly overhead, barely a couple of hundred feet above the broken masts, died away to a steady drone as the plane circled round the convoy.

'WT to escorts!' Vallery called quickly. 'Let him go—don't touch him! No starshells—nothing. he's trying to draw us out, to have us give away our position . . . It's not likely that the merchant ships . . . Oh, God! The fools, the fools! Too late, too late!'

A merchantman in the port line had opened up—Oerlikons or

Bofors, it was difficult to say. They were firing blind, completely blind: and in a high wind, snow and darkness, the chance of locating a plane by sound alone was impossibly remote.

The firing did not last long—ten, fifteen seconds at the outside. But long enough—and the damage was done. Charlie had pulled off, and straining apprehensive ears caught the sudden deepening of the note of the engines as the boosters were cut in for maximum climb.

'What do you make of it, sir?' Turner asked abruptly.

'Trouble.' Vallery was quiet but certain. 'This has never happened before—and it's not psychological warfare, as you call it, Commander: he doesn't even rob us of our sleep—not when we're this close to the North Cape. And he can't hope to trail us long: a couple of quick course alterations and—ah!' He breathed softly. 'What did I tell you, Commander?'

With a suddenness that blocked thought, with a dazzling glare that struck whitely, cruelly at singeing eyeballs, night was transformed into day. High above the *Ulysses* a flare had burst into intense life, a flare which tore apart the falling snow like filmy, transparent gauze. Swinging wildly under its parachute with the gusting of the wind, the flare was drifting slowly seawards, towards a sea no longer invisible but suddenly black as night, towards a sea where every ship, in its glistening sheath of ice and snow, was silhouetted in dazzling whiteness against the inky backdrop of sea and sky.

'Get that flare!' Turner was barking into the transmitter. 'All Oerlikons, all pom-poms, get that flare!' He replaced the transmitter. 'Might as well throw empty beer bottles at it with the old girl rolling like this,' he muttered. 'Lord, gives you a funny feeling this!'

'I know,' the Kapok Kid supplied. 'Like one of these dreams where you're walking down a busy street and you suddenly realize that all you're wearing is a wrist-watch. "Naked and defenceless," is the accepted term, I believe. For the non-literary, "caught with the pants down".' Absently he brushed the snow off the quilted kapok, exposing the embroidered 'J' on the breast pocket, while his apprehensive eyes probed into the circle of darkness outside the pool of light. 'I don't like this at all,' he complained.

'Neither do I.' Vallery was unhappy. 'And I don't like Charlie's sudden disappearance either.'

'He hasn't disappeared,' Turner said grimly. 'Listen!' They listened, ears straining intently, caught the intermittent, distant thunder of the heavy engines. 'He's way astern of us, closing.'

Less than a minute later the Condor roared overhead again, higher this time, lost in the clouds. Again he released a flare, higher, much higher than the last, and this time squarely over the heart of the convoy.

Again the roar of the engines died to a distant murmur, again the desynchronized clamour strengthened as the Condor overtook the convoy a second time. Glimpsed only momentarily in the inverted valleys between the scudding clouds, it flew wide, this time, far out on the port hand, riding clear above the pitiless glare of the sinking flares. And, as it thundered by, flares exploded into blazing life—four of them, just below cloud level, at four-second intervals. The northern horizon was alive with light, glowing and pulsating with a fierce flame that threw every tiny detail into the starkest relief. And to the south there was only the blackness: the rim of the pool of light stopped abruptly just beyond the starboard line of ships.

It was Turner who first appreciated the significance, the implications of this. Realization struck at him with the galvanic effect of sheer physical shock. He gave a hoarse cry, fairly flung himself at the broadcast transmitter: there was no time to await permission.

'"B" turret!' he roared. 'Starshells to the south. Green 90, green 90. Urgent! Urgent! Starshells, green 90. Maximum elevation 10. Close settings. Fire when you are ready!' He looked quickly over his shoulder. 'Pilot! Can you see—?'

'"B" turret training, sir.'

'Good, good!' He lifted the transmitter again. 'All guns! All guns! Stand by to repel air attack from starboard. Probable bearing green 90. Hostiles probably torpedo-bombers.' Even as he spoke, he caught sight of the intermittent flashing of the fighting lights on the lower yardarm: Vallery was sending out an emergency signal to the convoy.

'You're right, Commander,' Vallery whispered. In the gaunt

pallor, in the skin taut stretched across the sharp and fleshless bones, his face, in that blinding glare, was a ghastly travesty of humanity; it was a death's-head, redeemed only by the glow of the deep-sunken eyes, the sudden flicker of bloodless lids as the whip-lash crash of 'B' turret shattered the silence. 'You must be,' he went on slowly. 'Every ship silhouetted from the north—and a maximum run-in from the south under cover of darkness.' He broke off suddenly as the shells exploded in great overlapping globules of light, two miles to the south. 'You *are* right,' he said gently. 'Here they come.'

They came from the south, wing-tip to wing-tip, flying in three waves with four or five planes in each wave. They were coming in at about 500 feet, and even as the shells burst their noses were already dipping into the plane of the shallow attack dive of the torpedo-bomber. And as they dived, the bombers fanned out, as if in search of individual targets—or what seemed, at first sight, to be individual targets. But within seconds it became obvious that they were concenrating on two ships and two ships alone—the *Stirling* and the *Ulysses*. Even the ideal double target of the crippled merchantman and the destroyer *Sirrus*, almost stopped alongside her, was strictly ignored. They were flying under orders.

'B' turret pumped out two more starshells at minimum settings, reloaded with HE. By this time, every gun in the convoy had opened up, the barrage was intense: the torpedo-bombers—curiously difficult to identify, but looking like Heinkels—had to fly through a concentrated lethal curtain of steel and high explosive. The element of surprise was gone: the starshells of the *Ulysses* had gained a priceless twenty seconds.

Five bombers were coming at the *Ulysses* now, fanned out to disperse fire, but arrowing in on a central point. They were levelling off, running in on firing tracks almost at wave-top height, when one of them straightened up a fraction too late, brushed lightly against a cresting wave-top, glanced harmlessly off, then catapulted crazily from wave-top to wave-top—they were flying at right angles to the set of the sea—before disappearing in a trough. Misjudgment of distance or the pilot's windscreen suddenly obscured by a flurry of snow—it was impossible to say.

A second later the leading plane in the middle disintegrated in a searing burst of flame—a direct hit on its torpedo warhead. A third plane, behind and to the west, sheered off violently to the left to avoid the hurtling debris, and the subsequent dropping of its torpedo was no more than an empty gesture. It ran half a cable length behind the *Ulysses*, spent itelf in the empty sea beyond.

Two bombers left now, pressing home their attack with suicidal courage, weaving violently from side to side to avoid destruction. Two seconds passed, three, four—and still they came on, through the falling snow and intensely heavy fire, miraculous in their immunity. Theoretically, there is no target so easy to hit as a plane approaching directly head on: in practice, it never worked out that way. In the Arctic, the Mediterranean, the Pacific, the relative immunity of the torpedo-bombers, the high percentage of successful attacks carried out in the face of almost saturation fire, never failed to confound the experts. Tension, over-anxiety, fear—these were part of the trouble, at least: there are no half measures about a torpedo-bomber—you get him or he gets you. And there is nothing more nerve-racking—always, of course, with the outstanding exception of the screaming, near-vertical power-dive of the gull-winged Stuka dive-bomber—than to see a torpedo-bomber looming hugely, terrifyingly over the open sights of your gun and know that you have just five inexorable seconds to live . . . And with the *Ulysses*, of course, the continuous rolling of the cruiser in the heavy cross-sea made accuracy impossible.

These last two bombers came in together, wing-tip to wing-tip. The plane nearer the bows dropped its torpedo less than two hundred yards away, pulled up in a maximum climbing turn to starboard, a fusillade of light cannon and machine-gun shells smashing into the upper works of the bridge: the torpedo hit the water obliquely, porpoised high into the air, then crashed back again nose first into a heavy wave, diving steeply into the sea: it passed under the *Ulysses*.

But seconds before that the last torpedo-bomber had made its attack—made its attack and failed and died. It had come roaring in less than ten feet above the waves, had come straight on without releasing its torpedo, without gaining an inch in height, until the crosses on the upper sides of the wings could be clearly seen, until it was less than a hundred yards away. Suddenly, desperately, the pilot had begun to climb: it was immediately obvious that the torpedo release mechanism had jammed, either through mechanical failure or icing in the intense cold: obviously, too, the pilot had intended to release the torpedo at the last minute, had banked on the sudden decrease of weight to lift him over the *Ulysses*.

The nose of the bomber smashed squarely into the for'ard funnel, the starboard wing shearing off like cardboard as it scythed across the after leg of the tripod mast. There was an instantaneous, blinding sheet of gasoline flame, but neither smoke nor explosion. A moment later the crumpled, shattered bomber, no longer a machine but a torn and flaming crucifix, plunged into the hissing sea a dozen yards away. The water had barely closed over it when a gigantic underwater explosion heeled the *Ulysses* far over to starboard, a vicious hammer-blow that flung men off their feet and shattered the lighting system on the port side of the cruiser.

Commander Turner hoisted himself painfully to his feet, shook his head to clear it of the cordite fumes and the dazed confusion left by cannon shells exploding almost at arm's length. The shock of the detonating torpedo hadn't thrown him to the duckboards—he'd hurled himself there five seconds previously as the flaming guns of the other bomber had wrecked the bridge from pointblank range.

His first thought was for Vallery. The Captain was lying on his side, crumpled strangely against the binnacle. Dry-mouthed, cold with a sudden chill that was not of that Polar wind, Turner bent quickly, turned him gently over.

Vallery lay still, motionless, lifeless. No sign of blood, no gaping wound—thank God for that! Turner peeled off a glove, thrust a hand below duffel coat and jacket, thought he detected a faint, a very faint beating of the heart. Gently he lifted the head off the frozen slush, then looked up quickly. The Kapok Kid was standing above him.

'Get Brooks up here, Pilot,' he said swiftly. 'It's urgent!'

Unsteadily, the Kapok Kid crossed over the bridge. The communication rating was leaning over the gate, telephone in his hand.

'The Sick Bay, quickly!' the Kapok Kid ordered. 'Tell the Surgeon Commander . . . ' He stopped suddenly, guessed that the man was still too dazed to understand. 'Here, give me that phone!' Impatiently, he stretched out his hand and grabbed the telephone, then stiffened in horror as the man slipped gradually backwards, extended arms trailing stiffly over the top of the gate until they disappeared. Carpenter opened the gate, stared down at the dead man at his feet: there was a hole the size of his gloved fist between the shoulder-blades.

He lay alongside the Asdic cabinet, a cabinet, the Kapok Kid now saw for the first time, riddled and shattered with machine-gun bullets and shells. His first thought was the numbing appreciation that the set must be smashed beyond recovery, that their last defence against the U-boats was gone. Hard on the heels of that came the sickening realization that there had been an Asdic operator inside there . . . His eyes wandered away, caught sight of Chrysler rising to his feet by the torpedo control. He, too, was staring at the Asdic cabinet, his face drained of expression. Before the Kapok Kid could speak, Chrysler lurched forward, fists battering frantically, blindly at the jammed door of the cabinet. Like a man in a dream, the Kapok Kid heard him sobbing . . . And then he remembered. The Asdic operator—his name was Chrysler too. Sick to his heart, the Kapok Kid lifted the phone again . . .

Turner pillowed the Captain's head, moved across to the starboard corner of the compass platform. Bentley, quiet, unobtrusive as always, was sitting on the deck, his back wedged between two pipes, his head pillowed peacefully on his chest. His hand under Bentley's chin, Turner gazed down into the sightless eyes, the only recognizable feature of what had once been a human face. Turner swore in savage quiet, tried to prise the dead fingers locked round the hand-grip of the Aldis, then gave up. The barred beam shone eerily across the darkening bridge.

Methodically, Turner searched the bridge-deck for further casualties. He found three others and it was no consolation at all that they must have died unknowing. Five dead men for a three-second burst—a very fair return, he thought bitterly. Standing on the after ladder, his face stilled in unbelief as he realized that he was staring down into the heart of the shattered for'ard funnel. More he could not see: the boat deck was already blurred into featureless anonymity in the dying glare of the last of the flares. He swung on his heel, returned to the compass platform.

At least, he thought grimly, there was no difficulty in seeing the *Stirling*. What was it that he had said—said less than ten minutes ago? 'I wish they'd have a go at the *Stirling* once in a while.' Something like that. His mouth twisted. They'd had a go, all right. The *Stirling*, a mile ahead, was slewing away to starboard, to the south-east, her for'ard superstructure enveloped in a writhing cocoon of white flame. He stared through his night glasses, tried to assess the damage; but a solid wall of flame masked the superstructure, from the fo'c'sle deck clear abaft the bridge. He could see nothing there, just nothing—but he could see, even in that heavy swell, that the *Stirling* was listing to starboard. It was learned later that the *Stirling* had been struck twice: she had been torpedoed in the for'ard boiler-room, and seconds later a bomber had crashed into the side of her bridge, her torpedo still slung beneath the belly of her fuselage: almost certainly, in the light of the similar occurrence on the *Ulysses*, severe icing had jammed the release mechanism. Death must have been instantaneous for every man on the bridge and the decks below; among the dead were Captain Jeffries, the First Lieutenant and the Navigator.

The last bomber was hardly lost in the darkness when Carrington replaced the poop phone, turned to Hartley.

'Think you can manage now, Chief? I'm wanted on the bridge.'

'I think so, sir.' Hartley, blackened and stained with smoke and extinguisher foam, passed his sleeve wearily across his face. 'The worst is over . . . Where's Lieutenant Carslake? Shouldn't he—?'

'Forget him,' Carrington interrupted brusquely. 'I don't know where he is, nor do I care. There's no need for us to beat about the bush, Chief—we're better without him. If he returns, *you're* still in charge. Look after things.'

He turned away, walked quickly for'ard along the port alley. On the packed snow and ice, the pad of his rubber seaboots was completely soundless.

He was passing the shattered canteen when he saw a tall, shadowy figure standing in the gap between the snow-covered lip of the outer torpedo tube and the end stanchion of the guard-rails, trying to open a jammed extinguisher valve by striking it against the stanchion. A second later, he saw another blurred form detach itself stealthily from the shadows, creep up stealthily behind the man with the extinguisher, a heavy bludgeon of wood or metal held high above his head.

'Look out!' Carrington shouted. 'Behind you!'

It was all over in two seconds—the sudden, flailing rush of the attacker, the crash as the victim, lightning fast in his reactions, dropped his extinguisher and fell crouched to his knees, the thin piercing scream of anger and terror as the attacker catapulted over the stooping body and through the gap between tubes and rails, the splash—and then the silence.

Carrington ran up to the man on the deck, helped him to his feet. The last flare had not yet died, and it was still light enough for him to see who it was—Ralston, the LTO. Carrington gripped his arms, looked at him anxiously.

'Are you all right? Did he get you? Good God, who on earth—?'

'Thank you, sir.' Ralston was breathing quickly, but his face was almost expressionless again. 'That was too close! Thank you very much, sir.'

'But who on earth—?' Carrington repeated in wonder.

'Never saw him, sir.' Ralston was grim. 'But I know who it was—Sub-Lieutenant Carslake. He's been following me around all night, never let me out of his sight, not once. Now I know why.'

It took much to disturb the First Lieutenant's iron equanimity, but now he shook his head in slow disbelief.

'I knew there was bad blood!' he murmured. 'But that it should come to this! What the Captain will say to this I just—'

'Why tell him?' Ralston said indifferently. 'Why tell anyone? Perhaps Carslake had relations. What good will it do to hurt them, to hurt anyone. Let anyone think what they like.' He laughed shortly. 'Let them think he died a hero's death fire-fighting, fell over the side, anything.' He looked down into the dark, rushing water, then shivered suddenly. 'Let him go, sir, please. He's paid.'

For a long second Carrington, too, stared down over the side, looked back at the tall boy before him. Then he clapped his arm, nodded slowly and turned away.

Turner heard the clanging of the gate, lowered the binoculars to find Carrington standing by his side, gazing wordlessly at the burning cruiser. Just then Vallery moaned softly, and Carrington looked down quickly at the prone figure at his feet.

'My God! The Old Man! Is he hurt badly, sir?'

'I don't know, Number One. If not, it's a bloody miracle,' he added bitterly. He stooped down, raised the dazed Captain to a sitting position.

'Are you all right, sir?' he asked anxiously. 'Do you—have you been hit?'

Vallery shuddered in a long, exhausting paroxysm of coughing, then shook his head feebly.

'I'm all right,' he whispered weakly. He tried to grin, a pitiful, ghastly travesty of a smile in the reflected light from the burning Aldis. 'I dived for the deck, but I think the binnacle got in my way.' He rubbed his forehead, already bruised and discoloured. 'How's the ship, Commander?'

'To hell with the ship!' Turner said roughly. He passed an arm round Vallery, raised him carefully to his feet. 'How are things aft, Number One?'

'Under control. Still burning, but under control. I left Hartley in charge.' He made no mention of Carslake.

'Good! Take over. Radio *Stirling, Sirrus,* see how they are. Come on, sir. Shelter for you!'

Vallery protested feebly, a token protest only, for he was too weak to stand. He checked involuntarily as he saw the snow falling whitely through the barred beam of the Aldis, slowly followed the beam back to its source.

'Bentley?' he whispered. 'Don't tell me . . . ' He barely caught the Commander's wordless nod, turned heavily away. They passed by the dead man stretched outside the gate, then stopped at the Asdic cabinet. A sobbing figure was crouched into the angle between the shelter and the jammed and shattered door of the hut, head pillowed on the forearm resting high against the door. Vallery laid a hand on the shaking shoulder, peered into the averted face.

'What is it? Oh, it's you, boy.' The white face had been lifted towards him. 'What's the matter, Chrysler?'

'The door, sir!' Chrysler's voice was muffled, quivering. 'The door—I can't open it.'

For the first time, Vallery looked at the cabinet, at the gashed and torn metal. His mind was still dazed, exhausted, and it was almost by a process of association that he suddenly, horrifyingly thought of the gashed and mangled operator that must lie behind that locked door.

'Yes,' he said quietly. 'The door's buckled . . . There's nothing anyone can do, Chrysler.' He looked more closely at the grief-dulled eyes. 'Come on, my boy, there's no need—'

'My brother's in there, sir.' The words, the hopeless despair, struck Vallery like a blow. Dear God! He had forgotten . . . Of course—Leading Asdic Operator Chrysler . . . He stared down at the dead man at his feet, already covered with a thin layer of snow.

'Have that Aldis unplugged, Commander, will you?' he asked absently. 'And Chrysler?'

'Yes, sir.' A flat monotone.

'Go below and bring up some coffee, please.'

'Coffee, sir!' He was bewildered, uncomprehending. 'Coffee! But—but—my—my brother—'

'I know,' Vallery said gently. 'I know. Bring some coffee, will you?'

Chrysler stumbled off. When the shelter door closed behind them, clicking on the light, Vallery turned to the Commander.

'Cue for moralizing on the glories of war,' he murmured quietly. '*Dulce et decorum*, and the proud privilege of being the sons of Nelson and Drake. It's not twenty-four hours since Ralston watched his father die . . . And now this boy. Perhaps—'

'I'll take care of things,' Turner nodded. He hadn't yet forgiven himself for what he had said and done to Ralston last night, in spite of Ralston's quick friendliness, the ready acceptance of his apologies. 'I'll keep him busy out of the way till we open up the cabinet . . . Sit down, sir. Have a swig of this.' He smiled faintly. 'Friend Williams having betrayed my guilty secret . . . Hallo! Company.'

The light clicked off and a burly figure bulked momentarily against the grey oblong of the doorway. The door shut, and Brooks stood blinking in the sudden light, red of face and gasping for breath. He eyes focused on the bottle in Turner's hand.

'Ha!' he said at length. 'Having a bottle party, are we? All contributions gratefully received, I have no doubt.' He opened his case on a convenient table, was rummaging inside when someone rapped sharply on the door.

'Come in,' Vallery called.

A signalman entered, handed a note to Vallery. 'From London, sir. Chief says there may be some reply.'

'Thank you. I'll phone down.'

The door opened and closed again. Vallery looked up at an empty-handed Turner.

'Thanks for removing the guilty evidence so quickly,' he smiled. Then he shook his head. 'My eyes—they don't seem so good. Perhaps you would read the signal, Commander?'

'And perhaps *you* would like some decent medicine,' Brooks boomed, 'instead of that filthy muck of Turner's.' He fished in his bag, produced a bottle of amber liquid. 'With all the resources of modern medicine—well, practically all, anyway—at my disposal, I can find nothing to equal this.'

'Have you told Nicholls?' Vallery was stretched out on the settee now, eyes closed, the shadow of a smile on his bloodless lips.

'Well, no,' Brooks confessed. 'But plenty of time. Have some?'

'Thanks. Let's have the good news, Turner.'

'Good news!' The sudden deadly quiet of the Commanderr's voice fell chilly over the waiting men. 'No, sir, it's not good news.

'"Rear-Admiral Vallery, Commanding 14 ACS, FR77."' The voice was drained of all tone and expression. '"*Tirpitz*, escorting cruisers, destroyers, reported moving out Alta Fjord sunset. Intense activity Alta Fjord airfield. Fear sortie under air cover. All measures avoid useless sacrifice Merchant, Naval ships. DNO, London."' With deliberate care Turner folded the paper, laid it on the table. 'Isn't that just wonderful,' he murmured. 'Whatever next?'

Vallery was sitting bolt upright on the settee, blind to the blood trickling down crookedly from one corner of his mouth. His face was calm, unworried.

'I think I'll have that glass, now, Brooks, if you don't mind,' he said quietly. The *Tirpitz*. The *Tirpitz*. He shook his head tiredly, like a man in a dream. The *Tirpitz*—the name that no man mentioned without a far-off echo of awe and fear, the name that had completely dominated North Atlantic naval strategy during the past two years. Moving out at last, an armoured Colossus, sister-ship to that other Titan that had destroyed the *Hood* with one single, savage blow—the *Hood*, the darling of the Royal Navy, the most powerful ship in the world—or so men had thought. What chance had *their* tiny cockleshell cruiser . . . Again he shook his head, angrily this time, forced himself to think of the present.

'Well, gentlemen, I suppose time bringeth all things—even the *Tirpitz*. It had to come some day. Just our ill luck—the bait was too close, too tempting.'

'My young colleague is going to be just delighted,' Brooks said grimly. 'A *real* battleship at long, long last.'

'Sunset,' Turner mused. 'Sunset. My God!' he said sharply, 'even allowing for negotiating the fjord they'll be on us in four hours on this course!'

'Exactly,' Vallery nodded. 'And it's no good running north. They'd overtake us before we're within a hundred miles of them.'

'Them? Our big boys up north?' Turner scoffed. 'I hate to sound like a gramophone record, but you'll recall my earlier statement about them—too—late as usual!' He paused, swore again. 'I hope that old bastard Starr's satisfied at last!' he finished bitterly.

'Why all the gloom?' Vallery looked up quizzically, went on softly. 'We can still be back, safe and sound in Scapa in forty-eight hours. "Avoid useless sacrifice Merchant, Naval ships," he said. The *Ulysses* is probably the fastest ship in the world today. It's simple, gentlemen.'

'No, no!' Brooks moaned. 'Too much of an anti-climax. I couldn't stand it!'

'Do another PQ17?'[1] Turner smiled, but the smile never touched his eyes. 'The RoyalNavy could never stand it: Captain—Rear-Admiral Vallery would never permit it; and speaking for myself and, I'm fairly certain, this bunch of cut-throat mutineers of ours—well, I don't think we'd ever sleep so sound o' nights again.'

'Gad!' Brooks murmured. 'That man's a poet!'

'You're right, Turner.' Vallery drained his glass, lay back

---

1. PQ17, a large mixed convoy—it included over 30 British, American and Panamanian ships—left Iceland for Russia under the escort of half a dozen destroyers and perhaps a dozen smaller craft, with a mixed Anglo-American cruiser and destroyer squadron in immediate support. A shadow covering force—again Anglo-American—comprising one aircraft carrier, two battleships, three cruisers and a flotilla of destroyers, lay to the north. As with FR77, they formed the spring of the trap that closed too late. The time was midsummer, 1942, a suicidal season for the attempt, for in June and July, in these high latitudes, there is no night. About longitude 20° east, the convoy was heavily attacked by U-boats and aircraft. On the same day as the attack began—4th July—the covering cruiser squadron was radioed that the *Tirpitz* had just sailed from Alta Fjord. (This was not the case: The *Tirpitz* did make a brief, abortive sortie on the afternoon of the 5th, but turned back the same evening: rumour had it that she had been damaged by torpedoes from a Russian submarine.) The support squadron and convoy escorts immediately withdrew to the west at high speed, leaving PQ17 to their fate, leaving them to scatter and make their unescorted way to Russia as best they could. The feelings of the crews of the merchant ships at this save-their-own-skins desertion and betrayal by the Royal Navy can be readily imagined. Their fears, too, can be readily imagined, but even their darkest forebodings never conceived the dreadful reality: 23 merchant ships were sent to the bottom—by U-boats and aircraft. The *Tirpitz* was not seen, never came anywhere near the convoy, but even the threat had driven the naval squadrons to flight. The author does not know all the facts concerning PQ17, nor does he seek to interpret those he does know: still less does he seek to assign blame. Curiously enough, the only definite conclusion is that no blame can be attached to the commander of the squadron, Admiral Hamilton. He had no part of the decision to withdraw—the order came from the Admiralty, and was imperative. But one does not envy him. It was a melancholy and bitter incident, all the more unpalatable in that it ran so directly counter to the traditions of a great Service; one wonders what Sir Philip Sydney would have thought, or, in more modern times, Kennedy of the *Rawalpindi* or Fegen of the *Jervis Bay*. But there was no doubt what the Merchant Navy thought. What they still think. From most of the few survivors, there can be no hope of forgiveness. They will, probably, always remember: the Royal Navy would desperately like to forget. It is difficult to blame either.

exhausted. 'We don't seem to have much option . . . What if we receive orders for a—ah—high-speed withdrawal?'

'You can't read,' Turner said bluntly. 'Remember, you just said your eyes are going back on you.'

'"Souls that have toiled and wrought and fought with me,"' Vallery quoted softly. 'Thank you, gentlemen. You make things very easy for me.' He propped himself on an elbow, his mind made up. He smiled at Turner, and his face was almost boyish again.

'Inform all merchant ships, all escorts. Tell them to break north.'

Turner stared at him.

'North? Did you say "north"? But the Admiralty—'

'North, I said,' Vallery repeated quietly. 'The Admiralty can do what they like about it. We've played along long enough. We've sprung the trap. What more can they want? This way there's a chance—an almost hopeless chance, perhaps, but a fighting chance. To go east is suicide.' He smiled again, almost dreamily. 'The end is not all-important,' he said softly. 'I don't think I'll have to answer for this. Not now—not ever.'

Turner grinned at him, his face lit up. 'North, you said.'

'Inform C-in-C,' Vallery went on. 'Ask Pilot for an interception course. Tell the convoy we'll tag along behind, give 'em as much cover as we can, as long as we can . . . As long as we can. Let us not delude ourselves. 1,000 to 1 at the outside . . . Nothing else we can do, Commander?'

'Pray,' Turner said succinctly.

'And sleep,' Brooks added. 'Why don't you have half an hour, sir?'

'Sleep!' Vallery seemed genuinely amused. 'We'll have all the time in the world to sleep, just by and by.'

'You have a point,' Brooks conceded. 'You are very possibly right.'

FIFTEEN

Saturday Evening II

Messages were pouring in to the bridge now, messages from the merchant ships, messages of dismayed unbelief asking for confirmation of the *Tirpitz* breakout: from the *Stirling,* replying that the superstructure fire was now under control and that the engine-room watertight bulkheads were holding; and one from Orr of the *Sirrus,* saying that his ship was making water to the capacity of the pumps—he had been in heavy collision with the sinking merchantman—that they had taken off forty-four survivors, that the *Sirrus* had already done her share and couldn't she go home? The signal had arrived after the *Sirrus*'s receipt of the bad news. Turner grinned to himself: no inducement on earth, he knew, could have persuaded Orr to leave now.

The messages kept pouring in, by visual signal or WT. There was no point in maintaining radio silence to outwit enemy monitor positions; the enemy knew where they were to a mile. Nor was there any need to prohibit light signalling—not with the *Stirling* still burning furiously enough to illuminate the sea for a mile around. And so the messages kept on coming—messages of fear and dismay and anxiety. But, for Turner, the most disquieting message came neither by lamp nor by radio.

Fully quarter of an hour had elapsed since the end of the attack and the *Ulysses* was rearing and pitching through the head seas on her new course of 350°, when the gate of the bridge crashed open and a panting, exhausted man stumbled on to the compass platform.

Turner, back on the bridge again, peered closely at him in the red glare from the *Stirling*, recognized him as a stoker. His face was masked in sweat, the sweat already caking to ice in the intense cold. And in spite of that cold, he was hatless, coatless, clad only in a pair of thin dungarees. He was shivering violently, shivering from excitement and not because of the icy wind—he was oblivious to such things.

Turner seized him by the shoulder.

'What is it, man?' he demanded anxiously. The stoker was still too breathless to speak. 'What's wrong? Quickly!'

'The TS, sir!' The breathing was so quick, so agonized, that the words blurred into a gasping exhalation. 'It's full of water!'

'The TS!' Turner was incredulous. 'Flooded! When did this happen?'

'I'm not sure, sir.' He was still gasping for breath. 'But there was a bloody awful explosion, sir, just about amid—'

'I know! I know!' Turner interrupted impatiently. 'Bomber carried away the for'ard funnel, exploded in the water, port side. But that was fifteen minutes ago, man! Fifteen minutes! Good God, they would have—'

'TS switchboard's gone, sir.' The stoker was beginning to recover, to huddle against the wind, but frantic at the Commander's deliberation and delay, he straightened up and grasped Turner's duffel without realizing what he was doing. The note of the urgency deepened still further. 'All the power's gone, sir. And the hatch is jammed! The men can't get out!'

'The hatch-cover jammed!' Turner's eyes narrowed in concern. 'What happened?' he rapped out. 'Buckled?'

'The counter-weight's broken off, sir. It's on top of the hatch. We can only get it open an inch. You see, sir—'

'Number One!' Turner shouted.

'Here, sir.' Carrington was standing just behind him. 'I heard . . . Why can't you open it?'

'It's the *TS* hatch!' the stoker cried desperately. 'A quarter of a bloody ton if it's an ounce, sir. You know—the one below the ladder outside the wheelhouse. Only two men can get at it at the same time. We've tried . . . Hurry, sir. *Please*.'

'Just a minute.' Carrington was calm, unruffled, infuriatingly so. 'Hartley? No, still fire-fighting. Evans, MacIntosh—dead.' He was obviously thinking aloud. 'Bellamy, perhaps?'

'What is it, Number One?' Turner burst out. He himself had caught up the anxiety, the impatience of the stoker. 'What are you trying—?'

'Hatch-cover plus pulley—1,000 lbs.,' Carrington murmured. 'A special man for a special job.'

'Petersen, sir!' The stoker had understood immediately. 'Petersen!'

'Of course!' Carrington clapped gloved hands together. 'We're on our way, sir. Acetylene? No time! Stoker—crow-bars, sledges . . . Perhaps if you would ring the engine-room, sir?'

But Turner already had the phone in his hand.

Aft on the poop-deck, the fire was under control, all but in a few odd corners where the flames were fed by a fierce through draught. In the mess-decks, bulkheads, ladders, mess partitions, lockers had been twisted and buckled into strange shapes by the intense heat: on deck, the gasoline-fed flames, incinerating the two and three-quarter inch deck plating and melting the caulking as by some gigantic blow-torch, had cleanly stripped all covering and exposed the steel deck-plates, plates dull red and glowing evilly, plates that hissed and spat as heavy snowflakes drifted down to sibilant extinction.

On and below decks, Hartley and his crews, freezing one moment, reeling in the blast of heat the next, toiled like men insane. Where their wasted, exhausted bodies found the strength God only knew. From the turrets, from the Master-At-Arms's office, from mess-decks and emergency steering position, they pulled out man after man who had been there when the Condor had crashed: pulled them out, looked at them, swore, wept and plunged back into the aftermath of that holocaust, oblivious of pain and danger, tearing aside wreckage, wreckage still burning, still red-hot, with charred and broken gloves: and when the gloves fell off, they used their naked hands.

As the dead were ranged in the starboard alleyway, Leading Seaman Doyle was waiting for them. Less than half an hour previously, Doyle had been in the for'ard galley passage, rolling in silent agony as frozen body and clothes thawed out after the drenching of his pom-pom. Five minutes later, he had been back on his gun, rock-like, unflinching, as he pumped shell after shell over open sights into the torpedo bombers. And now, steady and enduring as ever, he was on the poop. A man of iron, and a face of iron, too, that night, the bearded leonine head still and impassive as he picked up one dead man after the other, walked to the guard-rail and dropped his burden gently over the side. How many times he repeated that brief journey that night, Doyle never knew: he had lost count after the first twenty or so. He had no right to do this, of course: the navy was very strong on decent burial, and this was not decent burial. But the sailmakers were dead and no man would or could have sewn up these ghastly charred heaps in the weighted and sheeted canvas. The dead don't care, Doyle thought dispassionately—let them look after themselves. So, too, thought Carrington and Hartley, and they made no move to stop him.

Beneath their feet, the smouldering mess-decks rang with hollow reverberating clangs as Nicholls and Leading Telegraphist Brown, still weirdly garbed in their white asbestos suits, swung heavy sledges against the securing clips of 'Y' magazine hatch. In the smoke and gloom and their desperate haste, they could hardly see each other, much less the clips: as often as not they missed their strokes and the hammers went spinning out of numbed hands into the waiting darkness.

Time yet, Nicholls thought desperately, perhaps there is time. The main flooding valve had been turned off five minutes ago: it was possible, barely possible, that the two trapped men inside were clinging to the ladder, above water level.

One clip, one clip only was holding the hatch-cover now. With alternate strokes of their sledges, they struck it with vicious strength. Suddenly, unexpectedly, it sheared off at its base and the hatch-cover crashed open under the explosive up-surge of the compressed air beneath. Brown screamed in agony, a single coughing shout of pain, as the bone-crashing momentum of the swinging hatch crashed into his right hip, then fell to the deck where he lay moaning quietly.

Nicholls did not even spare him a glance. He leant far through the hatch, the powerful beam of his torch stabbing downwards into the gloom. And he could see nothing, nothing at all—not what he wanted to see. All he saw was the water, dark and viscous and evil, water rising and falling, water flooding and ebbing in the eerie oil-bound silence as the *Ulysses* plunged and lifted in the heavy seas.

'Below!' Nicholls called loudly. The voice, a voice, he noted impersonally, cracked and shaken with strain, boomed and echoed terrifyingly down the iron tunnel. 'Below!' he shouted again. 'Is there anybody there?' He strained his ears for the least sound, for the faintest whisper of an answer, but none came.

'McQuater!' He shouted a third time. 'Williamson! Can you hear me?' Again he looked, again he listened, but there was only the darkness and the muffled whisper of the oil-slicked water swishing smoothly from side to side. He stared again down the light from the torch, marvelled that any surface could so quickly dissipate and engulf the brilliance of that beam. And beneath that surface . . . He shivered. The water—even the water seemed to be dead, old and evil and infinitely horrible. In sudden anger, he shook his head to clear it of these stupid, primitive fears: his imagination—he'd have to watch it. He stepped back, straightened up. Gently, carefully, he closed the swinging hatch. The mess-deck echoed as his sledge swung down on the clips, again and again and again.

Engineer-Commander Dodson stirred and moaned. He struggled to open his eyes but his eyelids refused to function. At least, he thought that they did for the blackness around remained as it was, absolute, impenetrable, almost palpable.

He wondered dully what had happened, how long he had been there, what had happened. And the side of his head—just below the ear—that hurt abominably. Slowly, with clumsy deliberation, he peeled off his glove, reached up an exploratory hand. It came away wet and sticky: his hair, he realized with mild surprise, was thickly matted with blood. It must be blood—he could feel it trickling slowly, heavily down the side of his cheek.

And that deep, powerful vibration, a vibration overlain with an indefinable note of strain that set his engineer's teeth on edge—he could hear it, almost feel it, immediately in front of him. His bare hand reached out, recoiled in instant reflex as it touched something smooth and revolving—and burning hot.

The shaft tunnel! Of course. That's where he was—the shaft tunnel. They'd discovered fractured lubricating pipes on the port shafts too, and he'd decided to keep this engine turning. He knew they'd been attacked. Down here in the hidden bowels of the ship, sound did not penetrate: he had heard nothing of the aircraft engines: he hadn't even heard their own guns firing—but there had been no mistaking the jarring shock of the 5.25s surging back on their hydraulic recoils. And then —a torpedo perhaps, or a near miss by a bomb. Thank God he'd been sitting facing inboard when the *Ulysses* had lurched. The other way round and it would have been curtains for sure when he'd been flung across the shaft coupling and wrapped round . . .

The shaft! Dear God, the shaft! It was running almost red-hot on dry bearings! Frantically, he pawed around, picked up his emergency lamp and twisted its base. There was no light. He twisted it again with all his strength, reached up, felt the jagged edges of broken screen and bulb, and flung the useless lamp to the deck. He dragged out his pocket torch: that, too, was smashed. Desperate now, he searched blindly around for his oil can: it was lying on its side, the patent spring top beside it. The can was empty.

No oil, none. Heaven only knew how near the over-stressed metal was to the critical limit. He didn't. He admitted that: even to the best engineers, metal fatigue was an incalculable unknown. But, like all men who had spent a lifetime with machines, he had developed a sixth sense for these things—and, right now, that sixth sense was jabbing at him, mercilessly, insistently. Oil—he would have to get oil. But he knew he was in bad shape, dizzy, weak from shock and loss of blood, and the tunnel was long and slippery and dangerous—and unlighted. One slip, one stumble against or over that merciless shaft . . . Gingerly, the Engineer-Commander stretched out his hand again, rested his hand for an instant on the shaft, drew back sharply in sudden pain. He lifted his hand to his cheek, knew that it was not friction that had flayed and burnt the skin off the tips of his fingers. There was no choice. Resolutely, he gathered his legs under him, swayed dizzily to his feet, his back bent against the arching convexity of the tunnel.

It was then that he noticed it for the first time—a light, a swinging tiny pinpoint of light, imponderably distant in the converging sides of that dark tunnel, although he knew it could be only yards away. He blinked, closed his eyes and looked again. The light was still there, advancing steadily, and he could hear the shuffling of feet now. All at once he felt weak, light-headed: gratefully he sank down again, his feet safely braced once more against the bearing block.

The man with the light stopped a couple of feet away, hooked the lamp on to an inspection bracket, lowered himself carefully and sat beside Dodson. The rays of the lamp fell full on the dark heavy face, the jagged brows and prognathous jaw: Dodson stiffened in sudden surprise.

'Riley! Stoker Riley!' His eyes narrowed in suspicion and conjecture. 'What the devil are you doing here?'

'I've brought a two-gallon drum of lubricating oil,' Riley growled. He thrust a Thermos flask into the Engineer-Commander's hands. 'And here's some coffee. I'll 'tend to this—you drink that . . . Suffering Christ! This bloody bearing's red-hot!'

Dodson set down the Thermos with a thump.

'Are you deaf?' he asked harshly. 'Why are you here? Who sent you? Your station's in "B" boiler-room!'

'Grierson sent me,' Riley said roughly. His dark face was impassive. 'Said he couldn't spare his engine-room men—too bloody valuable . . . Too much?' The oil, thick, viscous, was pouring slowly on to the overheated bearing.

'*Lieutenant* Grierson!' Dodson was almost vicious, his voice a whip-lash of icy correction. 'And that's a damned lie, Riley! Lieutenant Grierson never sent you: I suppose you told *him* that somebody else had sent you?'

'Drink your coffee,' Riley advised sourly. 'You're wanted in the engine-room.'

The Engineer-Commander clenched his fist, restrained himself with difficulty.

'You damned insolent bastard!' he burst out. Abruptly, control came back and he said evenly: 'Commander's Defaulters in the morning. You'll pay for this, Riley!'

'No, I won't.' Confound him, Dodson thought furiously, he's actually grinning, the insolent . . .

He checked his thought.

'Why not?' he demanded dangerously.

'Because you won't report me.' Riley seemed to be enjoying himself hugely.

'Oh, so that's it!' Dodson glanced swiftly round the darkened tunnel, and his lips tightened as he realized for the first time how completely alone they were: in sudden certainty he looked back at Riley, big and hunched and menacing. Smiling yet, but no smile, Dodson thought, could ever transform that ugly brutal face. The smile on the face of the tiger . . . Fear, exhaustion, never-ending strain—they did terrible things to a man and you couldn't blame him for what he had become, or for what he was born . . . But his, Dodson's, first responsibility was to himself. Grimly, he remembered how Turner had berated him, called him all sorts of a fool for refusing to have Riley sent to prison.

'So that's it, eh?' he repeated softly. He turned himself, feet thrusting solidly against the block. 'Don't be so sure, Riley. I can give you twenty-five years, but—'

'Oh, for Christ's sake!' Riley burst out impatiently. 'What are you talking about, sir? Drink your coffee—please. You're wanted in the engineroom, I tell you!' he repeated impatiently.

Uncertainly, Dodson relaxed, unscrewed the cap of the Thermos. He had a sudden, peculiar feeling of unreality, as if he were a spectator, some bystander in no way involved in this scene, this fantastic scene. His head, he realized, still hurt like hell.

'Tell me, Riley,' he asked softly, 'what makes you so sure I won't report you?'

'Oh, you can report me all right.' Riley was suddenly cheerful again. 'But I won't be at the Commander's table tomorrow morning.'

'No?' It was half-challenge, half-question.

'No,' Riley grinned. ''Cos there'll *be* no Commander *and* no table tomorrow morning.' He clasped his hands luxuriously behind his head. 'In fact, there'll be no nothin'.'

Something in the voice, rather than in the words, caught and held Dodson's attention. He knew, with instant conviction, that though Riley might be smiling, he wasn't joking. Dodson looked at him curiously, but said nothing.

'Commander's just finished broadcastin',' Riley continued. 'The *Tirpitz* is out—we have four hours left.'

The bald, flat statement, the complete lack of histrionics, of playing for effect, left no possible room for doubt. The *Tirpitz*—out. The *Tirpitz*—out. Dodson repeated the phrase to himself, over and over again. Four hours, just four hours to go . . . He was surprised at his own reaction, his apparent lack of concern.

'Well?' Riley was anxious now, restive. 'Are you goin' or aren't you? I'm not kiddin', sir—you're wanted—urgent!'

'You're a liar,' Dodson said pleasantly. 'Why did you bring the coffee?'

'For myself.' The smile was gone, the face set and sullen. 'But I thought you needed it—you don't look so good to me . . . They'll fix you up back in the engine-room.'

'And that's just where you're going, right now!' Dodson said evenly.

Riley gave no sign that he had heard.

'On your way, Riley,' Dodson said curtly. 'That's an order!'

'—off!' Riley growled. 'I'm stayin'. You don't require to have three—great gold stripes on your sleeve to handle a bloody oil can,' he finished derisively.

'Possibly not.' Dodson braced against a sudden, violent pitch, but too late to prevent himself lurching into Riley. 'Sorry, Riley. Weather's worsening, I'm afraid. Well, we—ah—appear to have reached an impasse.'

'What's that?' Riley asked suspiciously.

'A dead-end. A no-decision fight . . . Tell me, Riley,' he asked quietly. 'What brought you here?'

'I told you!' Riley was aggrieved. 'Grierson—*Lieutenant* Grierson sent me.'

'What brought you here?' Dodson persisted. It was as if Riley had not spoken.

'That's my—business!' Riley answered savagely.

'What brought you here?'

'Oh, for Christ's sake leave me alone!' Riley shouted. His voice echoed loudly along the dark tunnel. Suddenly he turned round full-face, his mouth twisted bitterly. 'You know bloody well why I came.'

'To do me in, perhaps?'

Riley looked at him a long second, then turned away. His shoulders were hunched, his head held low.

'You're the only bastard in this ship that ever gave me a break,' he muttered. 'The only bastard I've ever *known* who ever gave me a chance,' he amended slowly. 'Bastard' Dodson supposed, was Riley's accolade of friendship, and he felt suddenly shamed of his last remark. 'If it wasn't for you,' Riley went on softly, 'I'd 'a' been in cells the first time, in a civvy jail the second. Remember, sir?'

Dodson nodded. 'You were rather foolish, Riley,' he admitted.

'Why did you do it?' The big stoker was intense, worried. 'God, everyone knows what I'm like—'

'Do they? I wonder . . . I thought you had the makings of a better man than you—'

'Don't give me that bull!' Riley scoffed. 'I know what I'm like. I know what I am. I'm no—good! Everybody says I'm no—good! And they're right . . . ' He leaned forward. 'Do you know somethin'? I'm a Catholic. Four hours from now . . . ' He broke off. 'I should be on my knees, shouldn't I?' he sneered. 'Repentance, lookin' for—what do they call it?'

'Absolution?'

'Aye. That's it. Absolution. And do you know what?' He spoke slowly, emphatically. 'I don't give a single, solitary damn!'

'Maybe you don't have to,' Dodson murmured. 'For the last time, get back to that engine-room!'

'No!'

The Engineer-Commander sighed, picked up the Thermos.

'In that case, perhaps you would care to join me in a cup of coffee?'

Riley looked up, grinned, and when he spoke it was in a very creditable imitation of Colonel Chinstrap of the famous ITMA radio programme.

'Ectually, I don't mind if I do!'

Vallery rolled over on his side, his legs doubled up, his hand automatically reaching for the towel. His emaciated body shook violently, and the sound of the harsh, retching cough beat back at him from the iron walls of his shelter. God, he thought, oh, God, it's never been as bad as this before. Funny, he thought, it doesn't hurt any more, not even a little bit. The attack eased. He looked at the crimson, sodden towel, flung it in sudden disgust and with what little feeble strength was left him into the darkest corner of the shelter.

'You carry this damned ship on your back!' Unbidden, old Socrates's phrase came into his mind and he smiled faintly. Well, if ever they needed him, it was now. And if he waited any longer, he knew he could never be able to go.

He sat up, sweating with the effort, swung his legs carefully over the side. As his feet touched the deck, the *Ulysses* pitched suddenly, steeply, and he fell forward against a chair, sliding helplessly to the floor. It took an eternity of time, an infinite effort to drag himself to his feet again: another effort like that, he knew, would surely kill him.

And then there was the door—that heavy, steel door. Somehow he had to open it, and he knew he couldn't. But he laid hold of the handle and the door opened, and suddenly, miraculously, he was outside, gasping as the cruel, sub-zero wind seared down through his throat and wasted lungs.

He looked fore and aft. The fires were dying, he saw, the fires on the *Stirling* and on his own poop-deck. Thank God for that at least. Beside him, two men had just finished levering the door off the Asdic cabinet, were flashing a torch inside. But he couldn't bear to look: he averted his head, staggered with outstretched hands for the gate of the compass platform.

Turner saw him coming, hurried to meet him, helped him slowly to his chair.

'You've no right to be here,' he said quietly. He looked at Vallery for a long moment. 'How are you feeling, sir?'

'I'm a good deal better, now, thanks,' Vallery replied. He smiled and went on: 'We Rear-Admirals have our responsibilities, you know, Commander: it's time I began to earn my princely salary.'

'Stand back, there!' Carrington ordered curtly. 'Into the wheelhouse or up on the ladder—all of you. Let's have a look at this.'

He looked down at the great, steel hatch-cover. Looking at it, he realized he'd never before appreciated just how solid, how massive that cover was. The hatch-cover, open no more than an inch, was resting on a tommy-bar. He noticed the broken, stranded pulley, the heavy counter-weight lying against the sill of the wheelhouse. So that's off, he thought: thank the Lord for that, anyway.

'Have you tried a block and tackle?' he asked abruptly.

'Yes, sir,' the man nearest him replied. He pointed to a tangled heap in a corner. 'No use, sir. The ladder takes the strain all right, but we can't get the hook under the hatch, except sideways—and then it slips off all the time.' He gestured to the hatch. 'And every clip's either bent—they were opened by sledges—or at the wrong angle . . . I think I know how to use a block and tackle, sir.'

'I'm sure you do,' Carrington said absently. 'Here, give me a hand, will you?'

He hooked his fingers under the hatch, took a deep breath. The seaman at one side of the cover—the other side was hard against the after bulkhead—did the same. Together they strained, thighs and backs quivering under the strain. Carrington felt his face turning crimson with effort, heard the blood pounding in his ears, and relaxed. They were only killing themselves and that damned cover hadn't shifted a fraction—someone had done remarkably well to open it even that far. But even though they were tired and anything but fit, Carrington thought, two men should have been able to raise an edge of that hatch. He suspected that the hinges were jammed—or the deck buckled. If that were so, he mused, even if they could hook on a tackle, it would be of little help. A tackle was of no use when a sudden, immediate application of force was required; it always yielded that fraction before tightening up.

He sank to his knees, put his mouth to the edge of the hatch.

'Below there!' he called. 'Can you hear me?'

'We can hear you.' The voice was weak, muffled. 'For God's sake get us out of here. We're trapped like rats!'

'Is that you, Brierley? Don't worry—we'll get you out. How's the water down there?'

'Water? More bloody oil than water! There must be a fracture right through the port oil tank. I think the ring main passage must be flooded, too.'

'How deep is it?'

'Three-quarters way up already! We're standing on generators, hanging on to switchboards. One of our boys is gone already—we couldn't hold him.' Even muffled by the hatch, the strain, the near-desperation in the voice was all too obvious. 'For pity's sake, hurry up!'

'I said we'd get you out!' Carrington's voice was sharp, authoritative. The confidence was in his voice only, but he knew how quickly panic could spread down there. 'Can you push from below at all?'

'There's room for only one on the ladder,' Brierley shouted. 'It's impossible to get any pressure, any leverage upwards.' There was a sudden silence, then a series of muffled oaths.

'What's up?' Carrington called sharply.

'It's difficult to hang on,' Brierley shouted. 'There are waves two feet high down there. One of the men was washed off there . . . I think he's back again. It's pitch dark down here.'

Carrington heard the clatter of heavy footsteps above him, and straightened up. It was Petersen. In that narrow space, the blond Norwegian stoker looked gigantic. Carrington looked at him, looked at the immense span of shoulder, the great depth of chest, one enormous hand hanging loosely by his side, the other negligently holding three heavy crowbars and a sledge as if they were so many lengths of cane. Carrington looked at him, looked at the still, grave eyes so startlingly blue under the flaxen hair, and all at once he felt oddly confident, reassured.

'We can't open this, Petersen,' Carrington said baldly. 'Can you?'

'I will try, sir.' He laid down his tools, stooped, caught the end of the tommy-bar projecting beneath the corner of the cover. He straightened quickly, easily: the hatch lifted a fraction, then the bar, putty-like in its apparent malleability, bent over almost to a right angle.

'I think the hatch is jammed.' Petersen wasn't even breathing heavily. 'It will be the hinges, sir.'

He walked round the hatch, peered closely at the hinges, then grunted in satisfaction. Three times the heavy sledge, swung with accuracy and all the power of these great shoulders behind them, smashed squarely into the face of the outer hinge. On the third stroke the sledge snapped. Petersen threw away the broken shaft in disgust, picked up another, much heavier crowbar.

Again the bar bent, but again the hatch-cover lifted—an inch this time. Petersen picked up the two smaller sledges that had been used to open clips, hammered at the hinges till these sledges, too, were broken and useless.

This time he used the last two crowbars together, thrust under the same corner of the hatch. For five, ten seconds he remained bent over them, motionless. He was breathing deeply, quickly, now, then suddenly the breathing stopped. The sweat began to pour off his face, his whole body to quiver under the titanic strain: then slowly, incredibly, both crowbars began to bend.

Carrington watched, fascinated. He had never seen anything remotely like this before: he was sure no one else had either. Neither of these bars, he would have sworn, would have bent under less than half a ton of pressure. It was fantastic, but it was happening: and as the giant straightened, they were bending more and more. Then suddenly, so unexpectedly that everyone jumped, the hatch sprang open five or six inches and Petersen crashed backwards against the bulkhead, the bars falling from his hand and splashing into the water below.

Petersen flung himself back at the hatch, tigerish in his ferocity. His fingers hooked under the edge, the great muscles of his arms and shoulders lifted and locked as he tugged and pulled at that massive hatch-cover. Three times he heaved, four times, then on the fifth the hatch almost literally leapt up with a screech of tortured metal and smashed shudderingly home into the retaining latch of the vertical stand behind. The hatch was open. Petersen just stood there smiling—no one had seen Petersen smile for a long time—his face bathed in sweat, his great chest rising and falling rapidly as his starved lungs sucked in great draughts of air.

The water level in the Low Power Room was within two feet of the hatch: sometimes, when the *Ulysses* plunged into a heavy sea, the dark, oily liquid splashed over the hatch coaming into the flat above. Quickly, the trapped men were hauled to safety. Soaked in oil from head to foot, their eyes gummed and blinded, they were men overcome by reaction, utterly spent and on the verge of collapse, so far gone that even their fear could not overcome their exhaustion. Three, in particular, could do no more than cling helplessly to the ladder, would almost certainly have slipped back into the surging blackness below; but Petersen bent over and plucked them clean out of the Low Power Room as if they had been little children.

'Take these men to the Sick Bay at once!' Carrington ordered. He watched the dripping, shivering men being helped up the ladder, then turned to the giant stoker with a smile. 'We'll all thank you later, Petersen. We're not finished yet. This hatch must be closed and battened down.'

'It will be difficult, sir,' Petersen said gravely.

'Difficult or not, it *must* be done.' Carrington was emphatic. Regularly, now, the water was spilling over the coaming, was lapping the sill of the wheelhouse. 'The emergency steering position is gone: if the wheelhouse is flooded, we're finished.'

Petersen said nothing. He lifted the retaining latch, pulled the protesting hatch-cover down a foot. Then he braced his shoulder against the latter, planted his feet on the cover and straightened his back convulsively: the cover screeched down to 45°. He paused, bent his back like a bow, his hands taking his weight on the ladder, then pounded his feet again and again on the edge of the cover. Fifteen inches to go.

'We need heavy hammers, sir,' Petersen said urgently.

'No time!' Carrington shook his head quickly. 'Two more minutes and it'll be impossible to shut the hatch-cover against the water pressure. Hell!' he said bitterly. 'If it were only the other way round—closing from below. Even I could lever it shut!'

Again Petersen said nothing. He squatted down by the side of the hatch, gazed into the darkness beneath his feet.

'I have an idea, sir,' he said quickly. 'If two of you would stand on the hatch, push against the ladder. Yes, sir, that way—but you could push harder if you turned your back to me.'

Carrington laid the heels of his hands against the iron steps of the ladder, heaved with all his strength. Suddenly he heard a splash, then a metallic clatter, whirled round just in time to see a crowbar clutched in an enormous hand disappear below the edge of the hatch. There was no sign of Petersen. Like many big, powerful men, he was lithe and cat-like in his movements: he'd gone down over the edge of that hatch without a sound.

'Petersen!' Carrington was on his knees by the hatch. 'What the devil do you think you're doing? Come out of there, you bloody fool! Do you want to drown?'

There was no reply. Complete silence below, a silence deepened by the gentle susurration of the water. Suddenly the quiet was broken by the sound of metal striking against metal, then by a jarring screech as the hatch dropped six inches. Before Carrington had time to think, the hatch-cover dropped farther still. Desperately, the First Lieutenant seized a crowbar, thrust it under the hatch-cover: a split second later the great steel cover thudded down on top of it. Carrington had his mouth to the gap now.

'In the name of God, Petersen,' he shouted, 'are you sane? Open up, open up at once, do you hear?'

'I can't.' The voice came and went as the water surged over the stoker's head. 'I won't. You said yourself . . . there is no time . . . this was the only way.'

'But I never meant—'

'I know. It does not matter . . . it is better this way.' It was almost impossible to make out what he was saying. 'Tell Captain Vallery that Petersen says he is very sorry . . . I tried to tell the Captain yesterday.'

'Sorry! Sorry for what?' Madly Carrington flung all his strength against the iron bar: the hatchcover did not even quiver.

'The dead marine in Scapa Flow . . . I did not mean to kill him, I could never kill any man . . . But he angered me,' the big Norwegian said simply. 'He killed my friend.'

For a second, Carrington stopped straining at the bar. Petersen! Of course—who but Petersen could have snapped a man's neck like that. Petersen, the big, laughing Scandinavian, who had so suddenly changed overnight into a grave unsmiling giant, who stalked the deck, the mess-decks and alleyways by day and by night, who was never seen to smile or sleep. With a sudden flash of insight, Carrington saw clear through into the tortured mind of that kind and simple man.

'Listen, Petersen,' he begged. 'I don't give a damn about that. Nobody shall ever know, I promise you. Please Petersen, just—'

'It is better this way.' The muffled voice was strangely content. 'It is not good to kill a man . . . it is not good to go on living . . . I know . . . Please, it is important—you will tell my Captain—Petersen is sorry and filled with shame . . . I do this for my Captain.' Without warning, the crowbar was plucked from Carrington's hand. The cover clanged down in position. For a minute the wheelhouse flat rang to a succession of muffled, metallic blows. Suddenly the clamour ceased and there was only the rippling surge of the water outside the wheelhouse and the creak of the wheel inside as the *Ulysses* steadied on course.

The clear sweet voice soared high and true above the subdued roar of the engine-room fans, above the whine of a hundred electric motors and the sound of the rushing of the waters. Not even the metallic impersonality of the loudspeakers could detract from the beauty of that singing voice . . . It was a favourite device of Vallery's when the need for silence was not paramount, to pass the long, dark hours by coupling up the record-player to the broadcast system.

Almost invariably, the musical repertoire was strictly classical—or what is more often referred to, foolishly and disparagingly, as the popular classics. Bach, Beethoven, Tchaikovski, Lehar, Verdi,

Delius—these were the favourites. 'No. I in B flat minor', 'Air on a G string', 'Moonlight on the Alster', 'Claire de Lune', 'The Skater's Waltz'—the crew of the *Ulysses* could never have enough of these. 'Ridiculous', 'impossible'—it is all too easy to imagine the comments of those who equate the matelot's taste in music with the popular conception of his ethics and morals; but those same people have never heard the hushed, cathedral silence in the crowded hangar of a great aircraft carrier in Scapa Flow as Yehudi Menuhin's magic bow sang across the strings of the violin, swept a thousand men away from the harsh urgencies of reality, from the bitter memories of the last patrol or convoy, into the golden land of music.

But now a girl was singing. It was Deanna Durbin, and she was singing 'Beneath the Lights of Home', that most heartbreakingly nostalgic of all songs. Below decks and above, bent over the great engines or huddled by their guns, men listened to the lovely voice as it drifted through the darkened ship and the falling snow, and turned their minds inwards and thought of home, thought of the bitter contrast and the morning that would not come. Suddenly, halfway through, the song stopped.

'Do you hear there?' the speakers boomed. 'Do you hear there? This—this is the Commander speaking.' The voice was deep and grave and hesitant: it caught and held the attention of every man in the ship.

'I have bad news for you.' Turner spoke slowly, quietly. 'I am sorry—I . . . ' He broke off, then went on more slowly still. 'Captain Vallery died five minutes ago.' For a moment the speaker was silent, then crackled again. 'He died on the bridge, in his chair. He knew he was dying and I don't think he suffered at all . . . He insisted—he insisted that I thank you for the way you all stood by him. "Tell em"—these were his words, as far as I remember—"tell em," he said, "that I couldn't have carried on without them, that they are the best crew that God ever gave a Captain." Then he said—it was the last thing he said: "Give them my apologies. After all they've done for me—well, well, tell them I'm terribly sorry to let them down like this." That was all he said—just "Tell them I'm sorry." And then he died.'

SIXTEEN

Saturday Night

Richard Vallery was dead. He died grieving, stricken at the thought that he was abandoning the crew of the *Ulysses*, leaving them behind, leaderless. But it was only for a short time, and he did not have to wait long. Before the dawn, hundreds more, men in the cruisers, the destroyers and the merchantmen, had died also. And they did not die as he had feared under the guns of the *Tirpitz*—another grim parallel with PQ17, for the *Tirpitz* had not left Alta Fjord. They died, primarily, because the weather had changed.

Richard Vallery was dead, and with his death a great change had come over the men of the *Ulysses*. When Vallery died, other things died also, for he took these things with him. He took with him the courage, the kindliness, the gentleness, the unshakable faith, the infinitely patient and understanding endurance, all these things which had been so peculiarly his own. And now these things were gone and the *Ulysses* was left without them and it did not matter. The men of the *Ulysses* no longer needed courage and all the adjuncts of courage, for they were no longer afraid. Vallery was dead and they did not know how much they respected and loved that gentle man until he was gone. But then they knew. They knew that something wonderful, something that had become an enduring part of their minds and memories, something infinitely fine and good, was gone and they would never know it again, and they were mad with grief. And, in war, a grief-stricken man is the most terrible enemy there is. Prudence, caution, fear, pain—for the grief-stricken man these no longer exist. He lives only to lash out blindly at the enemy, to destroy, if he can, the author of his grief. Rightly or wrongly, the *Ulysses* never thought to blame the Captain's death on any but the enemy. There was only, for them, the sorrow and the blind hate. Zombies, Nicholls had called them once, and the *Ulysses* was more than ever a ship manned by living zombies, zombies who prowled restlessly, incessantly, across the snow and ice of the heaving decks, automatons living only for revenge.

The weather changed just before the end of the middle watch. The seas did not change—FR77 was still butting into the heavy, rolling swell from the north, still piling up fresh sheets of glistening ice on their labouring fo'c'sles. But the wind dropped, and almost at once the snowstorm blew itself out, the last banks of dark, heavy cloud drifting away to the south. By four o'clock the sky was completely clear.

There was no moon that night, but the stars were out, keen and sharp and frosty as the icy breeze that blew steadily out of the north.

Then, gradually, the sky began to change. At first there was only a barely perceptible lightening on the northern rim then, slowly, a pulsating flickering band of light began to broaden and deepen and climb steadily above the horizon, climbing higher to the south with the passing of every minute. Soon that pulsating ribbon of light was paralleled by others, streamers in the most delicate pastel shades of blue and green and violet, but always and predominantly white. And always, too, these lanes of multi-coloured light grew higher and stronger and brighter: at the climax, a great band of white stretched high above the convoy, extending from horizon to horizon . . . These were the Northern Lights, at any time a spectacle of beauty and wonder, and this night surpassing lovely: down below, in ships clearly illumined against the dark and rolling seas, the men of FR77 looked up and hated them.

On the bridge of the *Ulysses*, Chrysler—Chrysler of the uncanny eyesight and super-sensitive hearing, was the first to hear it. Soon everyone else heard it too, the distant roar, throbbing and intermittent, of a Condor approaching from the south. After a time they became aware that the Condor was no longer approaching, but sudden hope died almost as it was born. There was no mistaking it now—the deeper, heavier note of a Focke-Wulf in maximum climb. The Commander turned wearily to Carrington.

'It's Charlie, all right,' he said grimly. 'The bastard's spotted us. He'll already have radioed Alta Fjord and a hundred to one in anything you like that he's going to drop a market flare at 10,000 feet or so. It'll be seen fifty miles away.'

'Your money's safe.' The First Lieutenant was withering. 'I never bet against dead certs . . . And then, by and by, maybe a few flares at a couple of thousand?'

'Exactly!' Turner nodded. 'Pilot, how far do you reckon we're from Alta Fjord—in flying time, I mean?'

'For a 200-knot plane, just over an hour,' the Kapok Kid said quietly. His ebullience was gone: he had been silent and dejected since Vallery had died two hours previously.

'An hour!' Carrington exclaimed. 'And they'll *be* here. My God, sir,' he went on wonderingly, 'they're really out to get us. We've never been bombed nor torpedoed at night before. We've never had the *Tirpitz* after us before. We never—'

'The *Tirpitz,*' Turner interrupted. 'Just where the hell *is* that ship? She's had time to come up with us. Oh, I know it's dark and we've changed course,' he added, as Carrington made to object, 'but a fast destroyer screen would have picked us—Preston!' He broke off, spoke sharply to the Signal Petty Officer. 'Look alive, man! That ship's flashing us.'

'Sorry, sir.' The signalman, swaying on his feet with exhaustion, raised his Aldis, clacked out an acknowledgement. Again the light on the merchantman began to wink furiously.

'"Transverse fracture engine bedplate,"' Preston read out. '"Damage serious: shall have to moderate speed."'

'Acknowledge,' said Turner curtly. 'What ship is that, Preston?'

'The *Ohio Freighter,* sir.'

'The one that stopped a tin fish a couple of days back?'

'That's her, sir.'

'Make a signal. "Essential maintain speed and position."' Turner swore. 'What a time to choose for an engine breakdown . . . Pilot, when do we rendezvous with the Fleet?'

'Six hours' time, sir: exactly.'

'Six hours.' Turner compressed his lips. 'Just six hours—perehaps!' he added bitterly.

'Perhaps?' Carrington murmured.

'Perhaps,' Turner affirmed. 'Depends entirely on the weather. C-in-C won't risk capital ships so near the coast unless he can fly off fighter cover against air attack. And, if you ask me, that's why the *Tirpitz* hasn't turned up yet—some wandering U-boat's tipped him off that our Fleet Carriers are steaming south. He'll be waiting on the weather . . . What's he saying now, Preston?' The *Ohio*'s signal lamp had flashed briefly, then died.

'"Imperative slow down,"' Preston repeated. '"Damage severe. Am slowing down."'

'He is, too,' Carrington said quietly. He looked up at Turner, at the set face and dark eyes, and knew the same thought was in the Commander's mind as was in his own. 'He's a goner, sir, a dead duck. He hasn't a chance. Not unless—'

'Unless what?' Turner asked harshly. 'Unless we leave him an escort? Leave what escort, Number One? The *Viking*—the only effective unit we've left?' He shook his head in slow decision. 'The greatest good of the greatest number: that's how it has to be. They'll know that. Preston, send "Regret cannot leave you standby. How long to effect repairs?"'

The flare burst even before Preston's hand could close on the trigger. It burst directly over FR77. It was difficult to estimate the height—probably six to eight thousand feet—but at that altitude it was no more than an incandescent pinpoint against the great band of the Northern Lights arching majestically above. But it was falling quickly, glowing more brightly by the sound: the parachute, if any, could have been only a steadying drogue.

The crackling of the WT speaker broke through the stuttering chatter of the Aldis.

'WT—bridge. WT—bridge. Message from *Sirrus*: "Three survivors dead. Many dying or seriously wounded. Medical assistance urgent, repeat urgent."' The speaker died, just as the *Ohio* started flickering her reply.

'Send for Lieutenant Nicholls,' Turner ordered briefly. 'Ask him to come up to the bridge at once.'

Carrington stared down at the dark broad seas, seas flecked with milky foam: the bows of the *Ulysses* were crashing down heavily, continuously.

'You're going to risk it, sir?'

'I must. You'd do the same, Number One . . . What does the *Ohio* say, Preston?'

'"I understand. Too busy to look after the Royal Navy anyway. We will make up on you. Au revoir!"'

'We will make up on you. Au revoir.' Turner repeated softly. 'He lies in his teeth, and he knows it. By God!' he burst out. 'If anyone ever tells me the Yankee sailors have no guts—I'll push his perishing face in. Preston, send: "Au revoir. Good luck." . . . Number One, I feel like a murderer.' He rubbed his hand across his forehead, nodded towards the shelter where Vallery lay stretched out, and strapped to his settee. 'Month in, month out, he's been taking these decisions. It's no wonder . . .' He broke off as the gate creaked open.

'Is that you, Nicholls? There is work for you, my boy. Can't have you medical types idling around uselessly all day long.' He raised his hand. 'All right, all right,' he chuckled. 'I know . . . How are things on the surgical front?' he went on seriously.

'We've done all we can, sir. There was very little left for us to do,' Nicholls said quietly. His face was deeply lined, haggard to the point of emaciation. 'But we're in a bad way for supplies. Hardly a single dressing left. And no anæsthetics at all—except what's left in the emergency kit. The Surgeon-Commander refused to touch those.'

'Good, good,' Turner murmured. 'How do you feel, laddie?'

'Awful.'

'You look it,' Turner said candidly. 'Nicholls—I'm terribly sorry, boy—I want you to go over to the *Sirrus*.'

'Yes, sir.' There was no surprise in the voice: it hadn't been difficult to guess why the Commander had sent for him. 'Now?'

Turner nodded without speaking. His face, the lean strong features, the heavy brows and sunken eyes were quite visible now in the strengthening light of the plunging flare. A face to remember, Nicholls thought.

'How much kit can I take with me, sir?'

'Just your medical gear. No more. You're not travelling by Pullman, laddie!'

'Can I take my camera, my films?'

'All right.' Turner smiled briefly. 'Looking forward keenly to photographing the last seconds of the *Ulysses*, I suppose . . . Don't forget that the *Sirrus* is leaking like a sieve, Pilot—get through to the WT. Tell the *Sirrus* to come alongside, prepare to receive medical officer by breeches buoy.'

The gate creaked again. Turner looked at the bulky figure stumbling wearily on to the compass platform. Brooks, like every man in the crew was dead on his feet; but the blue eyes burned as brightly as ever.

'My spies are everywhere,' he announced. 'What's this about the *Sirrus* shanghaiing young Johnny here?'

'Sorry, old man,' Turner apologized. 'It seems things are pretty bad on the *Sirrus*.'

'I see.' Brooks shivered. It might have been the thin threnody of the wind in the shattered rigging, or just the iceladen wind itself. He shivered again, looked upwards at the sinking flare. 'Pretty, very pretty,' he murmured. 'What are the illuminations in aid of?'

'We are expecting company,' Turner smiled crookedly. 'An old world custom, O Socrates—the light in the window and what have you.' He stiffened abruptly, then relaxed, his face graven in granitic immobility. 'My mistake,' he murmured. 'The company has already arrived.'

The last words were caught up and drowned in the rumbling of a heavy explosion. Turner had known it was coming—he'd seen the thin stiletto of flame stabbing skywards just for'ard of the *Ohio Freighter's* bridge. The sound had taken five or six seconds to reach them—the *Ohio* was already over a mile distant on the starboard quarter, but clearly visible still under the luminance of the Northern Lights—the Northern Lights that had betrayed her, almost stopped in the water, to a wandering U-boat.

The *Ohio Freighter* did not remain visible for long. Except for the moment of impact, there was neither smoke, nor flame, nor sound. But her back must have been broken, her bottom torn out—and she was carrying a full cargo of nothing but tanks and ammunition. There was a curious dignity about her end—she sank quickly, quietly, without any fuss. She was gone in three minutes.

It was Turner who finally broke the heavy silence on the bridge. He turned away and in the light of the flare his face was not pleasant to see.

'Au revoir,' he muttered to no one in particular. 'Au revoir. That's what he said, the lying . . . ' He shook his head angrily, touched the Kapok Kid on the arm. 'Get through to WT,' he said sharply. 'Tell the *Viking* to sit over the top of that sub till we get clear.'

'Where's it all going to end?' Brooks's face was still and heavy in the twilight.

'God knows! How I hate those murdering bastards!' Turner ground out. 'Oh, I know, I know, we do the same—but give me something I can see, something I can fight, something—'

'You'll be able to see the *Tirpitz* all right,' Carrington interrupted dryly. 'By all accounts, she's big enough.'

Turner looked at him, suddenly smiled. He clapped his arm, then craned his head back, staring up at the shimmering loveliness of the sky. He wondered when the next flare would drop.

'Have you a minute to spare, Johnny?' The Kapok Kid's voice was low. 'I'd like to speak to you.'

'Sure.' Nicholls looked at him in surprise. 'Sure, I've a minute, ten minutes—until the *Sirrus* comes up. What's wrong, Andy?'

'Just a second.' The Kapok Kid crossed to the Commander. 'Permission to go to the charthouse, sir?'

'Sure you've got your matches?' Turner smiled. 'OK. Off you go.'

The Kapok Kid smiled faintly, said nothing. He took Nicholls by the arm, led him into the charthouse, flicked on the lights and produced his cigarettes. He looked steadily at Nicholls as he dipped his cigarette into the flickering pool of flame.

'Know something, Johnny?' he said abruptly. 'I reckon I must have Scotch blood in me.'

'Scots,' Nicholls corrected. 'And perish the very thought.'

'I'm feeling—what's the word?—fey, isn't it? I'm feeling fey tonight, Johnny.' The Kapok Kid hadn't even heard the interruption. He shivered. 'I don't know why—I've never felt this way before.'

'Ah, nonsense! Indigestion, my boy,' Nicholls said briskly. But he felt strangely uncomfortable.

'Won't wash this time.' Carpenter shook his head, half-smiling. 'Besides, I haven't eaten a thing for two days. I'm, on the level, Johnny.' In spite of himself, Nicholls was impressed. Emotion, gravity, earnestness—these were utterly alien to the Kapok Kid.

'I won't be seeing you again,' the Kapok Kid continued softly. 'Will you do me a favour, Johnny?'

'Don't be so bloody silly,' Nicholls said angrily. 'How the hell do you—?'

'Take this with you.' The Kapok Kid pulled out a slip of paper, thrust it into Nicholls's hands. 'Can you read it?'

'I can read it.' Nicholls had stilled his anger. 'Yes, I can read it.' There was a name and address on the sheet of paper, a girl's name and a Surrey address. 'So that's her name,' he said softly. 'Juanita . . . Juanita.' He pronounced it carefully, accurately, in the Spanish fashion. 'My favourite song and my favourite name,' he murmured.

'Is it?' the Kapok Kid asked eagerly. 'Is it indeed? And mine, Johnny.' He paused. 'If, perhaps—well, if I don't—well, you'll go to see her, Johnny?'

'What are you talking about, man?' Nicholls felt embarrassed. Half-impatiently, half-playfully, he tapped him on the chest. 'Why, with that suit on, you could *swim* from here to Murmansk. You've said so yourself, a hundred times.'

The Kapok Kid grinned up at him. The grin was a little crooked.

'Sure, sure, I know, I know—will you go, Johnny?'

'Dammit to hell, yes!' Nicholls snapped. 'I'll go—and it's high time I was going somewhere else. Come on!' He snapped off the lights, pulled back the door, stopped with his foot halfway over the sill. Slowly, he stepped back inside the charthouse; closed the door and flicked on the light. The Kapok Kid hadn't moved, was gazing quietly at him.

'I'm sorry, Andy,' Nicholls said sincerely. 'I don't know what made me—'

'Bad temper,' said the Kapok Kid cheerfully. 'You always did hate to think that I was right and you were wrong!'

Nicholls caught his breath, closed his eyes for a second. Then he stretched out his hand.

'All the best, Vasco.' It was an effort to smile. 'And don't worry. I'll see her if—well, I'll see her, I promise you. Juanita . . . But if I find *you* there,' he went on threateningly, 'I'll—'

'Thanks, Johnny. Thanks a lot.' The Kapok Kid was almost happy. 'Good luck, boy . . . *Vaya con Dios*. That's what she always said to me, what she said before I came away. "*Vaya con Dios*."'

Thirty minutes later, Nicholls was operating aboard the *Sirrus*.

The time was 0445. It was bitterly cold, with a light wind blowing steadily from the north. The seas were heavier than ever, longer between the crests, deeper in their gloomy troughs, and the damaged *Sirrus*, labouring under a mountain of ice, was making heavy weather of it. The sky was still clear, a sky of breath-taking purity, and the stars were out again, for the Northern Lights were fading. The fifth successive flare was drifting steadily seawards.

It was at 0445 that they heard it—the distant rumble of gunfire far to the south—perhaps a minute after they had seen the incandescent brilliance of a burning flare on the rim of the far horizon. There could be no doubt as to what was happening. The *Viking*, still in contact with the U-boat, although powerless to do anything about it, was being heavily attacked. And the attack must have been short, sharp and deadly, for the firing ceased soon after it had begun. Ominously, nothing came through on the WT. No one ever knew what had happened to the *Viking*, for there were no survivors.

The last echo of the *Viking*'s guns had barely died away before they heard the roar of the engines of the Condor, at maximum throttle in a shallow dive. For five, perhaps ten seconds—it seemed longer than that, but not long enough for any gun in the convoy to begin tracking him accurately—the great Focke-Wulf actually flew beneath his own flare, and then was gone. Behind him, the sky opened up in a blinding coruscation of flame, more dazzling, more hurtful, than the light of the noonday sun. So intense, so extraordinary the power of those flares, so much did pupils contract and eyelids narrow in instinctive self-protection, that the enemy bombers were through the circle of light and upon them before anyone fully realized what was happening. The timing, the split-second co-operation between marker planes and bombers were magnificent.

There were twelve planes in the first wave. There was no concentration on one target, as before: not more than two attacked any ship. Turner, watching from the bridge, watching them swoop down steeply and level out before even the first gun in the *Ulysses* had opened up, caught his breath in sudden dismay. There was something terribly familiar about the speed, the approach, the silhouette of these planes. Suddenly he had it—Heinkels, by God! Heinkel 111s. And the Heinkel 111, Turner knew, carried that weapon he dreaded above all others—the glider bomb.

And then, as if he had touched a master switch, every gun on the *Ulysses* opened up. The air filled with smoke, the pungent smell of burning cordite: the din was indescribable. And all at once, Turner felt fiercely, strangely happy . . . To hell with them and their glider bombs, he thought. This was war as he liked to fight it: not the cat-and-mouse, hide-and-seek frustration of trying to outguess the hidden wolf-packs, but war out in the open, where he could see the enemy and hate him and love him for fighting as honest men should and do his damnedest to destroy him. And, Turner knew, if they could at all, the crew of the *Ulysses* would destroy him. It needed no great sensitivity to direct the sea-change that had overtaken his men—yes, *his* men now: they no longer cared for themselves: they had crossed the frontier of fear and found that nothing lay beyond it and they would keep on feeding their guns and squeezing their triggers until the enemy overwhelmed them.

The leading Heinkel was blown out of the sky, and fitting enough it was 'X' turret that destroyed it—'X' turret, the turret of dead marines, the turret that had destroyed the Condor, and was now manned by a scratch marine crew. The Heinkel behind lifted sharply to avoid the hurtling fragments of fuselage and engines, dipped, flashed past the cruiser's bows less than a boat-length away, banked steeply to port under maximum power, and swung back in on the *Ulysses*. Every gun on the ship was caught on the wrong foot, and seconds passed before the first one was brought to bear—time and to spare for the Heinkel to angle in at 60°, drop his bomb and slew frantically away as the concentrated fire of the Oerlikons and pom-poms closed in on him. Miraculously, he escaped.

The winged bomb was high, but not high enough. It wavered, steadied, dipped, then glided forwards and downwards through the drifting smoke of the guns to strike home with a tremendous, deafening explosion that shook the *Ulysses* to her keel and almost shattered the eardrums of those on deck.

To Turner, looking aft from the bridge, it seemed that the *Ulysses* could never survive this last assault. An ex-torpedo officer and explosives expert himself, he was skilled in assessing the disruptive power of high explosive: never before had he been so close to so powerful, so devastating an explosion. He had dreaded these glider bombs, but even so he had under-estimated their power: the concussion had been double, treble what he had been expecting.

What Turner did not know was that what he had heard had been not one explosion but two, but so nearly simultaneous as to be indistinguishable. The glider bomb, by a freakish chance, had crashed directly into the port torpedo tubes. There had been only one torpedo left there—the other two had sent the *Vytura* to the bottom—and normally Amatol, the warhead explosive, is extremely stable and inert, even when subjected to violent shock: but the bursting bomb had been too close, too powerful: sympathetic detonation had been inevitable.

Damage was extensive and spectacular: it was severe, but not fatal. The side of the *Ulysses* had been ripped open, as by a giant can-opener, almost to the water's edge: the tubes had vanished: the decks were holed and splintered: the funnel casing was a shambles, the funnel itself tilting over to port almost to fifteen degrees; but the greatest energy of the explosion had been directed aft, most of the blast expending itself over the open sea, while the galley and canteen, severely damaged already, were no more than a devil's scrapyard.

Almost before the dust and debris of the explosion had settled, the last of the Heinkels was disappearing, skimming the waves, weaving and twisting madly in evasive action, pursued and harried by a hundred glowing streams of tracer. Then, magically, they were gone, and there was only the sudden deafening silence and the flares, drooping slowly to extinction, lighting up the pall above the *Ulysses*, the dark clouds of smoke rolling up from the shattered *Stirling* and a tanker with its after superstructure almost gone. But not one of the ships in FR77 had faltered or stopped; and they had destroyed five Heinkels. A costly victory, Turner mused, if it could be called a victory; but he knew the Heinkels would be back. It was not difficult to imagine the fury, the hurt pride of the High Command in Norway: as far as Turner knew, no Russian Convoy had ever sailed so far south before.

Riley eased a cramped leg, stretched it gently so as to avoid the great spinning shaft. Carefully he poured some oil on to the bearing, carefully, so as not to disturb the Engineer Commander, propped in sleep between the tunnel wall and Riley's shoulder. Even as Riley drew back, Dodson stirred, opened heavy, gummed lids.

'Good God above!' he said wearily. 'You still here, Riley?' It was the first time either of them had spoken for hours.

'It's a—good job I *am* here,' Riley growled. He nodded towards the bearing. 'Bloody difficult to get a firehose down to this place, I should think!' That was unfair, Riley knew: he and Dodson had been taking it in half-hour turns to doze and feed the bearing. But he felt he had to say something: he was finding it increasingly difficult to keep on being truculent to the Engineer Commander.

Dodson grinned to himself, said nothing. Finally, he cleared his throat, murmured casually: The *Tirpitz* is taking its time about making its appearance, don't you think?'

'Yes, sir.' Riley was uncomfortable. 'Should 'a' been here long ago, damn her!'

'Him,' Dodson corrected absently. '*Admiral von Tirpitz*, you know . . . Why don't you give up this foolishness, Riley?'

Riley grunted, said nothing. Dodson sighed, then brightened.

'Go and get some more coffee, Riley. I'm parched!'

'No.' Riley was blunt. '*You* get it.'

'As a favour, Riley.' Dodson was very gentle. 'I'm damed thirsty!'

'Oh, all right.' The big stoker swore, climbed painfully to his feet. 'Where'll I get it?'

'Plenty in the engine-room. If it's not iced water they're swigging, it's coffee. But no iced water for me.' Dodson shivered.

Riley gathered up the Thermos, stumbled along the passage. He had only gone a few feet when they felt the *Ulysses* shudder under the recoil of the heavy armament. Although they did not know it, it was the beginning of the air attack.

Dodson braced himself against the wall, saw Riley do the same, pause a second then hurry away in an awkward, stumbling run. There was something grotesquely familiar in that awkward run, Dodson thought. The guns surged back again and the figure scuttled even faster, like a giant crab in a panic . . . *Panic,* Dodson thought: that's it, panic-stricken. Don't blame the poor bastard—I'm beginning to imagine things myself down here. Again the whole tunnel vibrated, more heavily this time—that must be 'X' turret, almost directly above. No, I don't blame him. Thank God he's gone. He smiled quietly to himself. I won't be seeing friend Riley again—he isn't all that of a reformed character. Tiredly, Dodson settled back against the wall. On my own at last, he murmured to himself, and waited for the feeling of relief. But it never came. Instead, there was only a vexation and loneliness, a sense of desertion and a strangely empty disappointment.

Riley was back inside a minute. He came back with that same awkward crab-like run, carrying a three-pint Thermos jug and two cups, cursing fluently and often as he slipped against the wall. Panting, wordlessly, he sat down beside Dodson, poured out a cup of steaming coffee.

Why the hell did you have to come back?' Dodson demanded harshly. 'I don't want you and—'

'You wanted coffee,' Riley interrupted rudely. 'You've got the bloody stuff. Drink it.'

At that instant the explosion and the vibration from the explosion in the port tubes echoed weirdly down the dark tunnel, the shock flinging the two men heavily against each other. His whole cup of coffee splashed over Dodson's leg: his mind was so tired, his reactions so slow, that his first realization was of how damnably cold he was, how chill that dripping tunnel. The scalding coffee had gone right through his clothes, but he could feel neither warmth nor wetness: his legs were numbed, dead below the knees. Then he shook his head, looked up at Riley.

'What in God's name was that? What's happening? Did you—?'

'Haven't a clue. Didn't stop to ask.' Riley stretched himself luxuriously, blew on his steaming coffee. Then a happy thought struck him, and a broad cheerful grin came as near to transforming that face as would ever be possible.

'It's probably the *Tirpitz*,' he said hopefully.

Three times more during that terrible night, the German squadrons took off from the airfield at Alta Fjord, throbbed their way nor'-nor'-west through the bitter Arctic night, over the heaving Arctic sea, in search of the shattered remnants of FR77. Not that the search was difficult—the Focke-Wulf Condor stayed with them all night, defied their best attempts to shake him off. He seemed to have an endless supply of these deadly flares, and might very well have been—in fact, almost certainly was—carrying nothing else. And the bombers had only to steer for the flares.

The first assault—about 0545—was an orthodox bombing attack, made from about 3,000 feet. The planes seemed to be Dorniers, but it was difficult to be sure, because they flew high above a trio of flares sinking close to the water level. As an attack, it was almost but not quite abortive, and was pressed home with no great enthusiasm. This was understandable: the barrage was intense. But there were two direct hits—one on a merchantman, blowing away most of the fo'c'sle, the other on the *Ulysses*. It sheered through the flag deck and the Admiral's day cabin, and exploded in the heart of the Sick Bay. The Sick Bay was crowded with the sick and dying, and, for many, that bomb must have come as a God-sent release, for the *Ulysses* had long since run out of anaesthetics. There were no survivors. Among the dead was Marshall, the Torpedo Officer, Johnson, the Leading

SBA, the Master-At-Arms who had been lightly wounded an hour before by a splinter from the torpedo tubes, Burgess, strapped helplessly in a strait-jacket—he had suffered concussion on the night of the great storm and gone insane. Brown, whose hip had been smashed by the hatch-cover of 'Y' magazine, and Brierley, who was dying anyway, his lungs saturated and rotted away with fuel oil. Brooks had not been there.

The same explosion had also shattered the telephone exchange: barring only the bridgegun phones, and the bridge-engine phones and speaking-tubes, all communication lines in the *Ulysses* were gone.

The second attack at 7 a.m., was made by only six bombers—Heinkels again, carrying glider-bombs. Obviously flying strictly under orders, they ignored the merchantmen and concentrated their attack solely on the cruisers. It was an expensive attack: the enemy lost all but two of their force in exchange for a single hit aft on the *Stirling*, a hit which, tragically, put both after guns out of action.

Turner, red-eyed and silent, bareheaded in that sub-zero wind, and pacing the shattered bridge of the *Ulysses*, marvelled that the *Stirling* still floated, still fought back with everything she had. And then he looked at his own ship, less a ship, he thought wearily, than a floating shambles of twisted steel still scything impossibly through those heavy seas, and marvelled all the more. Broken, burning cruisers, cruisers ravaged and devastated to the point of destruction, were nothing new for Turner: he had seen the *Trinidad* and the *Edinburgh* being literally battered to death on these same Russian convoys. But he had never seen any ship, at any time, take such inhuman murderous punishment as the *Ulysses* and the obsolete *Stirling* and still live. He would not have believed it possible.

The third attack came just before dawn. It came with the grey half-light, an attack carried out with great courage and the utmost determination by fifteen Heinkel 111 glider-bombers. Again the cruisers were the sole targets, the heavier attack by far being directed against the *Ulysses*. Far from shirking the challenge and bemoaning their illluck the crew of the *Ulysses*, that strange and selfless crew of walking zombies whom Nicholls had left behind, welcomed the enemy gladly, even joyfully, for how can one kill an enemy if he does not come to you? Fear, anxiety, the nearcertainty of death—these did not exist. Home and country, families, wives and sweethearts, were names, only names: they touched a man's mind, these thoughts, touched it and lifted and were gone as if they had never been. 'Tell them,' Vallery had said, 'tell them they are the best crew God ever gave a captin.' Vallery. *That* was what mattered, that and what Vallery had stood for, that something that had been so inseparably a part of that good and kindly man that you never saw it because it *was* Vallery. And the crew hoisted the shells, slammed the breeches and squeezed their triggers, men uncaring, men oblivious of anything and everything, except the memory of the man who had died apologizing because he had let them down, except the sure knowledge that they could not let Vallery down. Zombies, but inspired zombies, men above themselves, as men commonly are when they know the next step, the inevitable step, has them clear to the top of the far side of the valley . . .

The first part of the attack was launched against the *Stirling*. Turner saw two Heinkels roaring in in a shallow dive, improbably surviving against heavy, concentrated fire at point-blank range. The bombs, delayed action and armour-piercing, struck the *Stirling* amidships, just below deck level, and exploded deep inside, in the boiler-room and engine-room. The next three bombers were met with only pom-pom and Lewis fire: the main armament for'ard had fallen silent. With sick apprehension, Turner realized what had happened: the explosion had cut the power to the turrets.[1] Ruthlessly, contemptuously almost, the bombers brushed aside the

---

1. It is almost impossible for one single explosion, or even several in the same locality, to destroy or incapacitate all the dynamos in a large naval vessel, or to sever all the various sections of the Ring Main, which carries the power around the ship. When a dynamo or its appropriate section of the Ring Main suffered damage, the interlinking fuses automatically blew, isolating the damaged section. Theoretically, that is. In practice, it does not always happen that way—the fuses may not rupture and the entire system breaks down. Rumour—very strong rumour—had it that at least one of HM capital ships was lost simply because the Dynamo Fuse Release Switches—fuses of the order of 800 amps—failed to blow, leaving the capital ship powerless to defend itself.

puny opposition: every bomb went home. The *Stirling*, Turner saw, was desperately wounded. She was on fire again, and listing heavily to starboard.

The suddenly lifting crescendo of aero engines spun Turner round to look to his own ship. There were five Heinkels in the first wave, at different heights and approach angles so as to break up the pattern of AA fire, but all converging on the after end of the *Ulysses*. There was so much smoke and noise that Turner could only gather confused, broken impressions. Suddenly, it seemed, the air was filled with glider-bombs and the tearing, staccato crash of the German cannon and guns. One bomb exploded in mid-air, just for'ard of the after funnel and feet away from it: a maiming, murderous storm of jagged steel scythed across the boat-deck, and all Oerlikons and the pom-poms fell immediately silent, their crews victim to shrapnel or concussion. Another plunged through the deck and Engineers' Flat and turned the WT office into a charnel house. The remaining two that struck were higher, smashing squarely into 'X' gun-deck and 'X' turret. The turret was split open around the top and down both sides as by a giant cleaver, and blasted off its mounting, to lie grotesquely across the shattered poop.

Apart from the boat-deck and turret gunners, only one other man lost his life in that attack, but that man was virtually irreplaceable. Shrapnel from the first bomb had burst a compressed air cylinder in the torpedo workshop, and Hartley, the man who, above all, had become the backbone of the *Ulysses* had taken shelter there, only seconds before . . .

The *Ulysses* was running into dense black smoke, now—the *Stirling* was heavily on fire, her fuel tanks gone. What happened in the next ten minutes, no one ever knew. In the smoke and flame and agony, they were moments borrowed from hell and men could only endure. Suddenly, the *Ulysses* was out in the clear, and the Heinkels, all bombs gone, were harrying her, attacking her incessantly with cannon and machine-gun, ravening wolves with their victim on its knees, desperate to finish it off. But still, here and there, a gun fired on the *Ulysses*.

Just below the bridge, for instance—there was a gun firing

there. Turner risked a quick glance over the side, saw the gunner pumping his tracers into the path of a swooping Heinkel. And then the Heinkel opened up, and Turner flung himself back, knocking the Kapok Kid to the deck. Then the bomber was gone and the guns were silent. Slowly, Turner hoisted himself to his feet, peered over the side: the gunner was dead, his harness cut to ribbons.

He heard a scuffle behind him, saw a slight figure fling off a restraining hand, and climb to the edge of the bridge. For an instant, Turner saw the pale, staring face of Chrysler, Chrysler who had neither smiled nor even spoken since they had opened up the Asdic cabinet; at the same time he saw three Heinkels forming up to starboard for a fresh attack.

'Get down, you young fool!' Turner shouted. 'Do you want to commit suicide?'

Chrysler looked at him, eyes wide and devoid of recognition, looked away and dropped down to the sponson below. Turner lifted himself to the edge of the bridge and looked down.

Chrysler was struggling with all his slender strength, struggling in a strange and frightening silence, to drag the dead man from his Oerlikon cockpit. Somehow, with a series of convulsive, despairing jerks, he had him over the side, had laid him gently to the ground, and was climbing into the cockpit. His hand, Turner saw, was bare and bleeding, stripped to the raw flesh—then out of the corner of his eyes he saw the flame of the Heinkel's guns and flung himself backward.

One second passed, two, three—three seconds during which cannon shells and bullets smashed against the reinforced armour of the bridge—then, as a man in a daze, he heard the twin Oerlikons opening up. The boy must have held his fire to the very last moment. Six shots the Oerlikon fired—only six, and a great, grey shape, stricken and smoking, hurtled over the bridge barely at head height, sheared off its port wing on the Director Tower and crashed into the sea on the other side.

Chrysler was still sitting in the cockpit. His right hand was clutching his left shoulder, a shoulder smashed and shattered by a cannon shell, trying hopelessly to stem the welling arterial blood.

Even as the next bomber straightened out on its strafing run, even as he flung himself backwards, Turner saw the mangled, bloody hand reach out for the trigger grip again.

Flat on the duckboards beside Carrington and the Kapok Kid, Turner pounded his fist on the deck in terrible frustration of anger. He thought of Starr, the man who had brought all this upon them, and hated him as he would never have believed he could hate anybody. He could have killed him then. He thought of Chrysler, of the excruciating hell of that gun-rest pounding into that shattered shoulder, of brown eyes glazed and shocked with pain and grief. If he himself lived, Turner swore, he would recommend that boy for the Victoria Cross. Abruptly the firing ceased and a Heinkel swung off sharply to starboard, smoke pouring from both its engines.

Quickly, together with the Kapok Kid, Turner scrambled to his feet, hoisted himself over the side of the bridge. He did it without looking, and he almost died then. A burst of fire from the third and last Heinkel—the bridge was always the favourite target—whistled past his head and shoulders: he felt the wind from the convulsive back-thrust that had sent him there, he was stretched full length on the duckboards again. They were only inches from his eyes, these duckboards, but he could not see them. All he could see was the image of Chrysler, a gaping wound the size of a man's hand in his back, slumped forward across the Oerlikons, the weight of his body tilting the barrels grotesquely skywards. Both barrels had still been firing, were still firing, would keep on firing until the drums were empty, for the dead boy's hand was locked across the trigger.

Gradually, one by one, the guns of the convoy fell silent, the clamour of the aero engines began to fade in the distance. The attack was over.

Turner rose to his feet, slowly and heavily this time. He looked over the side of the bridge, stared down into the Oerlikon gunpit, then looked away, his face expressionless.

Behind him, he heard someone coughing. It was a strange, bubbling kind of cough. Turner whirled round, then stood stock-still, his hands clenched tightly at his sides.

The Kapok Kid, with Carrington kneeling helplessly at his side, was sitting quietly on the boards, his back propped against the legs of the Admiral's chair. From left groin to right shoulder through the middle of the embroidered 'J' on the chest, stretched a neat, straight, evenly-spaced pattern of round holes, stitched in by the machine-gun of the Heinkel. The blast of the shells must have hurtled him right across the bridge.

Turner stood absolutely still. The Kid, he knew with sudden sick certainty, had only seconds to live: he felt that any sudden move on his part would snap the spun-silk thread that held him on to life.

Gradually, the Kapok Kid became aware of his presence, of his steady gaze, and looked up tiredly. The vivid blue of his eyes was dulled already, the face white and drained of blood. Idly, his hand strayed up and down the punctured kapok, fingering the gashes. Suddenly, he smiled, looked down at the quilted suit.

'Ruined,' he whispered. 'Bloody well ruined!' Then the wandering hand slipped down to his side, palm upward, and his head slumped forward on his chest. The flaxen hair stirred idly in the wind.

SEVENTEEN

Sunday Morning

The *Stirling* died at dawn. She died while still under way, still plunging through the heavy seas, her mangled, twisted bridge and superstructure glowing red, glowing white-hot as the wind and sundered oil tanks lashed the flames into an incandescent holocaust. A strange and terrible sight, but not unique: thus the *Bismarck* had looked, whitely incandescent, just before the *Shropshire*'s torpedoes had sent her to the bottom.

The *Stirling* would have died anyway—but the Stukas made siccar. The Northern Lights had long since gone: now, too, the clear skies were going, and dark cloud was banking heavily to the north. Men hoped and prayed that the cloud would spread over FR77, and cover it with blanketing snow. But the Stukas got there first.

The Stukas—the dreaded gull-winged Junkers 87 dive-bombers—came from the south, flew high over the convoy, turned, flew south again. Level with, and due west of the *Ulysses*, rear ship in the convoy, they started to turn once more: then, abruptly, in the classic Stuka attack pattern, they peeled off in sequence, port wings dipping sharply as they half-rolled, turned and fell out of the sky, plummeting arrow-true for their targets. Any plane that hurtles down in undeviating dive on waiting gun emplacements has never a chance. Thus spoke the pundits, the instructors in the gunnery school of Whale Island, and proceeded to prove to their own satisfaction the evident truth of their statement, using AA guns and duplicating the situation which would arise insofar as it lay within their power. Unfortunately, they couldn't duplicate the Stuka.

'Unfortunately', because in actual battle, the Stuka was the only factor in the situation that really mattered. One had only to crouch behind a gun, to listen to the ear-piercing, screaming whistle of the Stuka in its near-vertical dive, to flinch from its hail of bullets as it loomed larger and larger in the sights, to know that nothing could now arrest the flight of that underslung bomb, to appreciate the truth of that. Hundreds of men alive today—the lucky ones who endured and survived a Stuka attack—will readily confirm that the war produced nothing quite so nerve-rending, quite so demoralizing as the sight and sound of those Junkers with the strange dihedral of the wings in the last seconds before they pulled out of their dive.

But one time in a hundred, maybe one time in a thousand, when the human factor of the man

behind the gun ceased to operate, the pundits could be right. This was the thousandth time, for fear was a phantom that had vanished in the night: ranged against the dive-bombers were only one multiple pom-pom and half a dozen Oerlikons—the for'ard turrets could not be brought to bear—but these were enough, and more, in the hands of men inhumanly calm, ice-cool as the Polar wind itself, and filled with an almost dreadful singleness of purpose. Three Stukas in almost as many seconds were clawed out of the sky, two to crash harmlessly in the sea, a third to bury itself with tremendous impact in the already shattered day cabin of the Admiral.

The chances against the petrol tanks not erupting in searing flame or of the bomb not exploding were so remote as not to exist: but neither happened. It hardly seemed to call for comment—in extremity, courage becomes routine—when the bearded Doyle abandoned his pom-pom, scrambled up to the fo'c'sle deck, and flung himself on top of the armed bomb rolling heavily in scuppers awash with 100 per cent octane petrol. One tiny spark from Doyle's boot or from the twisted, broken steel of the Stuka rubbing and grinding against the superstructure would have been trigger enough: the contact fuse in the bomb was still undamaged, and as it slipped and skidded over the ice-bound deck, with Doyle hanging desperately on, it seemed animistically determined to smash its delicate percussion nose against a bulkhead or stanchion.

If Doyle thought of these things, he did not care. Coolly, almost carelessly, he kicked off the only retaining clip left on a broken section of the guard-rail, slid the bomb, fins first, over the edge, tipped the nose sharply to clear the detonator. The bomb fell harmlessly into the sea.

It fell into the sea just as the first bomb sliced contemptuously through the useless one-inch deck armour of the *Stirling* and crashed into the engineroom. Three, four, five, six other bombs buried themselves in the dying heart of the cruiser, the lightened Stukas lifting away sharply to port and starboard. From the bridge of the *Ulysses,* there seemed to be a weird, unearthly absence of noise as the bombs went home. They just vanished into the smoke and flame, engulfed by the inferno.

No one blow finished the *Stirling,* but a mounting accumulation of blows. She had taken too much and she could take no more. She was like a reeling boxer, a boxer overmatched against an unskilled but murderous opponent, sinking under an avalanche of blows.

Stony-faced, bitter beyond words at his powerlessness, Turner watched her die. Funny, he thought tiredly, she's like all the rest. Cruisers, he mused in a queerly detached abstraction, must be the toughest ships in the world. He'd seen many go, but none easily, cleanly, spectacularly. No sudden knock-out, no *coup de grâce* for them—always, always, they had to be battered to death . . . Like the *Stirling*. Turner's grip on the shattered windscreen tightened till his forearms ached. To him, to all good sailors, a well-loved ship was a well-loved friend: for fifteen months, now, the old and valiant *Stirling* had been their faithful shadow, had shared the burden of the *Ulysses* in the worst convoys of the war: she was the last of the old guard, for only the *Ulysses* had been longer on the blackout run. It was not good to watch a friend die: Turner looked away, stared down at the ice-covered duckboards between his feet, his head sunk between hunched shoulders.

He could close his eyes, but he could not close his ears. He winced, hearing the monstrous, roaring hiss of boiling water and steam as the white-hot superstructure of the *Stirling* plunged deeply into the ice-chilled Arctic. For fiteen, twenty seconds that dreadful, agonized sibilation continued, then stopped in an instant, the sound sheared off as by a guillotine. When Turner looked up, slowly, there was only the rolling, empty sea ahead, the big oil-slicked bubbles rising to the top, bubbles rising only to be punctured as they broke the surface by the fine rain falling back into the sea from the great clouds of steam already condensing in that bitter cold.

The *Stirling* was gone, and the battered remnants of FR77 pitched and plunged steadily onwards to the north. There were seven ships left now—four merchantmen, including the Commodore's ship, the tanker, the *Sirrus* and the *Ulysses*. None of them was whole: all were damaged, heavily damaged, but none so desperately hurt as the *Ulysses*. Seven ships, only seven: thirty-six had set out for Russia.

At 0800 Turner signalled the *Sirrus*: 'WT gone. Signal C-in-C course, speed, position. Confirm 0930 as rendezvous. Code.'

The reply came exactly an hour later. 'Delayed heavy seas. Rendezvous approx 1030. Impossible fly off air cover. Keep coming. C-in-C.

'Keep coming!' Turner repeated savagely. 'Would you listen to him! "Keep coming," he says! What the hell does he expect us to do—scuttle ourselves?' He shook his head too in angry despair. 'I hate to repeat myself,' he said bitterly. 'But I must. Too bloody late as usual!'[1] Dawn and daylight had long since come, but it was growing darker again. Heavy grey clouds, formless and menacing, blotted out the sky from horizon to horizon. They were snow clouds, and, please God, the snow would soon fall: that could save them now,

---

1. It is regrettable but true—the Home Fleet squadron was almost always too late. The Admiralty could not be blamed—the capital ships were essential for the blockade of the *Tirpitz*; and they did not dare risk them close inshore against the land-based bombers. The long awaited trap *did* eventually snap shut; but it caught only the heavy cruiser *Scharnhorst* and not the *Tirpitz*. It never caught the great ship. She was destroyed at her anchorage in Alta Fjord by Lancaster bombers of the Royal Air Force.

that and that alone. But the snow did not come—not then. Once more, there came instead the Stukas, the roar of their engines rising and falling as they methodically quartered the empty sea in search of the convoy—Charlie had left at dawn. But it was only a matter of time before the dive-bomber squadron found the tiny convoy; ten minutes from the time of the first warning of their approach, the leading Junkers 87 tipped over its wing and dropped out of the sky.

Ten minutes—but time for a council and plan of desperation. When the Stukas came, they found the convoy stretched out in line abreast, the tanker *Varella* in the middle, two merchantmen in close line ahead on either side of it, the *Sirrus* and the *Ulysses* guarding the flanks. A suicidal formation in submarine waters—a torpedo from port or starboard could hardly miss them all. But weather conditions were heavily against submarines, and the formation offered at least a fighting chance against the Stukas. If they approached from astern—their favourite attack technique—they would run into the simultaneous massed fire of seven ships; if they approached from the sides, they must first attack the escorts, for no Stuka would present its unprotected underbelly to the guns of a warship . . . They elected attack from either side, five from the east, four from the west. This time, Turner noted, they were carrying long-range fuel tanks.

Turner had no time to see how the *Sirrus* was faring. Indeed, he could hardly see how his own ship was faring, for thick acrid smoke was blowing back across the bridge from the barrels of 'A' and 'B' turrets. In the gaps of sound between the crash of the 5.25s, he could hear the quick-fire of Doyle's midship pom-pom, the vicious thudding of the Oerlikons.

Suddenly, startling in its breath-taking unexpectedness, two great beams of dazzling white stabbed out through the mirk and gloom. Turner stared, then bared his teeth in fierce delight. The 44-inch searchlights! Of course! The great searchlights, still on the official secret list, capable of lighting up an enemy six miles away! What a fool he had been to forget them—Vallery had used them often, in daylight and in dark, against attacking aircraft. No man could look into those terrible eyes, those flaming arcs across the electrodes and not be blinded.

Blinking against the eye-watering smoke, Turner peered aft to see who was manning the control position. But he knew who it was before he saw him. It could only be Ralston—searchlight control, Turner remembered, was his day action station: besides, he could think of no one other than the big, blond torpedoman with the gumption, the quick intelligence to burn the lamps on his own initiative.

Jammed in the corner of the bridge by the gate, Turner watched him. He forgot his ship, forgot even the bombers—he personally could do nothing about them anyway—as he stared in fascination at the man behind the controls.

His eyes were glued to the sights, his face expressionless, absolutely; but for the gradual stiffening of back and neck as the sight dipped in docile response to the delicate caress of his fingers on the wheel, he might have been carved from marble: the immobility of the face, the utter concentration was almost frightening.

There was not a flicker of feeling or emotion: never a flicker as the first Stuka weaved and twisted in maddened torment, seeking to escape that eye-staring flame, not even a flicker as it swerved violently in its dive, pulled out too late and crashed into the sea a hundred yards short of the *Ulysses*.

What was the boy thinking of? Turner wondered. His mother, his sisters, entombed under the ruins of a Croydon bungalow: of his brother, innocent victim of that mutiny—how impossible that mutiny seemed now!—in Scapa Flow: of his father, dead by his son's own hand? Turner did not know, could not even begin to guess: clairvoyantly, almost, he knew that it was too late, that no one would ever know now.

The face was inhumanly still. There wasn't a shadow of feeling as the second Stuka overshot the *Ulysses*, dropped its bomb into the open sea: not a shadow as the third blew up in mid-air: not a trace of emotion when the guns of the next Stuka smashed one of the lights . . . not even when the cannon shells of the last smashed the searchlight control, tore half his chest away. He died instantaneously, stood there a moment as if unwilling to abandon his post, then slumped back quietly on to the deck. Turner bent over the dead boy, looked at the face, the eyes upturned to the first feathery flakes of falling snow. The eyes, the face, were still the same, mask-like, expressionless. Turner shivered and looked away.

One bomb, and one only, had struck the *Ulysses*. It had struck the fo'c'sle deck just for'ard of 'A' turret. There had been no casualties, but some freak of vibration and shock had fractured the turret's hydraulic lines. Temporarily, at least, 'B' was the only effective remaining turret in the ship.

The *Sirrus* hadn't been quite so lucky. She had destroyed one Stuka—the merchantmen had claimed another—and had been hit twice, both bombs exploding in the after mess-deck. The *Sirrus*, overloaded with survivors, was carrying double her normal complement of men, and usually that mess-deck would have been crowded: during action stations it was empty. Not a man had lost his life—not a man was to lose his life on the destroyer *Sirrus*: she was never damaged again on the Russian convoys.

Hope was rising, rising fast. Less than an hour to go, now, and the battle squadron would be there. It was dark, dark with the gloom of an Arctic storm, and heavy snow was falling, hissing gently into the dark and rolling sea. No plane could find them in this—and they were almost beyond the reach of shore-based aircraft, except, of course, for the Condors. And it was almost impossible weather for submarines.

'It may be we shall touch the Happy Isles,' Carrington quoted softly.

'What?' Turner looked up, baffled. 'What did you say, Number One?'

'Tennyson.' Carrington was apologetic. 'The Captain was always quoting him . . . Maybe we'll make it yet.'

'Maybe, maybe.' Turner was non-committal. 'Preston!'

'Yes, sir, I see it.' Preston was staring to the north where the signal lamp of the *Sirrus* was flickering rapidly.

'A ship, sir!' he reported excitedly. '*Sirrus* says naval vessel approaching from the north!'

'From the north! Thank God! Thank God!' Turner shouted exultantly. 'From the north! It must be them! They're ahead of time . . . I take it all back. Can you see anything, Number One?'

'Not a thing, sir. Too thick—but it's clearing a bit, I think . . . There's the *Sirrus* again.'

'What does she say, Preston?' Turner asked anxiously.

'Contact. Sub contact. Gren 30. Closing.'

'Contact! At this late hour!' Turner groaned, then smashed his fist down on the binnacle. He swore fiercely.

'By God, she's not going to stop us now! Preston, signal the *Sirrus* to stay . . . '

He broke off, looked incredulously to the north. Up there in the snow and gloom, stilettos of white flame had lanced out briefly, vanished again. Carrington by his side now, he stared unwinkingly north, saw shells splashing whitely in the water under the bows of the Commodore's ship, the *Cape Hatteras*: then he saw the flashes again, stronger, brighter this time, flashes that lit up for a fleeting second the bows and superstructure of the ship that was firing.

He turned slowly, to find that Carrington, too, had turned, was gazing at him with set face and bitter eyes, Turner, grey and haggard with exhaustion and the sour foretaste of ultimate defeat, looked in turn at his First Lieutenant in a long moment of silence.

'The answer to many questions,' he said softly. 'That's why they've been softening up the *Stirling* and ourselves for the past couple of days. The fox is in among the chickens. It's our old pal the *Hipper* cruiser come to pay us a social call.'

'It is.'

'So near and yet . . . ' Turner shrugged. 'We deserved better than this . . . ' He grinned crookedly. 'How would you like to die a hero's death?'

'The very idea appals me!' boomed a voice behind him. Brooks had just arrived on the bridge.

'Me, too,' Turner admitted. He smiled: he was almost happy again. 'Have we any option, gentlemen?'

'Alas, no,' Brooks said sadly.

'Full ahead both!' Carrington called down the speaking-tube: it was by way of his answer.

'No, no,' Turner chided gently: 'Full *power*, Number One. Tell them we're in a hurry: remind them of the boasts they used to make about the *Abdiel* and the *Maxman* . . . Preston! General emergency signal: "Scatter: proceed independently to Russian ports."'

The upper deck was thick with freshly fallen snow, and the snow was still falling. The wind was rising again and, after the warmth of the canteen where he had been operating, it struck at Johnny Nicholls's lungs with sudden, searing pain: the temperature, he guessed must be about zero. He buried his face in his duffel coat, climbed laboriously, haltingly up the ladders to the bridge. He was tired, deadly weary, and he winced in agony every time his foot touched the deck: his splinted left leg was shattered just above the ankle—shrapnel from the bomb in the after mess-deck.

Peter Orr, commander of the *Sirrus*, was waiting for him at the gate of the tiny bridge.

'I thought you might like to see this, Doc.' The voice was strangely high-pitched for so big a man. 'Rather I thought you would want to see this,' he corrected himself. 'Look at her go!' he breathed. 'Just look at her go!'

Nicholls looked out over the port side. Half a mile away on the beam, the *Cape Hatteras* was blazing furiously, slowing to a stop. Some miles to the north, through the falling snow, he could barely distinguish the vague shape of the German cruiser, a shape pinpointed by the flaming guns still mercilessly pumping shells into the sinking ship. Every shot went home: the accuracy of their gunnery was fantastic.

Half a mile astern on the port quarter, the *Ulysses* was coming up. She was sheeted in foam and spray, the bows leaping almost clear of the water, then crashing down with a pistol-shot impact easily heard, even against the wind, on the bridge of the *Sirrus*, as the great engines thrust her through the water, faster, faster, with the passing of every second.

Nicholls gazed, fascinated. This was the first time he'd seen the *Ulysses* since he'd left her and he was appalled. The entire upperworks, fore and aft, were a twisted, unbelievable shambles of broken steel: both masts were gone, the smokestacks broken and bent, the Director Tower shattered and grotesquely askew: smoke was still pluming up from the great holes in fo'c'sle and poop, the after turrets, wrenched from their mountings, pitched crazily on the deck. The skeleton of the Condor still lay athwart 'Y' Turret. A Stuka was buried to the wings in the fo'c'sle deck, and she was, he knew, split right down to the water level abreast the torpedo tubes. The *Ulysses* was something out of a nightmare.

Steadying himself against the violent pitching of the destroyer, Nicholls stared and stared, numbed with horror and disbelief. Orr looked at him, looked away as a messenger came to the bridge.

'Rendezvous 1015,' he read. '1015! Good lord, 25 minutes' time! Do you hear that, Doc? 25 minutes' time!'

'Yes, sir,' Nicholls said absently: he hadn't heard him.

Orr looked at him, touched his arm, pointed to the *Ulysses*.

'Bloody well incredible, isn't it?' he murmured.

'I wish to God I was aboard her,' Nicholls muttered miserably. 'Why did they send me—? Look! What's that?'

A huge flag, a flag twenty feet in length, was streaming out below the yardarm of the *Ulysses*, stretched taut in the wind of its passing. Nicholls had never seen anything remotely like it: the flag was enormous, red and blue and whiter than the driving snow.

'The battle ensign,' Orr murmured. 'Bill Turner's broken out the battle ensign.' He shook his head in wonder. 'To take time off to do that *now*—well, Doc, only Turner would do that. You know him well?'

Nicholls nodded silently.

'Me, too,' Orr said simply. 'We are both lucky men.'

The *Sirrus* was still doing fifteen knots, still headed for the enemy, when the *Ulysses* passed them by a cable-length away as if they were stopped in the water.

Long afterwards, Nicholls could never describe it all accurately. He had a hazy memory of the *Ulysses* no longer plunging and lifting, but battering through waves and troughs on a steady even keel, the deck angling back sharply from a rearing forefoot to the counter buried deep in the water, fifteen feet below the great boiling tortured sea of white that arched up in seething magnificence above the shattered poop-deck. He could recall, too, that 'B' turret was firing continuously, shell after shell screaming away through the blinding snow, to burst in brilliant splendour over and on the

German cruiser: for 'B' turret had only starshells left. He carried, too, a vague mental picture of Turner waving ironically from the bridge, of the great ensign streaming stiffly astern, already torn and tattered at the edges. But what he could never forget, what he would hear in his heart and mind as long as he lived, was the tremendous, frightening roar of the great boiler-room intake fans as they sucked in mighty draughts of air for the starving engines. For the *Ulysses* was driving through the heavy seas under maximum power, at a speed that should have broken her shuddering back, should have burnt out the great engines. There was no doubt as to Turner's intentions: he was going to ram the enemy, to destroy him and take him with him, at a speed of just on or over forty incredible knots.

Nicholls gazed and gazed and did not know what to think: he felt sick at heart, for that ship was part of him now, his good friends, especially the Kapok Kid—for he did not know that the Kid was already dead—they, too, were part of him, and it is always terrible to see the end of a legend, to see it die, to see it going into the gulfs. But he felt, too, a strange exultation; she was dying but what a way to die! And if ships had hearts, had souls, as the old sailing men declared, surely the *Ulysses* would want it this way too.

She was still doing forty knots when, as if by magic, a great gaping hole appeared in her bows just above the waterline. Shell-fire; possibly, but unlikely at that angle. It must have been a torpedo from the U-boat, not yet located: a sudden dip of the bows could have coincided with the upthrust of a heavy sea forcing a torpedo to the surface. Such things had happened before: rarely, but they happened . . . The *Ulysses* brushed aside the torpedo, ignored the grievous wound, ignored the heavy shells crashing into her and kept on going.

She was still going forty knots, driving in under the guns of the enemy, guns at maximum depression, when 'A' magazine blew up, blasted off the entire bows in one shattering detonation. For a second, the lightened fo'c'sle reared high into the air: then it plunged down, deep down, into the shoulder of a rolling sea. She plunged down and kept on going down, driving down to the black floor of the Arctic, driven down by the madly spinning screws, the still thundering engines her own executioner.

EIGHTEEN

Epilogue

The air was warm and kind and still. The sky was blue, a deep and wonderful blue, with little puffs of cotton-wool cloud drifting lazily to the far horizon. The street-gardens, the hanging birdcage flower-baskets, spilled over with blue and yellow and red and gold, all the delicate pastel shades and tints he had almost forgotten had ever existed: every now and then an old man or a hurrying housewife or a young man with a laughing girl on his arm would stop to admire them, then walk on again, the better for having seen them.

The nesting birds were singing, clear and sweet above the distant roar of the traffic, and Big Ben was booming the hour as Johnny Nicholls climbed awkwardly out of the taxi, paid off the driver and hobbled slowly up the marble steps.

His face carefully expressionless, the sentry saluted, opened the heavy swing door. Nicholls passed inside, looked around the huge hall, saw that both sides were lined with heavy, imposing doors: at the far end, beneath the great curve of the stairs and overhanging the widely convex counter of the type usually found in banks, hung a sign: 'Typist Pool: Inquiries.'

The tip-tap of the crutches sounded unnaturally loud on the marble floor as he limped over to the counter. Very touching and melodramatic, Nicholls, he thought dispassionately: trust the audience are having their money's worth. Half a dozen typists had stopped work as if by command, were staring at him in open curiosity, hands resting limply on their machines. A trim young Wren, red-haired and shirt-sleeved, came to the counter.

'Can I help you, sir?' The quiet voice, the blue eyes were soft with concern. Nicholls, catching a glimpse of himself in a mirror behind her, a glimpse of a scuffed uniform jacket over a great fisherman's jersey, of blurred, sunken eyes and gaunt, pale cheeks, admitted wryly to himself that he couldn't blame her. He didn't have to be a doctor to know that he was in pretty poor shape.

'My name is Nicholls, Surgeon-Lieutenant Nicholls. I have an appointment—'

'Lieutenant Nicholls . . . HMS *Ulysses*!' The girl drew in her breath sharply. 'Of course, sir. They're expecting you.' Nicholls looked at her, looked at the Wrens sitting motionless in their chairs, caught the intense, wondering expression in their eyes, the awed gaze with which one would regard beings from another planet. It made him feel vaguely uncomfortable.

'Upstairs, I suppose?' He hadn't meant to sound so brusque.

'No, sir.' The Wren came quietly round the counter. 'They—well, they heard you'd been wounded, sir,' she murmured apologetically. 'Just across the hall here, please.' She smiled at him, slowed her step to match his halting walk.

She knocked, held open the door, announced him to someone he couldn't see, and closed the door softly behind him when he had passed through.

There were three men in the room. The one man he recognized, Vice-Admiral Starr, came forward to meet him. He looked older, far older, far more tired than when Nicholls had last seen him—hardly a fortnight previously.

'How are you, Nicholls?' he asked. 'Not walking so well, I see.' Under the assurance, the thin joviality so flat and misplaced, the harsh edge of strain burred unmistakably. 'Come and sit down.'

He led Nicholls across to the table, long, big and covered with leather. Behind the table, framed against huge wall-maps, sat two men. Starr introduced them. One, big, beefy, red of face, was in full uniform, the sleeves ablaze with the broad band and four stripes of an Admiral of the Fleet: the other was a civilian, a small, stocky man with iron-grey hair, eyes still and wise and old. Nicholls recognized him immediately, would have known anyway from the deference of both the Admirals. He reflected wryly that the Navy was indeed doing him proud: such receptions were not for all . . . But they seemed reluctant to begin the reception, Nicholls thought—he had forgotten the shock his appearance must give. Finally, the grey-haired man cleared his throat.

'How's the leg, boy?' he asked. 'Looks pretty bad to me.' His voice was low, but alive with controlled authority.

'Not too bad, thank you, sir,' Nicholls answered. 'Two, three weeks should see me back on the job.'

'You're taking two months, laddie,' said the grey-haired man quietly. 'More if you want it.' He smiled faintly. 'If anyone asks, just tell 'em I said so. Cigarette?'

He flicked the big table-lighter, sat back in his chair. Temporarily, he seemed at a loss as to what to say next. Then he looked up abruptly.

'Had a good trip home?'

'Very fair, sir. VIP treatment all the way. Moscow, Teheran, Cairo, Gib.' Nicholls's mouth twisted. 'Much more comfortable than the trip out.' He paused, inhaled deeply on his cigarette, looked levelly across the table. 'I would have preferred to come home in the *Sirrus*.'

'No doubt,' Starr broke in acidly. 'But we cannot afford to cater for the personal prejudices of all and sundry. We were anxious to have a first-hand account of FR77—and particularly the *Ulysses*—as soon as possible.'

Nicholls's hands clenched on the edge of his chair. The anger had leapt in him like a flame, and he knew that the man opposite was watching closely. Slowly he relaxed, looked at the greyhaired man, interrogative eyebrows mutely asking confirmation.

The grey-haired man nodded.

'Just tell us all you know,' he said kindly. 'Everything—about everything. Take your time.'

'From the beginning?' Nicholls asked in a low voice.

'From the beginning.'

Nicholls told them. He would have liked to tell the story, right as it fell out, from the convoy before FR77 straight through to the end. He did his best, but it was a halting story, strangely lacking in conviction. The atmosphere, the surroundings were wrong—the contrast between the peaceful warmth of these rooms and the inhuman cold and cruelty of the Arctic was an immense gulf that could be bridged only by experience and understanding. Down here, in the heart of London, the wild, incredible tale he had to tell fell falsely, incredibly even on his own ears. Halfway through, he looked at his listeners, almost gave up. Incredulity? No, it wasn't that—at least, not with the grey-haired man and the Admiral of the Fleet. Just a baffled incomprehension, an honest failure to understand.

It wasn't so bad when he stuck to the ascertainable facts, the facts of carriers crippled by seas, of carriers mined, stranded and torpedoed: the facts of the great storm, of the desperate struggle to survive: the facts of the gradual attrition of the convoy, of the terrible dying of the two gasoline tankers, of the U-boats and bombers sent to the bottom, of the *Ulysses*, battering through the snowstorm at 40 knots, blown up by the German cruiser, of the arrival of the battle squadron, of the flight of the cruiser before it could inflict further damage, of the rounding-up of the scattered convoy, of the curtain of Russian fighters in the Barents Sea, of the ultimate arrival in the Kola Inlet of the battered remnants of FR77—five ships in all.

It was when he came to less readily ascertainable facts, to statements that could never be verified at all, that he sensed the doubt, the something more than wonder. He told the story as calmly, as unemotionally as he could: the story of Ralston, Ralston of the fighting lights and the searchlights, of his father and family: of Riley, the ringleader of the mutiny and his refusal to leave the shaft tunnel: of Petersen, who had killed a marine and gladly given his own life: of McQuater and Chrysler and Doyle and a dozen others.

For a second, his own voice broke uncertainly as he told the story of the half-dozen survivors from the *Ulysses*, picked up by the *Sirrus* soon afterwards. He told how Brooks had given his lifejacket to an ordinary seaman, who amazingly survived fifteen minutes in that water: how Turner, wounded in head and arm, had supported a dazed Spicer till the *Sirrus* came plunging alongside, had passed a bowline round him and was gone before anything could be done:

how Carrington, that enduring man of iron, a baulk of splintered timber under his arms, had held two men above water till rescue came. Both men—Preston was one—had died later: Carrington had climbed the rope unaided, clambered over the guard-rails dangling a left-leg with the foot blown off above the ankle. Carrington would survive: Carrington was indestructible. Finally, Doyle, too, was gone: they had thrown him a rope, but he had not seen it, for he was blind.

But what the three men really wanted to know, Nicholls realized, was how the *Ulysses* had been, how a crew of mutineers had borne themselves. He had told them, he knew, things of wonder and of splendour, and they could not reconcile these with men who would take up arms against their own ship, in effect, against their own King.

So Nicholls tried to tell them, then knew, as he tried, that he could never tell them. For what was there to tell? That Vallery had spoken to the men over the broadcast system: how he had gone among them and made them almost as himself, on that grim, exhausting tour of inspection: how he had spoken of them as he died: and how, most of all, his death had made them men again? For that was all that there was to tell, and these things were just nothing at all. With sudden insight, Nicholls saw that the meaning of that strange transformation of the men of the *Ulysses*, a transformation of bitter, broken men to men above themselves, could neither be explained nor understood, for all the meaning was in Vallery, and Vallery was dead.

Nicholls felt tired, now, desperately so. He knew he was far from well. His mind was cloudy, hazy in retrospect, and he was mixing things up: his sense of chronological time was gone, he was full of hesitations and uncertainties. Suddenly he was overwhelmed by the futility of it all, and he broke off slowly, his voice trailing into silence.

Vaguely, he heard the grey-haired man ask something in a quiet voice, and he muttered aloud, unthinking.

'What was that? What did you say?' The greyhaired man was looking at him strangely. The face of the Admiral behind the table was impassive. Starr's, he saw, was open in disbelief.

'I only said, "They were the best crew God ever gave a Captain,"' Nicholls murmured.

'I see.' The old, tired eyes looked at him steadily, but there was no other comment. Fingers drumming on the table, he looked slowly at the two Admirals, then back to Nicholls again.

'Take things easy for a minute, boy . . . If you'll just excuse us . . . '

He rose to his feet, walked slowly over to the big, bay windows at the other end of the long room, the others following. Nicholls made no move, did not even look after them: he sat slumped in the chair, looking dejectedly, unseeingly, at the crutches on the floor between his feet.

From time to time, he could hear a murmur of voices. Starr's high-pitched voice carried most clearly. 'Mutiny ship, sir . . . never the same again . . . better this way.' There was murmured reply, too low to catch, then he heard Starr saying, ' . . . finished as a fighting unit'. The grey-haired man said something rapidly, his tone sharp with disagreement, but the words were blurred. Then the deep, heavy voice of the Fleet Admiral said something about 'expiation', and the grey-haired man nodded slowly. Then Starr looked at him over his shoulder, and Nicholls knew they were talking about him. He thought he heard the words 'not well' and 'frightful strain', but perhaps he was imagining it.

Anyway, he no longer cared. He was anxious for one thing only, and that was to be gone. He felt an alien in an alien land, and whether they believed him or not no longer mattered. He did not belong here, where everything was so sane and commonplace and real—and withal a world of shadows.

He wondered what the Kapok Kid would have said had he been here, and smiled in fond reminiscence: the language would have been terrible, the comments rich and barbed and pungent. Then he wondered what Vallery would have said, and he smiled again at the simplicity of it all, for Vallery would have said: 'Do not judge them, for they do not understand.'

Gradually, he became aware that the murmuring had ceased, that the three men were standing above him. His smile faded, and he looked up slowly to see them looking down strangely at him, their eyes full of concern.

'I'm damnably sorry, boy,' the grey-haired man said sincerely. 'You're a sick man and we've asked far too much of you. A drink, Nicholls? It was most remiss—'

'No, thank you, sir.' Nicholls straightened himself in his chair. 'I'll be perfectly all right.' He hesitated. 'Is—is there anything else?'

'No, nothing at all.' The smile was genuine, friendly. 'You've been a great help to us, Lieutenant, a great help. And a fine report. Thank you very much indeed.'

A liar and a gentleman, Nicholls thought gratefully. He struggled to his feet, reached out for his crutches. He shook hands with Starr and the Admiral of the Fleet, and said goodbye. The greyhaired man accompanied him to the door, his hand beneath Nicholls's arm.

At the door Nicholls paused.

'Sorry to bother you but—when do I begin my leave, sir?'

'As from now,' the other said emphatically. 'And have a good time. God knows you've earned it, my boy . . . Where are you going?'

'Henley, sir.'

'Henley! I could have sworn you were Scots.'

'I am, sir—I have no family.'

'Oh . . . A girl, Lieutenant?'

Nicholls nodded silently.

The grey-haired man clapped him on the shoulder, and smiled gently.

'Pretty, I'll be bound?'

Nicholls looked at him, looked away to where the sentry was already holding open the street doors, and gathered up his crutches.

'I don't know, sir,' he said quietly. 'I don't know at all, I've never seen her.'

He tip-tapped his way across the marble flags, passed through the heavy doors and limped out into the sunshine.

ACKNOWLEDGEMENTS

I wish to acknowledge my debt to my elder brother, Ian L. MacLean, Master Mariner, for the considerable technical help and advice on matters maritime given me in the preparation of this book.

To avoid possible confusion it must be clearly stated that there is no connection whatsoever between the HMS *Ulysses* of this book and the Ulster-class destroyer—now fully converted to a frigate—of the same name which entered operational service in the early part of 1944, some 12 months after the events described in this book. Nor is there any connection between any ship herein mentioned as being in Scapa Flow or participating in the convoy and any naval ship of the same name that has served, or is serving, in the Royal Navy.

A.M.

MacLean Goes Everywhere You Do

If you enjoyed this book by Alistair MacLean, look for ebook editions of his other thrilling blockbusters, available for your e-reader or smartphone for only $4.99:

ISBN 978-1-4027-9253-3
50499>
9 781402 792533

The Satan Bug 978-1-4027-9253-3

Behind the locked doors of E block in the fortress-like Mordon Research Centre, a scientist lies dead, and a new toxin of terrifying power has vanished. When the first letter is delivered threatening to unleash the virus, special agent Pierre Cavell is given just 24 hours to solve the mystery of the break-in and prevent a plague-born apocalypse.

Where Eagles Dare 978-1-4027-9251-9

A team of British special forces parachutes onto a mountainside in wartime Germany. Their mission: To rescue a captured American general from the Castle of the Eagle before the Nazi interrogators can force him to reveal secret D-Day plans. As team members start to perish along the way, the true purpose of the rescue turns out to be infinitely more complicated.

Bear Island

978-1-4027-9255-7

As the *Morning Rose* ploughs through wintry Arctic seas toward Bear Island, the ship's doctor Christopher Marlowe is kept busy attending to the seasick passengers, a film unit being sent to make a film so secret that none of them knows much about it. As passengers and crew begin dying, he realizes that the *Morning Rose* has a murderer on board. Once on the island, Marlowe must contend against weather, terrain, and ruthless adversaries as events build to a brutal climax in the darkness of the Polar night.

Caravan to Vaccares 978-1-4027-9247-2

From all over Europe, even from behind the Iron Curtain, gypsies make an annual pilgrimage to the shrine of their patron saint in Provence. But at this year's gathering, people are mysteriously dying. Intrepid sleuths Cecile Dubois and Neil Bowman join the caravan in order to uncover the truth behind the deaths, in the process revealing an international plot that the sinister Gaiuse Strome will stop at nothing to keep secret.

Force 10 from Navarone

978-1-4027-9249-6

The thrilling sequel to *The Guns of Navarone,* this book reunites members of the Allied team that silenced the giant guns of Navarone and sends them on a desperate bid to assist a ragtag group of Partisan forces trapped by two armoured divisions of the German army in the rugged mountains of Yugoslavia.